THE HEATHER HILLS OF STONEWYCKE

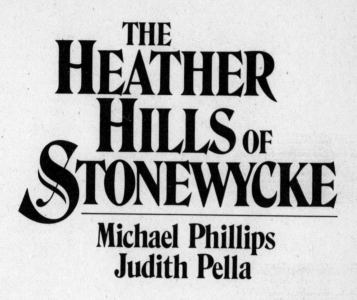

THE
HEATHER
HILLS OF
STONEWYCKE

Michael Phillips
Judith Pella

Published by Bethany House Publishers
A Division of Bethany Fellowship, Inc.
6820 Auto Club Road, Minneapolis, Minnesota 55438

Printed in the United States of America

Library of Congress Cataloging in Publication Data

Phillips, Michael R., 1946-
    The heather hills of Stonewycke.

    I. Pella, Judith. II. Title.
PS3566.H492H4 1985   813'.54   84-29771
ISBN 0-87123-803-9 (pbk.)

Dedication

To Brenda Scott, for her friendship, help, and encouragement.

The Authors

MICHAEL PHILLIPS, editor of the George MacDonald reprint series, has also authored ten books of his own. A magna cum laude graduate of Humboldt State University in Arcata, California, he owns and operates a chain of bookstores on the West Coast as well as carrying on a heavy writing schedule. He and his wife live in Eureka, California, with their three sons.

JUDITH PELLA, an avid reader and history buff, makes a home for her two children in Eureka, California. She received her nursing degree in 1971 and later a B.A. in Social Sciences from Humboldt State University. This is her first book.

The Stonewycke Trilogy

The Heather Hills of Stonewycke
Flight from Stonewycke
Lady of Stonewycke

Scottish Romances by George MacDonald retold for today's reader by Michael Phillips:

The Fisherman's Lady
The Marquis' Secret
The Baronet's Song
The Shepherd's Castle
The Tutor's First Love
The Musician's Quest
The Maiden's Bequest

Contents

Prologue

Like vanishing smoke, generations fade and life passes into life. Dreams are born, hopes kindled, families and tribes and nations rise and fall. But men and women return to the earth as they came. All that remains is the land—one enduring reality under heaven's eternal gaze. The land *remains*, while over it the inexorable march of history passes—man to man, woman to woman, child to child.

In its early days the Isle of Britain remained unmolested by the warring hordes that swept through the rest of Asia and Europe. But progress brought larger ships and broader horizons; eventually the slender estuary separating Britain from the European mainland no longer proved an obstacle to those desiring to cross and invade. The land was verdant and fertile. The climate, though not temperate, was equable and healthy. In the first century B.C. the Romans, under Gaius Julius Caesar, vanquished their natural fear and hatred of the sea, sailed across the channel, and within a century had subjugated the scattered groups of Britons into Roman Brittania.

Seeking refuge from the Romans in Gaul and South Britain, various tribes migrated north into the Scottish highlands and lowlands. Protected as these northernmost reaches were by rugged terrain and severe weather, these tribes, the Picts, settled the land. Uniting gradually under one king after another, by the sixth century they controlled the greater part of the territory north of the line between the Firth of Forth and Loch Linnhe.

The Picts were first to discover the massive heap of granite some four miles inland from the shore—five huge boulders piled on and about one another in apparently random fashion, thrown into their positions by the convulsive prehistoric quakings of the earth. In the early days of the settlement, the great stones provided a reference point of the ridge bordering the fertile valley. A youngster at play might have been the first to notice the narrow passage through two of the rocks and under a third which led to a secluded little dell, invisible from any point on the high moorland which surrounded it. The *wicket*, or little door (*through the stones* it came to be called), many a Pict child scampered through to elude his friends.

In the course of time, the Britons, the Angles, and the Celtic Scots

11

established themselves firmly, along with the resident Picts, in northern Britain above Solway Firth and the Cheviot Hills. All four peoples possessed individual backgrounds and histories, and there formed no obvious natural alliance between them. Inevitably, the Picts found themselves in perpetual conflict with the other three as each gradually encroached northwards on the kingdom the Picts had established.

A perilous balance thus continued in Scotland until the ninth century. The most powerful of the kings of the Picts, Oengus, had conquered the Scottish kingdom of Dalriada, and the kingdom of the Picts seemed well on its way to establishing a permanent united rule over the northern third of the British Isles.

But then from over the seas came the invading wave of Nordic pirates—ruthless, driven not by necessity or circumstances or cramped homelands but by the sheer appetite for pillage and conquest. If the soul of the Vikings lay in their thirst for adventure, the symbols of that quest were their sleek, long, fast ships—wicked and bright, finely carved with dragon-shaped prows and high, curving sterns. Along the sides sat the brutal Scandinavian rovers of the sea, with oars poised, swords ready, long rows of shields ranged along the sides.

The Viking storm broke in fury in 835. Huge fleets of three or four hundred vessels began plundering shore towns and villages, rowing up the rivers of England. Pict blood spilled freely in a desperate attempt to hold off the invaders from the north. The great granite heaps were stained with the blood of violent death; even a child could find no refuge behind the stone wicket. But if the Viking warriors came seeking the treasure about which they had heard, they found only the spoils of living victims.

As the Norse invasion disturbed the political balance of the north, the kingdom of the Picts gradually collapsed. Preoccupied with defending themselves against the Vikings from the sea, the Picts failed to recognize the growing menace of the Scots on their southern flank. By the time a Scottish party of settlers arrived at what had been the Pict village of *Steenbuaic*, all that remained was a ruinous reminder of the bloody annihilation of an unsuspecting village at the hands of the marauding Vikings. It now remained for the Scot children to discover anew the door under the mighty granite sentinel whose mute power had proved useless to stem the Nordic assault. From etchings on the rocks the ancient name was discovered and saxonized to *Stanweoc* and thereafter used to denote that heathland south of the new Scot village of Straithland on the coast where the Picts had once thrived.

The ancient kingdom of the Picts was thus lost in the warring wreckage of the ninth century, and within a hundred more years the Picts had been entirely supplanted by the Scots, who claimed this land as their right of conquest. Whatever influence and native individuality the Picts had once possessed was muted as the two cultures intermingled and the Picts were amalgamated into the whole.

Meanwhile, the Danish and Norwegian raiders stayed longer every year. In the summer, the fleets would sail from their homelands to plunder and destroy. But each year the tendency was to linger longer in the more genial southern climates. Eventually the warriors began to bring their wives and families; some intermarried with the natives of the lands they had pillaged. The familiar terrain and climate of sparsely populated Scotland especially suited them. As the Scots had assimilated the Picts, the colonizing Vikings mingled and were absorbed, becoming, like the Basques, the Celts, the Picts, the Angles, and the Britons before them, the ancestors of future Scottish generations.

The Viking domination of the island lasted less than a hundred years; in 1066 the Normans from the coast of France, themselves descended from the Vikings, invaded England under William the Conqueror. To the north, the Scots maintained a unity in spite of the individuality of their many distinct family clans. The Anglo-Norman clan Ramsaidh achieved prominence in the thirteenth century when King David I granted lands in Lithian near Glasgow to Simon de Ramsay. Simultaneously, the chief of the northern branch of the clan, Adam de Ramsay, was made baron of Banff while others of his family, bearing his crest, were settling in Strathy, the valley town just to the east.

Throughout the following centuries the Ramsays were conspicuously engaged in the border wars with England; for his great valor in the services of King James V of Scotland, Andrew Ramsay was given the marquisate of Stonewycke in 1539. The Stonewycke estate overlooked the rich valley of Strathy east of Banff. The granite sentinels lay within the estate some three miles to the south in the midst of a heath ridge which had centuries before been known as Branuaic. But no eyes turned toward those barren moors during the time of Andrew; all attention focused instead on the grand castle he had set out to build. Sir James Hamilton, the king's own architect, lent his talents to the raising of the magnificent structure, nearly seven years in the building. When completed it became known as the jewel of the northern coast, established on a lovely green hill; when lighted at night with candles and lanterns, it bedazzled many a fisherman who gazed in awe at the sight.

But the jewel dimmed some hundred and fifty years later when Iver Ramsay invested heavily in the ill-fated Darien Company. Losing his fortune, Iver only barely managed to hang onto the estate. The grandeur of the castle declined, and eventually Iver left Strathy altogether and was reported to have taken up residence in a simple Edinburgh townhouse. For the next twenty years the grand house of the Ramsay lineage fell to the mercies of mice, spiders, and decay. The empty rooms, stripped of their furnishings by the desperate lord, only whispered of past life; dust and cobwebs clung ghostlike to the gilt-edged mantels and ornate balustrades.

While Stonewycke slept, political upheaval and military conflict pitted Scottish against English in the battle for supremacy, possession, and ultimate rule of the wild and beautiful Scottish lands. Thomas Ramsay, son of Iver, fell in with the Jacobites, blaming, as he did, his father's financial demise on the English. Changing the spelling of his name to Ramsey as an act of individualism, Thomas determined to restore his ancestral home of Stonewycke to its former position of glory, prestige and influence. Life returned again to the turrets and towers, the ballrooms and corridors, the stables and grounds. But Thomas Ramsey died six years before his dream of a Jacobite rebellion against the English could be realized. But he passed on to his son Colin a passion for his homeland and its cause. Colin was among the first to join Bonnie Prince Charlie in his idealistic grasp for the throne in 1745, and was struck down to his death at Culloden in a desperate attempt to shield the Prince from a dreadful blow.

In honor of her husband's loyalty, Christina Ramsey harbored the fugitive Young Pretender and would-be king for a time. And it was at Stonewycke where Prince Charles Edward came distressingly close to discovery. A troop of English militia, acting on the word of an informer, stormed the castle, but a thorough search revealed no fugitive. Little Bobby Ramsey had taken the prince to a spot where the offspring of ancient Pict children still hid from one another in their play. And for the space of a few days, the sombre mounds surrounding the sunken dell and watched over by granite peaks became an unlikely palace for the man who dreamed of being king.

Finally, forty years after the humiliation of Scottish insurrectionists at Culloden Moor, King George III reinstated the heirs of the Scottish clan leaders to their former landowning positions as a gesture of unity and goodwill.

Robert Ramsey, son of Colin Ramsey and descended from Baron Adam de Ramsay and Andrew Ramsay, was endowed in 1784 with the estate of Stonewycke which had been his father's at the time of the uprising. He lived another twenty years, after which his son Anson became laird of the expansive and prosperous valley of Strathy on the northern coast. Greatly beloved by the people under him, Anson governed only another twelve years, when his life was suddenly cut short. His two sons had not been cast in his mold; their lusting hearts were set on riches rather than service to their people. The legend of the wealth of the ancient Picts still circulating, these ambitious sons, fearing disinheritment and loss of their chance at the treasure, grew increasingly estranged from their father until a mysterious hunting accident ended Anson's life. Measures to ensure the protection of the land he loved had been undertaken, but remained unfulfilled at his death. His unscrupulous son Talmud succeeded him.

Still the land remained, as generations of occupants rose and fell with the winds of history. Still the people tilled the soil and built their homes upon its hills. Rarely, however, did their eyes now turn toward that barren heath where this valley's first inhabitants had overturned the rocks to begin working the stubborn earth. But recognized or not, there still stood the immovable garrison of granite with its narrow wicket of stone, standing as a mute reminder of the ancient peoples who first populated this rugged northern land.

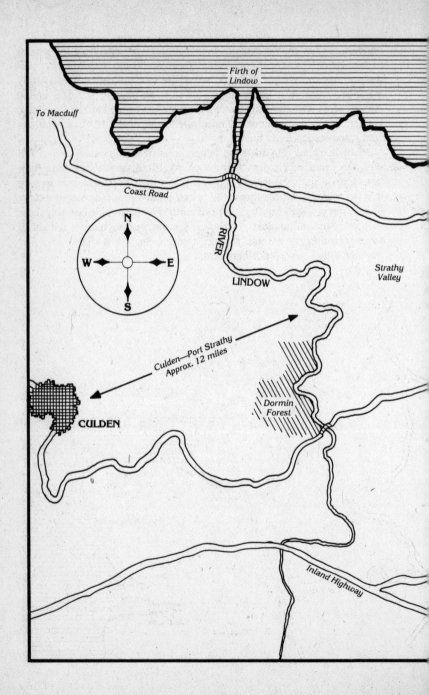

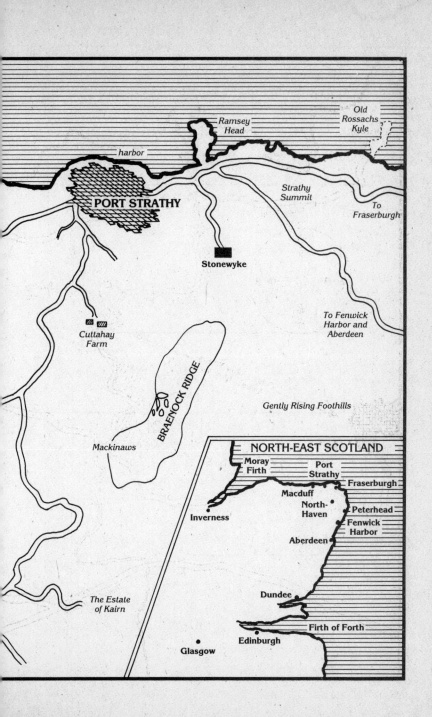

harbor

Ramsey
Head

Old
Rossachs
Kyle

PORT STRATHY

Strathy
Summit

To
Fraserburgh

Stonewyke

Cuttahay
Farm

To Fenwick
Harbor and
Aberdeen

BRAENOCK RIDGE

Gently Rising Foothills

Mackinaws

NORTH-EAST SCOTLAND

Moray
Firth

Port
Strathy

Fraserburgh

Macduff

North-
Haven

Peterhead

Inverness

Fenwick
Harbor

Aberdeen

The Estate
of Kairn

Dundee

Firth of Forth

Edinburgh

Glasgow

Ramsey Family Tree

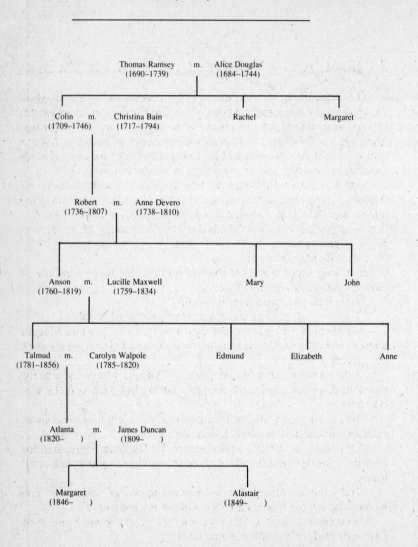

Thomas Ramsey   m.   Alice Douglas
(1690–1739)   (1684–1744)

Colin   m.   Christina Bain   Rachel   Margaret
(1709–1746)   (1717–1794)

Robert   m.   Anne Devero
(1736–1807)   (1738–1810)

Anson   m.   Lucille Maxwell   Mary   John
(1760–1819)   (1759–1834)

Talmud   m.   Carolyn Walpole   Edmund   Elizabeth   Anne
(1781–1856)   (1785–1820)

Atlanta   m.   James Duncan
(1820–   )   (1809–   )

Margaret   Alastair
(1846–   )   (1849–   )

1 / Root of Contention

The warm afternoon sun had passed its zenith and begun its slow descent west. Maggie had not been out of doors today—unusual for the thirteen-year-old girl who so loved the Scottish countryside of her upbringing. Today's mood had been thoughtful and melancholy, and the ordinarily vibrant youngster had instead spent most of the day haunting the solitary corridors and empty rooms of the great mansion.

In mid-afternoon she wandered into the library, not particularly enthusiastic about reading but having exhausted her other possibilities for amusement. She looked around at the endless stacks of books, took one down, sat on the sofa, and thumbed through it casually as her eyelids began to grow heavy.

Suddenly Maggie started awake.

How long she'd dozed off she had no idea, but there were voices close by, raised in heated debate.

"How dare you attempt such a thing!"

"I assure you, nothing was further from my mind. I only—"

"And behind my back!" interrupted a woman's voice which Maggie knew to be her mother's. Hearing the tone she could almost see the dark eyes flashing like flint.

"I didn't want to trouble you with—" Maggie's father began, for the other disputant was indeed the girl's father. But once again he was cut short.

"Ah, of course. You didn't want to worry my feminine head about such an uninteresting business transaction, is that it?"

"Of course, my dear," replied James. He had been unprepared for his wife's hostile outburst and now hoped to soothe her with conciliatory tones.

"Ha!" flared Atlanta, her voice revealing bitter sarcasm. "You would dare sell off Braenock Ridge without my consent?"

"You know as well as I that we need the money it will bring. And I've been pledged a handsome amount."

"*You* need the money you mean! You are determined to buy that brewery whatever it costs the estate."

"I've negotiated a shrewd deal," replied James confidently.

19

"You would sell off the land bit by bit for the sake of a profit." Atlanta's voice shook with emotion. "But," she went on, "I will not allow you to sell off generations of the Ramsey's lifeblood . . ." Her voice caught on tears she would not let rise to the surface.

Now James's own anger vent itself upon his wife.

"Not allow!" he fumed, spinning around to face her. "*Not allow!* You would dare challenge me in affairs of business?"

"You forget, dear husband," answered Atlanta, her tones cooling with her effort at self-control, "that this land is mine, not yours. Everything that goes on is my affair. You can do nothing without my approval."

"And you never allow me to forget it, do you, Atlanta?"

She said nothing.

Young Maggie crouched low behind the back of the sofa, stiff with terror lest she be discovered as a common eavesdropper. She had never intended to fall asleep. Yet once her parents entered and began their heated discussion, she desperately wished she could escape undetected. Now she remained motionless.

Her parents argued often. Maggie was well aware of the tense distance between them, even when their words were civil. This particular dispute seemed more dreadful than usual, the conflict perhaps heightened by the knowledge that she was a secretive listener to their private words.

The grim iciness of her father's tone, as he resumed the conversation, sent a chill through Maggie's body.

"We shall see," he said. "My solicitor is drawing up papers regarding Braenock. It's all legal, I assure you. My name is on the documents of this estate as well as yours."

Atlanta stared at her husband for a moment, her vacant gaze scarcely revealing a hint of the enmity churning within. Whatever love that may have existed between the two of them was far from visible at this moment. Both were strong and determined, and, during the past several years, their clashes over the future of the estate had grown more frequent as James's ambitions had widened.

"I warn you, James," she said at length, in deliberate and measured tones, "do not misjudge me. I still have more control than you may think."

"We shall see."

"James, don't push me too far. I will not be moved. You shall not sell Braenock."

"If you think to intimidate me, Atlanta, save your strength. I will do what I am compelled to do—for the good of the estate."

"Dispossessing our tenants is for no one's good," Atlanta replied. "And what of our children? If we followed your suggestion, they would end up with nothing. The land would all be gone!"

"They will applaud the wealth and prestige I will bring them."

"Not Margaret. Your money will mean nothing to her. She would applaud nothing that would destroy—"

"I can handle Margaret. And don't try to interfere with me. She is my daughter as well."

"And one with a mind of her own."

"A mind of her own, precisely," he shot back, "unless you try to fill her head with lies about me! But I am her father and she loves me. She will do what I say."

Atlanta did not reply.

Maggie, shielded behind the sofa and several towering bookcases, heard her father's footsteps retreat from the room followed by the final slam of the door. She felt, rather than saw, her mother's tall, proud form standing motionless, staring after her husband, observed only by a thousand dusty, leatherbound witnesses of ages past. Maggie remained still, and after another few moments heard the click of the door as it opened and closed. She had not even heard her mother's soft retreating footsteps.

Finally young Margaret stirred, rising slowly to peer over the edge of the sofa, still not sure she was truly alone. Trembling, she slid from the sofa and stood. A tear trickled down her cheek, and she bit her lower lip to still the quivering. What could it all mean?

How could her father speak so harshly to her mother? Maggie had always thought of him as such a loving and unselfish man. He loved her, didn't he, as only a daughter can feel loved by a father she adores and looks up to with pride and an almost reverent regard?

Was this the same man whose voice she had just heard? There had been arguments before, but none quite like this. And what had he meant when he'd said he could *handle* her?

Confusion surged through her. Her face was hot; her tears were rising again. She had to get out of the house—to ride, to forget. Maybe all would be different when she returned.

Maggie crept softly toward the stair, began her descent quietly; then halfway down she gave way to the pounding in her chest and broke into a run all the way to the stables.

2 / Cinder

From the house Maggie led her charcoal-gray mare north toward the road and then down the hill into Port Strathy. She had to find a place to run, and the beach west of town was one of her favorites.

Arguments between her parents may have grown more frequent lately, though she chanced to hear them only rarely. But when she did they were never pleasant. Her impulse was always to flee, especially when she sensed that she herself was somehow bound up in the conflicts which erupted over the land.

Though she and her mother were close, her father had always held a special place in her heart. His words of affection during her early years had struck deep root and she had grown up adoring him. And he had never given her any reason to suspect that the feeling wasn't mutual. True, they spent little time together; she often begged him to go riding with her, but he was usually too busy. Nevertheless, the carefree child rarely paused to think that the relationship might be one-sided, that while she had given all of her trusting and vulnerable young heart to him, her father might have larger matters to occupy his mind. She took for granted that the love in his heart matched the wellsprings from her own, and never dreamed of questioning his feelings for her. Indeed, at her tender age, how could she begin to fathom the grip of the world of Mammon upon such a man as her father?

Braenock Ridge, Maggie thought to herself. *What could be so special about that particular corner of the land?* The grand estate called Stone-wycke had been Atlanta's inheritance. Located in the north of Scotland, it occupied miles of rich pasture and farming land and accessible coast-line, unusual in the northern Scottish highlands. In 1860 it was, indeed, a marquisate of no small repute in Britain. James Duncan had married into the fortune, and on an estate containing such a rich heritage, he had never ceased feeling the outsider. Whether the disputes between Mother and Father stemmed from this fact would be hard to say.

But somehow their daughter found herself increasingly caught in the middle.

Avoiding the small fishing village of Port Strathy, Maggie at length arrived at the beach to the west of the harbor. The low tide offered a long, flat expanse of sand, hard and wide—just right for the gallop she needed. Maggie dug her heels into Cinder's flanks and swung the mare westward.

After a high, plunging kick, the horse tore into the wet sand and flew away into the afternoon sun. Within a few moments horse and rider dwindled to a mere speck on the distant coastline; no observer at the pier of the harbor would have been able to make them out. But at last, near the rocky shoal bordering the expanse of sand to the west, the speck swerved a little and grew steadily larger until once more horse and rider could be distinctly seen. Still Maggie urged the mare on as if her own emotions could be spent through the exhaustion of the powerful beast. The horse galloped along the water's edge, sending lumps of wet sand flying from its hooves like a random storm of loose-caked clods. In front its hooves scattered dainty wisps of foam, left behind by the ebb and flow of the incoming tide.

Halfway down the beach, Maggie suddenly wheeled the mare around and dashed headlong into the sea. At first the horse struggled, but her load was light, and when they reached the deep water she swam strongly with her head high out of the water. Nothing could have quieted the raging of Maggie's spirit more than the chill of sea water. Although the mare seemed laboring for her very life, Maggie knew her animal well enough to recognize that nothing could have pleased the mare more after such an energetic gallop.

When Maggie judged her mount had had enough, she turned back toward the shore. Out of the water they came, still at a run—the unusually colored gray mare and her small but confident mistress perched atop her soaking back—with a great splashing of foamy sea water and high-kicking hooves, much to the delight of the young rider, whose deep red curls flew out in the wind behind her.

Straight on Maggie drove Cinder, over the wide expanse of packed sand, and straight up the grassy dune which bordered the beach. Up the loose sand they charged, the sun-bathed dance of splashing water now followed by a stormy cloud of gray dust flying upward before the churning hooves.

At last, as they gained the small seashore summit, Maggie reined the mare in. Cinder stood, sides heaving as her great lungs gasped for air, the wide distended nostrils shooting out steamy breaths.

Maggie sat still, also exhausted from the effort. At last the array of confusing thoughts had subsided and her mind was clear. To be out with Cinder, astride the spirited animal, was what she always needed when life at home grew too overwhelming. She drew in a deep sigh, patted the horse gently on her black head, bent forward, and mumbled some soft words of affection. Then easing her gently forward, she descended the other side of the sandy slope.

"Let's ride out to Braenock, shall we, Cinder?" she said.

The summer afternoon was warm and Maggie steered a course directly away from the sea. Though she was still a child in many ways, she knew the countryside as well as any farmer several times her age. She and Cinder had ridden and explored everything between Rossachs Kyle and the Dormin Forest together. Riding through the fields and meadows, splashing through the streams, climbing the rugged hills, and exploring the coastline of her native home of northern Scotland, provided Maggie's one great pleasure in life. Notwithstanding that she was a Duncan who lived in the imposing mansion of Stonewycke, the farmers and fishermen loved young Margaret, for she seemed to feel about their beloved homeland much as they themselves did—a bond they were not accustomed to sharing with the titled landowners.

Leaving behind two or three ridges of dunes covered with pale sea-grasses, horse and girl came upon a stretch of rolling meadowland which lengthened out in the distance before them. This wide and fertile valley, for which Port Strathy had been named, was dotted here and there with small cottages of the farmers—the crofters, who worked the land on behalf of the Duncan estate, of which Maggie was the eldest offspring. To her right as she rode, some two or three miles distant, could be seen clumps of thick pines and fir which bordered the Lindow River as it wound its way leisurely from the mountainous south toward the North Sea. On her left, composing the opposite boundary of the valley, the terrain rose steadily into a range of high hills, of which Strathy Summit was the closest. She could make out her own house with its straggling stone walls and ancient turrets nestled among the firs about a third of the way up the summit. In the distance ahead of her to the south, the mountains rose gradually to peaks which had only recently doffed their white winter's cap.

The way Maggie now pursued lay straight up the valley, past numerous farms, none too prosperous, yet each with a certain charming flavor of its own. Usually there was a vegetable garden, half planted with potatoes, a few dozen chickens scratching about the grounds, and a cow or two. Without fresh milk furnished by the family cow, and the abundant supply of potatoes, many of the families would not have been able to make it through the long northern winters. *How much improved some of the dreary-looking cottages would look*, thought Maggie, *with a few flowers planted here and there about the yards*.

Maggie leaned low over Cinder's damp neck and spoke to her again in unintelligible tones, then veered toward the road which connected

Port Strathy with its nearest neighbor, the inland village of Culden, some twelve miles southwest across the Lindow. Reaching the road, Maggie followed it for about a mile, then diverged to the left, while the road continued its course westward toward Culden.

Maggie had learned to ride almost by the time she could walk, but only in the past four years or so had she taken to such extensive wanderings throughout the countryside. Cinder had been given to her—a foal barely three weeks old—by her father's groom Digory. He had been called from the estate to attend the mare's birth at the farm of one of the poorest, though most respected, families in the valley. The delivery grew complicated, lasted well into the night, and without Digory's assistance it is doubtful that either foal or mother would have survived. In gratitude the old farmer had presented Digory with the newborn animal. The filly was not a thoroughbred, to be sure, the old man had said, but her line had been part of Strathy's equine heritage for more than ten generations. The charcoal body and jet black head certainly presented such a striking picture that the horse could stand proud, unique among the most lettered of purebreds.

Digory accepted the gift thankfully and offered the foal to the ten-year-old young lady of the house he served. Maggie had instantly fallen in love with the filly, and the two had become inseparable.

On Maggie and Cinder walked, the shrubbery growing gradually thicker and the terrain more steep and rocky. On her right Maggie could make out the peak of Marbrae, with the sun descending behind it, standing as if to guard the peaceful Strathy valley to the north. Veering to the east Maggie eased Cinder carefully down the side of a steep, dry gorge, then re-ascended the opposite bank until she stood at last, nearly three miles south of the mansion, on the high moorland known as Braenock Ridge.

Three or four cottages were scattered over the surrounding plateau, but this land was clearly poorer than the lush, green valley and was used mostly for grazing. There were, of course, a number of families for whom this was home. The struggling flocks of sheep and free-grazing goats had been a traditional part of the land for as far back as anyone could remember.

It was neither the most beautiful nor the most prosperous section of the estate. Why would her mother object so adamantly to its being sold? On the other hand, why would anyone want to buy it? As long as Stonewycke's borders east of Rossachs Kyle and west of the Lindow were preserved, what could this remote southern parcel of arid, shrub-filled heath matter?

Sunk in her reverie, Maggie had not heard young Mackinaw come over the rise behind her. The ringing tinkle of the sheep's bells reached her ears just as the voice spoke.

"Aft'noon t' ye, Miss Duncan."

Maggie spun around in the saddle.

"Why, Stevie! I thought I was alone," she said. "You're out herding the sheep by yourself today?"

The boy appeared about Maggie's age, but was in reality two years younger. His lanky frame was lean and awkward, vacillating between boyhood and adolescence. In his face appeared already the hint of lines that would etch themselves deeper through years of looking at the sun and facing the harsh northern elements. His brown leathery skin gave the appearance of age beyond his years. The only assertively boyish feature was the massive crop of wiry red hair which shot out in all directions from his head.

"I have since the weather's turned fair," he replied. "My daddy's gettin' some too lame t' trample o'er these parts lookin' fer grass t' graze the sheep, ye know."

"I'm sorry to hear that, Stevie. Is your mother well? I haven't been out here for some time."

"Fair t' middlin', miss. Only this past winter was a rough one fer her. The wind's cold as ice sometimes."

"But surely you keep a fire going?"

"Yes'm," he replied. "But ye know, the peat be none too o'er warm when a body's sick. But noo that the sun's oot, we're feelin' right well, miss."

As the two spoke, the sheep following their master had edged their way over the rise and had begun to crowd about them. Cinder stamped nervously, but Maggie held her firm.

"Well, tell your mother and father I'll be by for a visit one of these days."

"They'll like that real good, miss," he said, looking away shyly as he pretended to tend the sheep. "An' thank ye, miss," he added. "An' good day t' ye!"

Maggie waved as she maneuvered Cinder through the herd. Then she urged the mare into a slow gallop and headed north, back toward the house along the ridge.

3 / Digory

Brilliant hues of pink and orange marked the early summer sunset as Maggie neared home. She loved the summer gloamin'. Darkness fell but for a few hours on those near-arctic reaches, and her freedom to roam about the countryside was greatly extended. Approaching the stables from the south, Maggie rode up without being seen. She dismounted and led the mare inside.

"Weel, lassie," came an ancient voice from the dimness of the interior. "I was beginin' t' wonder when we'd see ye again."

Startled, Maggie peered inside as her eyes adjusted to the darkness. At length she spied the old groom perched on a three-legged creepie stool. "Digory," she replied, "what do you mean?"

"They was frettin' aboot ye in the hoose."

"I was only out for a ride."

"Aye, an' a long one! But they haven't grown so accustomed t' yer ways as I have."

"Have I caused a stir?"

"Only a wee one, lass. They sent me oot t' look fer ye. But soon's I saw Cinder's empty stall I knew the two o' ye were oot together an' there'd be no use my traipsin' aboot lookin' fer ye."

"I hope I didn't cause you trouble," said Maggie.

"Ah, lass," he replied with a laugh that resembled a cackle, "ye'll hae t' be gone longer than that t' cause me trouble. Though ye be but a yoong lassie, ye been comin' an' goin' mostly as ye please fer long enough that I'm confident ye ken what ye're aboot."

"I wasn't planning to be gone so long. It was just that I . . . had to go, and—"

She looked up, her sincere eyes struggling to fight back tears at the remembrance of what had driven her from the house.

Digory stood, straightening his body by slow degrees. He reached out and placed his bony hand on her shoulder. "I'm sure ye meant no harm," he said. Then he approached the horse and reached gently for the reins. "Ye've had yersel' quite a ride, I can see."

He led Cinder toward her stall, began to unhitch the saddle, and whispered softly to her while stroking her back with his free hand.

Maggie could never understand his words at such times. But she had long since grown accustomed to his gaelic utterances to the animals he loved.

She watched in silence as Digory performed his ministrations to the horse. Normally she liked to rub the mare down herself, a routine contemplated with quiet pride by the groom, for he had taught her everything she knew about caring for a horse. But today Maggie was content to observe. Digory's actions were as natural to him as eating or laughing or breathing. Though his shoulders were bent with the unmistakable signs of age, he moved with a certain loving grace. His arthritic hands made up in tenderness what they lacked in dexterity as they curried the rich gray coat. At times, especially in mid-winter when drifts of wind-tossed snow piled higher against the north wall of the stable than the roofline, his hands became too painful to maintain their grip on the brush. Still, he bore his sinewy frame as a statement of his hardy Scottish endurance—a far more eloquent presentation of his character than his simple speech could attempt. His jagged facial features had frightened Maggie as a youngster, but as she had grown and begun to spend more time around the horses he tended for her father, the intimidation dissolved. The soft drawl of his deeply accented voice became to the growing girl a source of warmth and pleasure. Though her first introduction to prayer had been with James and Atlanta around the dinner table, such blessings had remained a formal affair. From the gentle voice of the groom Maggie had first heard of God as a tender and compassionate Father.

"Digory," Maggie began after some moments of silence, "you've been here a long time . . ." Her voice trailed off as if she were uncertain of what she was attempting to say.

"Aye, that I hae," he replied. "Yer grandaddy an' I used t' romp t'gether on the great lawns when we were jist wee bairns."

"You were born on the estate?"

"Aye. My own daddy served yer great-grandpa Anson. A great laird that man was—not that yer own daddy is na a fine laird too . . . if ye take my meanin'."

"I don't know much about him."

"Laird Anson Ramsey were special, least so my daddy always said. 'Tis a long time ago, t' be sure. Stayed his whole life at Stonewycke. Didna even keep a home in the city as most do. Cared fer the people o' the land, even the poor fishers an' crofters. Always was oot among them. The people, they loved him. 'Tis a shame he died so yoong an' his son had t' become laird at such a yoong age. I never thought I'd outlive yer grandaddy. He was a tough one, not at all like his father."

"Who was that?"

"Talmud . . . Talmud Ramsey. A hard man."

"Digory," said Maggie. "What's so different about Braenock Ridge?"

"Braenock . . ." Digory reflected and was silent a moment, then went on slowly. "There couldna be a more desolate piece o' land. How anythin' can live oot there, none can tell. But live they do—the goats, the sheep, an' the folks. An' they all be the hardier fer it. Maybe that's what makes it special. I've heard some call it godforsaken. But I'll not be believin' that. The Lord doesna forsake any o' His creation. Remember that, child, when ye're older an' ye think God's left ye alone. He's always there. An' maybe a place like Braenock Ridge holds a tender place in His heart jist because it never gives up. The wind sweeps icy o'er the moor. An' yet ye can still find a primrose or a tiny daisy peekin' oot from 'atween the rocks."

"My father wants to sell Braenock," Maggie said.

" 'Tis it so?" replied Digory, shaking his head slowly and thoughtfully. "Weel, he be the laird. He knows what's best. Still," he went on, his tone indicating the doubt he felt was not new to him, " 'tis a sad thing t' see him sellin' parcels here an' there on the corners o' the estate. But 'tis na my place t' be speakin' aboot it."

"I rode out there today," Maggie said. "I saw Stevie Mackinaw with his herd of sheep."

"There be several families that live oot there. Canna do much wi' it. But 'tis aboot the only place some o' them can afford t' live."

"What would happen to them . . . if Papa sold the land?"

"Who could tell?" replied the groom. "The Mackinaws an' the others there are like the land—they are the enduring ones . . . the survivors."

"Mrs. Mackinaw is sickly," said Maggie. "I hope Papa doesn't sell it."

Digory said nothing, but looked down and smiled at the young girl he loved as much as the daughter he'd never had. *She's a Ramsey, t' be sure,* he thought to himself. *She'll be a lady someday. Lovin' this estate as she does, Anson—an' who knows, maybe even hard-bitten ol' Talmud too—would be proud.*

" 'Tis good that ye care fer the folks, lass," he said at length. " 'Tis what holds Stonewycke an' all the people that make it t'gether."

4 / Mother and Daughter

The sun had nearly set now, and as Maggie walked slowly back to the house, the great stone walls of the ancient mansion rose up like ghostly shadows before her. The gray walls, covered intermittently with climbing ivy, presented a stark and chilling contrast with the congeniality of the stables she had just left. Austere as its name implied, Stonewycke was not the most inviting of places. But it was home, and one grows accustomed to one's surroundings, and usually even learns to love them.

Maggie was too young to care about, or even notice, the many outward adornments that accompanied her family's position of wealth and influence. Stonewycke was awe-inspiring to her for other reasons. Many were the times she had thought of all those who had lived within its walls before her. For long hours she had daydreamed about them, trying to imagine what her ancestors were like. What did they do as children? Did they ride, burrow through the straw in the hayloft, climb trees? Or were they kept inside by strict nannies and somber tutors? Did they wander through the endless maze of rooms, like her, looking for something interesting to do—but usually finding it out in the barn or stables instead?

Maggie turned the latch on the massive oak door and it swung open noiselessly. Every detail of the house, down to the monthly oiling of the door's hinges, was always kept in perfect order.

Inside she stopped, bracing herself to face her mother and father. They could not guess what prompted her evening's ride, yet she felt guilty knowing about their argument. As she glanced up her eyes fell on the grand stairway which swept from the ground floor toward the upper reaches of the house. Its rich walnut banister and rails curved gracefully up to the second floor—perfect for an exhilarating ride down—when no grown-ups were looking, of course. To the left of the stairs the entryway opened toward several large doors which led to drawing rooms, a banquet hall, and a smaller dining room for the family. Farther toward the rear of the house, and through two or three more corridors, lay the kitchen, the servants' quarters, and many additional rooms and passageways—each with its own nooks and crannies which Maggie had still not yet fully explored.

To the right of the stairs lay the grand ballroom. For the most part, she would always have chosen to be out of doors with Cinder rather than in just about any room of the house—with the possible exception of the library. But this one room always gave the young girl a thrill. The walls were decked with pale lavender gilt-edged flowers and walnut paneling, and splendid purple velvet curtains were pulled back from the tall windows with golden rope-ties. The floors, always polished to a high gloss, reflected like mirrors. But most striking of all was the crystal chandelier. When the sunlight came through the windows just so, striking hundreds of leaded prisms, thin shafts of color cascaded like gentle fairies all about the room.

Maggie could remember but one party in the ballroom, given about five years ago, before her grandfather had died. Maggie had been too young to appreciate it fully. All she could remember of that evening, besides the beautiful dresses of the ladies, was being scurried off to bed while the guests were still arriving.

Tonight she opened the door a crack and peeked into the ballroom for a moment. It was one of the few places she was not allowed to enter without permission. Turning away and easing the door closed, she heard her mother's step descending the stair.

"There you are, Maggie," Atlanta said, with the sharpness that often accompanies concern.

"Hello, Mother," she replied somewhat nervously, "I was out riding. I . . . I forgot the time."

"I was worried, my dear. I sent Digory off to find you. You must leave some report of your whereabouts if you are to continue these long rides."

"I'm sorry, Mother."

"Well, you are here now—and safe. Come along and have your supper. I had the kitchen keep it warm for you."

Atlanta led the way to the dining room where, at her bidding, the remnants of the recently completed light supper were brought to the table. With an inner sigh of relief Maggie cast her eyes quickly around and noticed her father was not present. For the moment, she was glad she didn't have to face them together. She didn't want anyone wondering where she had been and asking what had put Braenock into her head all of a sudden. Her younger brother, Alastair, was still seated at the table dawdling over a dish of butterscotch pudding. He barely seemed to notice as his mother and sister entered, but did manage to shoot Maggie as much of a smirk as he dared. Young Alastair always took special delight in his sister's misfortune, and on this occasion—having witnessed the growing cloud of worry as Maggie's absence had extended longer and longer into the evening—he had anticipated some disciplinary action. Though barely ten, he had learned an infinite number of cunning methods to manipulate his parents far more expertly than his older sister, and was adept at presenting himself as a model child—well-mannered and thoughtful in every way. His deception was bolstered by the fact that, through the years, it was usually Maggie who walked onto the carpet with muddy shoes, knocked over a prized piece of china, or appeared at the dinner table with smudged face. On the rare instances when little Alastair's misdeeds caught up with him, he was able to put on such an angelic and repentant face that he usually escaped punishment.

Maggie ate in silence. Afterward Atlanta announced that there was a nice fire burning in the hearth upstairs. As soon as he was excused, however, Alastair bounded away to his own room. Maggie followed Atlanta up the stairs to the cozy parlor where the family gathered on most evenings. The fire was blazing and sent waves of warmth out into the room. Maggie curled up on one of the low sofas while Atlanta sat down in a chair opposite and picked up a piece of needlework from her basket. With precise and deliberate motions she began to work the needle in and out of the cloth.

She was not a beautiful woman. Her features were too severe for beauty. But a stately, almost swan-like gracefulness caught the attention of any observer in an instant, and her surface plainness quickly receded into memory. In youth, Atlanta's hair had been golden, a reminder of her Saxon heritage. But now, at forty, it had begun to dim with encroaching strands of gray. She wore it pulled tightly back into a bun at the nape of her neck, and she often wore black taffeta as if in perpetual mourning. The rustle of the fabric as Atlanta moved about was to Maggie a soothing substitute to the gentle words her mother was unable to vocalize.

Maggie stole a glance at her mother. She loved to watch her while she sewed and stitched intricate designs with her nimble fingers. Atlanta sat straight and tall—her statuesque dignity reminiscent of the Normans, and the Vikings before them, who had inhabited the land from which she had sprung—in the high-backed mahogany chair, not once relaxing her disciplined frame. But her hands moved effortlessly at her work, never slowing, never erring.

"*The Lord is my shepherd, I shall not want,*" Atlanta murmured, then looked toward her daughter. "This is how I learned the scriptures as a child, Maggie, stitching them into cloth. My father always thought religion frivolous—best left to the women. I suppose one proof he was wrong was that he died an unhappy man. Yet on the other hand," she sighed, turning her eyes again to the work before her, "perhaps in one way we are all doomed to the same fate. I wish I had something more lasting to pass on to you than Bible verses sewn into linen."

"You've taught me many good things, Mother," Maggie offered, not quite certain how to respond to her mother's unusually candid thoughts.

"Not near enough, I'm afraid."

"Digory says the best teacher of religion is God himself," said Maggie.

"Good heavens. I hope you are not getting your religious education from our groom," replied Atlanta, more amused than alarmed, and leaving once more the realm of her pensive feelings. "We are paying Graham good money to fulfill the position of tutor. I had hoped he would include religion in his program."

She had *hoped* it, Atlanta thought to herself, even more strongly than she would admit to her daughter—or anyone else. For of late she had grown more aware of her own inadequacies in the area of faith, while at the same time the clashes with James—which revealed conflicts within herself—were convincing her more and more of its importance. But she forced her attention back upon her daughter who was speaking.

"Mr. Graham knows history and mathematics," said Maggie. "But it's different when I'm helping Digory clean out the stables, or when he's helping me groom Cinder. He knows so much about . . . well, everyday things. Today he was saying—"

She stopped short, suddenly realizing she had nearly breached treacherous ground.

"Saying what?" queried Atlanta, cocking her left eyebrow inquisitively.

"Oh, nothing important," returned Maggie with a momentary tremor in her voice.

"It must have been important for you to mention it," pressed Atlanta.

"No . . . not really." Maggie could feel the red rising to her neck and cheeks.

"Maggie," said Atlanta, growing impatient. "I would like to know what our groom has been telling you."

Maggie remained silent.

"He . . . he said," she finally began, unable to endure her mother's insistent gaze; "he said Braenock Ridge was not godforsaken as some call it."

Maggie swallowed slowly.

"And?" said her mother. "Is that all?"

"He said he thought such places held a special place in God's heart because they are so strong and hardy and never give up. He almost made it sound more beautiful than the valley."

"Why was he talking about Braenock?" Atlanta asked, forcing her words slightly, as if she also knew they had intruded upon delicate ground.

"I—I asked him about it," Maggie replied.

What had sparked Maggie's interest in Braenock Ridge Atlanta could not even guess. To be sure, there was a hesitation in the child's voice which hadn't been there earlier. Yet Atlanta could not bring herself to probe further. Was it her own vulnerability she feared? She would not have wanted to admit it. But forces were at work threatening to upset the balance in her life. She feared for the estate and what James might do to it. But even more she worried about her daughter who was fast growing up, and whom she feared she might lose in the feud with her husband. But she had learned early in life that a lady never caused a scene, never allowed tears to flow in public, never exposed her unguarded inner feelings. So Atlanta pulled her well-composed facade about her like the walls of a crypt, and said no more.

Watching her mother, Maggie saw only her dignified grace and, she thought, noble bearing. Little could her young mind begin to comprehend the inner struggles tugging at the heart of her proud Scottish mother. She saw but the shell of surface fortitude, interpreted it as a sign that all was well, and concluded that she had become upset for nothing by the words in the library.

"It's getting late," Atlanta said after a lengthy silence. "You had a long day, my dear. It's time you were in bed."

"Yes, Mother."

Maggie left the drawing room and made her way down the corridor, now dimly lit and cool as the evening advanced. When she reached the stairs she remembered she had failed to ask about her father.

5 / Stonewycke

The needle sank into Maggie's flesh. Quickly she thrust the finger into her mouth—the last thing she needed was to stain this pure white linen with a spot of blood.

"This is impossible!" she grumbled.

Maggie sat alone in the dayroom on the third floor of the great house. It was one of her favorite retreats in the early hours of the morning because its windows, facing east, caught the full glory of the rising sun. But even more importantly, it was seldom frequented by any of the household, and she knew she would not likely be disturbed.

Normally she would retreat here with one of the Waverly novels—or perhaps Shakespeare if she was trying to impress Mr. Graham. But today she had taken her sewing instead. She'd begun this embroidery project so many weeks ago that by now she had grown impatient with it. With summer bursting out all around her, bringing with it such glorious days for riding, she could barely manage to squeeze in a spare moment for anything else.

She looked down at how her work had progressed thus far. The colorful border of primroses and forget-me-nots was completed, and she openly admired how well it had turned out.

But now the tedious remainder, the seemingly endless names which had sparked her interest when she had begun, blurred together on the small piece of cloth. Atlanta had warned that she might have chosen something too difficult. But Maggie had resolved in her determined young mind to copy the large tapestry of her family tree which hung in her childhood nursery. Atlanta had helped her simplify the design, but there was little to be done to simplify the generations of names and dates which now had to be carefully outlined.

Maggie withdrew her finger from her mouth and, making sure there was no telltale blood to mar the cloth, began once more. An exacting girl, she wanted every letter to turn out precise and uniform—all the more so because Atlanta had stitched the original tapestry. Though her mother had been nineteen at the time, Maggie nevertheless hoped the finished product of what now lay in her young hands would be nearly as lovely as the original.

R-o-b-e-r-t R-a-m-s-e-y . . .

The *y* was causing her particular annoyance at the moment.

Her mind wandered back to the day several years earlier when she had first really taken notice of the tapestry. The brilliant colors had caught her attention before anything else. Then slowly other details came into focus.

"Mother," she had asked, "who are all those names?"

"They are your family, Margaret," had been Atlanta's answer. And though she could not have been more than seven or eight at the time, the note of pride in her mother's voice was by no means lost on the child.

"Do they live in London? I don't remember anyone by those names."

"They are all dead," replied Atlanta. "Except your father and me. These are your ancestors—all the lairds and ladies of Stonewycke. Not all, of course. I only began the family tree with Robert Ramsey."

"Why him?"

"It was to him that the land was reinstated after the Jacobite Rebellion," Atlanta replied. "So that was a significant time for us Scots, when King George III returned our land to us in the 1780s."*

---

*After the death of Charles II, King of England, in 1685, James II became king of a precariously united England and Scotland. Demonstrating bad judgment, he became increasingly unpopular. Thus in 1688 certain English parliamentary leaders invited William of Orange in the Netherlands to assume the English and Scottish crowns. James abdicated and took up refuge in France.

However, William was not as popular in Scotland as he was in England. The Scottish dissenters who still backed the displaced Stuart monarchy of James came to be known as Jacobites. In 1715 they followed the Earl of Mar in a hapless attempt to restore James's son, or "the Pretender," to the throne.

The Jacobites were still active a generation later when Prince Charles Edward Stuart, son of "the Pretender" and grandson of James II, came to the Highlands in 1745 to rally support for his claim to the throne. Having sailed from France with only seven friends, Bonnie Prince Charlie was a brave and hopeful leader. Soon the majority of Scotland's clan leaders were on his side.

The Highlanders marched to Edinburgh and there the Prince proclaimed himself King of Scotland. Then they blazed their way into England with an army of 6,000 men. But when the English army advanced north to meet them, the Highlanders were forced to retreat. Back in Scotland support for the Prince was eroding. The retreat continued through Glasgow and north toward Inverness. The English army pursued Bonnie Prince Charlie and met the insurrectionary forces at Culloden Moor east of Inverness on April 16, 1746. The rebel army of some 5,000 men was crushed and scattered in a final and decisive defeat. Miraculously the Prince escaped and wandered for months, a fugitive with an English bounty on his head.

King George II of England took the uprising of 1745 as an opportunity to humble Scotland for its insubordination and took their lands away from the Jacobite clan leaders. However, some forty years later, when the tide of anger had abated against the Jacobites, George III reinstated the heirs of the clans to their former landowning positions.

"Did Robert Ramsey know the king?" asked Maggie with wide eyes.

"I don't know, child," laughed her mother.

"Oh, I'd like to know!" said Maggie excitedly.

"He was my great-grandfather," said Atlanta, then paused, reflecting. "This family tree marks but a hundred years of our existence," she went on at length. "But the Ramseys had been at Stonewycke for almost two hundred years before that."

"Oh, I'd like to find out all about it!" exclaimed Maggie. "What about the Duncans, Mother?"

"That is your father's family," Atlanta returned rather crisply. She hesitated, and then softened almost imperceptibly. "They live mostly in London and have their own side of the family tree. Perhaps you should ask your father about that side of your family."

"Will there be no more Ramseys at Stonewycke?" asked Maggie innocently.

Atlanta winced but regained her composure before her daughter noticed.

"*You* are a Ramsey," Atlanta finally replied. "My father had but one child, a daughter instead of the son he would have preferred. But Stonewycke will not suffer because my name was changed to Duncan. Ramsey blood will never grow thin here—not as long as you love Stonewycke with your very soul, as I do."

"I do love it, Mother," young Margaret had replied, hardly aware of what she was saying, but moved by her mother's passionate eloquence.

"Always remember, my daughter, that it is more than the land you are loving. The lifeblood of the land comes from the people—not only these names you see before you, but also all those who live under our care and who work the land of the estate. As long as you love them, Stonewycke will be whole . . . whatever your name may one day become."

Maggie's thoughts drifted slowly back to the present as her eyes focused once again on the names in front of her. She wished her mother would fall into such reflective moods more often. But never again since that day had she heard her talk about her family or the love she obviously held deep in her heart for Stonewycke.

With a sigh Maggie turned her attention again to the *y* of Ramsey on the linen before her. Just then there was a sharp rap at the door.

6 / Father and Daughter

Maggie hadn't realized how quickly the time had slipped by, but glancing up she could see that the sun was now high in the sky. She was also puzzled to think who could have found her this far into the upper reaches of Stonewycke.

The door opened and James walked in. "There you are, Margaret," he said. "I hope you don't mind my disturbing you."

"Of course not, Father," she replied. Notwithstanding a certain awe she felt in his presence, Maggie was always glad to see her father. Like most impressionable young daughters, she adored him and lived for the moment when she might bask in the fleeting glow of one of his smiles or a tender word of praise. To please him was the one ambition in life; to be loved by him—for him to return but a glimmer of the exuberant and trusting childlike affection which beat in her heart for him—that was *everything*! But at almost fourteen Maggie was shy of disclosing herself, for James had not cultivated intimacy with his daughter. He rarely came near just to visit; there was always something specific on his mind.

James entered and closed the door behind him. He stood in the middle of the room for a moment with his hands clasped awkwardly behind him. Maggie put down her sewing and sat with hands folded in her lap and eyes focused on the pattern of the Persian rug on the floor. James cleared his throat.

"I'm surprised you are not out riding today," he said at length.

"Cinder threw a shoe and Digory is repairing it," Maggie answered, glancing up briefly, then back at the floor.

James formed his lips into a smile as if he were trying it on for size. He walked over to the window, feeling the awkwardness of the moment and not wanting to make it worse by sitting down. *She's grown up too deuced fast*, he thought to himself. Now she was at such an uncertain age. One moment he'd look at her and see his little baby; the next, he'd hardly recognize the changes taking place. It was no wonder he always felt a bit clumsy trying to make conversation. Even though she was his daughter, sometimes he scarcely knew her.

James was not an imposing man. At five-foot-eight he stood shorter than his wife, but he bore his small frame like a military officer—shoulders square, back straight as an iron rod. His dark, unwavering eyes penetrated their object, and he had always taken a special pride in being able to look another man in the eye and cause him to glance away first. Unfortunately this ability was equally as effective on his daughter as it was on business associates. By now she had learned to avoid rather than seek his face. It did not make for easy conversation.

"I hear you are becoming quite the little horsewoman," he said, gazing out the window. "It's been some time since we rode together. We shall have to go out again soon."

"That would be nice, Father," Maggie said.

"Where do you take your rides?" he asked.

"Different places. I like riding on the beach or in the valley."

"Do you?" he asked thoughtfully. "Well then, we shall have to go there one of these days."

"Perhaps we could—" began Maggie with uncertainty, then hesitated, suddenly losing her courage.

"Perhaps what, Margaret?"

"I was just thinking . . . I mean, I was going to ride out to visit the Mackinaws . . ."

"Whatever for?" asked her father, turning away from the window to face her. His voice contained a slight edge.

"I saw Stevie the other day. His mother's been sick. He said it had been a rough winter."

"My dear," replied James with an amused laugh, "you have much to learn about dealing with crofters. These tenants will do anything to gain our sympathies, even stoop to sending their children to appeal to the delicate sensitivities of the laird's daughter. You must learn to take a hard line or they'll walk all over you."

"They didn't send him," protested Maggie, confused.

"Of course it would never appear that way, but you must not allow yourself to be so easily fooled. My dear little Margaret," James went on, assuming a fatherly tone, "one day you may be mistress of the estate. It would be your duty to rule with wisdom. These rustic poor folk will lose respect for you if you are not firm. And, Margaret, you must always keep their respect."

"Yes, but—"

"No buts, Margaret. Giving in when they complain is a sure sign of weakness, and they will look down on you for it."

"Yes, sir," Maggie replied with a sigh which went unnoticed by her father as she cast her gaze back down at the carpet.

"Now, as to why I sought you out in the first place," James began

in a new vein; "tomorrow we shall have a special guest visiting Stonewycke. I want you to be on your best behavior—no running about the
house, that sort of thing. Lord Browhurst is a very important friend of
your father's. He and I have some serious business to discuss, and I
want him to have a good impression of Scotland, and of my family."

"I'll do my best, Father," Maggie replied, eager for a chance to
please him after his marked disapproval of her interest in the Mackinaws.
Yet she couldn't help feeling disheartened at his tone. He still addressed
her as if she were a little girl, just as he spoke to Alastair. She longed
for him to notice that she was growing into an attractive young woman.

"Fine . . . fine," James went on, oblivious to the conflicting struggles in the heart of his young daughter—the gleam of hope in her eyes
at the thought of gaining his favor, and the disillusionment at his condescending tone. Maggie's tender emotions and her need for approbation
were as foreign to James Duncan as the motives and pressures driving
him were to young Margaret. He turned and made his departure without
another word. Maggie's eyes followed him from the room, and her face
slowly fell. How she longed for him to put aside the hasty pace of his
schedule! She thought wistfully back to the simpler days of childhood.
Part of her still longed to climb up on his lap, to snuggle in his arms at
the end of the day. Oh, just to have a *papa*, she thought! But she had
never, even then—though her heart had been full of him—had that kind
of a *papa*. She had had instead a father who was away from home a
good deal and was more interested in his business pursuits than he was
in his growing daughter.

When the sound of his footsteps had died away, Maggie rose and
quietly left the house by another route. On such occasions Cinder was
always ready to yield a corner of her living quarters as a refuge for the
lonely child. Avoiding Digory, Maggie crept in the rear entrance to the
stables, sought out Cinder's stall, flipped up the rusty latch, walked in,
and closed the door behind her. The manger was full of fresh-cut grass
and Cinder was presently occupied at the far end, her long black head
buried in a trough of oats and fresh hay. She turned to see who this
visitor might be and gave an amiable snort of recognition as Maggie
came nearer and stroked her head and nose.

"Ah, you're a fine horse, my Cinder," she said softly.

She slipped her arms around the mare's neck and squeezed her tightly,
then stepped back. It was so cool and dark, and Cinder was such pleasant
company, that Maggie often sought seclusion here with the horse she
considered her closest friend in the world.

Maggie sat down near Cinder's head in a pile of clean straw; Digory
had no doubt refurbished the stall only moments before. Gradually the

fountain of tears which she usually managed to hold in check began to overflow their gates. And when their supply had been exhausted a few moments later, Maggie was sound asleep.

By instinct sensing the troubled spirit of her young mistress, Cinder bent toward Maggie and gave the peaceful face three moist licks with her long wet tongue. Then she turned back to the oats.

7 / James Duncan

Having left Margaret in the dayroom, James strode briskly down the hall. By the time he reached the stairs he was humming a little tune. He may not have Braenock, he thought—Atlanta had seen to that—but he *could* manage his children. Things would go his way in the end. It was especially important to maintain their loyalty, even more so since this cool distance between him and Atlanta had grown so pronounced. Margaret was a vital link in his future if he was to maintain control of Stonewycke.

She was not the only link, to be sure. He smiled smugly. *Let Atlanta have Braenock*, he mused. *It's nothing but wasteland anyway*. He would still obtain the brewery. That's why Browhurst was coming, after all. He determined to make sure everything was just right.

James carried himself with confidence and self-assurance. But to be practical, he had to admit that there were times when it would certainly have proved profitable had he been titled in his own right. It was only natural, then, that to make up for his provincial background, he occasionally had to find just the right way to impress a business associate. "Greasing the wheels of commerce," as he said, had long been his unspoken creed. James prided himself at having learned to disguise his art skillfully. Rarely did one of his colleagues know he was being manipulated, so adeptly did James ingratiate himself with favors and promises and indulgences.

Browhurst was, he thought, already in the palm of his hand. But if he could find one more weak spot in his character, one flaw he could exploit, one unfulfilled desire of Browhurst's that he could satisfy, then he would feel sure of the deal. He would have to keep his eyes opened once the old man arrived.

James reached the foot of the stairs, continued past the dining room, down several corridors, and finally arrived at the east wing of the house. In this little-used portion of the sprawling castle-like mansion, he maintained a private and secluded office. The rooms were small and plain and not kept up regularly like the rest of the house. In times past they had been used as a billet for soldiers. A persistent rumor in the family maintained that Bonny Prince Charles had spent several weeks here during the months following his rout at Culloden Moor. But some treachery on the part of one of the servants alerted the Earl of Cumberland to the Prince's place of hiding and the Young Pretender had had to flee for the Continent. Whether there was any truth to such reports, James had never bothered to consider. He hated superstition and old wives' fables in any form, and considered the Prince Charlie story as a hybrid of genuine legend and pure poppycock. Whatever their history, the rooms were now mostly empty except for a few used for storage.

James opened a door, ascended a narrow staircase, then paused before another door. The room he entered was little more than a cubicle, not more than twelve feet by fifteen feet with a single window looking out onto the rear portion of the grounds. Against one wall several shelves contained stacks of books, rarely used—mostly technical volumes, legal and surveying reports, and one set of ancient law whose backings of leather were badly cracked and chipped away, so brittle had they become with age. Most had come here during Anson Ramsey's time, and James had never so much as looked at them. On the wall opposite hung a variety of ancient weapons: several ornate swords, one encased in a leather sheath in no better condition than the law bindings; a dagger with jeweled handle; two pistols; and one round shield with curiously carved figures on it. Each obviously had its own silent history and many stories to tell.

James's attention for the moment, however, centered on a roll-top desk shoved against the wall underneath the window. The top was up; such was the clutter upon the desk itself that it would have been impossible to roll the top down. A multitude of papers and dusty old journals and ledgers lay in seeming disarray. A worn leather-covered oaken chair, the leather broken in half-a-dozen spots revealing the horsehair innards of the cushion, sat in front of the desk. At first glance the room seemed a most inappropriate setting for an office for such a one as James, with his lofty plans and high ambitions. But it suited James's needs perfectly.

Of course he maintained a finely appointed study upstairs, with a rich oak sideboard and handsome secretary, where he took brandy with friends and associates. But this cubicle was where he retreated to plan and plot out his major business dealings. Atlanta was, no doubt, aware of the existence of the room. She had, after all, grown up here. But she had never ventured to invade her husband's private domain. Even *she* knew that certain limits existed. Both strong in their own way, James and Atlanta had over the years established their distinctive battle lines beyond which the other dared not cross.

James moved aside a ledger on the desk, nearly overturning a bottle of ink. Sorting through a sheaf of papers, he at length found the one he had been seeking, pulled it out, and gazed at it with apparent satisfaction.

"Yes," he murmured to himself, "yes . . . this is just fine. Everything is in order."

James Duncan had known what he wanted early in life. He longed for the power and prestige his father's mismanagement had deprived him of. The family had owned a large estate in the central lowlands of East Lothian, but gambling and poor investments had finally forced Lawrence Duncan to sell the estate to pay his debts. In the end the family was left with only a tenuous hold on the privileges of the lordly circles they had once been so proudly a part of. Even Lawrence's own brother, the wealthy Earl of Landsbury, would have little to do with him and refused him so much as a shilling in assistance.

Lawrence Duncan aged more rapidly than his years accounted for and became a sickly recluse. Young James was forced to work in order to maintain for the family what little they had managed to keep. Having a temperament for the aristocratic life and a taste for life's finer pleasures, James bitterly resented his father's placing him in the position of a common laborer. With only two years at the university in Edinburgh, he could find little employment suitable for a gentleman, as he styled himself. But he possessed a quick mind, was adept at figures, and eventually secured a post in one of the city's mid-sized banks.

As demeaning as he considered the position, a bank did afford him the opportunity to rub shoulders with people of importance, and, more significantly, people of wealth. It did not take long for James to curry the bank president's favor. Though lowly situated in the company's hierarchy, aggressive young James Duncan grew to become the president's personal lackey and with the important man's eye upon him, he began to advance more rapidly than would have been appropriate under any other circumstances.

James met Talmud Ramsey, the eleventh marquis of Stonewycke, while the latter was in Edinburgh on bank business. The older man was so taken with young James that his good word further heightened the president's view of him; before long James Duncan, barely thirty-four, had been promoted into the office management of the bank, causing no little stir among his fellow employees of more advanced experience and greater tenure.

More important than occupational progress to James, however, were the fringe advantages accompanying his widening association with the Ramsey family. Invited by the marquis to visit their London home whenever bank business drew him to the south, James was drawn back into the coveted circles of English wealth and influence his father had relinquished.

The Marquis' only daughter rarely left the Ramsey estate in northern Scotland, though her father traveled to London six or eight times yearly and maintained a fully-staffed home there. But on one such excursion in 1843, twenty-three-year-old Atlanta decided to accompany her father. James Duncan chanced to be in London simultaneously, and the two met for the first time.

James immediately perceived that Atlanta was no beauty. But neither was she unsightly, and he had only a passing interest in beauty. His views on relationships were far too pragmatic for that. Atlanta was the daughter of the Marquis of Stonewycke, and what was more, heiress of the estate. She was certainly well mannered and refined—striking, he would say. He found no difficulty in persuading himself that he loved her—not that love was a necessary prerequisite to their union, but it did cast a sheltering veneer over his other, more utilitarian, motives.

Atlanta, on her part, found James perfectly suited to the ideal marriage she had already been forced to consider. Having no living brothers or uncles, she had long known the estate would pass to her. Though eleven years her senior, James was untitled; thus in marrying him she would be able to maintain control of Stonewycke, and thereby prevent its being swallowed up in the holdings of a suitor more affluent and powerful than James. If he could provide her with an offspring into whom she could pour herself and to whom she could in turn pass on the legacy, she would be satisfied. Love and romance were of equally little concern to Atlanta alongside the possibility of losing Stonewycke. She could endure any marriage, she thought, if it meant keeping control of her father's land and the heritage of the Ramsey name. And she had to admit, James *was* handsome. He was a magnetizing man whose blandishments were not lost on the young heiress. The marriage, of course, could not have been more to old Talmud's liking.

So in their union, James and Atlanta each found something they wanted, had hoped for more, and had undoubtedly been disappointed in the years since. But neither had been deluded, for happiness was not a commodity they sought, even now. If they harbored any silent regrets, they were too stubborn to admit they had grasped for the wrong things fifteen years earlier.

The birth of their first child brought a certain joyful optimism to the household. In those early days there even began to develop a degree of tenderness between Atlanta and James as husband and wife. But they were never to know if it could have matured into a greater bond of love, for it was all too suddenly shattered by the death of Atlanta's father. As the estate passed to Atlanta, James felt his dispossession more severely than ever. Of course, the husband held certain legal rights by virtue of his position, but he could not help feeling like an adopted orphan.

Perhaps even then the marriage would have held together if his subconscious resentment over what his father had done to him—aggravated by Talmud's death—had not led James into his terrible indiscretion. How he could have been so foolish he never knew. His anger at himself was worsened in that Atlanta had been almost gracious about it. A child by an ill-advised affair was bad enough, but he could easily have swept the situation under the carpet. When the child's mother died, however, James was presented with a regrettable responsibility. The fact that the child was a son made him all the more loathe to give him up, for he knew there would be no more children by Atlanta. He still wondered how he was able to convince Atlanta to take the infant in and, for the sake of propriety, claim him as her own. She claimed the child, but forever after rejected the father.

Atlanta had not set out intentionally to make James resent her dominant position. At first she was hardly aware that his apparent jealousy over her power was in fact a misplaced malice still seething in his heart against all those of rank and wealth and privilege—commodities which he felt by right should have been his but which had been torn from him. But as she saw more and more deeply into his soul, Atlanta realized she had no intention of allowing an outsider (which she considered him, husband or not) to become master of the estate. Stonewycke was her heart and life, and she could barely hide the disdain she felt each time James was referred to as the *laird* in her hearing.

But James did not sit back and accept the second post easily. He refused to allow a woman eleven years his junior to dominate him, no matter what her maiden name. He adopted the mantle of laird with sober determination. Thus the ensuing conflict was inevitable, for each met the other with stout resolve.

The recent dispute over Braenock Ridge was merely one brief skirmish in the ongoing war, a battle in which James grudgingly had to admit defeat. He would perhaps not have yielded quite so readily had he not seen another means to achieve his goal.

The paper he now held in his hands was precisely that means. And it needed only Lord Browhurst's signature to render it legal.

A mere name on the line . . . James thought confidently, running his finger along his short-cropped moustache. *That shouldn't be too difficult.*

8 / A Bargain Is Struck_____

Lord Browhurst ducked low to avoid cracking his head against the lintel of the carriage. A tall man, he had often remarked that carriage-makers must bear some special malice toward persons of full stature. His head cleared without mishap, and he stepped out to his first view of the manor known as Stonewycke.

These Scottish castles are always so dreary, he thought to himself.

Further speculation was cut short as his host stepped forward to greet him.

"How good of you to come!" said James with enthusiasm and an outstretched hand.

"I wouldn't think of refusing your kind invitation," Browhurst replied in a detached tone, "especially since Port Strathy offered such a convenient layover for my yacht."

"I trust you have enjoyed a pleasant sail?"

"Ah, yes. Fair winds and clear skies—couldn't have asked for better," he replied in a deep, resonant voice. At fifty-nine, Browhurst was a handsome man with gray eyes, ruddy complexion, and silver hair. His normally large frame, however, had taken on a few extra pounds of late, especially in his midriff and in a slightly doubled chin.

James presented his family, and Lord Browhurst extended his hand toward Atlanta, greeting her with a politeness that bordered on indifference. Atlanta's smile was strained, but she offered her hand to their guest. She was certain this visit was not purely social but had been unsuccessful in her attempt to discover what scheme James was concocting.

Browhurst cast but a passing glance toward the two children standing silently beside their mother.

After Browhurst had refreshed himself in his room, he and James took a leisurely stroll about the grounds. James was proud of Stonewycke, even if he was but a graft into the long line of generations which had built it. He took a great satisfaction in its grandeur, in the vast wild beauty of the lands. He was, after all, the laird of this mighty estate, and it necessarily reflected well on him.

"I hear you are something of a celebrated horseman," James ventured as they neared the stables.

"I gained a bit of renown in my youth for my equestrian pursuits," Browhurst replied, exhibiting a thin attempt at modesty.

"Then you shall definitely want to have a ride on our highland paths—an experience you won't soon forget."

"I bow to your discretion in the matter," said Browhurst with a good-natured laugh.

They reached the stables and found Digory puttering about with his routine chores. The guest sauntered down the row of stalls, admiring each animal in its turn.

"I must admit, Duncan, you have an impressive stock here."

"I have made horseflesh something of an avocation," said James modestly, knowing full well the other's consuming passion for a fine steed.

"Well, my friend, you have succeeded most admirably."

"Digory," James called. "Saddle up the bay and the gelding. We'll be taking them out right away."

Digory set down a pail and shuffled toward one of the stalls. He lifted the saddle and was about to heave it onto the bay when Browhurst's voice boomed through the quiet stable:

"Is there any reason I shouldn't take out this gray?"

He had come upon Cinder's stall and was gazing at the horse with admiration as if to suggest that perhaps Scotland was good for something after all.

"She were a wee bit lame yesterday, my lord," Digory answered. "She might be wantin' a rest today."

"Nonsense!" interposed James, approaching the stall. "You gave her a new shoe, didn't you? She should be perfectly fine. Saddle her up."

"But, my lord," Digory persisted, "I would not like t' see her—"

James turned on Digory, his black eyes glaring at the old groom. "Enough of your insolence! Do as I say or you'll feel the lash of my whip." Then turning to Browhurst, he added, "You have a fine taste in horseflesh. This one's from a long line of Scottish thoroughbreds. Not only is she unique in appearance, but she is as stout and surefooted as any I've seen."

"I shall be the judge of that," returned Browhurst.

"A favorite of my daughter's."

"Most unusual coloring. I don't know when I've seen such an extraordinary combination of black and gray. It's positively stunning."

Digory had sucked in a deep breath to calm himself and had then turned obediently to the task of saddling Maggie's mare. When finished he took one final look at the right front hoof which had caused the problem yesterday. He lifted the foot gently; even to his cautious eye it appeared perfectly sound. However, he still didn't like the idea of this Englishman riding the little lady's horse.

When the two men returned from their ride later in the afternoon, Browhurst was flushed both from exertion and pleasure. He had given Cinder several vigorous runs and found that James had not been idly boasting about her.

"Splendid creature!" he exclaimed. "Perfectly splendid!"

"Did I not tell you?" James replied with pride.

They dismounted and, leaving the horses in the care of Digory, who hovered protectively about Cinder, made their way back to the house.

"She would make a fine show in London," Browhurst continued, almost to himself. "I cannot get over the remarkable shades of her coat . . . never seen anything to match it."

"I have given that some thought," said James slowly. "But London is such a trip for a horse, and she is still young."

"I say, Duncan!" exclaimed Browhurst in a sudden burst of resolve, "what would you take for her?"

"Take?" responded James quizzically. "I don't quite follow you."

In reality, however, James understood all too well.

"Yes . . . how much? Every man has his price."

"Well, I don't know. You mean you—"

"Come, come, man!" Browhurst went on with rising impatience. "I want to buy the animal!"

"I've never given a thought to selling her," said James slowly.

"I don't want to haggle over the price. I'll give you whatever you ask."

"Indeed, I doubt I could put a price on such a grand animal—"

"Don't be coy, Duncan!" Browhurst snapped.

"As I was saying," James continued, apparently heedless of the interruption, "I could never put a price on her. But . . ."

He paused, drawing out his words for maximum effect.

". . . but," he went on, "I would happily present her to you as a gift, a token of Scottish hospitality."

Browhurst had hardly been prepared for this. The insistent words that had already begun to form on his lips fell immediately into silence as he fumbled for an appropriate response.

"I must say, Duncan," he began, recovering from his momentary shock, "I . . . ah . . . I hardly know how to respond. This is indeed a most unexpected gesture. I . . . I will certainly be forever in your debt."

James accepted the words of gratitude with due modesty, but inwardly could not help feeling extremely pleased with himself. Every

man did have his price, as his guest had indicated, and James congrat-
ulated himself that he had apparently found Browhurst's.

Later that evening, following dinner, James was able to bring his
plan to completion. He and Browhurst had returned to the formal setting
of James's sitting den, where they sipped an expensive brandy together
and relaxed as the conversation drifted to business. James found no
difficulty in bringing the brewery to the forefront of the discussion. From
reliable sources he had learned that Browhurst was exploring options of
expanding his financial base. He had, in fact, been making informal
verbal forays among his associates whom he thought he might interest
in investing in future breweries and distilleries to add to the four he
presently owned in England.

In his most skillful manner, avoiding all hint of coercion, James laid
out the details of his plans to produce a fine Scottish ale which would
eventually become one of the best known in England as well. He made
such a strong case that Browhurst might well have decided to throw in
with him regardless of the gift of the horse. But James had no regrets,
for there was little doubt that the mare had sealed the deal. When Lord
Browhurst signed his name on the document James had drawn up in
advance, James had difficulty containing his delight.

Browhurst was no less pleased with the arrangement. He had fully
realized that the gift would not be without strings; that was in the very
nature of such affiliations. He also had done his checking on James. He
knew him to be a calculating and opportunistic businessman and was
aware from the outset that the invitation from the Scottish laird undoubtedly contained ulterior motives. But the contract between them
was satisfactory, whatever the other man's designs. Now he not only
had a bloody fine horse, but also a reasonable investment in what he
deemed would become a highly lucrative venture.

9 / Loss

James had been absent the whole morning making preparations for shipping the horse to London. Browhurst's yacht, one of the largest vessels to sail into Strathy harbor in recent memory, was scheduled to continue its southerly voyage with the evening tide, and a suitable berth for Cinder had to be fashioned before that time. James had employed two local carpenters and Browhurst had overseen the operation, unable to contain the glow of satisfaction he felt in anticipating the envy his London associates would show upon his arrival.

James had not yet seen Maggie, and thus the dreadful news was all the more awful when the first hint of it came in sing-song jeers from Alastair's taunting voice, "Papa gave your horse away. Papa gave your horse away. . . ."

Not believing her brother, yet alarmed by his words, Maggie said nothing but ran immediately to the stables to check Cinder's stall. To her great relief Cinder stood inside calmly munching away at her supply of hay. But whatever relief she may have felt was short-lived, for Digory was there also, making what appeared to be ominous arrangements with a feedbag and a special harness Maggie knew was used only when one of the horses was to be transported.

"Digory," she asked in alarm, "is father taking a trip?"

"No, child," he answered in a voice which sounded peculiarly weak, "I dinna believe he is."

"Then why are you getting one of the horses ready to travel?"

He went on with his work, saying nothing. It was not like Digory to remain so subdued. A lump of fear began inching its way up into Maggie's throat from the pit of her stomach.

She turned and fled. Digory looked up only in time to see her heels vanish through the open doorway.

"Child . . ." he called after her, but she did not turn back.

He continued his gaze until a silent tear blurred his vision in one eye. He swept over it with the back of his rough hand, then bent himself once more to the loathesome task he had been given an hour earlier. No one but he could have grasped what damage the loss of this horse would inflict within the heart of the wide-eyed and sensitive child. He wept not only for her, but also for his master. For he doubted that James Duncan would ever after this day know his daughter again. And he ached with the anguish of realizing how the father's separation from the daughter would sharply wound the young girl he loved with all his heart.

"Oh, God," he prayed quietly, "protect the wee bairn from the bitterness o' this loss. Dinna let this break her heart, O Lord. Wrap yer great arms o' love aroun' her!"

Still disbelieving what her heart told her was true, Maggie ran straight to the house in search of Atlanta. The look of suffering on her face spurred Alastair's demon of cruelty on to greater heights and he took up his jibes once more.

"You were always jealous of Cinder!" Maggie screamed at him, then ran upstairs to Atlanta.

"Mother . . . Mother . . ." she began before the sobs overcame her.

Atlanta said nothing, but approached her forlorn daughter with open arms. Her fists had been clenched, but she relaxed the anger she harbored toward James long enough to offer comfort to Maggie who alone had to bear the most painful brunt of his selfish act. She held her daughter close to her breast and stroked her hair while Maggie went on crying. After a few moments she relaxed her hold and entreated the girl to lie down.

"You'll feel better after a rest," she said, feeling helpless.

But Maggie could not rest. Nothing could still the wracking throb in her chest. All she wanted was to be with the only friend she had—the friend who was being taken from her. At length she ran down the stairs, out the door, across the yard, and again to the stables. This time Digory was not present. Carefully she entered Cinder's stall. Oblivious to the machinations about her, Cinder gave a short neigh of pleasure to see her young mistress. Maggie moved forward, folding her arms about the long, gray, horsey neck, and lay against the hairy mane. After standing thus for some time, she sank to the floor and began crying again.

When her tears were spent she looked up at the horse, feeding away as if food were everything and a new master and a trip to London were nothing at all.

But a moment that is far off comes as inevitably as if it were the next instant, and Maggie's temporary feeling of peace in the stall beside Cinder did not stop the reality from approaching at the appointed time. The moment came shortly before noon when the horse was scheduled to be taken to its new temporary quarters. Still sitting on the floor of Cinder's stall, Maggie heard footsteps approaching. Then the latch was lifted and, to her dismay, two men she did not know came in, and, heedless of her presence, untied Cinder and began to lead the mare away before her very eyes.

Maggie jumped to her feet and threw herself at the bewildered pair, pounding at them with her small fists.

"Thieves!" she shouted.

Treating her gently, but with firm hands, one of the men restrained her, trying to soothe her with kindly words. In the end, realizing she was powerless to stop them, Maggie abandoned her struggle. Staring after them with tearful eyes, she stood alone, forsaken in the stall which had been Cinder's.

When Maggie finally came to her senses, she rushed from the stable back across the yard into the dark house which no longer held any promise of comfort for her. Dashing up the stairs to her own room, she threw herself onto the bed, buried her face in the pillow, and overcome with grief, wept herself to sleep.

She had not moved when James found her about four o'clock that afternoon. He knocked softly on the door, and when no answer came he turned away, resolved to try again later. But a sensation he couldn't readily identify—being none too acquainted with the pangs of conscience—compelled him to enter the room.

He turned back toward the door, tested the handle, eased the door open, and walked in.

Afternoon shadows lay across the room.

"Maggie, dear," he whispered.

She made no response from the bed.

He cleared his throat and searched his mind for what to say next. "Your mother tells me you are upset about the horse," he began feebly. "I can't understand . . . that is, I had no idea it meant so much to you."

Maggie rolled over and faced him, shot through with a sudden ray of hope. It had been a mistake after all!

"You—you will get Cinder back?" she said with rising expectation.

"I'm afraid that is impossible," her father answered. "The yacht has already sailed."

"Sailed!" shrieked Maggie with a wail of agony. "Father, how could you!"

She threw herself back on the bed sobbing uncontrollably.

"You must understand, dear," he said, trying out his businessman's logic on her, remaining erect where he stood. "Losing a horse is but a small sacrifice for the good of our family and our financial future."

"What could possibly be worth losing Cinder?" cried Maggie through fresh choking sobs.

"It's only a horse, child," James began again. "You shall have another. The last time I was in London a fine thoroughbred mare had given birth to a grand chestnut—the owner knew I was interested and I'm sure the foal is still available." He forced cheer into his voice, attempting to portray as much optimism as possible. "In fact, I'll write this very afternoon. It shall be your very own horse . . . and a thoroughbred to boot!"

"I don't want your old London horse!" Maggie shouted, spitting out the words. "I don't care about a thoroughbred. Cinder is the only horse I could ever care about!"

"Margaret, be reasonable," James began. His tone revealed his growing frustration. He was trying to make up for her loss. He knew she liked the horse. But she was carrying her affection for the beast beyond the limits of his tolerance.

"Cinder was the only friend I had!"

"Nonsense!" said James, his impatience bursting through the restraints of his self-control. "You have your mother and me. And of course Alastair."

Maggie's only reply was a new outburst of sobs, partially stifled in her pillow.

"Well, well," he added checking himself and trying to lighten the tension in the room with a slight chuckle, "you shall feel differently once you see the new animal. Why before you know it, you will forget the other horse ever existed!"

"I'll *never* forget Cinder," came Maggie's reply, taut with emotion.

"You will see," he said, ". . . you will see."

Maggie did not respond.

James turned to leave the room. Just before the door closed behind him he heard his daughter speak again. But this time her words were cold and impersonal, sounding more like a solemn vow than an outburst of childish anger:

"And I'll never forget what you did to me today."

He hesitated briefly but did not turn around again. Then, deciding he had done all he could to rectify the situation, he closed the door behind him and continued on down the hall.

After all, he reasoned as he descended the stairs, he was master of his home and laird of the Duncan estate. What kind of man would he be if he allowed the females, not to say his very children, lord it over him? He had to do what was best for business, best for the estate, and best for him. These confounded vixens! Now Margaret was beginning to act just like Atlanta, taking it into their heads they could dictate what he should do. He had done the right thing, James was sure of that.

Browhurst was no small man to have given such a magnificent favor. He wouldn't forget. Yes . . . they would all thank him one day for his shrewd foresight.

Maggie did not leave the room for the rest of the afternoon or evening. Atlanta had some food sent up, but it remained untouched on the bureau.

10 / The Passing of Childhood_____

Digory stretched tall and rubbed the soreness from his lower back. He was glad for the onset of warm weather, but even the long sunny days would not keep away advancing age.

"Weel, the Lord be praised," he rasped as he hoisted the saddle to the workbench in front of him. "I'll soon be wi' Ye, I reckon."

He stooped down, picked up a dirty rag, scooped a handful of a brown, oily substance from a tin, and began to rub it into the leather. Others used what they called saddle soap, but Digory swore by the concoction handed down to him by his father. The smell was strong, and it browned the hands that used it for at least three days. But the half dozen or so native Scottish ingredients moistened even the toughest leather and preserved it as nothing else could. Digory had done it so many times he scarcely gave the oily rubbing down of one more saddle a second thought—especially today, when his mind was occupied with his young mistress. He had laid eyes on her only once or twice in the three weeks since Cinder's departure, and then only at a distance. She had not ventured near him or the stable in all that time. The somber atmosphere throughout the estate made clear to everyone, servants and family alike, that something had snapped inside the once cheerful girl—everyone, that is, with the possible exception of her father. Digory had not seen her speak to anyone in all that time, but had only seen her walking slowly about, without apparent purpose, with a glazed expression of empty distance in her eyes. The redness from her tears was gone, replaced by a steely resolve never to let herself be hurt like that again. Digory prayed for her morning and night, fearful that James's selfishness might scar his own relationship with Maggie and cause her to shut him out as she had everyone else.

So engrossed was the groom in his mingled thoughts and prayers for his near fourteen-year-old friend that Maggie entered the stable unnoticed. The soft dirt floor sprinkled with sawdust muted her footfalls, and she approached without being heard. An aromatic blend of hay and feed, with an occasional whiff of manure from the pit in back, added to the special atmosphere of the place. On this particular morning the streams of sunlight pierced the cracks in the eastern wall of the barn, and millions of brilliant motes danced in the narrow shafts of sun. Here and there the snort of a horse could be heard, but most were still busily engaged with the breakfast Digory had given them earlier.

"Hello, Digory," said Maggie quietly as she approached.

He looked up from his work, and the trace of a smile parted his lips. If he was startled by her sudden appearance, he gave no sign of it.

"Mornin' to ye, lassie," he said. His voice sounded as normal as he could make it and did not betray the surge of joy he felt in seeing the girl once more in the stable. "Can I be saddlin' up a horse fer ye?"

"No, not today. Thank you."

She hadn't intended to ride. Even the thought of sitting astride a horse again evoked memories too painful to be exhumed. She just wanted to be in the stable again, to breathe in the sweet fragrances and hear the gentle stomping and scuffling and snorting of the horses in their stalls. Even the steady drone of flies somehow soothed her spirit. And to be near Digory again. She knew—whether they spoke openly of it or not— that he understood what the past weeks had been like for her.

Maggie wandered slowly from one end of the stable to the other, rekindling her fondness for the place she had always loved so dearly, reaching in occasionally to pat one of the horses that glanced up toward her. Digory went on with his work, saying nothing. She was quiet, even detached and withdrawn. Her voice rang with—he couldn't be sure exactly—a new degree of independence. Or was it a form of maturity? Had these past three weeks aged her beyond a mere twenty days? Indeed, Digory could see hiding beneath her eyes a new appearance—was it the look of dawning womanhood? But as quickly as the change appeared and the old man thought he had grasped hold of it, suddenly it was gone, retreating once more below the surface features of childhood, awaiting its time. Still her face wore the pained expression of undeserved hurt; for had she not been betrayed by one she had trusted and to whom she had given all?

He watched her noiselessly as she explored again all the old familiar crannies of the stable, fiddling with the equipment, kicking against the burlap bags of feed, as if she were discovering new relationships with the stuff with which horses were cared for all over again. One moment he was observing his youthful friend Maggie as he had so many times in the past, the next he was watching a stranger he had just met for the first time. Her face and body seemed to hover awkwardly between childhood and womanly adolescence.

Digory sensed that the events of the past three weeks had in some deep way stricken the innocence of Maggie the child, out of whose death was even now beginning to emerge Margaret, the future lady of Stonewycke.

The groom's reverie was broken as out of the corner of his eye he saw Maggie pause for a long moment in front of the black mare's stall. The horse was snorting steadily and pounding its hoof against the hay-strewn floor. A length of rope was twisting back and forth in the hay. Noticing it, Maggie realized the mare's back hoof had become tangled in the loose cord.

She opened the door and stepped in. "Take it easy," she said softly, rubbing the horse's white face. "What have you got yourself into here?" She continued murmuring gently while edging her way to the mare's hindquarters. She knew full well what a restive animal could do if approached carelessly from behind. Slowly she knelt down to loosen the rope which had by now become snarled between both hind feet.

"There, Raven . . . that's better, isn't it?" she said, running her hand along the shiny black flank. It was the first time she had been in the horse's stall, although her father had owned the mare for more than a year. Still, she knew the name of every horse on the estate.

"She's a braw one, she is," came Digory's voice behind her.

"I suppose so," Maggie replied.

" 'Cept I been so busy here o' late," he continued, "that her coat's gone a bit scraggly. She could use a good currin'."

Maggie said nothing.

She had always felt so close to Digory, even wanted to be like him. She had envied the peace she had sensed within him, had hungered to feel the same way toward God as he felt. But now, everything seemed changed—even Digory. Or was she just imagining it? Withdrawing to protect her own feelings from further hurt at the hands of those she loved, she hardly realized that she had pulled back from him, too.

"Ye wouldn't be wantin' to give an old man a wee hand, would ye, lass?"

"Digory," answered Maggie flatly, "I'll never forget Cinder." Her voice quavered slightly as she spoke the name.

"An' I'll not be wantin' ye t'."

"You weren't trying to trick me into—" began Maggie with a note of mistrust clinging to her voice.

"Ye remember 'twas me that brought Cinder into the world. She was some special horse t' me too, lass, an' I'll be missin' her sore mysel'."

"I'm sorry," replied Maggie, her old tenderness toward the groom reviving momentarily. "I thought you were trying to make me forget with another horse."

"Oh, lassie, my poor lassie," he said, placing a bent and workworn hand on her shoulder. "I wouldn't be wantin' ye to forget her. She was a fine . . . such a fine horse—"

"I hate him for selling her!" interrupted Maggie, the cold, distant *woman* taking charge of her personality again.

The words stung the old man almost as if they had been directed at him. What he feared most was that bitterness would take root in her tender young heart. And clearly the shoots had already reached down to lodge deep in her memory. How could she, at her impressionable age and with feelings so delicate, understand that only forgiveness could provide the healing balm—not only to rectify her relationship with her father, but also to cleanse the agony of loss within her own heart?

"Lassie," Digory began slowly, realizing his mere words could never bring healing in themselves, "when ye try t' punish others when they wrong ye, weel . . . ye're more than likely the only one who'll be hurt."

"But I've already been hurt," she said cynically.

"Ay, but not so much as ye will be when ye strike back wi' hatred."

"He deserves it!"

"Maybe 'tis so. Only the Lord knows. An' 'tis true that ye didna deserve what he did t' ye. But t' hate him only heaps wrong upon wrong."

"It's all I've got left," she replied bitterly.

" 'Tis only one way t' heal the hurts ye don't deserve, child, an' it comes from yer own heart, an' God in it. To begin wi', it has almost nothin' t' do with yer father an' what he's done t' ye."

"I don't understand you, Digory."

"Forgiveness is a sorely complex thing," said Digory as a perplexed wrinkle added itself to his already creased brow. "I don't understan' all aboot it mysel'. But I do know it begins when ye open yer heart first t' God's love."

"How could I ever forgive him?" said Maggie, growing hostile once more. "He's off in London—he probably doesn't care at all, doesn't even remember."

"I doobt that's true, lassie. Ye never ken what kind o' pain people are carryin' aroun'—even men like yer father. Seein' them wi' God's eyes, that's the beginnin' o' true forgiveness. But time will tell," Digory replied.

"You may be right," Maggie said. "But right now I can't forgive him . . . I *won't!*" She spoke the words through clenched teeth as if to give even more force to her resolve.

Time will tell many things, Digory thought mournfully, as he uttered a silent prayer that it would also help mend Maggie's wounded and resentful heart.

"Now, Maggie," he went on, trying with a positive voice to divert her attention, "this poor horse hae been sorely neglected.. An' I'm too old t' gi' her the workout she needs. She'll gi' ye a good ride."

"Perhaps . . . well, maybe I could," replied Maggie slowly. "After being all tangled in that rope, it would probably help her to feel better."

"I'm sure o' that, lass!"

Together Digory and Maggie saddled the mare known as Raven. She did seem anxious to get out of the confinement of her stall, and Maggie's anticipation rose at the prospect of being out in the countryside once again. She was soon astride the silky black mare, and in her blue frock with her red curls falling about her shoulders, she looked, Digory thought, just like a figure from a picture book.

With a crisp click of her tongue, Maggie urged the horse forward in a slow, uncertain cantor. But within a few strides the enthusiasm she had been suppressing gained the upper hand and she dug her heels into the animal's flanks, and Raven glided quickly into a full gallop. She barely slowed as they passed through the great iron gates leading away from the grounds.

Digory's brown face broke into a grin. It not only pleased him to see horse and rider enjoying themselves, but he knew that a victory—however small—had just been won. The bitterness toward her father might take some time to mend: she had been devastated by his action and the results would not quickly or easily disappear. But at least one obstacle had been overcome on the road toward healing—she had turned her eyes away from herself long enough to once again enjoy God's creation. It was a small, but necessary, beginning.

"She'll be doin' fine," he murmured. "May take some time, but He'll see her o'er this thing."

The bairn is growin' up, he thought. *Why, t' see her from this distance, one might already mistake her fer a grown woman, the grand lady of Stonewycke she is destined t' become.*

11 / The Birthday Celebration

A warm breeze swept over Stonewycke from the south. Perhaps it portended rain, but for the moment it resulted in an invigorating late-summer's evening.

The light wind carried the full fragrance of the foothills, where the heather had only recently exploded into brilliant purple bloom. The spring of 1863 had been unusually wet, bringing rains well into the summer months, and the trees and fields were still green and luscious.

Some of the guests, having traveled great distances, had already been on the estate one or two days. Those just arriving by carriage and coach from Inverness, Fraserburgh, Aberdeen, and even Dundee took full, sweet draughts of the pure northern air before entering the great house where the rugged highland landscape gave way to the influences of London.

Inside, Atlanta's efforts at adornment were evident. The ballroom floor shone as it had never shone before, and the grand crystal chandelier sparkled. The servants had worked for days preparing the mansion for this particular day; now they scurried about, carrying away hats and coats, serving beverages and hors d'oeuvres and caring for the other hundred details that inevitably were part of such a gathering.

Atlanta stood at the foot of the stairs in an elegant brown velvet-and-taffeta gown, greeting the new arrivals. Though her hand was cool, her smile was pleasant and she spoke a personal word of welcome to each who passed her stately and gracious form—every inch the marchioness she was.

But this was not her evening; it was Maggie's. This was the long-awaited day to celebrate the coming out of the young lady who would one day assume her mother's mantle and carry the Ramsey blood and the Duncan name into the future. That Alastair also bore the name, she hardly considered. The line of the blood was what mattered most to Atlanta.

She had to remind herself again that Maggie was now seventeen years old—a woman, almost. How difficult it was to concede entirely to her daughter's maturity. The guests, when they saw her, would no doubt exclaim that young Margaret was truly a woman. But Atlanta could still make out the faint shadow of the little girl about her. Something in her mothering instinct clung to that part of Maggie which receded further into the distance with each passing day. Atlanta knew how difficult womanhood could be, and she desperately wanted to protect Maggie from the heartache she herself had known. She had hoped to celebrate Maggie's seventeenth birthday with only a quiet family gathering. But Maggie had insisted on the party.

"In the ballroom." Her words had been emphatic. "And I will stay up until the very last guest leaves!"

Therewith Atlanta proceeded to plan for her daughter a festive event that would not soon be forgotten by any who attended. She invited barons and earls, lords and ladies, from throughout Scotland and several from as far away as London. If her only daughter must become a woman, then let all of British society behold what a grand lady she was.

"Sorry to have deserted you like that, my dear," James's voice broke into Atlanta's reverie. But she only barely heard it above the din of the guests and the orchestra. "Byron Falkirk cornered me," James went on to explain, "and I only this moment got away."

"I would have thought you could refrain from business—on this day, at least," Atlanta replied. Her words were terse, and for a brief second her smile faltered.

"I intended to," he began coolly, but before he could say anything further he was interrupted by a new arrival. "Ah, Lord Cultain. How very good to see you! And Lady Cultain, you do look lovely this evening."

James lifted the woman's plump hand to his lips and kissed it lightly.

A casual observer would scarcely have detected the tension between host and hostess, so cleverly did they masquerade their feelings, so skillfully did they play their respective roles, greeting the guests warmly and graciously.

"Where is Margaret?" James asked when there was a lull.

"She'll be down soon," Atlanta answered.

"Planning to make a grand entrance, is she?" said James with a chuckle.

Before Atlanta could answer, another arrival diverted James's attention. A solitary young man approached them; he was tall and angular, and to all appearances between twenty and twenty-five. He carried himself well, moving through the crowd as if he were accustomed to commanding respect. When he reached his hostess, he took her hand and kissed it with a grace far exceeding his years. He gave a slight bow to James and asked after his health.

"Never better, George," James answered. Then turning to Atlanta, he added, "Atlanta, you remember Falkirk's son, don't you?"

"Of course," Atlanta replied, her smile firmly in place. Had she been totally truthful, she would have had to beg his indulgence for a slight lapse in her memory, for he had been a mere child when she saw him last, and she would never have recognized him. She had to admit that he had grown into quite a dashing figure of a man. "But you were away in London for some time, were you not?"

"Yes, I was, my lady," he replied with a gleam in his eye Atlanta could not quite identify. "But I am residing once again at Kairn, reacquainting myself with the workings of the estate."

"The high-society life of the south too much for you, eh, George?" burst in James with an attempt at wit.

"I wouldn't say that, Mr. Duncan. The fashionable London season is not without its allure, I must say. I still visit the south from time to time."

"To see the young women there, no doubt," added James with a sly grin. Young Falkirk rejoined with a laugh but said nothing.

"Then you are planning to remain in Scotland?" asked Atlanta.

"Yes, my lady. How could one stay away from our bonny homeland for long?"

"And we hope," James added, patting the young man on the back, "that we shall be seeing more of you, George."

"I will look forward to that," he answered.

Before the words were fully out of his mouth, a hush descended over the crowd and all eyes instinctively turned to the top of the stairway. The face of the young gentleman from the neighboring estate of Kairn looked upward as well; first astonishment, then a broad smile broke out across his countenance when his eyes reached their object.

Maggie had been waiting days . . . weeks, for this moment.

Now as she stood on the landing, every eye riveted to where she stood, her stomach quivered and her lips suddenly felt very dry. She tried to smile, then took a tentative step forward and began her descent.

The guests were evidently stunned by the young heiress of Stonewycke. Her shimmering silk gown reflected the pink of the heather in full bloom. The fitted bodice, studded with pearls, outlined every curve of her small but shapely figure. Around her neck hung a single strand of pearls, creamy and lustrous like her skin. Her auburn tresses fell to the middle of her back, adorned with sprigs of heather and baby's breath.

Ignoring the trembling of her knees beneath her, she made her way slowly down the stairs. Halfway down a voice called, "Bravo!" Then followed a chorus of encouraging words and praises which at length erupted into a round of applause. By the time she reached the last step, Maggie's faintheartedness had vanished. She glanced toward her mother, who returned her smile and reached out to give her hand a heartening squeeze. This was her day, and she now had no reason to believe it would not be everything she had hoped.

From his vantagepoint near the foot of the stair, George Falkirk had already begun to reconsider his earlier estimation of the evening's entertainment. He had come to Stonewycke principally as a courtesy to his father, and because he needed a base from which to reestablish his own position and reputation with respect to acquaintances in the area. True, he was not lord of Kairn yet. But it certainly never hurt to plan early with an eye toward such eventualities. He knew his father had been shrewdly courting the Laird of Stonewycke. Though the older Falkirk had been subtle about it, George was no fool. His father had designs of his own, and he was well aware that a marriage uniting the two estates had been discussed by the two older men.

George was sufficiently a traditionalist to recognize his duty. He would accede willingly to whatever his father arranged for him—even if he never laid eyes on Margaret Duncan ahead of time. He would do it, for the estate, for his own claim on the future. Whatever his commitments in Scotland, he always had a bonny lass or two awaiting him in London. But now, as he looked upon the lovely figure descending the stairway, he had to admit to himself that duty need not always prove odious.

Moving past her mother and father, Maggie's face was drawn to his, for it was not a countenance a young girl could easily miss. Falkirk smiled and offered a suave bow. Maggie returned his smile, then swept past him into the ballroom.

George Falkirk, however, was not one to stand back waiting for an engraved invitation. In two quick strides he was at her side.

"My lady," he said, stopping her with a hand on her arm, then bowing deeply, "I would count myself the most fortunate of men if you would honor me with the first dance."

"But I don't even know you!" Maggie protested, the hint of a coy smile playing at the corners of her lips.

"I am George Falkirk, son of the Lord of Kairn. You are a picture of loveliness this evening, my lady. And if you will but grant my request, I will be the most blessed of men."

"Then how can I possibly refuse you?" Maggie replied, extending her hand with another smile and a curtsey. He took her offering gently, and led her to the middle of the dance floor.

The orchestra, as if awaiting their cue from the handsome couple, immediately struck up a rousing Strauss ländler. George reached firmly around Maggie's waist with his right hand, took her right in his left, and led forward, much to the delight of the onlookers. His sure steps and authoritative lead relaxed Maggie as she followed his experienced motion, and she smiled up at him. Together they flowed with the music as if they had been dancing with one another for years.

Before long other couples joined in and the ballroom soon became a swirling palette of shimmering color, music, and movement. A waltz followed, again by the Viennese Strauss, and again Maggie found herself in the arms of George Falkirk. Not to be outdone, a number of other eligible young bachelors made their way forward to contest for her attentions. Waltz followed waltz, with now and then another ländler or a polka, and Maggie whirled back and forth between Falkirk and several other handsome gentlemen in turn. She had dreamed of this day since the day she was nine and had only been able to glimpse the grand ball from afar.

"A toast to our guest of honor!" cried a voice as the last notes of a waltz faded to an echo in the great hall.

Glasses were lifted toward Maggie amid scattered toasts and cheers.

"Good show, Duncan!" said someone in James's direction.

"Lord Duncan," cried out another, "a dance with your daughter!"

"Splendid idea!" James laughed. "Though I've scarcely been able to get near her all night with all these young bucks vying for her."

"Come on, James," urged another. "Let us see the turn of your feet!"

Enjoying the limelight and smiling broadly, James set down his drink, sought his daughter, took her hand, and led her to the middle of the dance floor.

Maggie complied, and not even the most trained observer could have detected the sudden coolness of her demeanor or the stiffness in her bearing as she followed her father through the strains of the perfunctory waltz. Even James himself, hardly adept at reading his daughter's innermost feelings, never knew that the smile which she forced to remain on her lips could never substitute for the smile that had drained out of her eyes.

When the dance was over James released her to revel in the congratulatory praises of his friends while Maggie, the color of her cheeks and the sparkle in her eyes returning, was swept in another direction by a troop of waiting admirers.

An hour later, out of breath and a little dizzy, she came to stop near the refreshment table. Three young men scurried off to fetch her a glass of punch at once, but it was Atlanta's hand instead that held out a glass to her.

"Mother," Maggie laughed, "isn't it grand!"

"I'm glad you are enjoying yourself," Atlanta replied. She was truly proud of her daughter. Not only was she lovely, she also carried herself as her station demanded. She walked, spoke, even danced with growing confidence. Atlanta had to remind herself that only three years earlier Maggie had cared for little but horses.

"I'll never forget this, Mother," Maggie was saying. "Thank you for making it happen!" Impulsively she kissed her mother on the cheek.

"You're welcome, dear," replied Atlanta. Her voice was soft, and in the excitement of her surroundings Maggie did not detect the slight quiver in her words. Atlanta was struggling to check the tears which had risen dangerously near the surface.

Just then one of the young men returned with a glass of punch which he eagerly shoved in front of her.

She held up the glass Atlanta had given her and smiled as if to say, "Sorry . . . I already have one."

The boy glanced around sheepishly, feeling more embarrassment than the slight awkwardness would account for, until Maggie laughed good-naturedly. She grabbed the glass from his hand, turned and handed both glasses to her mother, took his hand, and led him out to the dance floor once again.

12 / Harsh Words

For two days it rained. But Maggie's lingering exhilaration following the party in her honor could hardly be dampened by a few thundershowers.

And neither could her father's. James glanced out the library window into the gloomy mass of gray, but the sullen atmosphere outside did not for a moment quench his spirits. He re-read the letter in his hand, and smiled again. Then he laughed outright.

Even in his most wildly optimistic moments he could not have foretold that in a mere two years' time the brewery would have created such a substantial revenue. Yet the figures before him did not lie. Nor did the cheque which had been tucked in with the letter. Though the sum represented but a pittance to a man like Lord Browhurst, James knew he would be well pleased. It would add a stamp of credibility to this venture. The other investors, including Byron Falkirk, would now look upon James in an elevated light and view his future proposals with greater respect.

Not that Falkirk's respect mattered that greatly to James, but he had placed his family's future on the line to persuade his neighbor from Kairn to throw in the final sum needed to turn the brewery into a reality. At the time the elder Falkirk was still reeling from the loss of Braenock Ridge, the purchase of which—for reasons James could never quite grasp—he had set his heart upon. Why Falkirk had been so determined to obtain that barren stretch of moor, seemingly at any price, Duncan couldn't guess.

In any case, once Atlanta stepped in to kill all further negotiations between them, James had found it necessary to do some hasty talking before Falkirk would concede to part with his money. How James despised having to curry the favor of the old buffoon! But sometimes such condescension was necessary in the world of business and finance. *And Falkirk will whistle another tune now*, James thought with smug satisfaction. "He'll be crawling to me," he said to himself, "begging to be let in on my next deal."

The door opened and Atlanta walked into the room. "Excuse me," she said, stopping abruptly. "I didn't mean to disturb you," she added, preparing to retreat.

"No, I was hoping to see you anyway," he replied quickly. "Do come in."

Atlanta walked forward to the desk where James sat and stood stiffly with her hands folded in front of her.

"I wanted to share with you my good fortune," James continued, making only a modest attempt to hide his arrogance. "I have just received the annual report from the brewery, and I'm happy to say it has produced a tidy little sum."

"Is that so?" said Atlanta, preparing to leave again.

"Will you never be able to admit that I made the right move?" he asked with a mocking conceit in his voice.

Atlanta remained motionless.

"But the real problem," James went on, "is that I did it without a single farthing of yours, without so much as one pound from the estate. That's it, isn't it? You know your power over me is slipping. Yet in the end it will be *my* brewery and *my* other ventures which will keep Stonewycke intact!"

"Stonewycke will stand without the assistance of your enterprises and speculations!"

"Open your eyes, Atlanta," James returned. "Can't you see what is happening to landowners these days? They are no longer able to hide behind the sanctity of their vast acreage or their titles or their ancestral birthrights."

"Hiding! Is that what you call it?"

"That's exactly what you would choose to do. We could have sold Braenock for a handsome profit. But no. You place more value on your own sentimentalities than on the course of the future."

"It's more than sentimentality. You know what this land means to me."

"I know that judicious investments would be a wiser way to put our resources to work than for them to just sit idle while the heather grows and our debts pile up."

"The land means more than your financial undertakings."

"But it's accomplishing nothing!" retorted James, his blood now running hot. Why couldn't she see the benefits of progress and shrewd investments?

"Will you never understand, James? The land, and the people who work it—*they* are the resources of Stonewycke. Do you actually think selling parcels here and there, or building a profitable brewery, is going to replace all that?"

"It has already generated a considerable income, that much is clear to anyone with eyes to see," he returned, waving the cheque he still held in front of her face. "*This*," he went on with considerable weight to his tone, "is far more dependable than a scraggly assortment of dirt crofters and poor sheepherders."

"It's not the money, is it?" Atlanta said with derision in her voice. "It's England, it's rubbing shoulders with that Duke of wherever-he's-from. It's powerful men like Browhurst whose egos you massage to get at their pursestrings. It's Parliament . . . making a name for yourself in the south. That's what it's really all about, isn't it?"

"Oh, Atlanta, you are so naive! Look around. Those who fail to broaden their base are certain to go bankrupt. If you want to keep Stonewycke in one piece, you must make concessions. That's how the game is played."

"But that has little to do with it, keeping Stonewycke in one piece. Whom do you think you're fooling?"

"I'm trying to fool no one. I'm simply taking the measures of a prudent businessman."

"You would parcel off Stonewycke and sell the fragments to the highest bidder if it would advance your career!"

"I care about this estate too, my dear."

"Ha! It's all for yourself—your own success! That's all you care about!" Atlanta accused.

"My political aspirations are none of your affair!" James shot back angrily. "If you were half the wife you ought to have been, you would try to support me rather than destroy me!"

Atlanta sucked in a sharp breath. As much as she despised James in this moment, perhaps the words were too close to the truth for her to respond with anything but contrition. Yet that was a step she was unprepared to take.

Without another word, she turned on her heel and left the room.

13 / The Estate of Kairn _____

Two hours later James Duncan stood in the center of the study at the house of Kairn. The estate, not nearly so sizable but more sprawling, bordered Stonewycke to the south.

The room was one of the most masculine James had ever seen. Swords and paintings of battles and various war momentos made up the greater part of the room's decor. The study seemed especially out of place when contrasted with the rest of the house, which was garishly decorated in spindly French Provincial and delicate lace.

Byron Falkirk had done a fifteen-year military stint in India before malaria forced him home. As officer in charge of a military hospital, Falkirk had been sent to India in 1850, stationed at Delhi. Four years later, when the War of the Crimea broked out and England was drawn into the conflict, he had initially been disappointed to have been removed so far from the center of action. When reports reached him of the terrible sufferings of the English army, however, he began to congratulate himself on his good fortune.

The Crimean War was hardly over when England had to face another conflict, this time closer to Falkirk's post. Without warning in 1857 the sepoy mutiny broke out. But Byron Falkirk's blessed life had continued, for only a year before he had been reassigned to the newly annexed district of the Punjab to oversee a new medical facility. When the rebellion broke out, the first march of the natives was to Delhi where many English soldiers and their families were massacred. But the uprising did not spread so far west as the Punjab, and by the end of the following year it had been completely stamped out.

Though he had seen no action, Falkirk managed to puff up his importance somewhat by encouraging those to whom he related his heroic exploits ''on the front'' to think of him as occupying a position closer to the smell of gunpowder than had actually been the case. He did little to discourage the conclusions they might draw from his suggestive comments, enjoying, perhaps, the sense of heroism—realities clouded by the passage of time—when returning to his native land from a war-torn battle across the sea. How he longed to have been sent home with a live battle wound (a small one, granted) rather than suffering from the indignity of a vile eastern malady.

Upon his return to Scotland, Falkirk brought with him a ten-year accumulation of Indian culture and "war momentos," as he called them—everything in the room chosen to further the impression that Byron Falkirk had indeed been one of the realm's finest military men. All his paraphernalia had to be crowded into this single room, for Lady Falkirk would have none of it in any other part of her home. She despised India, and perhaps for good reason. It had not been a pleasant experience for her. In the beginning she had tried to endure it for her husband's sake. But after two years she simply could take no more and returned home. If Falkirk could have obtained a transfer back to the Isles, he never tried. As hard-pressed for medical help as the army in Turkey was, he feared they might send him there instead. Better let well enough alone.

By the time hostilities were over in Turkey, the sepoy uprising was about to begin, and a transfer at that time would have been out of the question. Finally, in 1858, malaria forced him to accept early retirement and make the voyage home. James could not help wondering, however, if even India—with malaria—might not be preferable to the overbearing Lady Falkirk. But now that the man was here, his only retreat into the world he had once loved was this single room where, alone, he could bask in past glories, envisioning himself a valiant leader of men.

James stood in front of the flagstone hearth admiring the magnificent tiger skin which hung above it; Falkirk returned to his guest, carrying a tray laden with a decanter of brandy and matching glasses.

"Ah, India!" the host remarked dreamily. "A dirty, uncivilized land—how I loved it!" Here he paused to enjoy his wit. "Rotten malaria! Still get bouts of it now and then—bloody business."

James shook his head in appropriate gesture.

"Did I ever tell you how I managed to get out of Delhi just before the insurgents from Meerut arrived? Was lucky to escape with my life! They were hell-bent to put one of their old Mongo descendants on the throne and kill every bloody one of us. Right over there," he went on, gesturing to a sideboard where a number of knives and daggers lay, "is the dirk I was wearing when—"

He stopped abruptly.

"—but I'm certain you didn't come all this way to hear of my exploits during the war years."

Byron Falkirk stood some six inches taller than James, but he was thin to the point of being gaunt. In his earlier years he had been muscular and even a bit handsome, though timid. One of his favorite stories, considerably embellished and in which actual truth did not seem to be a necessary ingredient to his enjoyment of the telling, involved two Indian sisters—daughters of a Marharish—who nearly killed each other over him. But malaria and inactivity since returning home had quickly reduced him to a shadow of his former self.

"Well, perhaps another time," James replied, sipping his brandy. It was the worst brandy he had ever tasted and he could not help but pity Falkirk who, despite their wealth—inherited, not saved from officer's salary—could not persuade his wife to buy better.

"Yes," said Falkirk, swallowing the unfinished portion of his tale. He glanced up at the tiger on the wall and remembered the moment he had shot it. "Now *that* is a grand story to tell!" he said aloud, almost in spite of himself. "Out in the jungle stalking the big game, what a time to remember! The animal charged toward us in full flight. I raised my rifle to my shoulder just in time to get off two shots . . ."

His voice trailed off as the memory of the incident grew clearer. *Wasn't it the native guide who brought down the animal?* he recalled. *Yes, that was it. He had been the one to put a bullet through his head from about ten paces. Cagy fellow, that guide. Wouldn't take anything less than two pounds to keep quiet and tell the story my way. Yes,* he thought, *quite a story!*

Jarring himself loose from his reverie, he turned to James and said, "You were saying you had good news?"

James pulled the envelope from his breast-pocket. "This may interest you," he said with a broad smile.

Falkirk slowly opened the envelope. He gazed at it a moment, obviously baffled by the contents. What did this have to do with the Punjab? He seemed momentarily bewildered, lost between past and present. Faint recognition began slowly to spread across his face, a glimmer of mild interest.

"Our brewery," James prompted.

"Ah yes . . . of course! The brewery," said Falkirk, his face lighting. "I'm afraid I'd forgotten. It seems to have done well."

James held his tongue and clasped his hands behind him so tightly that the nails dug into his skin. *The man is exasperating!* he thought. *Perhaps the malaria has advanced the onset of senility.*

"Lord Duncan," said a feminine voice, entering the room behind him. "I had heard you were visiting. How good to see you!" She extended her hand, which James took politely.

"Lady Falkirk," he replied, "you look well, as always."

Agnes Falkirk was as short, round, and robust as her husband was the complete opposite. Her gray hair was mounded atop her head in a a futile attempt to convey the impression of height. Even with her upright carriage and hair piled high, she only reached her husband's shoulder.

But she more than accommodated for her diminutive stature with her irrepressible vitality.

Her small black eyes immediately caught sight of the envelope in her husband's hand and squinted imperceptibly. Falkirk handed her the envelope.

"James rode over to bring us this," he said.

Lady Falkirk scrutinized the contents and the cheque with a far keener display of interest than her husband had shown.

"This is indeed a pleasant surprise," she remarked. "Yes, this is very impressive. It's doing well, then?"

"Of course," James answered, eager at last for the opportunity to boast of his business acumen. "After a mere two years of operation, I would say extremely well. That is why I decided to deliver this cheque in person—I thought our joint venture deserved a bit of a toast."

"It is apparent you possess keen business sense, Lord Duncan," the lady said in measured tones. It was just the sort of thing James wanted to hear. "Now, let me refill your glass."

"I still have plenty," replied James. "Don't trouble yourself."

"No trouble," she insisted, taking the crystal decanter from its tray and pouring another ounce of brandy into his glass, then her husband's. She took none herself. Smiling, James lifted his glass toward Falkirk, then raised the glass to his lips once more.

"It occurs to me," his hostess went on, "that we have another happy event to toast as well."

James lowered his glass slightly and replied with a puzzled expression.

"Certainly you haven't forgotten the little compact we made on the day we agreed to invest in your brewery? A *bargain* I believe is what we called it at the time . . . concerning your daughter."

"Oh, that," replied James. "Certainly not. I haven't forgotten."

"I presume we may still anticipate . . ." Her voice trailed off in unspoken implication. Though polite and steady, a hard glint could be detected deep in her eyes which said far more than her words could convey.

"In fact, I saw your son the other night," James went on.

"And. . . ?"

"I gave my word," James replied tersely.

"Yes, of course," the lady said. "And I would never disparage the integrity of a promise from the lips of one so highly respected as yourself. But I have been thinking it might be well for us to think in terms of a more tangible evidence of our mutual accord. A public betrothal, perhaps—"

"The girl is a mere child!"

"The young lady that graced the ballroom of Stonewycke two nights past is certainly no child," Agnes Falkirk returned with a cunning laugh. "One look at her will tell you that."

"Neither a book nor a child may be judged by its cover," James answered. "She is but seventeen—your son would be more content if we waited two or three years."

"I was barely sixteen when I married," the lady replied, as if sealing the argument against further rebuttal.

James was tempted to inquire how that fact had affected the Falkirks' marriage, but he checked the remark. He had to control himself. He needed the Falkirks' money more than they needed the prestige an alliance with his daughter would bring. He had to refrain from alienating this lady. Soothing words of conciliation were needed. He could manage Agnes Falkirk if only he didn't cause her to lose her temper.

"Come now, Agnes," Falkirk interceded. "These things do take time. Young George has been home only a short while. Waiting can never hurt a marriage."

"Waiting has its limits," she replied. "And I have mine. Just make sure, Lord Duncan, that you don't protract this so-called period of waiting too long and force me to take action on my own. I would greatly prefer, for the sake of appearances, that the announcement came from you two men. But I will not be put off forever."

James said nothing, but nodded as if to give an affirmation to her words, and she turned and left the room.

Returning to Stonewycke later in the afternoon, James wondered if he did not feel greater apprehension concerning Atlanta than Lady Falkirk. Of course, she need never know the full details. If she ever so much as suspected that he had traded away the hand of their daughter in exchange for his brewery, he had little doubt that she would resort to murder. But he feared she would guess it one day. And while he could manage her for the most part, if she ever bent the full power of her position against him, he knew she could make life unendurable for him. He had little fear of standing up to her. He had done so before, and would do so again. But he knew what he had conceived that day in the secretive study at Kairn with the man and woman he had just left was a despicable act in her eyes, well deserving of Atlanta's most violent wrath.

To his advantage, at least George Falkirk was a handsome young man, desired by a good many women. He stood to gain a fine inheritance from his father, appeared to have a good turn for business, and would no doubt double his wealth before he was forty. There was also an uncle somewhere in the family, childless and an earl, who could one day further his wealth and even bring him a title to accompany the vast holdings in and about Strathy which would be his. Surely Margaret would have no complaints. The girl would have to be promised eventually. At least he had chosen for her a respectable match.

If only he could fare so well for Alastair. But that would be a trifle more tricky, with the complications of the estate and the inheritance. It would be he, after all, who would carry on the Duncan name, if nothing else. Atlanta and all her talk of the Ramsey clan could not change the fact that the Ramsey name was gone forever from Stonewycke, however much of its precious blood flowed through the veins of their high-strung daughter. It was his now. The north of Scotland would one day look to the Duncan name for its future—and to him, James Duncan, to lead the way.

Let Atlanta rave. What he had done was not so sinister. Didn't they seem made for one another on the dance floor the other night? If the brewery hadn't been involved, Maggie might easily have chosen young Falkirk herself.

14 / Request from the South

Had the letter not first fallen into Atlanta's hands, James would have torn it up, and that would have been the end of it.

But even though she had seen it and appeared favorably disposed to the idea, he could hardly have been less concerned himself. The boy's problems were none of his worry, and he wasn't about to begin charity work at this stage of life.

His uncle's family had shunned him in the years since his father's death—never a word, never an invitation. Not that he would have lowered himself to pay his high-browed London relatives a visit—but how ironic it was that now, in their time of need, they would turn to him! The presumption of requesting a month's respite for their wayward son in *his* home! Anger burned red behind James's eyes. How could Atlanta understand the humiliation he had suffered at their hands, or the despair of his father when his own brother had turned his back at his hour of need?

"I'll not hear another word about it!" James said with finality. Though dinner had barely begun, the mood around the table had already grown tense.

"But, James," Atlanta continued in a tone more appeasing than was her custom, "the lad has nothing to do with what his grandfather may have done. I'm sure he bears no animosity toward you."

"It is enough that he is Landsbury's grandson!"

"The poor child has problems."

"And when were you struck with this sudden round of compassion?" asked James caustically.

Atlanta winced, but held her composure. "I only thought we might be able to help him," she said.

"He can burn in hell for all I care!"

"James—the children!"

Alastair stabbed diligently at his potato, pretending not to hear but, in fact, hanging on every word. Maggie squirmed uncomfortably in her seat, quickly losing whatever appetite she may have had.

"It is well the children know about the Earl of Landsbury." He spoke the words as if about to proceed with a dissertation on the evils of sin. "It is well they know that though the Earl and his descendants bear the name of Duncan, they shall never have any part with us."

"But the boy—"

"A common troublemaker!" James resounded. "Just what I would expect such a family to produce. His parents would have us believe a visit to the country would have a calming effect on him."

"Scotland is more peaceful than London."

"Rubbish! They only want to burden us with him, to get him out of their way. *You* read it," he said, waving the letter toward his wife in a mocking gesture. "Surely you can see the fine hand of deceit between the lines. And what do you care, anyway? You've always despised my side of the family."

Atlanta shrugged. "I don't know," she said with a sigh. "I suppose I thought a change of pace might do us all some good."

"A change of pace! The boy's been an embarrassment to them. I've heard of Theodore Duncan's escapades. Believe me, we don't want his sort upsetting our sleepy little village of Port Strathy."

"Of course, that is a good point," Atlanta replied, conceding at last to her husband's point of view. "I can see what you mean."

"Well," said James, his ruffled feathers settling back into place.

"You are certainly within your rights to turn the lad away. Your cousin no doubt expects that very thing. And I would guess he might even be somewhat relieved not to find himself beholden to you."

James stared at her with a puzzled expression.

Pretending to take no notice, Atlanta continued, "I expect it would gall him to have to thank you for your help."

The light gradually dawned in James's countenance and a cunning smile spread over his lips. *Atlanta and I may have our differences*, he thought to himself, *but I have to admire the woman*. She could be every bit as crafty as any man he had known. And he had to admit—he hadn't considered that particular aspect of the earl's request. It would be a sweet revenge, indeed, to see him grovel in appreciation. Not to mention the glowing reports of the wealth and prestige of Stonewycke and its laird that the lad would undoubtedly send back to the Earl of Landsbury.

What could have sparked Atlanta's sudden wave of charity he had no idea. Some scheme of her own, no doubt. But aside from that, her words rang with good sense.

"Ah, Atlanta, my dear, you are a clever one," he replied with a smug grin. "I don't know what possible interest you could have in our acceptance of cousin Roderick's request. But you are absolutely right. I would, of course, be loathe to put Roderick in the position of being indebted to me." He paused for a moment, then went on with a wily twinkle in his eye, ''Still, how can I turn away the young man when we may be his only hope for redemption. Send a reply off immediately to Landsbury telling him his son is more than welcome for a visit here. Yes, more than welcome.''

Later that evening, alone in his cluttered cubicle, James pondered further the merits of allowing the visit of his cousin's son. What would a month or two hurt? With Alastair going off to school in a few weeks, Atlanta's hours were bound to become idle. She would have all the more time to meddle in his affairs, a prospect she would undoubtedly greet with relish. And she should be kept occupied as he orchestrated the union of their daughter with Falkirk's son. He had to devise a plan to marshall events to bring the two young people together without any suspicion of design.

Atlanta had to be kept out of the way—and young Theodore Duncan would provide the perfect and fortuitous solution to that problem. If all reports were true about the boy, Atlanta would indeed have her hands full. The second son of the Earl of Landsbury was rumored to be a reckless gambler, and reports charged him with heavy drinking as well. With a chuckle James recalled one story he had heard about a brawl in a certain disreputable public house which had supposedly left the young rogue with a nasty scar across his forehead. He had been hauled before the magistrate several times, but his father's name and reputation had preceded him, and justice was not to be had in the court. At twenty years of age, Theodore Ian Duncan had certainly made his mark in the world, albeit a notorious one.

Despite the unsettled feeling of discomfort in the pit of his stomach, James considered this a most providential turn of events after all. Young Duncan would stir things up enough to make a marriage proposal seem the blessed event he intended it to be. *It couldn't be more perfect*, he resolved.

His chair creaked as James leaned back and began to consider how he should go about arranging a second meeting between Margaret and young Falkirk.

15 / The House on Braenock Ridge_____

She feared she had not made this ride often enough, and now that she was returning to Braenock Ridge, she hoped she wasn't too late. Prompting Maggie's decision was a chance rumor that Mrs. Mackinaw's health was failing quickly. The very next day she rode out to Braenock Ridge.

There were no trees about the place, only some scraggly shrubs, rocks and stones, and a brawling stream some fifty feet behind the house, tumbling its way from the mountains to the south into the valley, and on into the Lindow.

The small cottage stood in the middle of the barren moorland, built with an outside wall of rough stone and lime, with another wall of turf within, lined here and there with fir planks. The roof was thatched and a huge pile of cut peat stood against one wall as fuel for the fire which burned constantly inside. On two sides of the cottage stood a half-cultivated area where a small field of oats, a large square of potatoes, and several stocks of cabbage and kale struggled to survive under the harsh conditions. Mrs. Mackinaw had tended the garden until a few weeks ago, while her husband and Stevie had charge of the sheep in the fields. Now the sheep would have to rely solely on the boy for shepherding, and the father would have to coax what food he could for them from the obstinate soil. He was growing old too, but had not yet begun to feel the burden of age as had his wife.

When she had taken to bed, her husband and Stevie had set themselves to pull what quantities of heather they could from the surrounding hills. Binding the heather into tight bunches they squeezed them close together and boxed them in the board frames of a bed. The top made a dense surface, which, when covered with two or three blankets, made a far more luxurious bed for prolonged use than the usual ones of oat chaff. Upon this handmade bed of love Maggie found the old woman, lying against the southern wall of the cottage, which was always the warmest. Her nearly transparent skin stretched thinly over her high cheekbones and large eye sockets. She had been rather a large woman at one time, and the thickness of her bones accentuated her present frailty all the more. The once bright and lovely eyes, now covered with sagging lids, were a rheumy brown.

Maggie knelt down on the earthen floor beside her and grasped one of the woman's thin hands. The bones seemed to groan silently at the very touch, but she managed a tremulous smile as she gazed up into her visitor's face.

"Weel, my leddy," she said, her voice straining over the words, "what brings ye t' oor humble cottage?"

"I heard you were ill, Mrs. Mackinaw," Maggie replied.

"Nothin' fer ye t' be concerned aboot, jist a bit o' trouble that comes wi' age, ye know." Even as she said the words, however, a spasm of pain assailed her which Maggie could see reflected in her eyes.

"I've brought you a few things," Maggie said, trying to make her voice sound cheerful. "There's some chamomile—it'll help you rest. And Nellie was baking fresh bread as I was about to leave, so she made me wait long enough to bring you a loaf."

" 'Tis kind an' neighborly o' ye, an' Nellie too—she's a sweet girl," Mrs. Macknaw replied. "But I'm feared I'll na be much company fer ye, lass."

"Don't worry. You just rest while I brew you a nice pot of chamomile tea."

The woman nodded wordlessly and closed her eyes. Maggie rose and walked to the hearth—little more than a hole in the middle of the earthen kitchen floor surrounded by a ring of flat stones. A peat fire burned in the hole. There was no chimney, only a small hole at the peak of the roof. The smoke rose into the thatch, keeping the cottage very warm and dry, but also very sooty. Finding the shortest route to the outer air, the smoke filtered through the many cracks and fissures in the walls and roof. Over the fire a pot hung on a heavy iron tripod, along with hooks to hold various other implements for the fire. The peat had burned low and Maggie set to work with the poker and a small hand-bellows which hung nearby. Within a few minutes a satisfactory blaze appeared. She filled the kettle from a bucket of what appeared to be clean water and then hung it from one of the hooks over the fire.

As she waited for the water to boil, Maggie took stock of the cottage. It was hardly a wonder that Bess Mackinaw was so ill and appeared twenty years older than her fifty-three years. The cottage was composed of a single large room and, though stout, its walls could hardly insulate against the severities of the weather of the place. The floor was hard and cold, and the single window emitted little light. Maggie knew what the icy winter wind was like as it blew down from the snow-covered slopes of Kincairnmor over the foothills now covered with heather, and across the moor that had come to be known as Braenock. This tiny hovel could hardly keep out the chill of a summer evening, much less provide substantial shelter from that frozen blast. Yet the Mackinaws had lived in this very house for years beyond Maggie's time.

She sat down on a stool near the fire. What kind of a world was it where such poverty could exist within sight of the grandeur of the Castle Stonewycke? Was there nothing that could be done . . . should be done? If she were ever in the position to exercise control over the affairs of the estate, she would certainly have some decent homes built for these people. Were they not the charge of her family? Did they not work the land and pay their due to the estate from the proceeds? Why should they have to feel the bite of the cold without even the small comfort of a rug at their feet?

The face of her father rose before her mind's eye, and her cheeks grew red as a judgment against him. For the past three years, since the day she sat weeping in the empty stall over the loss of Cinder, Maggie's bitterness toward him had mounted. He was a wealthy man, growing wealthier by the day with his brewery and other "investments," as he called them. Why hadn't some of his good fortune gone toward improving the lot of his tenants?

Unaware that the ills of the land existed long before James Duncan's time, she considered him a villain, blaming her father for every grievance she could heap upon him. *He could change all this*, she thought angrily, *but he cares about no one but himself.* He had demonstrated that again and again. He had given away her horse, and now he cared nothing that one of his own people lay in poverty, sick and dying.

All at once this surge of enmity was interrupted by the sound of boiling water. She rose quickly and looked around for a thick rag with which to grasp the iron handle of the kettle. When she had removed it from the fire she scooped two large spoonfuls of the dried chamomile leaves into the water. It steeped a few minutes, then she poured the steaming tea into a coarse wooden mug.

As Maggie finished the process she was suddenly struck by the ludicrousness of waking the poor woman to give her a tea designed to help her rest. But Bess Mackinaw's feeble voice drew Maggie immediately to the bedside.

"Ye're still here, are ye, lass?" she said. "Ye are a patient child."

"I made some tea."

"I been a-watchin' ye. Ye're at home in a poor woman's cottage, though ye come from a great mansion. 'Tis t' yer credit, child."

Maggie smiled in gratitude at the words. "Won't you have some tea?" she offered.

" 'Tis somethin' o' a difficulty t' take anythin' by mouth . . ."

"I'll help." Maggie knelt on the floor and gently eased her hand under the woman's frail gray head and lifted it slightly. She raised the cup to her lips and the woman took a sip or two. Then she motioned for Maggie to lay her back down.

"I'm reminded o' somethin' I read jist the other day in my Book," she said. Maggie fancied that her voice sounded a little stronger already. " 'Fer I was an hungred, an' ye gave me meat,' " she continued. " 'I was thirsty, an' ye gave me drink. Naked, an' ye clothed me, sick, an' ye visited me. Fer inasmuch as ye hae done it unto one o' the least o' these my brethren, ye hae done it unto me.' Sweet words, don't ye think, my leddy? An' true. An' ye hae been wonderful t' me an' I'll never ferget it. An' neither will oor Lord—ye are truly His servant, my leddy."

She stopped and sighed deeply. "Oh, my! My auld husban' says I shouldna talk so much—it wears a body oot." She smiled at Maggie and gave a weak chuckle.

Uncomfortable at her words, Maggie turned away for a moment. She felt compassion for Bess Mackinaw, but she could hardly admit to being the Lord's servant when she knew so little about Him. Her former friendship with Digory, who had so openly talked to her about God and His ways, now seemed far in the past and remote. Then, quickly, she looked back and returned Bess's smile.

Recalling the incident in later years, the mere memory of poor Mrs. Mackinaw would bring tears to Maggie's eyes. Her brave attempt at laughter amidst the hopelessness of her life, and the woman's kindly words toward her when her own father could have eliminated their poverty, or certainly, at the very least made it easier to bear, revealed to her the fibre from which Bess Mackinaw was made. A quality of spirit was demonstrated to the young girl that she had seen in only one other, her old friend, Digory.

"You deserve far more than I could ever hope to give," Maggie murmured, wondering if Mrs. Mackinaw had fallen asleep again.

"I only wish—" the woman began again. ". . . but I reckon I'll ken soon enough. My reward be na too far away, I think."

"You mustn't say such a thing," Maggie answered, suddenly afraid of the death which the old woman so took for granted. "A good rest and a proper diet will see you as good as new. I'll see that some food is brought out."

"Save yer strength, lass. I'll ne'er be good as new." Again she attempted a laugh. "Not till I see my Lord face t' face . . ."

For a brief moment her mottled countenance shone. "Dyin' be na such a bad thing when there's the hope o' a better life on the other side. An' when folks get t' a certain age, lass, they begin t' sense when their time is comin'."

A better life . . .

Maggie pondered the words. Was that what this woman's faith was all about? And yet here was she, Maggie Duncan, an heiress, who had a *better life* by all appearances, yet she still felt a deep emptiness within. What gave Bess Mackinaw her strength, her hope, her *better life* in the midst of this destitution all around her? Was Digory's God her God? Was their faith in Him what set her apart from them?

But she could no longer continue to fill her mind with such questions. How could she admit that alongside Digory and Bess, she was empty of life's greater meaning? Having made the initial admission, she might further have to ask *why*, to wrench open a part of her heart that even after three years she kept tightly shut against all intruders—including herself.

"I hope the Lord'll fergive me fer sayin'," Bess went on, unaware of Maggie's thoughts, "but I'll sorely miss auld Hector, an' little Stevie too. Although he's na so little anymore. He'll be a help t' his daddy. I only wish his brothers hadna had t' go—but it couldna be helped . . ."

There had been two older Mackinaw sons, but they had migrated years ago, one to London and the other to America. A sister had died during an outbreak of cholera and another girl, the youngest, had died in childbirth. Drummond had returned to visit twice from London. But Mrs. Mackinaw had not seen her eldest son Drew since he sailed from Port Strathy to Aberdeen, thence to London and finally New York, over twelve years earlier. Eking out a scant farmer's living with his family in America, Drew Mackinaw had improved his lot over what it would have been in Scotland, but saving money for a visit to his homeland was out of the question.

Bess Mackinaw endured a multitude of sufferings before this present illness had come upon her, yet she never appeared disheartened. Notwithstanding that she had lived most of her days in a ramshackle hovel on the bare edge of existence, she always had a cheerful word to offer. "Weel, lass," Maggie remembered hearing her say once long ago, "it may be a desolate moor, cold in the winter an' dry in the summer, but leastways ye always know what t' be expectin'." As a youngster Maggie had laughed; almost a joke it had seemed at the time, followed as it was by Bess's hearty and infectious laughter. *But it is hardly humorous now*, Maggie thought, tears welling up in her eyes. Quickly she brushed them away, but not before the older woman had noticed.

"Dinna be pityin' me, lass," she said. "I hae no pity on mysel'—I hae had a good life wi' a fine man who couldna hae loved me more, an' fine sons fer me t' love t' carry on after me. A woman couldna ask fer one thing more . . ."

Love, Maggie reflected. Was that it? Was that the well from which Bess drew her hope, her meaning in life?

The ancient voice began to weaken toward the end of the touching speech and finally disintegrated into a paroxysm of coughing. Flecks of dark blood appeared at the corners of Bess's mouth.

"An' now, lass, if ye dinna mind," she went on, when the coughing had subsided, "I'd like t' see my menfolk, if ye could find them fer me."

"Of course," said Maggie, "and then I'd best be going."

"Oh no, lass, ye mustn't leave jist yet," interposed Bess. "Much as I hate t' impose on the laird's daughter t' run erran's fer me, 'tis so nice t' hae another one o' oor kind aroun', ye know, what wi' my own daughters gone. God's been good t' me, lass, an' given me what strength I need, but it's still a sore trial t' lose two daughters."

"I'm sorry."

"Na, na, we'll hae no sorriness aboot here. We're told t' be thankful in all things, an' mostly I am. 'Tis jist nice t' hae ye here, that's all. Especially that I hae not been able t' get t' town or t' the kirk on Sundays fer some months now. Sometimes it jist gets lonely oot here. Now, if ye'll get my man fer me, I'd be obliged even more t' ye."

Maggie found Hector Mackinaw shambling about the byre, a makeshift affair attached to the west wall of the cottage to house the family's single cow and what few chickens they managed to keep. The dejection on the man's face could find no relief even in the many tasks to which he was attending about the croft. As Maggie approached, the color drained from his ruddy cheeks, making him appear all the more wretched.

"She wants to see you, Mr. Mackinaw," said Maggie.

He dropped the pail in his hand and hurried out of the byre with scarcely a word. He stopped abruptly in the doorway and glanced back. "Would ye mind fetchin' Stevie?" he asked. "He's oot in the pasture."

Maggie found Stevie climbing among the rocky ledges of Braenock Ridge, so named for its position between the valley and the rising hills to the east. She called his name, but he did not heed her. A large granite boulder spanned a small cleft in the earth, and Stevie was struggling to lower himself down. Drawing closer, Maggie saw that the boulder was supported by two even larger stones, creating a rude bridge over the narrow opening between the two upright ones. Then she realized why he had ignored her. A lamb was tangled in a patch of thistles growing between the two large rocks. Stevie climbed down from the top one, smashed away the brush as best he could in the narrow opening, and at last retrieved the lamb. Seeing Maggie watching him from above, he called out.

"Take the lamb, will ye, my leddy?" He held it up with his arms outstretched.

Maggie knelt down, and reaching as far as she was able, barely managed to lay hold of the tiny animal.

"Grab a handful o' its wool an' hold on tight," Stevie called.

Maggie obeyed.

"Okay, my leddy, now pull it up t' ye."

Maggie did so, and in a second or two the lamb was returned to the safety of the tableland.

Stevie scrambled up the huge rocks the way he had come and was soon at Maggie's side. "Thank ye," he said. "This be some fearsome trap fer the sheep when they wander too close. Kind o' a little ravine here an' they hae not the sense t' stay back from the edge. There's lots o' other rocks close by all aboot an' it attracts them t' the place. I used t' play here, hidin' in amongst the huge rocks an' that little door between them. But 'tis all growed o'er wi' brambles now."

He was still the same Stevie Maggie had always known, only taller and more gangly as manhood tugged more firmly at his body with each passing year. The effusion of red hair remained the same. His friendly grin revealed two chipped front teeth.

"Weel," he said, "ye be some far from home, an' wi' no horse aboot neither."

"I came to visit your mother," Maggie replied. "She's not doing well, is she?"

Stevie only nodded.

"She sent me out here to get you—"

The broad grin on the boy's face had suddenly disappeared.

"Then the time has come," he said numbly.

"No," replied Maggie abruptly, searching for some word of comfort and refusing to believe the look on his face. "She . . . she only wanted to see you. She—"

Yet suddenly, in the very poverty of her words, Maggie sensed that perhaps Stevie knew better than she why his mother had summoned him.

Stevie ran toward the cottage and Maggie followed as quickly as she could. She was not as accustomed to the exertion as he, nor was she used to the feelings roused within her by this family crisis into which she had inadvertently stumbled. Somehow she sensed that, because of her place, her station, she should *do* something to help ease their pain. Yet events were moving beyond her control, and she was powerless to stay forces that only the heavens truly understood.

Stevie well outdistanced Maggie to the cottage. When she arrived some moments later, out of breath, she entered quietly. Father and son were kneeling by the bed of heather. Hector's frame was rigid, his stone face revealing little of the emotions raging inside. But tears streamed down fourteen-year-old Stevie's smudged and dirty cheeks.

"Ye'll get along jist fine." The feeble voice sounded distant, as if it had already been enveloped in mists from the other side. "I love the two o' ye, my two *men*, wi' all my heart."

"Oh, Lord!" burst out Hector, "strengthen my woman!"

"Strengthen me t' die wi' yer grace, Lord," prayed his wife.

"Amen," whispered Hector in a faint voice, seeming for the first time to accept the reality of what was taking place.

"I'm countin' on ye, Stevie," she went on, stretching out a frail hand and placing it on top of the weeping boy's head, "t' help yer daddy. An' the both o' ye keep the hope in yer heart. An' give my love t' Drummond an' t' Drew when ye write them next. We'll be together one day . . . one day soon. An' know when ye dream aboot me, I'm that very moment thinkin' aboot ye wi' all the love in my heart from somewhere above."

Then noticing Maggie standing just inside the door, the aged face brightened. She extended her hand and motioned Maggie forward.

". . . an' ye too, lass. Keep the hope o' the Lord in yer heart . . . always—"

Her head fell back on the pillow.

Stevie burst into a sobbing wail. Hector rose up on his knees and stretched his great arms around the withered body.

"I'm . . . I'm goin'—" Maggie could barely make out the scarcely audible words, "—goin' where there's no more—Hector . . . Stevie—"

The final word remained unfinished as her final breath slowly departed from her body in one long sigh. As the earthly light faded away, the look of troubled suffering on her face gradually gave way to an expression of radiant contentment, and Bess Mackinaw was gone, folded in the loving arms of husband and son.

_____

Maggie had never seen death before.

She had always pictured it as a frightful, hideous thing. Yet Bess Mackinaw seemed but to slip into sleep—the most peaceful sleep she had ever known. As she rode away from the ridge, Maggie could not erase from her mind the faint smile on the thin, blue, wrinkled lips.

Man and boy had both wept openly. Even stoic Hector Mackinaw could not contain his grief, though he made scarcely a sound as his tears flowed and his broad shoulders shook with convulsive agony. Maggie felt like an intruder, her presence shattering the intense exclusiveness of the awful moment. Without a word she slipped from the cottage and within moments was astride Raven, charging over the moor at a full gallop. She had no destination, she only had to ride.

By now she had crossed the wide moor and was racing up the expansive hills of heather that rose higher and higher toward the south and east. Where the estate of Stonewycke ended and that of Kairn began, Maggie neither knew nor cared. Tears streamed down her face, and on she sped.

These were new emotions erupting within her, and she did not know how to respond to them. Her mind reeled with conflicting thoughts and unanswered questions. She barely knew the woman; why was she suddenly flung into such depths of despair by her death? Was it because of the two men Bess was leaving behind? Was it because her life had been so hard and her death seemingly so friendless and forlorn?

A new sensation welled up in Maggie—*anger*. Anger that people should have to live like the Mackinaws. No one at Stonewycke had caught the cholera. No one in the castle was exposed to the harsh winter weather. They were not forced from their home because of a scanty harvest when there was not sufficient food to go around. Where was the justice in the world? Why did some have so much and others have so little? How could the woman have received her so graciously when the Mackinaws had every right to be bitter over their treatment by the laird of Stonewycke, the laird of their little plot of ground on the most desolate corner of the magnificent estate? Why didn't they hate their masters? How could they open their hearts with such love toward her? Was she not a Duncan as well?

Digory had spoken of God's love. Even old Bess Mackinaw had talked about the Lord as if He were her friend. But where was that love? What had He done for her?

Maggie slowed Raven to a walk, her tears spent for the moment. She stopped, dismounted, and sat down on the ground. This had always been one of her favorite rides. Behind her Braenock Ridge spread out on each side and the valley opened up in the distance, stretching to the sea. She looked around from her high vantage point halfway up the steadily steepening foothills. It was a good land, a rich land despite the many areas too stony and arid to grow anything. When the hills burst into their brilliant shades of pink and purple late in the summer, as they were now, she wished the whole earth was covered with heather. Carefully Maggie plucked a sprig of the wiry plant and held it up to the sunlight.

Scottish heather . . . the distinctive feature of her beloved homeland.

Yet, she thought, the melancholy of her former mood returning, *what do purple hillsides of heather and lush green rolling valleys really mean when old women can die in such poverty? The heather is beautiful*, she mused, *but the life of the poor is often ugly.*

How can they occupy the same land? Why does God allow it? How can God allow a man like my father to control it?

The instant her father's face came to mind, all Maggie's confusion and frustration came into focus as an indictment against him.

I hate him! she thought. *He killed her. Not the cold winters, not the sickness—he killed her, just like he did Cinder! God . . . I hate him!*

She threw the heather from her hand, but even as she did so, Digory's words of so long ago rushed back into her memory. She had tried to block them out, but they had remained: "When ye try to punish others when they wrong ye, ye're the only one who'll be hurt. To hate him only heaps wrong upon wrong. Forgiveness begins when ye open yer heart first to God's love."

"I won't forgive him!" she stormed aloud. "I won't! Not for Cinder, not for Bess Mackinaw!"

She jumped on Raven's back, turned, and headed back, down the hill toward the cottage. In the midst of her irrational thinking she realized that if her father had been responsible for the old woman's death, she must do what she could for the husband and son.

Back at the cottage Maggie rode up slowly, dismounted, and quietly went inside. Stevie was not there; Hector still knelt at the bedside.

"Is there anything I can do?" Maggie asked softly.

Slowly the stricken man rose and turned. "There's naught that any can be doin' now," he said.

"If I could . . . well, perhaps I should send someone out—to help," said Maggie in a faltering voice, struggling in her youthful way to atone for the loss.

"That's kind o' ye, miss."

The door opened and Stevie reentered the house, his red eyes swollen but temporarily dry. He walked to his father, and the large man enfolded him in his arms and pressed the boy tightly to his chest. Once again Stevie burst into a torrent of fresh tears.

Embarrassed at the touching scene, again Maggie turned to go.

"Thank ye, mem," said Hector. "Thank ye fer yer visit—an' fer stayin' here wi' us fer a spell."

"I wish I could do more," replied Maggie.

"Maybe ye could jist tell the beadle aboot poor Bess so he can make the arrangements. We'll be wantin' a proper funeral, ye know—she deserved that."

"Don't worry. I'll take care of it."

"Thank ye kindly, mem," Hector returned. "We'd be honored fer ye t' attend, if ye are o' a mind t'."

"Of course," Maggie said. "I will be there."

She turned, left the humble cottage, and began the ride home to Stonewycke.

17 / The Funeral

The day of the funeral the sky hung low, gray and overcast.

A fine mist drizzled down as Maggie walked to the stable to saddle Raven. She had told no one in the house where she was bound.

As the Mackinaws' cottage was several miles from the village and unsuitable for such an occasion, the mourners gathered at the church for the service instead. Tying her horse, Maggie walked in and sat down, hoping to avoid any undue attention. Every eye, however, turned toward her for an uncomfortable instant. The fact that a member of the laird's family was in attendance at a crofter's funeral could hardly go unnoticed. No doubt it would be talked about for days.

A moment later a man in shirtsleeves, dressed—like all those present—in black, appeared at the door of a side room to the main hall.

"If any o' ye wants t' see the corpse, now's the time," he said to the company, "afore I fasten down the lid."

No one responded to his offer and the carpenter turned and reentered the room. A few moments later the solitary sound of a hammer could be heard, driving home the last few nails into the covering of the coffin. Throughout the proceedings all present sat in utter silence. Hector Mackinaw and Stevie occupied the front row, composed and still.

Most of the parish seemed to be in attendance, for though the Mackinaws were likely the poorest members, they were nonetheless loved. Bess was always ready to help a neighbor in need, and she was not forgotten on this, the final day of her earthly pilgrimage. As Maggie sat awkwardly in the midst of so many unfamiliar faces, she knew the tears being shed around her were genuine, the grief deeply felt.

At length Hugh Downly, the parish minister, arrived, walked to the front of the church with somber gait, opened his Bible, and began the service. He read Isaiah 55 and the second chapter of 1 John, reminding his listeners that they were Bess Mackinaw's favorite passages. As Maggie listened to the scriptures, the words seemed descriptive of the saintly woman and of the love for the Lord which was in her heart. They sounded warm and inviting, and Maggie found herself wishing that she understood them better:

Incline your ear and come unto me: hear, and your soul shall live. . . .

Seek ye the Lord while he may be found, call ye upon him while he is near. . . . For as the heavens are higher than the earth, so are my ways higher than your ways, and my thoughts than your thoughts. For as the rain cometh down, and the snow from heaven, and returneth not thither, but watereth the earth, and maketh it bring forth and bud, that it may give seed to the sower, and bread to the eater: so shall my word be that goeth forth out of my mouth: it shall not return unto me void, but it shall accomplish that which I please, and it shall prosper in the thing whereto I sent it. For ye shall go out with joy, and be led forth with peace: the mountains and the hills shall break forth before you into singing, and all the trees of the field shall clap their hands. Instead of the thorn shall come up the fir tree, and instead of the brier shall come up the myrtle tree. . . .

As the reading of the Word ended and the traditional prayers of the Scottish funeral ceremony began, Maggie could not help thinking that the mountains and the hills of the scriptures were the mountains of snow and hills of heather upon which Bess Mackinaw had lived her life. Were those same hills and mountains, at this very moment, rejoicing in song at the triumphant entering into life of Bess Mackinaw?

Hardly had the prayer drawn to a close before the sounds of trampling feet in the adjoining room bore witness that one Simon Cready, the undertaker, and his assistants had already hoisted the coffin from the table and were trooping out to the horse-drawn hearse which stood waiting. The company gradually rose from their seats, withdrew from the room, watched in silence as the box was loaded, and then fell in behind it and began to move in an irregular procession toward the graveyard, some three hundred yards distant. Maggie followed on foot at the back of the column.

The sonorous tone of the beadle's bell deepened the hush of the crowd as they walked along, the nodding plumes atop the hearse silently waving in the gentle breeze. On the way they were joined by several who had not been in attendance inside, until at last they arrived at the final resting place of the dead. Just before they reached their destination, a few patches of blue peeked out from behind the clouds, and through one shot a beam of sunlight, as if to proclaim: "She for whom you grieve is not dead but alive! Cast off your burdensome cloaks of mourning, for behold the light of her *morning* has come!"

But few of the dour faces took notice, and within moments the patch of light was clouded over once again.

The beadle opened the gate to the cemetery and the procession filed in, finally coming to a stop beside the freshly dug grave. The graveside ceremony was brief. With hats clutched in hand, all heads bent downward in one final parting look as the humble box was lowered into the earth. Tears streamed down Maggie's face as the first spadeful of dirt slammed against the lid of the pine coffin with an echoless thud. She wiped her eyes, bit her lip firmly, and remained stoically in place. And though the wind blew and the drizzle grew steadily heavier, not a soul moved from the spot until the hands of Bess Mackinaw's friends and neighbors, assisting with spade and shovel, heaped the sheltering earth high over the grave.

As soon as the labor was ended, the gathering began to retreat from the graveside, not in formal recessional as they had come, but randomly, each in his own direction.

At the gate Maggie heard one of the farmers remark, "Weel, auld Jake MacKale'll be free t' go t' his reward noo."

"Aye," replied another. "An' let's hope poor Bess has a good long watch."

"My Bess'll na be waitin' by no gate," interposed Hector Mackinaw's trembling voice. "She's sittin' this very minute with her Lord an' she'll hae no part in yer superstitions o' one deceased keepin' watch o'er the yard till the next burial!"

"We meant no harm, Hector," returned the first. "We was only sayin' we hope there na be another death in oor parts anytime soon."

"Let none deny that she's sittin' there this very minute," went on Mackinaw, heedless of the apology. "The Book says so plainly. 'Tisn't that so, Mr. Downly?"

"Why—ah—yes," replied the Reverend who, walking behind the others, had been paying little attention to the gist of their conversation. His was a quiet nature who could speak easily in front of his Sunday morning congregation with the sure aid of a sheaf of notes. But in the more intimate relations of man to man, his was not a nature that found ease expressing itself. "Let me see," he went on, "the exact passage is—"

"Today shalt thou be with me in paradise," interrupted Stevie's voice, sounding almost manly in its tone, as if he meant to verify that his mother's deathbed faith in him was well placed. "I was readin' it this very mornin'."

"Yes—ah—that's it . . . of course," said Downly, plainly relieved. "Our Lord himself said those words to the thief who—ah—asked for mercy." Inside he was comforted to know that he had, at least, found the text for his sermon the following Sunday when he would be much better equipped to expound on this important truth to his congregation.

Returning toward the church, Maggie politely declined an invitation to attend the gathering following the funeral, and instead mounted Raven and slowly made her way home.

The images of the faces she had seen remained vivid in her mind. Even in the midst of the inevitable pain of such an occasion, she could sense a staunch strength and pride within these people: a pride in their land, in their humble dwellings, in the hard-won victories they gained over the land and the severity of the northern elements. She sensed the caring bonds of relationship which bound them together in intimate community with one another. At a birth they gathered to celebrate each the other's joy; through life they lifted strong arms and caring hands to bear one another's burdens; and now, at death, they gathered once more, this time quietly and reverently to share another's painful loss. Maggie found herself regretting her position, supposedly so far above these peasant people. Did they not, in fact, possess a quality of life which she and her family had never known?

But what would happen to Hector and Stevie now that Bess was gone? Surely they were indeed part of the community of caring; somehow they would get by. Their friends and neighbors would see to that. Yet it would not be easy for them. Bess Mackinaw was one of those persons who lent strength and support to those around her, even though it was scarcely noticed at the time. She would be greatly missed; such a void is never easy to fill. Already the haggard look in Hector Mackinaw's countenance was clearly visible. And Maggie wondered if she would ever be able to push from her mind the bitter tears Stevie had shed on the day of his mother's death. If only the two older brothers, and their families, were not so far away!

Maggie turned into the entry of Stonewycke, hardly noticing that the great iron gates stood wide open. Though preoccupied as she was, she could not help but see the unfamiliar black coach sitting in front of the stables. The horses had been unharnessed and were apparently now inside. There was not a soul to be seen about the place.

She had been so absorbed in the events surrounding Bess Mackinaw's death and the funeral that the impending arrival of her father's cousin had completely slipped her mind.

But even had she remembered, the sight of the coach would have remained a mystery. For Theodore Ian Duncan had made his appearance a week ahead of time.

18 / The Guest from London

As Maggie entered, the house seemed inordinately quiet.

She closed the solid oak door slowly, but as it thudded shut, the echo reverberated through the hall. Certainly she had been alone in the solitary mansion on previous occasions. But with Alastair now off to school at Eton, the absence of his high-pitched voice left a strange—though welcome—emptiness. Coming from the gloomy atmosphere of the graveyard into the deserted house deepened Maggie's pensive mood.

Wondering where everyone had gone, Maggie walked to her room. All was equally cheerless there. She wandered aimlessly toward the library. Perhaps now was the time to seek out a friendly book to divert her mind from the grief of Hector and Stevie Mackinaw.

She reached the library, opened the door, and walked in. Less than five feet in front of her stood a young man before a shelf of books.

"Oh, dear!" she gasped at the sight of the stranger, stopping in mid-step. "I . . . I didn't expect anyone—you startled me!"

He glanced up, revealing little surprise. If he was in any way caught off guard at being burst in upon suddenly by such an exquisite specimen of youthful womanhood, the only hint was a slight raising of his eyebrows.

"It seems I find myself in just the opposite position," he replied in a slightly mocking tone. "I came expecting someone, but found no one."

His impertinence caught Maggie by surprise. Unsure what answer to give, whether to excuse herself or demand what he was doing in their house, she stood silently for a moment. Suddenly she became aware that his eyes reflected amusement at her discomfiture.

"I beg your pardon," Maggie sputtered, annoyed, "but what are you doing here?"

"Doing here? Why I am a guest, of course," he replied with more presumption than Maggie could well tolerate.

"I'm afraid you will have to leave until my father—"

He interrupted her with a laugh. "Of course," he said, "you have no idea who I am." He offered a graceful, if exaggerated, bow toward Maggie. "I am Ian Duncan. And I have no doubt you are Lady Margaret Duncan."

Embarrassed by her outburst, Maggie struggled to regain her composure. "You must be my father's cousin," she surmised, "but I thought your name was Theodore."

"True, but I am generally known as Ian. And I am your father's *second* cousin," he corrected pointedly.

He continued to stare toward Maggie in a most disquieting way. Although provoked by his intrusive manner, she could not help noticing that the eyes which returned her gaze were attractive, brown as chestnuts. Though of medium height, his erect posture gave the semblance of greater stature, and the cut of his tweed jerkin emphasized straight, assertively broad shoulders. He was but twenty, and his tanned face contrasted richly with the golden coloring of his hair.

"Well, Mr. Duncan," said Maggie rather formally, "perhaps I should apologize that no one was here to greet you upon your arrival."

"No need," he replied. "I am quite adept at entertaining myself."

"So I have heard," replied Maggie with a hint of sarcasm in her voice.

This time he threw his head back in a merry laugh.

"I see my reputation precedes me," he said at length. "But surely it can't be that bad?"

Her initial testiness thawing in the presence of his infectious geniality, Maggie tried to make up for her caustic remark, "Oh, no . . . not really. It's just that my father said—"

She stopped abruptly, realizing she was only making it worse.

"Oh?" he asked, the amusement never leaving his countenance. "What did your father say?"

"Nothing . . . much," Maggie replied, wishing she had never spoken.

"Please, you mustn't spare me."

"Well, if you must know," she replied finally, giving way to his cheerful insistence, "he said you were a common troublemaker."

"Oh, did he!" replied Ian with another great laugh. But as the laughter faded, something akin to a cynicism crept into the corners of his mouth. This was clearly not the first time he had been confronted with such an accusation. Just as quickly the caustic expression dissolved into another laugh, "Well, I must heartily disagree!" he went on buoyantly. "I am the second son of the Earl of Landsbury. Therefore, I am in no way *common*!"

He laughed again, and this time Maggie laughed with him.

"When did you arrive?" Maggie asked.

"Only long ago enough to unhitch my horses, find them some oats in the stable, knock on the door of the house, admit myself, look around for a soul to welcome me, and stumble through various corridors until I came upon the library, where I had been about ten minutes before you came to rescue me in my wandering.''

"You drove alone?''

"My father never would, of course. But then he considers his second son a ne'er-do-well in need of the proper barnyard skills and all that. Besides, he doesn't provide me with a servant or groom of my own.''

"It's too bad your arrival had to be like this.''

"Never fear, my lady. I'm used to fending for myself . . . as you've no doubt also heard, eh?'' he added, with eyebrow cocked.

"I'll say nothing further this time,'' returned Maggie with a timid smile. "I can't imagine where the servants are. Mother must have given them the afternoon off.''

"No matter,'' said Ian.

"But you must get settled in and be shown about your new quarters.''

"And I can't think of a better guide than yourself, my young cousin,'' said Ian with a jovial grin. "Even if you are several years my inferior, you seem equal to the task of taking care of your wild and roguish cousin from the south. Lead on!''

Not quite sure how to take his words, Maggie hesitated, then turned and led the way out of the library with Ian, smiling broadly, delighted at the prospects for amusement this young demoiselle would no doubt afford him.

Later in the evening, dinner was at best an uncomfortable affair.

James occupied the head of the table, stiff and silent. He had offered little more than the most perfunctory welcome to his guest when he and Atlanta had returned from Kairn, apparently forgetful of his earlier enthusiasm over the idea. Once he had given his approval to the visit by the boy, he considered his obligation fulfilled. He cared not whether the young malcontent carried reports back to Landsbury of his kindness and generosity—only of his wealth and power.

Atlanta made several weak attempts at conversation, mostly in the way of inquiring innocuously about Ian's life in London. But it was clear either the afternoon's ride or her visit to the neighboring estate had been unsettling, and when Ian's answers to her questions proved disconcerting, she also fell silent.

For the first time in her life Maggie found herself actually wishing Alastair was present, if for no other reason than at least to keep a chattering conversation going. The only one enjoying himself was Ian. Observant enough to note the uneasiness Maggie felt at the silence of her parents, he was yet blithe enough to relish the awkward turn of affairs.

He found the entire inter-family feud senseless. He knew he could never curry James's favor, nor did he desire it. He therefore saw no reason to feel injured over his cool reception.

The moment dinner was completed, James rose and left the room without a word. Atlanta delayed long enough to appear civil and then followed, murmuring a hurried apology. Maggie and Ian sat at the table for a few moments in silence. Searching her mind for the best inroad toward conversation, Maggie was relieved when Ian at last spoke.

"Your father is quite a conversationalist, isn't he?" he said with a smile.

"I don't think he means to be rude," replied Maggie, trying to put Ian at his ease. "But he's . . ."

"Less than cordial on occasion?"

"That would not be an untrue way to phrase it," replied Maggie, recalling her own hurt at the man's words.

"I can't help but wonder why he sent me an invitation. It begins to appear he disdains me as much as he does my father."

"I think my mother may have had more of a hand in it than you realize."

"Oh?" replied Ian with a drawn-out, half-inquisitive tone.

They were interrupted that moment by Alice, the serving girl, who appeared at the door to the dining room.

"Mr. Duncan, sir," she said somewhat sheepishly. "Beggin' yer pardon, but his lairdship has requested the honor o' yer presence in the east parlor fer an after-dinner brandy—if ye would care t' join him."

"Please thank the laird for his kindness, miss," Ian replied graciously. "Tell him I will be happy to join him."

Alice turned and darted from the room. Ian rose to leave.

"I'd best not keep the man waiting," he said by way of parting remark. "Perhaps I misjudged his coolness at dinner."

"Such invitations are few and far between," said Maggie.

"Especially to kin of the Earl of Landsbury, no doubt," Ian replied.

"The family tensions. It seems they never go away."

"One could hardly be a Duncan without coming under the influence of this ridiculous feud. Rather droll, if you ask me. But then I suppose every family must have its black sheep."

"And who might *that* be?" Maggie asked, stiffening at the apparent affrontery, but more for the sake of pride in her particular branch of the family tree than for any concern about her father's reputation.

"That's a good question," Ian replied with a laugh. "I can certainly tell you who the black sheep is in *my* part of the family. As for your father's role in the larger question, I would not care to venture a guess."

"Does everything always entertain you so?" asked Maggie, not knowing how to characterize this London cousin of hers.

"Life, *my lady*," he said, stretching out the words in a facetious manner for maximum effect, "would be sheer hell if one were not able to laugh at it."

Hardly realizing he was poking fun at her with the feigned use of her title, she replied, "I've never thought of life as *that* bad."

"Ah, of course," he said, assuming even more of the merry tongue-in-cheek, "but you see, Miss Duncan, when you have lived as long as I have, and have gained the benefits of my worldly experience and wisdom, then things will take on more of their true perspective."

"I doubt I'll share your cynicism, even when I'm—"

"Twenty," he answered for her.

"Even when I'm twenty." Why Maggie was taking the side of optimism she couldn't have said, for before this day she would have considered herself as skeptical as anyone regarding the possibilities for happiness in life. Perhaps she was just making conversation. Or perhaps something in her wanted to take the opposite point of view, merely as a way to test the doubts she was afraid to voice herself.

"You'll never convince me," he replied. Briefly the edge of his voice sharpened. But just as quickly the flash of a smile supplanted the momentary peculiar look. "Good evening, *my lady*," he said, again emphasizing the title whimsically, then turned and walked toward the door.

Maggie watched him for a moment, then suddenly opened her mouth before she had a chance to think about the words. "Do . . . do you ride, Mr. Duncan?" she blurted out impulsively after him.

"I've been known to," he replied with a sly grin as he stopped. "A bit too recklessly for some."

"Stonewycke is reputed for its fine stable."

"Will I find you there?" he asked.

"On most days," Maggie replied.

"Then I shall most assuredly find my way there in the morning," he said, and closed the door behind him.

19 / Ian Duncan

Ian Duncan had not wanted to come to Scotland. He had grown comfortable with his somewhat rowdy London lifestyle. Perhaps something within him needed to play the knave, although he had never considered the question. He only knew it afforded him an identity, a sense of recognition and esteem. Women smiled at him, his drinking cronies laughed at his escapades, and he was able to glean a certain satisfaction from their approval. Barely past adolescence, he never stopped to reflect on what his habits signified. Beyond an undefined sense of occasional disquiet it never dawned on him that his happy-go-lucky roguery was in reality a mask to cover the anger hidden deep within, never entered his mind that he was a youth on the run, hiding from the one person he feared most to look straight in the eye—himself. Taking refuge behind his affected rough exterior and ever-present—and occasionally chafing—sense of humor, Ian laughed his way recklessly through life, giving the impression that to him the world was a stage and he was the principal actor in its comedy of chance.

The constant activity functioned like a stimulant to an addict—the frenzied pace sustained him. Or rather, it served to prevent his having to face what he dreaded most. He would have been unable to name his fears, would have readily denied any apprehensions in life whatsoever. But in the furthest corner of his soul, where the unrecognized angst of misgiving resided, he nevertheless felt the sting of the reality upon which those fears were grounded—the rejection he had received at the hand of his father.

For Ian was, after all, only the *second* son.

Roderick Clyde Duncan, the Earl of Landsbury, was the kind of man who could focus his attentions only on one thing at a time, to the exclusion of all else. Unfortunately for Ian, the whole of his time, energy, and devotion had been lavished on his firstborn. When a second son came along, five years younger than his brother, there was little left in the way of fatherly devotion for him. By then the Earl's affections were well entrenched. A second baby boy failed to move him as his first—*his heir*—had done.

Early in life young Ian had learned that misdeeds were the only sure way to earn attention from his father. So unconsciously his actions directed themselves along an increasingly frenetic path to garner that attention any way he could. However, while certainly gaining the attention he desired, the boy found himself criticized and rejected all the more. He and his father drifted further and further apart, and by the time Ian was fourteen no mending of ways could have healed the wound on either part. Ian grew to hate his life at home and turned to the streets, where, in his laughter and toughness, he discovered an identity—albeit a disreputable one. The more he laughed, the more he drank, the more he played the part of the genial ruffian, the more he found himself accepted by those around him. True, his revelry often landed him squarely in the midst of trouble. But it was rarely serious enough to worry about. Besides, he could laugh or talk his way through most anything. And his father's wealth and position were pledges sufficient to insure him few serious difficulties with the law.

When his mother had suggested Scotland, he had laughed outright. *A change, a diversion*, she had called it. *A diversion from what?* he had asked. He needed no change.

But it did not take long before he learned he had little choice. Only a few days before, he had once again fallen into the hands of the magistrate. But this time the charges had been more serious—assaulting an officer of the Crown. He had been hauled away and locked up without so much as a routine questioning. Ian was furious. He had been driven to the act, he insisted, only when the man, himself having had one toddy too many, persisted in his coarse treatment of one of the barmaids in Ian's favorite pub. All that mattered to the authorities to whom the case was turned over, however, was that Ian had a previous history of causing trouble and that the woman was a known prostitute.

At first the earl refused to ransom his second son.

"He can sit there and rot for all I care!" he had raged to his wife. "That boy is a blot on my name. What he needs is a good stint behind bars!"

She attempted to pacify him with reason. "But what will people say?"

"The people can say what they bloody well please!"

"But it will reflect on you, dear," she went on, in a softer tone. "What will they think of you when they learn that your son is sitting in the tollbooth?"

The earl paused in his outrage and thought for a moment.

"Let me send him away for a while, out of London," she went on.

"Hmmm . . . perhaps you're right," replied the earl slowly, considering the stake of his own reputation in the decision.

"I can arrange everything," she said, her hope rising that she had at last discovered a way to mediate between father and son.

"Yes—yes," the earl continued, "that's a possibility . . . a bloody good idea, actually. Get the boy out of London, away from his carousing friends. Yes, do it. A clever idea."

"And you'll talk to the authorities?"

"Yes, of course. I'll talk to them immediately. Just get the black-guard out of town, and out of my sight, for a while. A good long while!"

The Earl had not known until it was too late that his wife intended to send the lad north to Stonewycke. When he discovered that the would-be benefactor of his renegade son was none other than his cousin James, old Landsbury was so enraged that Ian began to look more favorably on the prospect. If his father were so dead set against it, he reasoned, it must have promising possibilities. The mother had managed to keep the boy out of further difficulty until plans for the journey were set, and now here he was, in the wild north—with no bright and inviting London streets beckoning to him with their evening life, no pubs, no women, no friends, no tables strewn with cards and money and ale, no sounds of laughter—no sounds *at all* after nine o'clock except that infernal chirping of crickets, the faint sound of running water from a stream outside his window, and an occasional snort from the stables. But he had always prided himself in making the best of it in any situation, and one way or another he would survive this rustic prison as he had London's worst.

His drink with James was brief, and, though cordial enough, did not altogether dispel Ian's earlier reservations concerning the man about whom he had heard all his life. Climbing the stairs to the room he had been given earlier in the day, Ian entered, walked toward the window, opened it, and peered out. All was blackness . . . and quiet. Deathly quiet!

He reassured himself that he missed the streets of the city. But a disquiet had been stealing over him; it had begun during dinner. He couldn't identify it, but whatever it was he would brush it aside with a laugh. He would never let this sort of life *get to him*. He couldn't. He wouldn't permit it.

He rose again and paced about the room. He opened the window again and listened. The faint rustle of the trees could be heard gently moving in the breeze. The stream below sang its way toward the sea. He sucked in a deep draught of the night air, and swore under his breath.

He threw the window shut with a crash—angered at the peacefulness of the still night air, angered at the crickets, angered at that tomfool horse who couldn't sleep and insisted on keeping the stable awake—

and returned to his bed where he threw himself down.

A diversion . . . *a change*—his mother's words came back to him. He hadn't wanted to come in the first place. He had been coerced into it by circumstances. Why the very thought of this place *moving* him was . . . well, it was downright preposterous!

20 / A Country Ride_____

A good night's sleep banished for the time Ian's discomfort with his new surroundings. The up-and-down nature of his emotional constitution always enabled him to bounce back from any difficulty with a smile and a cheery face. His optimistic personality managed to find possibilities in whatever circumstances it found itself. Thus the damp chill of the following dawn found him in the stable outfitted in leather jerkin and breeches, along with fine black riding boots.

The place seemed deserted. The only sounds present were the horsey noises coming from behind the walls of the stalls. In the light of morning the stomping and snorting and munching wasn't nearly so upsetting. Actually, they were nice sounds, with a hint of the musical in them. Looking about, Ian realized the girl had certainly not been exaggerating about the fine stock. He drew a deep breath, sucking in the fresh, crisp, hearty air, blended in sweet and fragrant mixture with the odors of hay, oats, straw, manure, and horseflesh.

Ian couldn't remember the last time he had been up so early. But he had to admit, it felt positively refreshing. All that worry last night was over nothing. *Yes*, he thought, *a fine collection of thoroughbreds. Perhaps this out-of-the-way little Scottish burgh has possibilities after all*.

Just then he heard the shuffling of feet, turned, and beheld the ancient visage of Digory.

"Ye must be none other than the laird's cousin," the old man said, studying the youth as best he could in one hasty glance.

"At your service," Ian replied with a friendly extension of his hand.

A good handshake, Digory thought. *Firm and confident*. But he'd heard too much about this youngster not to remain a little on his guard.

"I was told I would be welcome to a ride," Ian said.

"If the weather holds up," replied Digory noncommittally. He then turned and began to busy himself with the feeding of the horses. In the midst of what had always been his domain, his natural caution asserted itself in the presence of a stranger.

Ian walked slowly along the rows of stalls and finally came to a halt in front of Raven's quarters. As he stretched out his hand to rub the animal's silky white muzzle, Digory's voice interrupted him—

"That'll be Lady Margaret's horse."

"Oh," said Ian, aware that Digory had been keeping a watchful eye on his movements. He found the old groom's apparent protectiveness of the girl humorous. "Can you recommend another for me, then?" he added with the trace of a smile.

Realizing his comment had been construed as impertinence, Digory returned the smile, and softening said, "Hoots! Dinna mind me. I'm only the auld groom. 'Tis hardly my place t' tell ye what horse t' ride. But I wouldna want ye t' try this one; that is, except ye'd talked t' Lady Margaret hersel', fer she's partial t' Raven here."

"Raven, eh?" replied Ian, then backed away and continued down the row of stalls. He stopped and eyed the groom curiously for a moment as Digory entered Raven's cell with a bucket of feed. He had known household servants like this. They'd been around so long and outlived so many different masters that many times they wielded more power than the masters themselves. He knew it was not wise to cross their paths. He had no idea if such was the case with this guardian of the stables of Stonewycke. But he was a man worth watching, nonetheless.

Yes, Ian thought, *this might be an interesting place after all.*

"How about this chestnut?" he asked at length. He had progressed down three or four bays until his eye had caught the chestnut whose mane and tail were ebony black.

" 'Tis a fine horse," Digory replied, proud of the selection of animals and well-pleased that the lad could pick out a mount equal to Raven. "Ye've made yersel' a braw choice. Let me saddle her up fer ye!"

"Thank you kindly," said Ian, caught off his guard by the warming charm of this unique old groom. "What's her name?"

"Maukin," Digory answered as he found the saddle.

"An odd name," Ian remarked, "if I comprehend my Scottish aright."

Another voice answered his remark.

"You'll see when you ride her, Mr. Duncan," said Maggie, entering the stables behind him, "why we named her a *hare*. For she is fast. If you are in the least rusty, you might consider another mount."

Ian noted the twinkle in her eye and the coquettish set of her lips. Not a trace of the previous afternoon's occasional antagonism was left in her voice. A night's sleep had apparently put to rest some of her doubts, as well as his own. A second look revealed that Maggie had donned a fine riding habit in the anticipation of an outing with their houseguest. Her woolen skirt was the red and black Ramsey tartan, the black leather jacket fit her delicate waist snugly, and a black silk bonnet, tied about her neck with a ribbon of black velvet, stood out in rich contrast to her auburn tresses and creamy skin. Ian could hardly help but take a second look. *Indeed*, he thought again, *an interesting place after all*.

"I've never been known to back away from a challenge," he laughed merrily. He chose to ignore the fact that he was indeed a trifle rusty, for carriage and cab had been his usual mode of transportation of late in the city, though he tended to drive his carriage as fast as safety permitted, and often faster.

"A ride suits my mood today," said Maggie. "I could show you our lovely countryside."

"Thank you, my lady," Ian returned with a twinkle in his own eye, and casting a playful wink in Digory's direction. "I should be honored. Once again . . . lead on, fair maiden!"

They rode west and south as a gentle breeze played at their backs off the sea and a sky dotted with only a few patches of blue hung overhead. But the gloomy late-summer day could not diminish the brilliance of the blooming heather on the rolling hills nor the gay spirits of the youth who had never seen the likes of such rustic landscape in his life.

Still carrying the trace of a self-satisfied grin on his face, Ian followed Maggie along, smug in the thought that he was humoring this inexperienced country miss with his presence. But he was quite unprepared for the gradual changes which crept over him as he rode. Slowly the same thoughts which had so disturbed him the night before returned. But today they were not nearly so fearsome. The true face of Nature rarely made an appearance on London's streets and was never noticed by Ian Duncan when it did. But as they rode, the heady fragrances of heather, earth, wild grasses, trees, with just a hint of salt spray from the sea, mingled together, filling him with an intoxication of a sort with which he was quite unfamiliar. A lark winged overhead and his ears caught the sound of its silvery voice. *Was this the first time he had ever in his twenty years heard a bird sing?* How could it be? At least it was the first time he remembered the striking and simple beauty of the sound. He glanced around himself with pleasure. As far as his eye could see in all directions there was not another human being to be found. The two of them rode in a solitude he had never experienced, always shied away from. Today, however, the earth, the sky—it all seemed so big . . . so overwhelming . . . so majestic!

What was happening to him? The countryside of peasant farmers had always been something he had scorned. The bustle of the city was his lifeblood. What, then, was this strange feeling welling up from the depths, the sense of joyful lightheartedness, of jubilant exhilaration in the midst of this remote wilderness? What was this strange tingling within, almost like a memory of a memory, of something that had never been, rising out of the distance, not of years but of centuries; an intense longing of unfulfilled desire containing yet a feeling of great bliss? He was lifted into huge clean regions of vacant northern sky, feeling both the intense pleasure, and the piercing stab of pain which accompanies the longing for the unknown.

Ian threw his head back and laughed.

"What is it?" asked Maggie, joining in the laughter with him.

"It's . . . it's *wonderful!*"

"What?"

"Everything! Don't you see? It's all so . . . huge—so empty—so pure!"

Maggie said nothing and they rode on in silence for a few moments. Turning reflective, Ian at length stopped his horse, dismounted, and bent down over a small lonely flower which had struggled to the surface in the midst of weeds and taller field grasses.

"Look at it. It's so small, so delicate. Yet its leaves are rough and thick and hearty. And it's so alone!"

"They usually bloom in the early spring. I suppose it took this one all this time to push out of the undergrowth."

"What's it called?" Ian's voice was barely more than a whisper.

"Why, it's a primrose," answered Maggie. "I thought you knew. They grow like weeds here."

Ian tenderly plucked the thick stalk, eyed it intently for a moment, then handed it to Maggie. "Well, Margaret Duncan," he said with a voice full of energetic urgency, "thank you for introducing me to this tiny wonder. And however many there may be, there aren't enough! Why, I don't ever remember seeing such a lovely face in all of London. The gardens should be full of them! Every house—in London . . . in Scotland . . . *everywhere!* Every house should be surrounded with primroses, I tell you!"

He stretched out his arm in a sweeping circular motion. "You should all be growing primroses!" he shouted to the empty hills of purple and green. "Do you hear me? Primroses!"

Now it was Maggie's turn. She laughed enthusiastically.

"I must say," she said finally, "I didn't quite expect this. You seem altogether overcome with the exuberance of our countryside."

"I didn't expect it myself," returned Ian, settling into a quieter, more thoughtful tone.

He mounted his horse and they continued along their ride. "In fact," he went on, "I don't know what got into me."

"Scotland is like that," said Maggie. "So are these heather hills in the late summer and autumn. They get into you. They draw you, they lure you, and before you know it—"

She left the sentence uncompleted.

"Before you know it . . . what?" asked Ian.

"I was going to say that before you know it the land has become part of you. And you're in love with it."

Neither spoke for a moment. All at once, without warning Maggie urged Raven to a gallop. For a few seconds Ian forgot to follow as he watched her glide away, her hair streaming out behind her. She was like a goddess astride a cloud of black velvet. Suddenly he came to himself, shook off the reverie, mounted and spurred his own horse after her.

"Come on, Maukin!" he yelled.

Sitting rather precariously in the saddle, Ian felt as if he were riding a lumbering elephant in contrast to Maggie's graceful figure receding in the distance. He did not reach her until after she had come to a stop atop a small knoll about three furlongs away.

Maggie dismounted and stood watching his cumbersome gallop. Unwilling to slow the animal for fear Maggie's lead would increase all the more, he had given her full rein and Maukin had risen to a pace that gave her name credit. As they drew closer, the horse slowed not a whit, only pulling up at the final moment in reluctant obedience to her rider's urgent commands and frantic yanks on the reins.

When Ian caught his breath and regained his composure, he managed a sheepish grin. It was the first Maggie had seen of the lingering boy in him, previously hidden behind the facade of feigned manhood.

"Perhaps I overestimated my riding ability," he said.

Suppressing a giggle, Maggie replied. "You held your seat well, Mr. Duncan. Not many can on Maukin. She is truly a hare, always in search of a good scamper."

"Well, I intend to improve," he replied earnestly. "That will be a good occupation for me during my stay at Stonewycke."

"To keep you out of mischief?" suggested Maggie playfully.

"Touché!"

Ian dismounted and looked about him. "It's an absolute sea of heather!" he exclaimed. "Truly worth nearly breaking my neck over."

"Our Scottish poets are always extolling the virtues of the heather. Everyone becomes a poet in August."

"I can see why. Only a cold heart indeed would not be moved by such a scene as this."

"But besides being pretty," said Maggie, "it's just a wiry little shrub, not good for anything."

"Except decorating the hills in August," replied Ian. "Might not that be reason enough to justify the Maker's creation?"

"Perhaps."

"It's opening my eyes," said Ian pensively. "At least it's starting to."

"Opening your eyes?" said Maggie. "To what?"

Ian looked away, scanning the distant hills, then sweeping his gaze around northward toward the sea.

"To myself, I suppose," he replied at length. "But," he went on, seeking to divert the gist of the conversation from himself, "recite me a poem about the heather."

"Oh, I couldn't," said Maggie. "I don't know any."

"I bet you know a dozen. All I'm asking for is one. Come now, for your cousin from the city who's never seen or heard the likes of all this."

"Oh, all right," said Maggie. "Since you put it like that, how can I refuse?" She sat down on the grass, looked away, tried to imagine herself alone as she so often had been here, and in a soft dreamy voice, began:

Fair wast the heather, 'pon hill and muir,
   Fair wast my luve's smile in that sweet place.
So fair the heather 'neath leafy birk,
   An' still fairer the one wha's joy did melt my hert.
But winter steals 'way heather an' birk,
   An' 'way my luve must gang frae me,
   A fechtin' Highlan' wars.
To come again 'pon hills o' heather sweet,
   Like autumn in its verdant grace.

Her voice fell still and for a moment Maggie remained silently enfolded in the mood of the old poem. Suddenly she remembered her companion, and a blush stole into her cheeks.

"That was lovely," Ian said. "Is it your own?"

"Oh no," she laughed. "I discovered it in an old worn book of my mother's. I bring it out this time every year and reread it again and again."

"The poet of those words must truly love Scotland."

"Yes," Maggie agreed. "I suppose that's why I like the verse so. I can feel her love for the land and its people and its history."

"What did the poet mean, 'A fechtin' Highlan' wars,' if I remember the words."

"The poet was a woman. She said her 'love must go from me, a-fighting Highland wars.'"

"When were the *Highland wars*?"

"There were no specific wars by that name. But the inhabitants of the north of Scotland, the highlands, have always been a fighting people. We fought the Vikings when they first began to invade, and all throughout our history there has been fighting, until more recently when we fought the English at Culloden Moor west of here. That's probably the most famous battle."

"What happened?" asked Ian, growing more and more intrigued, both by this maiden cousin and the land from which she had sprung.

"There was a huge massacre. The English troops had marched into Scotland after our Bonnie Prince Charlie who tried to establish himself as King of Scotland. Your King George II didn't like that at all. Many Scotsmen died. But there have been battles and clan feuds and border skirmishes against the English down through the centuries, always taking young men away from their ladies."

The two continued to gaze out over the purple expanse of the hillside. "But despite our colorful past, Mr. Duncan, you will probably find the Scotland of the present rather dreary after London."

"So I thought myself," he replied. "But I surprise even myself. I am discovering that it, too, may have its merits."

"I agree."

"It may even turn out that I will grow fond of it. Perhaps my mother was right after all."

"In what way?"

"Saying I was ready for a change."

"What made you choose to come to Scotland?"

Ian laughed dryly. "Believe me, it was hardly by choice that I came. But it was preferable to the other alternatives facing me. I must remind you that you have welcomed a completely unsavory fellow into your home."

"So my father says," replied Maggie turning toward him. "But I find that hard to believe. How much harm could you have done?"

Ian grinned, wondering if he should tell her the truth of his latest caper. Part of the rowdy city-Ian slowly began to surface, relishing the lark of shocking the innocent girl with tales of being thrown into prison after a drunken brawl over a low-bred prostitute.

"I was exiled from my home as an alternative to a lengthy stay in Newgate," he said.

"Why? Whatever did you do?" asked Maggie with alarm.

"I doubled up my fist and applied it with great speed against the nose of one of the Crown's officers," replied Ian, attempting to add a touch of levity to an incident which had been no laughing matter once the dust settled.

"Well, then," Maggie replied, neither laughing nor showing signs of the shock Ian had halfway anticipated, "Scotland must indeed look rather good to you."

A shadow of self-reproach crossed Ian's face, and another part of him struggled to free itself from the unseen perils and fears of the past. Even as he found the old half wanting to boast in its villainy, the unfamiliar new half wished himself free to take advantage of the opportunity to start fresh presented in this new environment.

He threw his head back and laughed, but there was a quality of defeat in the tone that drained it of its mirth. To lay down his past would never be accomplished without an equal—and painful—laying down of pride.

"Truly spoken, indeed, my lady," he replied, saying the words of titular respect for the first time sincerely. Perhaps it was time to begin acting the part of the gentleman he was supposed to be.

Ian was the first to remount, and he kept a healthy pace all the way back to Stonewycke. Suddenly he had become afraid of those heather-covered hillsides. He rode hard to escape the tiny purple eyes which seemed bent on penetrating the depths of his soul, forcing him to face truths about himself he had managed to keep hidden—until now. His youthful mind was filled with possibilities that had assaulted him unbidden and which he had never considered before.

Maggie did not see her cousin for the rest of the day.

21 / A Dinner Invitation _____

James made no mention of the fact that he had orchestrated the invitation from the Falkirks. It had arrived the previous day and even Atlanta seemed remotely pleased with the idea.

Plans were progressing well. Their visit to Kairn last week was cordial enough despite Atlanta's annoyance over Lady Falkirk's brusqueness, and would pave the way for her later acquiescence to the notion of George as a suitable son-in-law. And today's visit, when George himself would be present, fairly teamed with opportunity, if only he could keep his impetuous daughter in tow. The only flaw was the presence of that boy—Theodore, or Ian, or whatever his name was. He couldn't very well leave their houseguest behind with no explanation. But he wasn't about to drag him along, either.

Shortly before eleven he sought the boy out in his room. Ian had risen only a short while earlier. He had not been up with the cocks again since the morning of his ride with Maggie two days earlier.

"Well, my boy," James began, "what do you think of our northland so far?"

"A far cry from the streets of London, that much is certain," replied Ian, wondering to what he owed this sudden overflow of friendly hospitality.

"Not to your father's liking, of that I am sure," said James. "But how about you?"

"I'm growing more accustomed to it every day."

"Ah, good for you. I have some business at a neighboring estate this afternoon. You don't mind more-or-less fending for yourself for the rest of the day, do you?"

"Not at all," answered Ian, more than a trifle confused. Not having seen James more than two or three times since his arrival, Ian could not help feeling a natural curiosity about the laird's sudden concern for his welfare.

"Fine, fine! By the way," James continued, as an apparent after-thought, "my wife and daughter will be accompanying me to Kairn, sort of a family matter, you understand. I'll have the cook set something out for you this evening."

111

He turned and left the room.

Ian smiled to himself. *Why all the deceit?* he wondered. *Why didn't he simply tell me I'd be dining alone this evening?*

He shook his head, walked to the window, and looked out. The sun was already high in the sky. "I really should try to get up earlier," he said to himself. "That morning of the ride was positively glorious."

Several hours later Maggie, along with her father and mother, rode up to the house on the estate of Kairn. When the young groom reined in the two horses and brought the carriage to a stop, the three stepped down and walked to the door. The driver took charge of the horses and carriage, and a servant showed them in through a spacious hallway and into the drawing room where Lady Falkirk awaited them.

"I'm so happy you could come," she said warmly, "and especially you, my dear," she added, turning toward Maggie. "I haven't seen you since your birthday last month."

Before Maggie could respond a door at the opposite end of the room opened and Lord Falkirk, followed by his son, walked in. Falkirk extended his hand toward James while George, bowing politely but hastily in Atlanta's general direction, walked straight toward Maggie.

"Welcome to Kairn, Lady Margaret," he said, taking her hand and raising it gently to his lips. "I must say, you look nearly as lovely today as you did in your pink silk the night of the ball."

"Thank you," replied Maggie, feeling the heat rising in her neck. "How could you possibly remember what I was wearing? I thought men paid no notice of such frivolity."

"I make it a point of remembering beautiful things," he answered with an arresting smile.

His eyes lingered on her face momentarily. Then he turned to greet James. "Good day, Lord Duncan," he said. "It's an honor to have you visit our home."

"The honor is mine, George," said James, pleased with the strong grip of the young man's handshake. "This is quite a son you've got here, Byron," he said, still holding onto George's right hand. "He'll make some young lassie in these parts a manly husband." He shot a quick wink at the young man and then released his hand.

"And an ambitious one," replied Falkirk.

"No doubt—no doubt!" laughed James.

As Lady Falkirk led the way into the dining room, George offered Maggie his arm. She placed her hand lightly in the crook of his elbow and they followed, while the two fathers brought up the rear. The two elder men sat at opposite heads of the table and, after seating her most graciously, George took his place next to Maggie.

As they were being served, George remarked, "I see you so rarely, Lady Margaret. Now that you have come of age, it would be proper of you to be out among the local gentry more frequently. Would you consider allowing me to call, and perhaps take you to visit some of the neighboring estates?"

"Yes . . . of course, certainly," replied Maggie.

"May I also call, just to visit *you*, Lady Margaret?"

"I suppose there would be no harm in that," said Maggie, glancing uncertainly toward her mother.

Atlanta smiled and gave a slight nod.

"I would consider that a pleasure," George went on. "Ever since that night when we first danced together, I've found myself—hullo! what's this?" he exclaimed as a servant placed directly in front of him a platter displaying a large roasted pheasant.

"You said you wanted to carve it, Master George," the man said.

"Oh, yes, so I did," said George. "Shot it myself only this morning," he remarked to no one in particular. "Thought I'd complete the sport by turning my hand to the knife. May I slice you a nice thick wedge of breast, Lord Duncan?" he asked.

"Thank you, George. That will be perfect," replied Maggie's father, fully delighted with the course of events.

As the dinner progressed it was some time before George spoke again to Maggie directly.

"I would like to call on you, Lady Margaret," he said at length. "I would be privileged to take you for a ride in my gig."

Maggie glanced away bashfully, then back. "That sounds like fun. But we do have a guest—"

"Nonsense!" interrupted James. "Come right over, George, at your convenience. The girl will be only too pleased to go with you."

"I don't want to interfere," replied George, displaying genuine concern.

"Rubbish!" said James. "The boy's a no-account cousin of mine from London. Nothing but a troublemaker. His mother sent him to me to see if I couldn't make a man of him, but it's useless. Got too much of his father's blood in him for his own good."

"He's not quite the rogue James makes him out to be," said Atlanta. "But the boy's been in some trouble, and we agreed to offer him a change of environment."

"Perhaps I ought to call on *him*," said George with a laugh. "Sounds like he needs to be taught some old-fashioned Scottish manners."

"Capital idea, George!" roared James, "positively splendid! We'd have the young blackguard straightened out in no time.''

Reveling in the merriment of the idea, George went on, ''I'd be happy to show the lad around, Lord Duncan, that is if I could be of some help to you. I imagine I could hold my own, even when pitted against a knave from London.''

''No fear of his getting the best of you, George,'' said James, wiping his eyes from the laughter. He couldn't remember when he'd had such a good time. ''The lad's three inches shorter and at least four years younger than you. A mere boy alongside a strapping man like yourself.''

George brushed off the compliment with a laugh, but could hardly help the pleasure he felt at James's words, glancing out of the corner of his eye to see whether Margaret had taken notice.

''So, it's all settled, then,'' said James, heartily anticipating the potential diversion such a visit by young Falkirk would provide. Landsbury's son would discover soon enough that the men of Scotland were no country bumpkins to be toyed with. ''We'll look for your visit with eagerness—won't we, my dear?'' he added turning toward his daughter.

Maggie smiled sweetly, but said nothing.

Driving back to Stonewycke early in the evening, James was in obvious good spirits, and even Atlanta seemed considerably warmed to the notion of a closer bond of relationship with the family of Falkirk. George had not spent the entire force of his blandishments on Maggie, but had reserved a good share for her mother as well. And his engaging and likable manner had not gone unnoticed. Atlanta had gone to Kairn on her guard, but had come away positively aglow. Witnessing this proceeding, James noted with satisfaction that Lady Falkirk had apparently communicated his scheme most adroitly to her son, and he had carried out his part with all the sophistication of a gentleman far more advanced in the ways of the world than his years would indicate.

''Why so silent, Margaret?'' asked James, detecting, in an uncharacteristic moment of sensitivity, his daughter's somber countenance.

''No particular reason, Father,'' she replied. In truth, she had been considerably rankled by the sport James had made over Ian at the dinner table, and now driving home she was reminded again of how she despised the way he treated people to serve his own ends. Her smoldering anger at her father, however, had not diminished the attraction she had felt for George Falkirk. He was, indeed, a captivating and dashing man. And notwithstanding the embarrassment of his obvious and forward attentions, she had to admit that his words had warmed her within.

''Come, come! Are you not thinking of young Falkirk?'' her father insisted. "The young man was clearly taken with you. How could you not have noticed?"

"Of course I noticed," she snapped, with a trace more emotion in her voice than she had intended. "But the way you were all eyeing us, what could I do? It was awkward to say the least."

"Nonsense!" replied James, not the least pleased with his daughter's tone. "The man was simply paying you the courtesies of a gentleman."

"It's not hard to see that George likes you, dear," said Atlanta in a moderated, motherly tone. "We only want you to be happy, and George certainly is charming."

"I know, Mother," replied Maggie blushing. "Of course I find him attractive. Naturally—it's . . . but he's so much older than I am—so traveled—educated. I'm only seventeen."

"But a beautiful seventeen, darling," added Atlanta. "You're a woman, dear, not a girl. Many young ladies are married at your age. And men stand up and take notice of a face like yours."

"Especially when you have the figure to match!" said James, still feeling jovial from the four glasses of wine he had consumed after dinner.

"Father!" said Maggie. "If you don't mind, I would appreciate your keeping your opinions of my body to yourself!"

Shocked at such a rebuff from his daughter, James held his peace. But it would not take many more such outbursts before he would respond in kind. He couldn't allow a daughter of his to talk with such affrontery. He would let it pass this time, just this once. Perhaps he had spoken out of turn, anyway. If so, it was the fault of that cheap wine of Falkirk's!

"But if he does call, dear," went on Atlanta, "we'll try not to interfere. You never know, you might grow rather fond of him."

"Mother," said Maggie, "I *have* been fond of him, as you put it, ever since he asked me to dance at my party. I just don't want Father hovering around trying to push me into the man's arms!"

James remained silent. Just so long as Falkirk married the ill-tempered vixen, he could hold his tongue. But, by Jove, she'd better watch herself! As long as she was under his roof, his daughter would keep a civil tongue in her mouth!

Meanwhile, he sat back and tried to enjoy the ride, at least to the extent that the pitted and rocky road would allow. Maggie lapsed again into the silence of her own thoughts, determined to stand up to her father if he ever again made an attempt to draw her into his personal schemes. She sensed more behind his good spirits leaving Kairn than a fine meal with neighbors. If he was up to something, she would have no part of it.

I couldn't prevent his taking Cinder, she remembered bitterly. *Next time he will not so easily have his own way.*

Meanwhile, she smiled at the memory of the meeting just past. George Falkirk *was* an appealing man. And handsome!

Since Bess Mackinaw's death a gradual desire had stolen upon Maggie to be closer to the people of Strathy valley. No longer, she felt, could she take such a vague and detached interest in their lives and well-being. Though she never dreamed of having much influence where her father was concerned, she felt compelled to become more involved in their affairs. She sensed her union with them in a common birthright, jointly linked by blood and by history to the land and the Scottish heritage they shared—by virtue of their ancient ancestors rather than by accidents of pedigree and breeding.

She resolved, therefore, to continue making calls on Hector and Stevie. At the same time Maggie found herself increasing the frequency of her visits to the town and the church, and thus progressively widening her circle of humble acquaintances in the tiny village. When her father learned she had visited the Gillies family and offered to teach their crippled daughter to read, he flew into a rage.

"As if you were a common domestic!" he exclaimed.

"She wants to read," Maggie argued, "but she can't get to the school."

"She can be taught by others!"

"There is no one else," Maggie insisted. Why couldn't her father accept her growing maturity and independence? Why did he insist on rejecting all the things she held dear, forcing the rising woman within her to rebel all the more strenuously against him?

"No daughter of mine will be tutor to a crofter's child!"

"But—"

"Remember your place, Margaret," said her father.

"My place is as one of these people!" she snapped.

"You are a *lady*," he returned. "*That* is your place!"

"Then isn't it my responsibility," asked Maggie, making one last attempt to reason with him, "to show kindness to our people?"

"Your responsibility," he answered with cold finality, "is to do as I say! *And nothing else!*"

Maggie turned and left the room, seething with bitterness. When she learned soon afterward that Lucy Krueger had just given premature birth to her firstborn child—who was not expected to live—she began immediate preparations to visit the girl. Her father could upbraid and denounce and punish her all he wanted—she was going to see Lucy!

The two girls, while not friends in the strictest sense of the word, had for years been as fond of one another as the distance between their respective stations would conveniently allow. Lucy could never have hoped to be on intimate terms with someone like Maggie, of course, but she had instinctively been drawn to the laird's daughter. They were separated by two years—Maggie the younger of the pair—and had from time to time seen one another on certain festival days when the laird's family had joined in with the crofters. Once, when they were mere children, Maggie had impulsively given the girl one of her favorite dolls, and Lucy had been thoroughly devoted to her since that day. The previous Christmas, Lucy and Maggie had visited at length. Lucy had only recently married, and Maggie was genuinely interested in her new life as Charlie Krueger's wife.

Maggie was saddling Raven to ride out to the Krueger farm when Ian ambled into the stable.

"How about a ride?" he asked.

"I'm sorry," she explained, "I'm on my way to visit a girl whose baby is about to die—they think so, at least."

Ian's disappointment was obvious, but a spark of human concern flickered near the regions of his heart at the same time. "Perhaps when you return," he said.

"I may be gone most of the day," said Maggie.

Unable to bear the prospect of another boring day alone, Ian suggested, "Might I join you?"

Hesitating a moment, Maggie answered, "Of course . . . if you can be ready in five minutes."

"It'll only take me three. I won't be in the way?"

"I don't think so. But not a word to my father of this!"

Relishing a mystery, Ian flashed a grin and ran off to find a saddle for Maukin. He could saddle her himself in a fraction of the time it would take to find Digory and explain the situation to him.

True to his word, in three minutes he exited the stable into the bright sunshine, leading Maukin on foot.

The morning was clear and warm, one of the last such they could expect as summer ebbed into fall. Again Ian took great pleasure in the splendid countryside. They made their way west until they struck the road which joined Port Strathy with Culden some twelve miles southwest. This road they followed for perhaps a mile before veering off south. In the craggy foothills between the valley and Braenock Ridge, the Krueger place was situated on the last tolerably tillable patch of rising land before the desolation of the moor began. Even at that it was considerably more rugged than the grassy farmland of the main expanse of the fertile valley. Sheep could be seen grazing among the rocky crags, and in the small plot of soil stalks of wheat and oats struggled to grow.

The cottage was built after the fashion of the Mackinaws', only larger and more protected from the harsh blasts of the elements. The one notable distinction, however, lay in a small plot of ground directly in front of the house which had been lovingly worked by Lucy until she had been able to produce a bright bed of nasturtiums and begonias. The dirt path to the front door divided this colorful little garden with flowers growing abundantly on either side. Approaching the cottage, Ian was filled with pity at the hopeless attempt to cover the wretchedness of the hovel with the contrasting cheeriness of the flowers. *How can anyone call such a place home?* he wondered. London had been rife with poverty, yet it had never touched him personally. Now, face to face with actual men and women and children struggling to survive, he found the sight all the more poignant.

Charlie Krueger strode out of the byre to meet them. He was tall and muscular, but his round, homely face was gaunt with anxiety and his eyes revealed sleepless nights. Shading his eyes from the sun with his left hand, he smiled a wan welcome to his esteemed visitors and extended his right hand to Ian. Then he turned to Maggie.

"Weel, my leddy," he said, his voice thick with self-conscious reserve, "what can I be doin' fer ye? Though I'm doubtin' there's aught a poor crofter can do fer the likes o' yer leddyship."

"I heard about Lucy, Mr. Krueger," Maggie replied. "I thought I might pay her a visit. I thought—"

She hesitated, searching for the right words so as not to seem condescending to the poor, proud farmer. Perhaps her father had been right— it wasn't her place to interfere. But before her thoughts went any further, a gentle voice from the doorway of the cottage put her questions to rest.

"Why, ye didna need t' do that, my leddy," said Lucy, "but it's so nice t' hear yer sweet voice again."

Maggie turned toward the cottage where Lucy, looking pale, stood leaning against the doorjamb. The moment she had heard Maggie's voice outside, she had hastily wrapped a blanket about her shoulders and come to the door.

"Oh, Lucy, my dear!" said Maggie, turning toward her haggard friend. "You look so tired!"

Lucy smiled and opened her arms to the young heiress of Stonewycke. "Never too tired fer a visit from ye," she said.

"I brought some bread and cheese," said Maggie.

"That's kind o' ye," said Lucy. Then in a different tone she turned to her husband. "Weel, Charlie, show the leddy an' gentleman in, an' gi' Leddy Margaret a han' wi' her bag." Charlie obeyed somewhat sheepishly, took the parcel from Maggie's arm, and led the way clumsily into the cottage.

"We'd be proud fer ye t' bide a wee wi' us," Lucy continued. "Ye can see oor little bairn."

"We'd love to," Maggie replied.

Maggie followed Lucy into the cottage. Ian stood for a moment hesitating, then followed the others inside. He blinked in the darkness and when his eyes finally adjusted to the dim light, he saw a peat fire in the center of the room with its trail of smoke lazily drifting upward through the ceiling. A kettle bubbled over the fire, indicating that Lucy had been busy despite her weakness.

Maggie and Lucy were already huddled over the coarse wooden cradle.

"Come, sir," Lucy invited Ian proudly. "Have a wee peer at oor sweet bairn."

"She's beautiful!" exclaimed Maggie. "What's her name, Lucy?"

"Weel, since she was christened last night, we named her Letty."

"Christened last night!" said Maggie. "You mean you've had her out already?"

"Hoots! no, my leddy. She was born but three days ago. Na, na. Mr. Downly came oot himsel', seein' that she weren't expected t' live. But jist look at her!" Lucy beamed. "She'll hae a proper church christenin' yet!"

The infant was tiny, utterly helpless, neither knowing nor caring that its very life hung on a slender thread. *But why should she struggle so to live?* thought Ian as he glanced around. *What does she have to look forward to? Nothing but a life of poverty and deprivation.*

"She has your eyes, Lucy," said Margaret.

Awkwardly searching for something to say as he stood over the cradle, Ian was suddenly horrified to see a large kitchen knife tucked in beside the child in the mattress.

"I say!" he exclaimed. "I think you've misplaced something."

He reached in to remove the knife, but Lucy placed a restraining hand on his arm.

"Oh no, sir," she said. "Leave the knife be, though 'tis there mainly fer Charlie's daddy's sake."

"What in heaven's name for!"

" 'Tis t' keep the fairies from stealin' away oor wee Letty an' re-

placin' her wi' a changelin'," she answered. "I told Fergus Krueger
that God'll be watchin' o'er oor Letty an' we needed no such auld
superstitions aroun' here. But he said a person couldna be too careful
an' he is the child's gran'father an' has a certain right t' speak his mind.
But 'twas the Lord that brought the child safe through that first night,
an' the nights since, an He'll keep her safe from any ol' fairies."

"She's a strong child, then," said Maggie. "She truly is."

" 'Tis kind o' ye t' say," replied Lucy.

"A braw one, 'tis what we would say," interposed Krueger, finally
breaking the silence from the uncertainty he felt at having such guests
in his poor home.

"Aye, the Lord's given us such joy o'er oor little one," said Lucy.
" 'Tis why we named her Letty."

"I don't understand," said Maggie.

"Letty . . . 'tis from the name *Letitia*; it means *happiness*."

"How wonderful!" exclaimed Maggie in delight.

"An' we are happy, my leddy, aren't we, Charlie?"

Blushing imperceptibly, Charlie nodded his head.

"Aye," Lucy went on, "the Lord's promised us the wee one will
live t' be strong an' healthy an' will someday make her mark fer the
good o' this land we all love. 'Deed, my leddy, the Lord has blessed us
more than we can deserve!"

A brief silence descended, which was broken after a moment by the
sound of Maggie's laughter. "Well, I'm so happy for you, Lucy . . .
and you too, Charlie," she added turning to face him. "A braw wee
bairn indeed!"

"Ye do right well wi' the sound o' yer native land on yer lips, my
leddy!" said Lucy with delight.

Lucy rose, walked toward the hearth, and began to fix her guests
some tea. But Maggie could see that she had already been on her feet
too long.

"You lie back down, Lucy," she said. "I can warm water and stir
up a pot of tea."

"I couldna have a leddy like yersel' waitin' on *me*!" expostulated
Lucy.

"Nonsense!" returned Maggie. "Besides, I insist. I'm giving you
no choice in the matter."

Uncomfortable with the reversal of roles, yet glowing from the combined radiance produced by motherhood and having the lady of the estate
take such a personal interest, Lucy yielded and sought out the bed upon
which she had been lying before her guests arrived.

"I was jist tendin' my animals when ye came," said Krueger. "If ye'd like t' see the byre, sir, ye can follow me while I finish my chores.''

"Certainly, my good man," replied Ian, enthusiastic about any prospect other than baby-watching with two women.

He followed the lumbering farmer out of the cottage and into the barn, which was attached to one wall of the house in the rear.

"Here's the byre," he said, "where we keep the livestock."

Entering the darkened structure, which was in reality little more than a huge shed, Ian was struck by the destitution of the place. *If this is what the man considers livestock*, he thought, *there isn't much here*. Two cows shuffled impatiently at the far end. Krueger walked straight toward them, unlatched the stall, and proceeded to lead them out of the building.

"I was jist readyin' t' let the nowt oot t' pasture," he said. "The field's not far. They're mighty hungry by now, I reckon."

Ian followed Krueger through the byre and walked alongside—the gentleman from London in clean, pressed riding clothes; and the humble farmer in dirt-smeared dungarees—as they accompanied the two lean black-and-white cows toward a fenced area about two hundred yards from the house. He could not think the little available grass afforded them much to look forward to in the way of breakfast.

"Don't you also feed them oats or hay?" he asked, making conversation.

"Hay, when'er I'm able," answered Krueger. "But na oats. They're too precious fer oursel's, ye know. But the beasts get by."

Returning to the barn, Krueger grabbed two handfuls of some kind of seed and scattered it over the fence of a small coop where some dozen or so chickens immediately flurried about pecking at the ground for every morsel of grain each could hoard to itself.

Back into the barn Ian noticed for the first time two lethargic pigs lying in a filthy and odiferous mixture of mud and manure. Into the feeding trough Krueger scooped a measure of some horrible concoction. At the sound of its splat onto the wooden slats at the bottom, the two pigs leaped to their feet snorting furiously, then plunged their snouts into the mass in a frenzied attempt to consume as much as possible in the shortest amount of time.

To Ian the whole ritual appeared pathetic, eking a bare subsistence from what the rocky ground and scraggly farm animals could produce. How could this man and his wife actually claim to be *happy*? Was there a wholesome purity that filled Charlie Krueger with a sense of life's fulfillment as he struggled—just he and his family and his plot of ground— against the elements of nature? Was it the challenge of the hard life that imbued this man and this woman with their happiness? What else could it be?

It was certainly a challenge he had never known . . . would never know. Life—if by life one meant food, clothing, shelter, money, and possessions—had always come easy for him. He'd never had to work a day in his life. Krueger's arms, on the other hand, were rough and brown, his hands cracked and tough from daily contact with the earth and its demands. Those hands, and what he managed to do with them, put oatmeal on their table and kept potatoes boiling in the kettle—hands that were not afraid to work the stubborn ground until they were black, hands that were not afraid of the stinging winter's cold.

Ian glanced down at his own hands—soft and white, the hands of a gentleman, the son of an earl, not the hands of a man who had to use them vigorously in order to eat dinner that same day.

Ian could not help but envy Krueger in a way; the farmer at least had something truly to call his own. It wasn't much—hardly more than twenty acres with little to show for it. But as humble as his cottage was, and as few and gaunt his animals, at least it was by his own labor that they were sustained. And now he had a wife and a child to care for, to provide for, to protect, and to love. What more could any man desire? *Yes*, he thought, *maybe there is happiness here.* Perhaps the little baby's name signified more than simply a momentary joy that God had chosen to deliver her from her danger and give her into their hands to love and nurture. Perhaps the child was somehow symbolic of the life marked out for its parents to live.

There *was* something here. Maggie was right. The people and their love for the earth beneath them could not help but affect any observer. Something was tugging at him, pulling at a deep longing in his heart to experience this elusive, intangible dream called *happiness* which Lucy and Charlie Krueger shared.

Leaving Krueger to complete his chores himself, Ian turned from the barn. He had come here intending simply to idle away a few pleasant weeks and then return to London as if nothing had happened. But something *was* happening inside him which he couldn't explain, for which he had been totally unprepared. Everything had changed since that first ride in the country. The place and its people were touching him, moving him. He was struck by the impression that the real significance of life was to be found—of all places!—*right here*, and not in London at all!

And then there was the girl Margaret, tantalizing wisp of maturing femininity, he had to admit, but so full of contrast! Silent one moment, angered over some verbal injury the next, and then bold and vivacious. Tender and open to Lucy Krueger; heartless and cold toward her father.

Was her initial reticence toward him born out of a fear of letting anyone draw too close? He had observed that often in James's presence, she stiffened into a frigid statue of marble.

What could he do, he wondered, to thaw her heart? Not that he was *interested* in her, he would have hastily added. After all, had he not been seen with some of London's finest on his arm? This young Margaret was but a country cousin—attractive, to be sure, but a tad young. She was an intriguing case, certainly full of powerful emotions—some of which surfaced; others, he concluded, which she kept locked away for no eyes but her own.

With such thoughts swirling in confusion through his brain, Ian began the ride home with Maggie an hour later. She too had been profoundly moved by the visit, for the tears were rising and only her tough Ramsey heritage kept them firmly in check.

Neither spoke, and they were some way down the rocky path when a breathless voice shouted after them from behind.

"My leddy . . . my leddy, hold!" It was Krueger.

The two reined in their mounts and turned to look back. He had been running to catch them, and when he stopped it took a moment for him to catch his breath before he could deliver the message. Finally he said: "My wife, she wanted ye t' hae this as thanks fer all yer kindness." He held up a handkerchief of bright white linen trimmed in tatted lace. Two bright pink primroses decorated one corner. "She made it hersel'," he added proudly, little realizing how infinitely more precious this made the simple gift.

Deeply moved, Maggie reached down for it, hardly daring to speak lest she be overcome. With a husky and tremulous voice, she managed a soft, "Thank you."

Then she turned Raven toward home and, with Ian following a few lengths behind, she trotted off. The urge to be alone had come upon her and she pressed the pace. But Ian spurred Maukin and managed to pull up even with Raven in time to see the unguarded tears streaming down Maggie's pale cheeks.

"Miss Duncan?" he said, for he knew of no other words to offer.

"Forgive me, Mr. Duncan," she replied, brushing away the tears and holding her trembling lips tight, swallowing hard. "This is deplorable!"

"No . . . no, it's not," he answered, and for one of the few times since his arrival his voice contained not a trace of sarcasm. "It's completely understandable. I would be a willing listener if you need one."

"Thank you, Mr. Duncan," she replied, gathering her reserve around her once again. "I am fine." She was not quite ready to offer him that much trust just yet.

Maggie tucked the handkerchief into her pocket and offered not another word until they parted at the door of the stables.

Perhaps I do need a listener, Maggie thought. *But not someone in any way reminiscent of my father.* She had trusted him as a child; she had loved him. And worse, she thought he loved her! Until the incident with Cinder she had never realized how little he cared for her feelings, or cared what was important to her. She had never recovered from the shock of what he had done, and had vowed that very day never to trust him again. Never again would she allow herself to be hurt like that— by him, by any man! She wasn't about to risk cracking the shell of self-protection she had been able to build by now opening her soul and confiding in this cousin of her father's. He would probably find an equally suitable opportunity to laugh in the face of something which was important to her—like this beautiful little handkerchief. He had already shown a great fondness for poking fun at life wherever he could. But it would not be at her expense!

Perhaps such hidden motivations lay at root in Maggie's vigorous pursuit of the friendship of the crofters. Not only did she love the land and the people who worked it, something in the subconscious well of her soul no doubt realized that, since by rank and position they were separated beyond reach from her, she would never have to encounter with them the potential pain of intimacy . . . the heartache of not being loved in return. Or worse—as had been the case with her father—of losing a love she thought she had by discovering it had never existed in the first place.

Yes, Mr. Duncan, perhaps I do need a listener. But the price is far too high.

23 / The Bluster 'N Blow

The next day might have ended on a better note if Maggie had been about. But no sooner had they returned from Lucy Krueger's than she disappeared. After a token appearance for dinner, she retired immediately for the night.

The visit to the Kruegers' had left Ian's emotions in disarray, and when he arose the following morning nothing had been resolved. Not knowing why, he sought out Maggie, if for no other reason than to be around someone to take his mind off his thoughts. Another ride, perhaps—this time just to ride, not visit.

He searched the stable, wandered through the house, poked his head into the library, then back to the stable. Digory had seen nothing of her, and Raven had not left her stall.

Reentering the house he encountered Atlanta. She stopped and made an attempt to engage him in friendly conversation. But his mood was not one that lent itself to small talk, the interview grew awkward, and Atlanta—either remembering or inventing an urgent errand—quickly excused herself.

Ian was thoroughly disgusted with the turn of the day. Coming here was a gigantic mistake. Where in blazes was Lady Margaret?

The flighty thing has probably had her fill of me, he thought, *and is now off amusing herself in the company of those pathetic crofters! It's no wonder she enjoys their company more than mine. She's cut of the same cloth. All the people up here are a hundred years behind the times! Dirty, miserable creatures! Bloody crime to bring a child into the world under such conditions!*

But just then the angel clothed in Scottish tartan rose to put the demon of his past life to sleep momentarily. In his mind's eye Ian again saw the picture of Lucy Krueger beaming down with radiant face at her newborn child, her eyes filled with something Ian had witnessed too little of in his life—simple, honest, pure, and total *love.* Did the child, in fact, have more to look forward to in life than he himself?

Ian laughed. But the sound which came from his throat had little of its usual enthusiasm and more resembled a dry groan. *What would that pathetic baby—what was its name? Letty, that's it. Happiness!*

He laughed again. *No doubt! no doubt! What would she think of having more to look forward to in life than the son of an earl!*

What was it about these people? At first he had pitied them. Was he actually now—unbelievably!—*envying* Charlie Krueger? A sensation he had not experienced since childhood suddenly took him by surprise: a warm, moist tear rose in his eye and without warning flowed down his cheek. Quickly the back of his hand obliterated the evidence of his momentary tenderness, and he turned and began pacing nervously.

Alas! The angel's stay was but a brief one and the demons once more asserted themselves.

I must be going mad! The thought of envying a wretched farmer like Krueger! Why, the thing is unthinkable!

Blast that Margaret! he thought. *Where could she be?*

Well, there must be something to do in this ridiculous place without her.

In the purposelessness of his turmoil, he left the house and hastened to the stable, asking Digory gruffly to saddle Maukin.

"And make it lively!" he said. "I'm in a hurry."

He remembered passing through a little village on the way to Stone-wycke. Strath—Port something or other! Surely there must be something there. He leapt on Maukin's back and tore off almost too fast to control the galloping hare.

Reaching Port Strathy it was not difficult to locate the place he sought, the only establishment of its kind for miles. The local inn stood on a promontory overlooking the shore, only a few long strides along the path down the embankment to wet sand. Its stone walls were perhaps the newest in the village, and the carved wooden sign bearing the name *Bluster 'N Blow* was freshly painted.

Tying his horse in front, Ian caught a fragrant whiff of tangy salt spray and the crusty odor of herring. The oaken door of the inn swung open before him with a creak. The interior of the premises would have been dim had it not been for the early afternoon sun streaming through skyline windows, located toward the tops of all but the wall where the door was located.

"Guid afternoon t' ye, yer lairdship," called a woman from across the room. She was the only one inside.

"I trust you are open," Ian said as he strode toward a table.

"Would ye be wantin' a room?" she asked, eyeing him almost greedily. She was a tall, large woman with muscular arms showing out below the short sleeves of her drab gray frock. She was clearly no stranger to hard work; the inn sparkled from her efforts. Her small black eyes were sharp and truly bespoke her shrewd character. For in addition to working hard, she was a cagey businesswoman. Her thick hair, about the color of her dress, was cut rather short. She hated any encumbrance that interfered with the handling of her duties.

"No," replied Ian, "but I am thirsty."

"Weel, yer lairdship. I'm none too accustomed t' servin' the barley bree fer another hour or so."

"Surely you would stretch your regulations for a guest of the Lord of Stonewycke."

"Ow, ye must be the nephew visitin' from Lonnon, yer lairdship?"

"Cousin," Ian corrected. "Second cousin to be exact. A distant relation, I assure you."

"Any relation o' the laird's be a gentleman in these parts," the lady said.

"And furthermore," Ian went on, "I'm not 'yer lairdship'—I am lord of nothing. Mr. Duncan will suffice."

"As ye wish."

"Now, how about that drink?"

"Right ye are, yer—er, Mr. Duncan. I suppose I can allow one or twa fer ye, special guest that ye are."

In reality she allowed nearer to three or four tall tumblers before the regular evening guests began to arrive a few hours later. Ian chatted easily with the buxom woman, laughed heartily at her stories concerning a few of the more notable locals, and found himself far more at home than he had felt since leaving London.

"You have a fine place here, Mistress—" Ian said after his first glass of whiskey.

"Mistress Rankin," she replied as she filled his glass again. "But everyone round here calls me Queenie."

"Well, it's a fine pub," said Ian again. "And I should know. I am well acquainted with every such establishment to be found in London."

"Thank ye fer speakin' well o' the Bluster 'N Blow. My husban' an' mysel' began buildin' it na twa years ago. The other inn was brought right doon in the muckle storm that year. 'Course it was near ready t' fall doon anyway."

Ian drained his glass and extended it toward her for another refill.

"That Scotch whiskey's mighty powerful stuff, Mr. Duncan. Would ye like t' try a glass o' oor finest ale? Brewed down by Glasgow, it is. Fine ale!"

"Pour me a round!" replied Ian with a hearty laugh. "I'll drink your ale and your whiskey and whatever else you have!"

She complied.

"Well," said Ian lifting his glass high. "Here's to you and your inn, Mistress Rankin. May no storms ever dampen your door again. Here's to stout walls and fair weather from here on out!''

When the first of the locals began to trickle in some time later, they were at first cautious and soft-spoken around the youthful stranger. But Ian was a master of the trade and had soon livened up the crew with his infectious laughter—aided not a little by the whiskey that had by then reached his blood, and the blood his brain—his stories of derring-do in the south, and most importantly, by the round of drinks he ordered for the whole lot. By the time the sun had been down an hour, the sounds of raucous laughter and merry singing could be heard from outside the Bluster 'N Blow.

Queenie had by now lost count of the number of drinks her young guest had taken, but she had begun to eye him with some concern. His fine English accent was slurred almost beyond recognition, and with each new toast he offered he managed to spill nearly as great a quantity as passed between his lips.

Finally, lifting one final glass toward the red-faced and tipsy gathering, he rose to his feet on shaky legs and attempted to climb on top of the bench on which he had been sitting. He quickly recognized the impossibility of such a proceeding, however, and thus contented himself with merely remaining on the floor and—for the moment—on his feet.

"Here's ta the heath, the hill, an' the heather," he began with his tongue so thick he could scarcely pronounce the words, *". . . the bonnet, the—the—"*

One of his companions stood up at his lapse of memory, threw his arm around him, and supplied the missing line—

"—the plaidie, the kilt, an' the feather!"

"That's it!" exclaimed Ian with exuberance. *"Here's ta the song—that auld Scotland can boast. May her name never die! Tha's a Highlandman's toast!"*

On the last line everyone joined in so boisterously that the sound no doubt reverberated throughout a good portion of the village. Much laughter and applause followed, and Ian's comrades, themselves inebriated far beyond their normal limits, hardly noticed that their new young friend had slumped back onto the bench, nearly unconscious.

No one noticed but Queenie, who was always alert to the state of her guests. She made her way toward him, and as gently as her fat and calloused hand could manage, patted his cheek.

"Mr. Duncan," she said. "Mr. Duncan. I'm thinkin' 'tis time ye were on yer way."

Ian pulled his wobbly head away from the back of the bench. "Lemme shee, ye're Queenie, arn' you?"

"Aye, yer lairdship—"

"Mussen call me tha, Queenie, my frien'."

" 'Tis gettin' late. Hae ye a way home? I can hitch up the wagon—"

"No, no, my dear Queenie," he replied, pulling himself halfway toward a sitting position. "I'm fine . . . fine—never needed anyone to take me home yet."

He rose to a wobbly stand, unable to discern whether he or the room was spinning in a slow circular motion. "Where's the door?" he asked.

Queenie took his arm and led him outside. The crisp night air should have helped the young rouster's condition. Instead, Ian grasped for Queenie's arm.

"I'm gon'ta be sick, Queenie," he moaned.

"Jist suck in a breath o' that clean air," she replied.

" 'Tis the air that's makin' me sick."

He clutched her arm and tried to focus on his horse.

"Are ye sure ye can make it, Mr. Duncan?"

"I'll be home an' a'tween my covers afore ye're rid o' the rest o' those wastrels in there," he said, attempting a laugh which was merely an echo of his already-spent mirth.

At last the night air began to clear a few of the cobwebs away and he was able to climb, awkwardly to be sure, onto Maukin. The horse, perhaps sensing his master's unsteady seat, took a slow and gentle gait back to Stonewycke. Queenie watched with some trepidation for several moments, then returned to her guests in the inn.

Had Ian been more sober, he would have been surprised to have made it back at all. He hardly knew the road, the night was dark, and his senses were blurred. As it was, he barely noticed the great iron gates as he passed. He left Maukin to her own devices, staggered toward the door of the great house, pondering whether to go in at all. What if the spectre of his host stood waiting on the other side, ready to storm at his insolence and seize this opportunity to throw him out for good?

Closing the door carefully behind him, Ian found to his great relief all was dark and quiet. Fumbling through the entryway, he kicked against a pedestal, heard a rattle, and his hands just laid hold of the vase sitting on top of it in time to prevent its falling to destruction on the floor. As gently as possible, he replaced it, then crept by inches through the hallway, and eventually found the stairs. Clutching the rail he began his ascent. When he arrived safely at the first landing, Ian's confidence grew. He turned to the left, took two steps, then suddenly heard a suppressed gasp.

"Mr. Duncan!"

"Oh, my lady," he replied, realizing he'd nearly collided with the one whose absence had sent him on this binge in the first place. He attempted a bow, but wavering, he steadied himself against the wall instead. "Wha' a surprise t' fin' you here."

"I couldn't sleep. I thought a glass of milk—" She stopped abruptly.

"I don't have to explain myself," she stated flatly. "What are *you* doing here?"

"Milk! Ah, yes," said Ian, ignoring her question. "I remember such a drink—helps you sleep, but not forget. Have no use for it my-sel'."

"Mr. Duncan, you're quite drunk!"

He threw his hand to his mouth in mock dismay and shock. "So that's what it is! Thank God! I thought I was dying."

He laughed at his own feeble joke.

"Hush! You'll wake the whole household!"

"Heaven forbid! We mussen disturb anyone's time in slummerlan', must we?"

"Mr. Duncan," Maggie returned, "you are rude and disgusting."

"*My lady*," he said, assuming a grave and serious tone, "I told you that your father had welcomed an unsavory reprobate into his home." He was unable to hold back his laughter any longer. "Now you know I never lie," he said, letting it loose.

"Go to your room! And for goodness sake, hush, or my father will hear you!"

"You're a sassy wench, my lady," he said with a drunken grin.

"Don't call me that!" she snapped with a flash of hot temper. "My name is Margaret Duncan—*Miss* Duncan to you!"

"Forgive me," he said, with somber expression; but he could hardly hold it, and dissolved into another outburst of laughter.

Maggie turned on her heel and went back to her bedroom, forgetting the milk.

She never noticed that Ian turned also, descended the stairs the way he had come, and went back out the front door.

24 / Digory and Ian

Digory arose while it was still dark, as that was his custom. He lit a lamp; that, too, was his custom, the only time he ever lit a lamp except once more at night before he retired. Both times the lamp only remained lit for a short while as he read. All other tasks he could perform in the dark if there was no sunlight.

He occupied two small rooms over the stable. They formed, in actuality, little more than a loft with a straw mattress, a rough wooden table and chair, and a small cast iron stove—and, of course, the lamp, and a small bookcase. They were humble lodgings. But to Digory it was home. As a trusted servant, indeed almost as a family member, he could have had any quarters he chose. He could have taken up residence in the great house, and Atlanta upon several occasions had tried to persuade him to do so. But he neither needed nor desired more. His tastes were simple, and year after year he remained where he was. All his needs were met—he took meals with the other servants, but found great satisfaction in the solitude of the life he lived.

Stonewycke had been Digory's home these many years since he had become groom in charge of the laird's stables. His father, who had occupied the position before him, had possessed a cottage on the property. But Robert Macnab had had a brood of six children, and even the roomy cottage had been a tight squeeze for the large family.

Now Digory was the only one left in the vicinity. His parents had gone years ago; the cottage had long since been rented out to others; two older brothers had died; another brother and two sisters had migrated to other parts of Scotland.

Digory Macnab followed his father into the service of the laird. He had never married and thus had no family. As a boy he had been something of a loner and as he grew, though personable and friendly, he remained meek and introverted. Casual acquaintances considered him a recluse. But those who were in closer contact with him soon came to realize that his retiring nature was simply a personality trait that in no way precluded a great love for the people around him. He was devoted to those he served, tried not to speak or think ill of his superiors, and loved young Maggie perhaps more profoundly than anyone at the estate realized, caring for her like the daughter he had never had. A new servant in the house from time to time would consider him stand-offish. But such thoughts rarely lasted more than a month or two. Among the permanent staff he was liked and enormously respected. The soft-spoken, almost mystical presence which haunted the barn and stable was a source of pride to the servants, for he was one of their own.

Digory found his Bible on the table and opened the well-worn leather cover. The pages had been turned so often that they practically opened on command. He read his customary Psalm—that was how he always began his morning, saving a corresponding chapter of the Gospels or Epistles for the evening. Then he bowed his head and murmured the Lord's Prayer in the old tongue, as he had learned it so long ago from his father:

Uor fader quhilk beest in Hevin, Hallowit weird thyne nam. Cum thyne kinrik. Be dune thyne wull as is in Hevin, sya po yerd. Uor dailie breid gif us thilk day. And forleit us uor skaiths, as we forleit them quha skaith us. And leed us na intil temptatioun. Butan fre us fra evil. Amen.

His head remained silently bowed for some moments afterward; then he slowly inched his way out of the chair. The arthritis was always worse in the chill of the morning, but he did not bother stoking up the fire, for soon he would be down in the stable. The hot breath and close bodies of the horses, along with the renewed activity of work, would soon warm and lubricate his stiff joints and sleepy limbs.

He closed the book and set it tenderly on the table. Then, seemingly as an afterthought, he bowed his aging head once more and, remaining standing, said, "An', Lord, I near fergot t' mention oor houseguest—that is t' say, the laird's houseguest. I dinna ken the lad, nor ken what t' pray, but ye do, Lord, an' 'tis enough. Amen."

Pulling on his wool cap, he made the slow descent from his quarters down creaky steps to the stable below. He began with his rounds to each compartment, giving a word and pat on the nose to each of the occupants. "Ye'll be wantin' fresh hay an' summat t' eat," he muttered. His charges were always fed before he had his own breakfast. He ran his stable like a fine boarding inn, and considered the animals under his care with as much respect as a thoughtful innkeeper. His morning began so early that breakfast at the house would not be for several hours.

Digory shuffled to a great haystack where he began to fill a rusty-wheeled wooden cart. It took several trips before the stalls were properly supplied. As his pitchfork was sifting through the hay for his third load, he heard a muffled inhuman groan and perceived a remote portion of the stack beginning to move. The ancient groom was hardly flustered, but curious to know the source of the sound. He ceased his labor and immediately walked around the huge pile to find what the mystery could be.

As he parted the hay with his hand, a light dawned upon his countenance.

"Mornin' t' ye, Mr. Duncan!" he said calmly, as if discovering a gentleman asleep in the midst of the horses' breakfast were nothing out of the ordinary.

Ian cracked open one bloodshot eye and squinted painfully up at the old groom. He tried to speak but found his mouth so dry he could not force a single intelligible sound from it.

"Weel, sir," Digory went on, "ye're a lucky man that ye chose a place no nearer my fork fer yer bed. In this hazy dawn I might never hae seen ye."

Ian stirred and tried to sit up. But his head was throbbing so severely that he fell back again into the soft pile with a groan.

"God have mercy!" he swore thickly.

"That He will, lad," Digory replied. "That He will."

Ian looked at him dumbly.

"I ken jist what ye'll be needin', lad," Digory said brightly. "Now, bide right where ye are. I'll be back 'fore ye ken."

Ian could hardly have moved if he had wanted to. The best he could hope for was to lie in the hay with the rich horsey smells floating through the still morning air about him. He fell back into a partial doze and by the time Digory returned, Ian had nearly forgotten him.

"Now, drink this, lad," the groom entreated.

Painfully Ian shook his head, "I—I couldn' . . . my head—"

"Come now, laddie."

"I don't think I can drink anything."

" 'Tis Nellie's special brew," Digory persisted. "It'll cure all that ails ye."

"I'm not sick. I was only—"

He paused, trying to remember how he had come to fall asleep in the stable.

"—I am sick, but only because I am drunk—or was last night."

He wondered if the words were coming out right from his jumbled brain. "I hardly know what I am. Maybe I am sick. Rude and disgusting, that's no doubt what I am," he added as memory began to creep over him. He had engaged in worse pub-crawls dozens of times in London. Why, now, did the thought of what he had done the previous night ache worse than his hangover?

Digory could detect hints of shame in the lad's disheveled countenance. He recalled his prayer of the morning and realized that now he had something more specific to talk to his God about when he next offered up a prayer for the laird's young cousin.

"There, laddie, ye drink this—ye'll be good as new in no time." Despite his arthritic knees, Digory knelt down and tried to prop up Ian's head with his hand to enable him to sip the potent compound.

Ian raised the cup to his lips absently. His mind reeled with cloudy images and bare fragments of thought. What did it matter if he was ever good as new? Everything here had turned upside-down. Wouldn't his father relish a glimpse of him now? It would prove once and for all that his second son was indeed a good-for-nothing derelict!

"Worthless," he mumbled, hardly realizing he had spoken.

"Jist give the brew a chance t' work—"

"I'm a contemptible fool," he said, with as much anger as repentance, wincing at the reverberation of his own voice in the early quiet of the stable. "And why are you helping me unless you're as much of a fool as I am?"

"Ye've had a bad night, son."

"Why don't you kick the hay over me and get the laird? Let him mete out my punishment. No doubt he would enjoy it tremendously!"

"Nobody's wantin' t' punish ye, laddie. Punishment's an ill way o' settin' things right."

"Ha!" laughed Ian contemptuously. "Tell that to my father and to the judges who would like to lock me away. Isn't that what life's all about—God judging the wicked, like me? Hell—the great tollbooth to come—is where sinners like me wind up, haven't you heard!"

"Oh, laddie," sighed Digory with a pained tenderness in his voice, " 'tisn't like that at all. We ken nothin' o' the Lord's punishment. We only ken what the Word's told us, that the Lord disciplines the ones He loves. He disciplines—not punishes, laddie—t' make us able t' bear more o' His love."

"He may discipline those He loves," said Ian, "but for those reprobates like me—"

"Son," interrupted Digory, "there is *no one* ootside the fold o' God's love. It says He loves the whole world. He jist wants t' love ye, laddie. 'Tis all the Lord wants."

"The *Lord*, maybe," consented Ian, tired of disputing the point, "but I wager it would be another reaction altogether from the *laird*."

"I'm sure if the laird knew—"

"What does it matter anyway," said Ian, half to himself. "How can I face *her* again?"

"If ye're meanin' Lady Margaret," said Digory, "she wouldna hold sich a thing against ye."

"She would have every right," Ian replied. "If only I could slip away from this place unseen."

"Ye wouldna be fair na t' give the lass a chance," Digory said, "an' the rest o' the family too. Ye mustn' be too hard on yersel', lad."

Ian glanced up at the persistent groom. *What does he care anyway?* he wondered.

As if divining his thoughts, Digory added, "If ye'd jist give yersel' a second chance, lad, I think ye might find ye'd like it here. And t'would warm my heart t' see ye fergive yersel' fer this one mishap. Fer, ye see, I've already begun t' grow a little fond o' ye."

Ian stared at him a moment longer, wondering what was behind that peculiar look in his eyes. Then he turned away, swallowed the remainder of the mysterious potion, and lay back in the hay. The churning in his stomach began to calm almost immediately, but it took five or ten minutes for the throbbing in his head to begin to subside.

Deciding he was best left alone, Digory returned to his morning chores. He had no intention of referring to the incident in the laird's presence. He shrank from any form of deceit. But equally foreign to him would have been the bringing of trouble down upon another without some specific motive toward good. In Ian's case, he did not judge that a disclosure would accomplish anything but further alienation.

Feeling gradually better, Ian lay on the haystack silently watching the old groom in the increasing light of day. He always felt this way after a drunken spree—the physical distress was nothing alongside the emotional turmoil which assailed him. Before the end of the morning he had usually come to the point of laughing it off, and by the following night had all but forgotten the mental confusion such incidents caused him.

The corner of his mouth turned up into a crooked grin. At least the night had been good for one thing—he had been able to get a rise out of Margaret. Why, she had been utterly scandalized at the whole interview. That *was* something to laugh about.

But try as he might, he could find no well of resident laughter within him. This bloody place! He would have been better off in Newgate. At least there he would have had the ever-present hope of escape, and the camaraderie of those of his kind.

But how could he escape *this* asylum, where he himself was the jailor, and his mind was the prison?

He remembered telling his mother he would use the time in the country to sort out his life.

Of course he had been patronizing her, saying the words she wanted to hear. He never took himself seriously. Introspection had been unknown in London. Day followed night . . . night followed day. Life went on, and he bounced through it. *Sort out his life*—he didn't even know what the words meant.

But the mental torment of this hangover was new to him. This time the torrent of embittered thoughts was not directed toward his father or his family or the bobby who had hauled him off to prison, but instead inward, at himself. And through his groggy brain tumbled a menacing array of confusing thoughts. He had always been proud that the tough exterior he'd managed to convey made people stand up and take notice. Suddenly he looked upon himself with disgust.

He pulled himself slowly to a sitting position.

Clutching the wall for support, he gained his feet. The room spun a little and his knees remained weak. He engineered a few tentative steps. Perhaps there was something to the groom's brew after all, for all at once he didn't feel nearly so bad.

25 / Breaking the Ice

Atlanta knew Maggie was in the dayroom.

She'd wanted to speak with her daughter, but was nevertheless reluctant to seek her out. She longed once in a while just to put her arms tenderly around her as she had when Maggie was a child. But Margaret was a little girl no longer. *It is harder now*, Atlanta thought. Harder to overcome her own natural reserve. *And besides*, Atlanta rationalized, *the dayroom is where Maggie goes to be alone*. But she had waited too long. Something was troubling Maggie; and as much as she didn't want to intrude, she could not put it off any longer.

Maggie could be so distant at times, so withdrawn into the solitude of her private thoughts. Atlanta had hoped the arrival of their young relative might draw her out. At first Maggie had seemed more cheerful. She and Ian had seemed to enjoy several rides together. But then suddenly the walls of silence around her had returned. Had the young man done something to offend her? Was it James again? He always seemed at root one way or another, ever since Maggie's remoteness toward them had begun two or three years earlier.

She had to know. She turned and mounted the steps to the dayroom.

Reluctantly Maggie put down her sewing and rose to answer the soft knock on the door. Still trying to come to grips with her own feelings, she couldn't possibly make her mother understand. She hardly understood herself. Why had Ian's visit and a simple gift from a poor farmer's wife pulled so at her heart? Suddenly her resolve not to open her heart again was giving way in the immediacy of relationships she was coming to value. It was already too late. Her heart was already open. And from within it, love was beginning to flow. But she didn't want to love again! Loving meant being hurt. She didn't want to love—not her mother, not Lucy, not George Falkirk, not anybody!

"I—I missed you at breakfast," Atlanta began nervously.

"I'm sorry," Maggie replied.

"It's only that I'm concerned—for your health." Why couldn't the love in her mother's heart find words better than this? "You hardly touched your dinner last night."

"I guess I wasn't very hungry."

"That doesn't sound like my little Maggie," said Atlanta, forcing a laugh.

"That's just it, don't you see?" Maggie burst out, not intending to lash out at her mother but having no one else present. "I'm not *little Maggie* anymore."

"I didn't mean anything by it."

"Oh, I know, Mother," said Maggie sincerely. "It's not you, it's—"

"It's what, dear?"

"I don't know. It's . . . everything! Lucy Krueger gave me this little handkerchief," she went on, handing the small piece of linen to her mother. "Something about it just—"

She stopped and looked away.

"What is it, Maggie?"

"I'm just confused. About Lucy and her baby, about what to say if George Falkirk does come to call, about the estate, about who I'm supposed to be anyway. Father shouts at me for visiting people I care for and want to see. George Falkirk pays me compliments for my face and my dress. But I don't think he cares about *me*, the real *me*." She paused, then continued in a different tone. "Mother," she said, "have you ever wished you could be someone other than who you are?"

Atlanta tried to conceal her surprise. "I suppose everyone has at some time or another."

"I mean really wished it," said Maggie. "Sometimes I think Lucy Krueger is happier in her life than I ever will be. Sometimes I wonder if all this, being part of an important family, if it isn't all worthless. Sometimes I just wish I could be a farmer's wife."

Misunderstanding her daughter, Atlanta's heart sank within her. So that was what had been on Maggie's mind; she wanted no part of her heritage—of Stonewycke, of carrying on the Ramsey line, of all that Atlanta held dear. Misinterpreting Maggie's struggle to face the crisis within herself, Atlanta swallowed to conceal her own hurt and disappointment.

"Do you know what I mean, Mother?"

"I have never wanted to be anyone but who I am—the marchioness of Stonewycke," she answered boldly, the compassionate mother in her submerging below the surface once more. "The Ramsey heritage is all I desire. Of course I care for the people, but not so much that I would become one of them. And this is always what I have desired for you too, my child, that you should follow me as governess of this great estate."

Maggie was silent and Atlanta remained still after her empassioned speech.

"Yes, Mother, you're right," answered Maggie at length, but her voice lacked conviction. "I know the heritage of the land and our place in it is more important than anything. You've always told me so. But . . . somehow I have to find what it means on my own."

She turned and looked out the window for several moments. "I hadn't noticed that the sun was already so high. I'd better go look in on Raven."

She turned back into the room and made her exit as quickly as possible.

Atlanta remained motionless in the middle of the room.

Maggie hurried through the house and out the door, crossed the lawn, and walked briskly toward the stables. She knew well enough that Raven would be well provided for without her. In addition, she was reluctant to run into Ian after last night's awkward encounter on the darkened landing when she had spoken so harshly to him. Of course he deserved it; yet still, she was timid about seeing him again.

But she couldn't face another moment with her mother just then. How could she convey to her what was on her own heart when she herself didn't even know? She loved Stonewycke. Why else would she have refused her father's many urgings that she attend school in Edinburgh or London? Yet despite that love for her family's estate, right now she might be far happier had she been born Digory's daughter, or if her last name had been Mackinaw or Krueger or Pike or MacDonald or . . . anything but Duncan. Her mind's eye caught a picture of herself running barefoot over Braenock Ridge, herding the sheep. Wasn't there something more than being a *lady* . . . a *marchioness*?

Maybe she was afraid of George Falkirk, afraid of his drawing her steadily away from the simple peasant folk she had come to know. He wanted to escort her into society, a gentleman with his lady friend from Stonewycke. But in her heart of hearts, she wanted opportunities to visit Lucy Krueger, and others like her, not the upper crust of the neighboring estates. *Ha!* thought Maggie. *Imagine what it would be like to take George Falkirk to the Kruegers' for a visit!*

Ian had known he must see Margaret again. Returning to his room, he cleaned up and remained there until the greatest part of his physical distress had subsided. He had just left the house through the scullery door when he spied her, apparently hastily on her way to the stables. He took a breath for courage, and called: "Lady Margaret."

Maggie stopped and turned. Ian could not at first glance tell whether she was annoyed or simply surprised. He hastened toward her as quickly as his aching head would allow.

"I've been hoping to find you," he began, ". . . to say I am sorry. I behaved despicably."

Interrupted in the midst of her own thoughts—which at that moment had been flitting to and fro about the person of George Falkirk—Maggie's sole response was a dumb stare.

"I would understand," Ian went on, "if you didn't wish to see me again. But I had to at least make my apologies before I left."

"Before you left!" exclaimed Maggie, coming to herself. "You're leaving Stonewycke?"

"Under the circumstances I think that would prove the best course— I don't want to cause any further trouble or embarrassment here."

"But where would you go?" asked Maggie, thinking he sounded more sober and sincere than she had yet seen him. "You can't return to London."

"I've thought about that. Perhaps my father was right, and it would be best for me to—"

"You don't mean prison! That would be dreadful!"

"It would be different for me," Ian replied objectively. "I have money. I would be able to buy certain privileges." Suddenly he stopped short and laughed. "Listen to me! I'm making it sound like Buckingham Palace."

Then just as quickly the laughter left his voice and his face grew solemn. "But to tell you the truth, I'm not quite ready to leave this place."

"Then why insist on it?" asked Maggie.

"I don't know. Actually, I don't know what I ought to do. You don't know how I feared coming here. And still do! Before I came I was afraid simply of the boredom. I was so used to London. But now . . . now I fear more what it's doing to me—making me see parts of myself I've tried to hide from."

Maggie eyed his face intently. What a new side of her cousin this was! She had thought his attitude toward life was restricted to laughing and poking fun at those around him. But he was just as confused, just as uncertain as anyone—as she herself.

"How I'd love to run away!" he went on. "A part of me yearns to get back on the London streets. That's my home! But then another part of me—a part of me I didn't know existed—whispers that there is something here for me, something I can't run from, something I can't afford to lose, as if a destiny of some kind is calling out to me. But the other part of me—the London part—doesn't want to listen."

"Don't listen to the London part. Stay!" said Maggie emphatically, hardly knowing why. Just moments ago she was angry with him.

"After last night, I just don't—"

"No one knows about last night."

"You know. Your groom knows."

"I will say nothing. And I assure you, Digory is as good as gold."

"I didn't exactly drink alone either."

"Oh—the villagers," Maggie said with an unconcerned wave of her hand. "They won't care. If anything it'll raise your estimation in their eyes. Especially with the harvest just beginning. They'll have plenty of things to occupy their minds besides you."

Relieved, Ian stood still, saying nothing for a moment, apparently thinking.

"Come . . . walk with me," said Maggie. "I want to show you a little garden nearby."

He nodded his assent and followed.

"It's one of my favorite spots. The way you were taken with the beauty of the fields the other day, I thought you'd enjoy it."

At the back of the house stood a small iron gate. A cursory glance might easily fail to reveal it altogether. And if one did chance to see it and became curious, he would undoubtedly find it locked. Maggie led Ian straight toward it, reached up to a broken piece of rock in the top of the stone hedge above her head, and brought down a key, large and rusty, apparently very old. This she inserted into the keyhole in the gate and with some effort the lock finally yielded and the two cousins entered.

No larger than a good-sized parlor, the garden was surrounded by a stone wall overgrown with hedge shrubbery and ivy. At either end sat two stone benches. A large leafy birch in the center had already begun shedding some of its leaves, a reminder that fall was near. In general it was an unkempt place with overgrown rhododendrons and azalias, and other folliage in sore need of trimming. But something about its wildness lent a mystic air of solitude to the place, and Ian could quickly see why Maggie said she loved it.

"I think I'm the only one who comes here," Maggie said as they seated themselves on the far bench. "I'm glad, though. If it were more used my mother would decide to fix it up. But I like it just the way it is." She stopped and thought for a long moment. All was silent about them. A light breeze rustled through the birch and several more golden leaves floated to the ground.

"Tell me, Mr. Duncan," Maggie went on at length, "would your father really prefer to see you in the hands of the magistrate?"

"My father . . ." Ian mused thoughtfully. Then he continued as if he had forgotten her question. "Do you know why there is a rift between our two families?"

"Only bits and pieces," Maggie replied.

"My grandfather was your grandfather's brother. When your grandfather lost his fortune, my grandfather turned away from him. They were brothers, but he wouldn't give him a farthing. My grandfather had everything—the money, the title, the estate—and yet he refused his own brother even enough to sustain his family. I understand your father's hatred. It always seemed to me that Lawrence Duncan hardly needed to be punished further. Even his self-respect was shattered. All he needed was some simple compassion, and no more money than my grandfather would have thoughtlessly spent on a new filly. But Grandfather would have called it pampering, and he steadfastly refused to give in to the pressure coming from other members of the family."

Ian stopped and exhaled a long sigh. Maggie stole a glance at his face. She could see his turbulent emotions reflected in his features.

"So when you ask about my father," he went on, "all that immediately comes into my mind. I suppose my own father comes from the same school. He learned compassion at the hands of his father—who had none."

"He's like your grandfather."

"Like father, like son," said Ian. "No pampering—especially in the case of an outcast second son."

"Outcast? You?"

"You should see my older brother, a perfect cast from the family mold. He'll make my father proud, carry on the family tradition, and all that. And maybe my father is right. Maybe I am no good. Only it would still—"

"You wish he cared about you anyway?" said Maggie, completing the thought for him.

He looked at her for a long moment. How could she see so deeply something he'd only just realized himself? "How could a father not love his own flesh and blood?" he pleaded, not so much to Maggie as to himself, and to anyone greater who might be listening.

"I've asked myself that very question," said Maggie quietly.

"You have?"

"Many, many times."

"But why? Your parents love you?"

"It's a long story."

"Would you tell me about it?"

"Not now," Maggie replied. "But sometime, if you stay long enough. Let's just say that my father, like yours, has peculiar notions about how he demonstrates familial affections. It's strange. In many ways my father has grown into a type of the very man he has always hated, your grandfather.''

"The Duncan blood is common to them both. Perhaps that is why I'm so wayward—the demon blood of the Duncans!''

They both laughed. Then silence once more enfolded the small garden until Ian finally broke it.

"I'm not accustomed to talking like that. To another person, you know. I usually make it a point of keeping my feelings inside.''

"It's not an easy thing to do. I'm not very used to it myself.''

"But it felt good. Thank you for listening . . . Maggie.''

Maggie stood and walked over to the great birch, the remainder of its yellow and green leaves rustling gently in the breeze.

"It sounds nice for you to call me by name.''

"You're not offended?''

"I don't like to be called *my lady*. I want to be Maggie. I don't want to be a *lady* to people like Lucy. I want to be a friend.''

"I understand.''

Breaking out in a merry laugh to escape the reflective mood, Maggie said, "The day is still fresh, Mr. Duncan. Shall we take the horses out for a ride?''

"Only if you promise to call me Ian,'' he replied.

She smiled and nodded. He rose from the stone bench and followed her back out through the gate and toward the stables.

26 / The Race

George Falkirk smiled a broad smile of satisfaction.

This was good land, he thought. *So much better than Father's.* Of course, land was land and he in no way despised the 640 acres he would someday inherit. But his father had not made the most discriminating purchases through the years. And he had done little to develop his holdings. He had contented himself instead with letting his stockpile of wealth simply accumulate in the bank. Thus, as he surveyed his prospects for the future, young George realized he would one day be very rich, but with little else to show for his name—no estate of renown to enhance the prestige of his reputation.

Thus, long before his recent return to Scotland, George had determined to make the most of what opportunities presented themselves. Not only was he the only son of a wealthy earl, he was skilled, educated, and—he had been told—a better-than-average looking man. He would keep his eyes and ears open and eventually, he was confident, something would turn up.

Thus the fortuitous discussion with his parents had coincided nicely with his personal ambitions. The laird of the neighboring estate, they told him, had a daughter. A trifle young, perhaps, but growing quickly into womanhood, and reported to be pretty. In ten years' time she would no doubt be a beautiful lady of some renown. Best of all, they said, complexities in the future of the estate—there was a younger brother—rendered the possibility quite likely that she would inherit a good portion of the land, possibly the estate in its entirety. And a fine estate it was, bordering Kairn along the ridge they called Braenock, and thence extending east and west and all the way to the sea, encompassing all of the fertile Strathy valley.

Indeed, his mother had said, if the two young people could come to the point in a relationship—which she was certain could be discreetly arranged—where a union of the two estates seemed likely, it would certainly enhance young George's position as a landowner in the area and propel him into prominence. George said little, keeping his opinions to himself. But ever since the girl's birthday party he had increasingly found his thoughts turning northward over the hills toward Stonewycke.

This could indeed be just the opportunity he had been looking for. He would simply have to bide his time, see how things developed with the girl, gain the influence of the father, and then wait for the proper moment to make his move. Along with his recent discovery concerning Braenock, having the girl at his side would indeed represent quite a coup. After all, waiting for his father's inheritance could entail another twenty years. There was no reason not to begin flexing the muscle of his position immediately, if he could just lay his hands on that money.

But he would worry about that later. Right now he was on his way to accompany a young lady on a ride, and his anticipation mounted each mile as he neared her home.

Ian and Maggie first saw George Falkirk riding around the corner of the house as they were making their way toward the stables.

"Good morning, Lady Margaret," he said, stopping to dismount and walking toward them. "I was hoping I might persuade you to take a ride with me," he went on, ignoring Ian.

"What a coincidence," Maggie replied. "We were just about to do that very thing. Mr. Falkirk, this is my father's cousin from London, Ian Duncan."

"Ah, yes . . . Mr. Duncan," said Falkirk as the two shook hands rather stiffly. "Reports of your visit have already spread to Kairn. I had hoped I might meet you while you were here."

Ian said nothing.

"Perhaps you could join us, Mr. Falkirk," said Maggie.

Falkirk's displeasure at Ian's unfortunate presence was only barely noticeable as a faint contortion played momentarily around the edges of his mouth. But there was no apparent way to get rid of the fellow, so he might as well make the best of it.

He waited while the two saddled their mounts, wondering if there might be some way to lose the city boy in the country. Then the three rode at a brisk trot out the gates and cantered away toward the south.

Maggie had intended to ride once again to the hillsides where she and Ian had gone their first day out together, but Falkirk edged his golden stallion to the front and led instead across the gentle hills toward the rockier and steeper fells. He kept a healthy pace, and the terrain gave the more inexperienced Ian all he could manage.

At length she drew Raven to a stop and said breathlessly, "I had hoped we could go at a slower pace and take a moment to admire the scenery, since Mr. Duncan is so new to Scotland."

"I am sorry, Lady Margaret," Falkirk replied, turning his mount and drawing up next to her. "It was most inconsiderate of me to set such a pace for your guest."

"Don't worry about me," said Ian gaily. In truth he was relieved they had stopped, for he had never before ridden in such rough country.

"It helps to have such a worthy mount as that chestnut," Falkirk said smugly. It was the first time he had addressed Ian.

"I suppose if yours was as good," replied Ian somewhat carelessly, "you'd probably be up on that far ridge by now."

A smile crept slowly across Falkirk's face. "Do I detect a challenge in your words?" he asked with a glint in his eye.

A challenge could not have been further from Ian's mind. But he rather enjoyed toying with the pomposity of this debonair gentleman. "You may take whatever meaning you wish from my words," he replied with a good-natured grin and a nonchalant wave of his hand.

"It sounded as though you meant to imply that your horse was faster than mine."

Ian merely shrugged, in baiting good humor.

"I must warn you that this stallion is northern champion in both cross country and steeplechase," Falkirk boasted.

"Well, Mr. Falkirk," Maggie put in, "I know something of Maukin's bloodline. And though she has never competed, if I were a man I'd wager my last guinea on her."

"It seems we have not only a challenge, but a wager as well!" exclaimed Ian, greatly enjoying the spirit of the moment. "There is but one missing element, Mr. Falkirk."

"To the top of that ridge and back," Falkirk enjoined.

Without another word the two riders were off. Falkirk made it a point to hold back for the first several strides, thus giving Ian the advantage of starting with a brief lead. He would not have it said when he won the race that he had enjoyed an edge at the starting gate.

Within a hundred yards he had taken the lead from Ian and maintained it thereafter. Watching from Raven's back, Maggie could see that Falkirk's form was flawless—he appeared one with his steed, flowing in perfect unison with the stallion's every motion.

Ian, however, now several lengths behind, seemed to hold little, if any, control over Maukin, who refused to restrain her great power now that the word had been given. Yet Ian seemed unconcerned with the clumsy picture he presented. If his horse was to have control, then he was willing to concede as long as he was carried along in her glory.

The golden stallion flew across a gully. Maukin followed easily. Ian swayed in the saddle, looked about to fall, but managed to right himself again. Shouting commands, Falkirk dug his heels unmercifully into his stallion's flanks, clutching the horse tightly with his knees as they scrambled up a rocky ascent where the footing was less sure, gained the ridge, and turned for home.

He masked the surprise on his face when, on wheeling around, he discovered that Ian was a mere four lengths behind him.

"Keep your horse clear, Falkirk!" shouted Ian with a broad grin on his face. "I'm about to let Maukin loose!"

Falkirk's only reply was a series of unintelligible words into the stallion's ear followed with a fresh round of lashings on his hindquarters with the crop he held in his hand.

Ian laughed, made the turn, bent low as Maukin eased down the rocky slope, then gave her the rein. "Now, Maukin," he urged, "go after that stallion."

Shading her eyes against the sun, Maggie could hardly distinguish the two riders, but it appeared they had drawn closer together as the tiny specks they had become now gradually grew in size once more.

Suddenly a chill ran through her body. *Could it be?* she thought. *Are these two men competing because of me?* A smile played on her lips, and she could not avoid the momentary ripple of pleasure that shot through her. Two handsome men—fighting over her?

But her girlish reverie was suddenly broken by the sounds of approaching shouts and thundering hooves. The terrain had leveled and the sheer test of speed was on. Maukin had narrowed the gap to less than two lengths and the expressions of both riders were more determined than ever. Without knowing what had come over her, Maggie found herself yelling wildly at the riders, hardly caring whether they heard her or not.

Falkirk's face displayed genuine concern. Riding hard, yet conscious of the pounding hooves gaining beside him, he could take the pressure of the unknown no longer. Suddenly he committed what was taboo for any rider in a race: he turned back and looked over his shoulder. Maukin was so wild with speed by now that all it took was that one lapse in concentration, that one fatal error in judgment. The next instant she had pulled even.

Falkirk watched his rival with desperation. Maukin's ears lay flat against her head and her reddened nostrils were flared. Ian was no master of her speed now, and only clung on for his life, exhilarated with fear and joy together.

In one final lunging effort, Falkirk flailed the stallion with his whip and pumped the heels of his boots into its sides, and as the two riders shot past Maggie in full reckless gallop, it was the stallion's head that sped by first. Maggie continued to cheer wildly. Maukin slowed of her own accord. Falkirk tugged at his rein and swung the stallion around so as to be first to arrive back at Maggie's side.

Maggie turned to reward the victor with a flushed smile. "Well, Mr. Falkirk," she said, "it seems you and your stallion are as good as your word."

Before he could reply, an exuberant Ian trotted up and dismounted, panting as hard as his sweating horse. "Wonderful race, Mr. Falkirk!" he said, extending his hand to the other, still mounted. "What a ride!"

Falkirk dismounted, smiling but stiff. The victory had apparently not contained the satisfaction he had anticipated. He lifted his stallion's left hind foot and examined the shoe.

"Is something wrong?" Maggie asked.

"I think my horse took a stone on the ridge," he replied.

To Maggie's eyes the hoof looked fine.

"I can see why the stallion is a champion," said Ian. "You gave me more than I bargained for."

"As did you, Duncan," replied Falkirk. "Well run, indeed. You gave me quite a scare. But glory in your near-win while you can. I'll not allow you so close next time."

As he spoke his final words, his eyes turned toward Maggie and an involuntary chill crept up her back.

Ian brushed back a tousled lock of hair, threw his head back, and laughed without restraint.

27 / An Afternoon Conspiracy————————

George Falkirk seethed with anger.

He had had different intentions for his day at Stonewycke. How could the miserable blighter have made him look like such a buffoon? Riding home, Margaret had been full of praise for Duncan's loss of the race with hardly so much as a mention of his own victory.

So the trouble-making young Duncan would vie for the favor of Lady Margaret, would he? His laughing good nature fooled no one. *Well, let him try*, thought Falkirk coolly. He was a practical man, and he realized that anger would not best serve the achieving of his goal. Duncan's momentary advantage of being in closer proximity to the little prize would gain him nothing. Hardly one to be influenced by modesty, Falkirk remained confident that he could sweep the young mistress of Stonewycke off her feet at will. He had only to contrive to see her more often, and her father would help in that, he was sure.

But he could take no chances. With young Duncan roaming about, anything might happen. And he was not about to let the *real* prize slip through his fingers—it was too close. And with that safely in his grasp, he wouldn't need Margaret or Stonewycke at all, if worse came to worst. But with all three in his possession, everything he had dreamed about would be his. He knew his desire for the lady and control of Stonewycke went beyond a mere quest for wealth and worldly position. But with the lady and with her estate and with the wealth he was soon to lay his hands upon, the ultimate power he sought would all be his.

He directed the golden stallion not south toward Kairn, but rather into the village of Port Strathy. When he reached the village he, like his competitor of two hours earlier, sought out the new stone inn, the Bluster 'N Blow.

It was late afternoon and the streets were quiet. The fisherfolk were readying themselves for the evening out on the sea in search of the herring. The farmers were busy gathering their crops, for the harvest season was upon them. Only a few women and children walked along the dirt street that led past the dry-goods store, a chandlery, and one or two other shops, toward the inn. Falkirk rode past them with hardly a notice. His eyes remained fixed straight ahead, although some of the passers-by hazarded a curious look or two at the fine steed and its lordly rider.

Falkirk dismounted at the inn and strode inside, finding it dark and empty. But Queenie, hearing the creak of the door, hurried out from her kitchen in an instant. A smile stole onto her lips. *Two gentlemen in one week!* she thought.

"What can I do fer ye, yer lairdship?" she said with as welcome a tone as her gruff voice would allow.

"I'll have a pint of ale, if it's fit to drink," he replied. Without waiting for her to answer, he found a place at one of the eight or ten tables which were spaced around the room. He brushed the table off with a handkerchief and waited.

He did not have to wait long. For though Queenie went to the cellar to break open a small cask of her best ale, she did not take her time about it. Perhaps word about her inn was spreading to some of the area's regal circles, and she intended to impress this lord with her finest brew.

Falkirk lifted his glass and took a leisurely swallow. *It's a good thing I didn't come here for the ale*, he thought, pursing his lips. Queenie stood by, awaiting his approval. Falkirk merely nodded, offered no word, and took another long draught.

In a few moments the door opened, emitting a bright stream of afternoon light. Falkirk continued to sip from his glass, not even casually acknowledging the new arrival.

A tall man, stocky and unkempt, shuffled up to the oaken counter. He rapped on the wood surface with the knuckles of a grubby hand. Queenie, who had reentered the kitchen for a moment, hurried back out, thinking her distinguished guest was beckoning her. But when her eyes fell on the man at the counter, no words of welcome rose to her lips.

"Oh, 'tis you, is it, Martin Forbes," she said. "What'll ye be wantin'?"

"What do ye think I came here fer, woman!" he snarled. "Certainly it'll na be yer fine cookin'."

"Weel, 'tis too early," she replied flatly.

Forbes shot a glance at Falkirk who remained totally disinterested.

"Ye're a hard woman, Queenie," Forbes said at length, then turned and left.

A moment later Falkirk drained his glass and rose to leave, first tossing a coin on the table. It rolled to the floor, but there he left it, as if intending the proprietress to retrieve her earnings from the floor.

Queenie waited until the lord was out the door, then she scooped up the coin, tucked it into her dress, and swore softly to herself. Her distinguished visitor the previous night might have been a bit on the drunk side, but she decided he was the better-mannered of the two. Had he not only this morning sent her money well and above the cost of his uproarious evening with a kindly note of thanks and apology?

As Queenie reflected on these things, Falkirk ambled around toward the back of the inn and took the steep path down to the water's edge. From out of the tall grass emerged a figure which approached him.

"I dinna ken what all the secrecy be aboot, yer lairdship," said the man.

"Don't worry about it, Forbes," said Falkirk with a tone of superiority. "As long as you do as I say."

"Aye, my lord," Forbes replied. "Didna I follow yer orders? Ye said t' look fer yer horse an' when I saw it t' come int' the inn but pretend I didn't ken ye. That's what ye said. I'll do right by ye, yer lairdship—ye can be sure o' that."

"I'll have to," Falkirk replied. "Now listen carefully. You know the place we spoke of the other night? I want you to go there tonight—there's a full moon so you shouldn't need any other light. Look for the opening we spoke of. There should be a little hollow, almost like a small valley. If you don't find it tonight, keep at it for as many nights as it takes. If you find it, touch nothing! Come immediately for me, do you understand?"

Forbes nodded.

"I'll know if anything has been tampered with. If you cross me you'll be sorry you ever sucked a stinking breath."

"Did I ever give yer lairdship reason na t' trust me?" exclaimed Forbes. "I'm na a greedy man."

"Yes, yes," replied Falkirk dubiously. "I'll trust you when hell freezes over. But until then, you just do exactly as I say. You stand to gain quite a tidy sum yourself—but if you try anything I don't like, there won't be a hole you can find to hide in where I won't find you." He glared at the man, then added, "Do you have any questions?"

"Nay, my lord—I'll poke aroun', then report back t' ye."

"Can you write?" Falkirk asked.

"Not o'er much."

"Can you write *yea* or *nay*?"

Forbes nodded.

"Then," Falkirk continued, "if you find the opening, come to Kairn at night and leave a note saying *yea* with the stableboy. I'll meet you the following night at the place. Start tonight."

With these words Falkirk spun around and stalked up the hill to his horse.

Maggie rose from her bed with a tingle of excitement.

She sprang to the window, looked out, and smiled. The sun would grace the land at least once more with its vibrant warmth. *It's a perfect day!* she thought. She dressed quickly and skipped down the stairs.

"Oh, Mother," she said, "it's lovely out!"

"Yes. I can tell you are excited," said Atlanta, showing more than usual good cheer herself. She was relieved that the awkwardness of her previous talk with Maggie seemed, for the moment at least, to be forgotten.

Ian walked into the dining room where the preparations were nearly complete for breakfast.

"Won't you come with us, Ian?" Maggie asked.

"Of course," he replied breezily. "I'm always ready for an adventure. Come where?"

Maggie laughed. "Of course, how could you know?" she said. "Today is the *Maiden*—the day when the last sheaf of the harvest is reaped. The crofters celebrate with a huge feast."

"One of our Scottish traditions," added Atlanta.

"I never miss it!" said Maggie.

"Well, then," said Ian, "how could I think of remaining behind? Will your friend Falkirk be there?"

"My friend?" said Maggie, casting her mother a quick glance. If Atlanta had a reaction to Ian's question, she did not show it. "He's no more my friend than yours."

"Ha!" laughed Ian good-naturedly. "I doubt he was calling on me last week! And after that horse race I don't think he considers me on the friendliest of terms."

"Well, I seriously doubt we'll see the Falkirks today," said Atlanta. "The neighboring lords and ladies don't usually make it much of a habit to mix with the people of the land."

"Too bad," said Ian. "I was just beginning to like the chap!"

Ian finished his breakfast while Maggie chatted gaily with Atlanta about preparations for the day. It being the crofters' holiday, Atlanta tried not to make an ostentatious show of the participation of the Duncan family. But the feast was a community ritual of brotherhood among all classes, everyone bringing what he was able; she always added several dishes to the large tables of food. James usually managed to be away at such times, and on this occasion had conveniently been forced to Edinburgh on business. His sentiments did not generally lie with those who worked his land, and he found their observances tedious indeed. Though she could appear aloof at times, Atlanta, on the other hand, missed no opportunity to mingle with the people of the land. She, too, had her friends such as Maggie's Lucy among them, and stole out not infrequently to take a basket of fruit or a loaf of fresh bread to a fisher wife or farmer's daughter.

By mid-afternoon the company from Stonewycke was ready to depart. Sam, the servant boy who helped Digory in the stables from time to time, brought out the open wagon which would not only provide a bumpy ride to the celebration but also a platform from which to observe the proceedings. Ian jumped aboard and lifted up the three large baskets of food as Atlanta handed them to him. He extended his hand and helped up Atlanta to her seat next to Sam, then he assisted Maggie, who joined him on the large, flat, wooden-planked bed behind them.

The celebration was to take place about a mile southwest of Port Strathy in a large grassy meadow lined with resplendent birch and oak trees, turning brilliant shades of yellow and red as autumn approached. When the wagon from Stonewycke castle arrived, over a hundred of the locals were already on hand, an assemblage which would swell to twice that size within the hour. Men were busily setting out boards to make tables to hold the food and drink. In the center Charlie Krueger was engaged in the important task of getting the huge bonfire underway, while instructing Stevie Mackinaw and a dozen other eager youngsters concerning the procurement of additional firewood.

Atlanta and Maggie took their baskets to the tables while Ian strolled over to the bonfire, greeted Krueger, and mingled with the other men gathered around, two or three of whom he hazily recognized from his ill-fated night at the Bluster 'N Blow.

As the hour drew near, the guests came trooping in from all directions, some from as far as Culden. From the direction of Port Strathy came mostly the fishermen and their wives. From the valley to the south came the crofters who worked the fertile, and the infertile, soil. It was their celebration, those by whose labor and sweat the wheat and oats and barley had at last been cut and stored away in great barns for the winter. But for longer than anyone could remember, the farmers had welcomed those others of their rank and class who similarly earned their living from the sea, and the *Maiden*, at least in the environs of Port

Strathy, had indeed become a community gathering of shared good will and thankfulness.

It had long been customary for the Ramseys to attend the *Maiden* celebration, and the peasants accepted their presence gladly. Atlanta walked about among the people—much more easily than she would have been able to had James been present—talking to the wives, smiling at the children, and generally living out the love she harbored in her heart with a genuine courtesy which fostered deep admiration in the minds of all those present. Maggie, likewise, joined her, flitting about on her own from time to time, and soon won all the hearts of the people. She was indeed becoming a lady, many commented, and a handsome one who did Stonewycke proud.

Lucy Krueger shyly sought out the Lady Margaret to show her the little baby girl who was nearly two weeks old.

"Oh, Lucy!" Maggie exclaimed in the merry spirit of the day. "Your little Letty is so pink and healthy."

"Didna I say the Lord would be watchin' oot fer her?" Lucy replied.

"You look as happy as your name," Maggie cooed to the child.

"I'd be honored if ye'd hold her."

"I've never held a baby before, Lucy," said Maggie.

" 'Tis the most natural thing in life fer womenfolk," said Lucy, "be ye high or low bred. Here, my leddy, 'tis the easiest thing in the world." She thrust the baby toward Maggie and helped her to arrange her arms properly. " 'Tis jist important that ye hold the wee head, fer it still be weak."

"Oh, my," Maggie breathed. But after only a few moments her arms relaxed and the baby fit perfectly in the crook of her arm.

Atlanta watched the scene and a great warmth welled up within her. For so long Atlanta had clung to her daughter's childhood that she had never so much as imagined the thought of grandchildren. Suddenly a vision formed in her mind of Maggie someday—a day perhaps not far away—cradling her own little one. The thought was precious to Atlanta; her own little baby was practically a woman.

"Oh, Mother," said Maggie, "look . . . look at Lucy's darling little baby girl."

Atlanta smiled. "She's beautiful, Lucy."

"Thank ye, my leddy," replied Lucy with timid pride.

"You and your husband Charlie can be very proud," Atlanta continued.

"Her name means *happiness*," said Maggie to her mother.

"And a fitting name it is," said Atlanta to Lucy. "I can see it on your face. The name, as well as your daughter, is no doubt a gift from the Lord.''

Beaming, Lucy reached out her arms, and Maggie tenderly handed the small Letty back to her.

All at once the distant wail of bagpipes could be heard. Everyone put down his preparations in various stages of completion, and clustered in small bunches to watch the approaching procession.

Two pipers in kilt and tam led the way, rejoicing the watchers with a rousing and glorious pilbroch of the Highland hills. Behind them creaked an old wagon filled with hay and drawn by a single, slow-stepping Clydesdale. Atop the hay sat Alice Macondy, daughter of a crofter, the proclaimed Queen of the Festival. She held the honored last sheaf in her arms as tenderly as if it had been a bouquet of long-stemmed roses from a London flower shop. But in this northern province of Scotland, in the autumn of a successful harvest, no rose could smell so sweet to the people of the land as the final sheaf of grain. Behind the wagon, completing the processional, walked a parade of crofters, marching and dancing to the skirl and drone of the pipes.

From the surrounding meadow now poured forth all those who had already arrived, to join and further swell the ranks of the merry-makers. Songs and cheers rose higher and higher until the procession finally reached the bonfire. There they all spread in a wide circle, several persons deep, and joining hands sang several choruses and folk songs extolling the blessings of their beloved homeland. With a final shout, as caps and bonnets were thrown high into the air, the company at last disbanded.

Then began the joyous task of consuming all the food which had so lovingly been prepared. Indeed, the feast would continue on and off throughout the remainder of the evening, interspersed with numerous other activities, for as long as food and drink held out.

Gradually the sun sank into the mountains of the west and the rosy glow of the bonfire became the center of the celebration. Blankets were produced and spread on the grass to sit upon. Others leaned against, and some of the more energetic boys scampered up into, the birches and oaks. When the bags of the pipes and lips of the pipers had given their all and finally grown silent as darkness descended, Clare Brown caught up his fiddle and struck up a merry melody. The time for ballads and stories had come.

Atlanta found Maggie and Ian close to the fire and sat down beside her daughter. None of them noticed that young Sam had taken up with the group of older youths standing around the keg of ale.

As Clare Brown began to sing, the music washed over Maggie's senses and she realized she had not felt so contented at any time she could remember. For this present moment the turmoils of her life had receded out of sight in the peaceful and dreamy atmosphere of the evening.

"Why don't ye sing the ballad o' the Douglas?" someone called out to Clare.

"Surely na such a sad song on such a gay night as this," he replied.

"Aye, 'tis sad," came the answer, "but ye sing it so well!"

"Aye. Ye'll have yer way wi' me, will ye!" said Clare with a laugh. "So here 'tis then":

"Rise up, rise up, now, Lord Douglas," she says,
    "An' put on yer armour so bright;
Let it never be said, that a daughter o' thine
    Was married to a lord under night."

Rise up, rise up, my seven bold sons,
    An' put on yer armour so bright,
An' take better care o' yer youngest sister,
    For yer eldest's awa the last night.

He's mounted her on a milk-white steed,
    An' himsel' on a dapple grey,
With a bugelet horn hung doon by his side,
    An' lightly they rode away.

Lord William lookit o'er his left shoulder,
    To see what he could see,
An' there he spy'd her seven brethren bold,
    Come ridin' o'er the lea.

"Light down, light down, Lady Marg'ret," he said,
    "An' hold my steed in yer hand,
Until that against yer seven brothers bold,
    An' yer father, I mak a stand."

She held his steed in her milk-white hand,
    An' never shed one tear,
Until that she saw her seven brethren fall,
    An' her father hard fighting, who lov'd her so dear.

"O hold yer hand, Lord William!" she said,
    "For yer strokes they are wond'rous sair;
True lovers I can get many a ane,
    But a father I can never get mair."

O she's ta'en out her handkerchief,
    It was o' the holland sae fine,
And aye she dighted her father's bloody wounds,

That were redder than the wine.

"O choose, O choose, Lady Marg'ret," he said,
  "O whether will ye gang or bide?"
"I'll gang, I'll gang, Lord William," she said,
  "For ye hae left me no other guide."

He's lifted her on a milk-white steed,
  An' lifted himsel' on a dapple grey,
With a bugelet horn hung down by his side,
  An' slowly they baith rade away.

O they rade on, an' on they rade,
  An' a' by the light o' the moon,
Until they came to yon wan water,
  An' there they lighted doon.

They lighted doon to tak a drink
  O' the spring that ran sae clear;
An' doon the stream ran his gude heart's blood,
  An' sair she 'gan to fear.

"Hold up, hold up, Lord William," she said,
  "For I fear that ye are slain!"
" 'Tis nothin' but the shadow of my scarlet cloak,
  That shines in the water sae plain."

O they rade on, an' on they rade,
  An' a' by the light o' the moon,
Until they cam to his mother's ha' door,
  An' there they lighted doon.

"Get up, get up, Lady Mother," he says,
  "Get up, an' let me in!—
Get up, get up, Lady Mother," he says,
  "For this night my fair lady I've win."

"O make my bed, Lady Mother," he says,
  "O make it braid and deep!
An' lay Lady Marg'ret close at my back,
  An' the sounder I will sleep."

Lord William was dead lang ere midnight,
  Lady Marg'ret lang ere day—
An' all true lovers that go t'gither,
  May they hae mair luck than they!

Lord William was buried in St. Marie's kirk,
  Lady Marg'ret in Marie's quire;
Out o' the lady's grave grew a bonny red rose,
  An' out o' the knight's a brier.

> An' they twa met, an' they twa plat,
>> An' fain they would be near;
> An' al' the world might ken right weel,
>> They were twa lovers dear.

> But by an' rade the Black Douglas,
>> An' wow but he was rough!
> For he pull'd up the bonny brier,
>> An' flang't in St. Mary's loch.

Maggie was only vaguely conscious of the melancholy words. She turned to look at Ian. As the fire reflected on his face, she saw deeper thought there than she had yet noticed. When Clare began a gayer tune, the pensive look remained momentarily, then gradually subsided. He turned, aware that she had been gazing at him, and smiled. No words seemed appropriate, or necessary.

As Clare began his final song, the great fire had burned down to bright orange embers. As the last notes died away into the still night air, as if waking from a peaceful slumber that it might go home to bed, the crowd slowly began to stir. The men stretched their tired legs, the women gathered children and baskets, and reluctantly the families of the Strathy valley began to make their way home.

Ian forced himself to a standing position, took Maggie's hand and lifted her to her feet, and went off in search of Sam. It took several minutes to discover him, nestled against the trunk of a tree, sound asleep with a smile on his face. Ian hoisted him into the back of the wagon where he sprawled out and quickly fell asleep once more.

Ian helped Maggie and Atlanta up, then jumped up himself, and, taking the reins, urged the horses forward with a click of his tongue and a flip of the reins in his wrists.

Little was said on the way back to Stonewycke, as if by common consent each wished the evening could have gone on and on.

The evening couldn't go on forever, of course. James returned late the following afternoon and with him returned the tensions he had taken with him. But James's first stop before riding back through the gates of Stonewycke had been Kairn. The visit had been a brief one, but long enough for George Falkirk to indicate subtly the difficulty he had found in getting near Lady Margaret. James extended to his neighbor's son an invitation to Stonewycke for the next day, assuring him the matter would be taken care of.

The day could not have been more ill-chosen for courting had it been contrived as a plot against the suave young Falkirk. The morning dawned cloudy, and as the hours wore on, the deep mass of gray gave way to thick menacing clumps of black storm clouds blowing down from the mountains in the south. By noon the rain had begun in earnest and by the time Falkirk arrived an hour later, all the inhabitants of Stonewycke were shut in together and the mood had grown gloomy.

Delighted with Falkirk's appearance, James put on a great show of friendliness before awkwardly beginning the task of contriving some distraction for Ian. Unsuccessful, at length he fabricated a story of a business associate he wanted his cousin to meet, passing—as chance would have it—through Port Strathy that very day. Duncan, unconvincing, deceived none of those present; and his case was hardly strengthened by the fact that he had previously made such a concerted effort to ignore Ian altogether.

Under the circumstances, however, Ian was hardly able to refuse; he consented to the ride despite the nasty weather, and went to his room for cloak and hat. Leaving Maggie in Falkirk's presence disturbed him more than he would have thought possible, even yesterday. But after the night of the *Maiden*, she had been on his mind almost constantly. All morning he had been making efforts to find a way to speak to her himself. Falkirk's inopportune arrival and James's clear ploy to thrust the two young estate neighbors together plunged him into a vortex of mixed emotions.

He had come north for reasons undefined, with expectations obscure. Now suddenly rising within him were feelings he hadn't expected, in the center of which swirled the face of his seventeen-year-old cousin Margaret. As he sat beside James in the covered gig and pulled his hat down tightly against the wind, he found his heart fairly pounding in his chest at the prospect of leaving his adversary alone with her.

As for the young master of Kairn, he had stepped unknowingly into what was for him an awkward encounter. Maggie was detached, at times downright rude to him, then suddenly turned to baiting him with coy glances of encouragement. He had only to surmise that her disagreeable nature stemmed in one way or another from the presence in the house of that wretched cousin of hers. *Not that her affections really matter in the end*, he told himself. It was all being arranged. Once she came to see him in a different light, she would come round to her senses, of that he was sure—even if it took some time.

In the meantime, he had to get her alone. When Atlanta was called away to attend to some difficulty in the kitchen, Falkirk breathed an inner sigh of relief.

When he had arrived, he had been shown into the east parlor. Atlanta and Maggie had been sitting on the setee, where they had remained for the duration of his visit thus far. Falkirk had taken a wing-backed chair adjacent to them. The moment Atlanta had left the room with the servant, he rose and strolled casually to the huge carved mantle over the fireplace.

"You don't know, Lady Margaret," he began, "how pleasant it has been to have this opportunity to visit you."

Maggie relaxed slightly, thinking he was about to take his leave.

"From the moment I met you," he continued, "I knew I must become more closely acquainted with you."

He paused for effect. Maggie squirmed slightly.

"Do you remember the day?"

Maggie nodded.

"Your party," he went on. He turned and began to move toward her. "The coming-out celebration for a young lady who is a girl no longer . . . but a woman."

He dropped down next to her on the setee.

"How grand you were that night!" he continued. "The most beautiful person there."

"Please, Mr. Falkirk," said Maggie, "you are making me uncomfortable."

"Your beauty has grown even greater to me since that day," he went on, ignoring her.

The words should have pleased Maggie, but instead she felt suddenly stifled and hot, as if she needed a window opened. The feeling intensified as Falkirk drew nearer. She found herself inching away from him.

"Margaret, my heart pounds when I think of you, and nearly stops now that we are together."

He grasped her hands. They were cold and trembling. Perceiving that she was nervous, he moderated his advance.

"You must think me terribly forward, even impetuous. Forgive me."

Maggie forced a smile and nodded her concurrence.

"But the throbbing of my heart compels me to speak thus. Please grant me permission to see more of you."

Maggie tensed again.

It was all too clear what George Falkirk wanted. He was a forceful man, with sophisticated manners and a fine inheritance to press his claim. Why wasn't she flattered by his attentions?

Wavering between outrage at his presumption and pleasure at his flatteries, Maggie floundered for an answer.

"Why, Mr. Falkirk," she began, "I . . . I don't know what to say. There are so few people in the neighborhood of my age—of course, it would be nice to share your company—"

"That's not exactly what I had in mind," he cut in sharply; then the edge in his voice immediately softened. "That is to say, I had hoped you might allow me, as I mentioned before, to act as your escort to some of the neighboring estates, and perhaps to some social functions."

"I'm not ready to make that kind of decision, Mr. Falkirk," said Maggie.

"What's to decide? I am a young man with experience. You are a beautiful young woman. Why shouldn't we be seen together? I see no reason—"

"I'm still very young," said Maggie feebly.

"The time must come, Lady Margaret, when you enter into your calling as the future mistress of the estate."

"What do you know about the future of Stonewycke?" asked Maggie pointedly.

Realizing he had revealed too much about what he knew, Falkirk attempted gracefully to soothe her.

"I only meant," he said, "that *should* you ever become the mistress of the estate—should your brother choose to advance his career in London, for instance—then it would behoove you to give thought to your calling."

She seemed temporarily mollified by his explanation. As he spoke he eased closer to her and slipped his arm around her onto the back of the setee. "Before long you will have suitors lined up at your door. And—sooner than you might think—the time will come when you must think of marriage."

"My marriage plans are my own concern," replied Maggie, on her guard again. "Marriage is too far in the future for me to think about. Besides, as I said before, I am still young. I have much to learn."

"Then let me be your teacher," he said, drawing so near that Maggie felt the heat of his breath on her face. "It's time you learned what life has to give you. Let me be the one to water the lovely bud of Stonewycke, the Lady Margaret Duncan."

He had pressed so close that his lips brushed her cheek. A fleeting pulse quickened her heartbeat. She wanted to yield to his words of affection, but suddenly she felt hot and trapped. She could feel the red rising up the back of her neck and into her cheeks.

"I . . . I just—" she began, then as if by impulse she jumped up from the setee and moved quickly to open the large window. She drew a deep breath of the air and immediately felt her flushed face cool.

But the next instant Falkirk's unsolicited hands slipped around her waist. "I must tell you," he whispered in her ear, "that I cannot so easily distract my mind from its infatuation with you, and I intend—"

At that moment Atlanta's step could be heard on the landing outside the door.

Falkirk immediately pulled away with a silent curse as she entered the room. Maggie's hands rose to her reddened cheeks while she continued to gaze out the window, saying nothing. Surveying the scene, Atlanta discerned that she had returned none too soon. More perturbed than flustered, Falkirk smiled and began an immediate conversation with Atlanta about nothing of particular consequence.

Later in the day James returned with Ian, having been unable to locate his friend, but taking advantage of the time for several minor items of business he had been putting off. Falkirk returned to Kairn, somewhat disconcerted at the effort it was apparently going to take to further his advance toward the headstrong little heiress. But he was pleased with himself nonetheless. He had laid his cards on the table and was confident. The little lady would capitulate in time; especially with the father advancing his cause, there was little need for concern. The veneer of her reluctance was all too transparent. His words of love would win her over. They had worked for him before, and she was no different than all the rest.

The rain had ceased but the sky remained black as he rode through the gates of Kairn. He was softly whistling a tune, feeling in good spirits, and relishing the thought of a tall mug of cold stout after his long ride. The stableboy took the horse, relieved that the young lord, who could be a hard master when things were not to his liking, was in an agreeable mood.

The boy led the horse to a stall, then stopped abruptly.

"My Lord!" he called out, hoping not to get his ears boxed for nearly forgetting.

"What is it?" demanded Falkirk, turning.

"A man brought ye this earlier. Tole me t' give it t' ye."

He handed the dirty, crumpled paper to Falkirk, who would have indeed boxed the boy's ears had he not been absorbed in the message.

It simply read *yea*.

30 / The Dormin

The ancient forest called Dormin stood on the west bank of the River Lindow which ran through the western portion of the Stonewycke estate. It stood in solemn splendor just as it had stood perhaps a thousand years ago—nearly untouched by man because some good king ages ago had laid eyes on it, and had loved it so that he passed laws against killing its animals or felling its trees or harming so much as a petal of the tiniest flower. Disobedience had been punishable by death.

In later years, of course, the severity of the punishment had been moderated, but the Dormin still remained under royal protection. Every so often a poacher would be found and arrested, but usually he faced only a stiff fine, and was not imprisoned unless the penalty went unpaid.

Yet few were bold enough to tread the tangled paths of the forest. Its treasures, therefore, remained all the more preserved for the infrequent beholder. Dozens of mosses clung to the trees, some so rare and exquisitely delicate that even botanical experts had not seen the like. The Dormin's trees—massive and ancient—appeared rather like living sentinals—old Scots fir, birch, aspen, alder, rowan, and oak—custodians of the past, guarding against intruders of the present. Interspersed between them were thick growths of high heather and other wet and woodsy shrubbery, pervaded by the ever-present hint of decay—rotting logs, fallen leaves and needles, and the continually dying, cyclically renewing dense underbrush. Even flowers could be found in their season, wherever they could push their lovely faces out of the tangled mass—crocuses, primroses, daffodils. Watching over them, from atop their higher perch, as king of the Dormin's flowering shrubbery, were the many-colored blossoms of wild rhododendron, ready to bestow the sweet pleasure of their faces to the more adventurous forest wanderer.

Maggie always experienced a shiver of apprehension as she approached the forest. Here her great-grandfather Anson Ramsey had been mysteriously killed one gray autumn day. She remembered well the story of his final days at Stonewycke. *A hunting party had driven three stags from the forest near the castle. Two were killed almost immediately, but the third, a magnificent pale animal, received only a superficial wound. The party tracked it for the remainder of that day, certain it could not get far.*

But at dusk the white stag still ran free, and the party was ready to concede defeat and turn for home. All, that is, except for Anson, who convinced his two sons, Talmud and Edmond, to keep up the hunt with him. They continued to trail the blood track and prints on the ground all night and into the next morning. Though they wandered in great circles, never heading for the high mountains, they were still unable to approach the mighty animal but could only make out the silhouette of its great antlered head over the next brae. During the afternoon of the second day, Anson tracked it across the Lindow only to watch his prey disappear into the depths of the Dormin: The great stag paused as he gained the opposite bank of the river, turned toward Anson as if to remind him that the last man to kill his prey in the forest behind him had been hanged, then bounded over a log and quickly disappeared from sight.

Anson knew the stag would easily elude them in the dense forest within moments, but too much time had been invested by now; he could not simply stand by helplessly, allowing the animal its victory without one final attempt.

Shouting for his sons to follow, he charged across the river and into the Dormin with renewed vigor and speed. Edmond and Talmud followed not far behind.

But Anson returned home that day with no prize.

He was draped over his horse, dead of a broken neck. His sons recounted that they had found him in the forest sprawled on the ground. They could only speculate that his steed had stumbled on a fallen branch and thrown the lord; in death, his disappointed gaze was still focused in the direction of the lost stag.

But family history was far from Maggie's mind today.

Raven and Maukin splashed across the shallow ford of the Lindow. Ian whistled gaily as they clambered up the opposite bank and beheld the seemingly impenetrable wood immediately before them. He stopped and gazed with wonder, sensing the mystery of the place. It seemed to emanate forgotten secrets and undiscovered histories. Maggie plunged Raven ahead into the labyrinth of vines and bushes and ferns, and Ian cautiously urged Maukin to follow. *It is almost a challenge,* he thought, *merely to cross the invisible threshold of this wood's border.* He wondered if that soft rustling sound was not some murmur of the trees, for there was no wind that fine September morning. But whether their leafy voices spoke welcome or boded ill, he could not tell.

After riding a few minutes, they stopped and dismounted, speaking in hushed tones. They stepped lightly on the carpet of fallen leaves and moss which graced the small clearing where they stood. Around them the few shafts of sunlight which were able to penetrate the foliage shone on a resplendent array of autumn reds and golds and yellows and browns, spread like fairy dust over the greenery beneath. Ian's eyes looked upward as he walked about; suddenly Maggie's soft but urgent voice warned him of a huge root protruding dangerously from the ground in front of his foot.

He avoided stumbling over it, thanked her, and bent his gaze toward the forest floor.

"Not only am I ungraceful in the saddle," he said; "it seems I need a guide for my feet, too!"

Maggie laughed softly.

"This is marvelous!" he exclaimed. "You could truly forget yourself here."

"If you wanted to forget," said Maggie. "I think it's the kind of place that would allow you to be whatever you needed to be."

"You've been here before, I can tell," said Ian.

"Many times."

"You make it sound almost reverent."

"I suppose I do reverence this place," she replied, "almost like a garden of Eden. It's so . . . so ancient."

"And that's what makes it holy?" asked Ian seriously.

"I don't know. It makes it awesome, that much is certain. But then I think Digory would say it isn't age that makes a thing holy, but . . ."

"But what?"

"I don't know what I was going to say exactly."

"Purity," said Ian, hardly realizing such an answer was in him.

"Purity . . . innocence? Then the more pure a thing is, the closer to holiness it comes. Is purity the same as godliness, do you suppose?"

"Well," said Ian briskly, trying to shake the spell of the place, "that's a question I will never have to worry about."

"Why?"

"I'm no philosopher. I'm just a fun-loving Englishman!"

"So I've discovered," replied Maggie with a laugh. "But you know people are not always what they appear on the surface," she went on with a playful gleam in her eye.

"Is that something else Digory would say?"

Maggie smiled.

"Come on," she said, "before we spend all day philosophizing when I've so much for you to see."

She grabbed his hand and would have skipped forward if the terrain had allowed it.

"Will we be able to find our way out of here?" Ian asked, though there was more laughter than anxiety in his voice.

"If we ever want to leave," she replied, "I know the way. I'm your guide, remember?"

Leaving the horses where they had tied them, Maggie led deeper into the forest. Gradually the light dimmed; only patches of sunlight and pale blue sky could occasionally be seen between the trees as they formed a lattice overhead like a fine lace mantilla.

They followed a tiny stream for a ways, stopping beside a freshet for a drink of icy mountain water. How long had it been since anyone had drunk from it? Or were they the first?

As she stood up from the stream, Maggie realized Ian was gazing at her instead of the forest, his eyes bright. *What is he thinking?* she wondered. Had she been able to see inside that head topped with tousled golden hair, she would have seen that he was chiding himself for his flippant attitude when they had first met. It seemed so long ago; in reality it had only been a matter of weeks. But that short time had added years to his life, extended his horizons of awareness—both of the world around him and of himself. Indeed, as he gazed deep into her eyes he realized that he regarded Maggie as a gift he had been given, a gift which stimulated his new discoveries and insights. But looking up to meet his gaze, Maggie knew none of this.

"Oh, look!" Maggie had spotted a tiny purple and white primrose, nestled among several dead branches; she whispered, as if her voice might somehow cause it to fold up its leaves and hide from them.

They stooped down together to observe it more closely. Ian moved back some of the leaves and branches and stretched out his hand to pluck it.

"Stop! Don't pick it," Maggie cried, placing her hand on his and drawing it away.

He turned, keeping hold of her hand. "I was going to give it to you," he said.

They drew apart, then, as if moved by the same impulse, and sat down on the ground, staring in the direction of the solitary primrose.

"Thank you," said Maggie. "I didn't mean to pounce on you so."

Ian said nothing, only glanced away, restlessly.

"Is anything wrong?" Maggie asked.

"No," he replied. "I mean . . . there's something—"

"What is it?"

Ian hesitated. "I've been . . . you know—in London. Playing the part of the carouser, the lady's gentleman. Words of love falling off my tongue more easily than the ale poured down my throat. But . . ."

Heat rose up the back of Maggie's neck. Her heart was pounding within her chest so loudly that she feared Ian must hear it, so loudly it echoed in the silence of the forest; but not loudly enough to silence the words she knew Ian was struggling to say. The fear now burning hot in her cheeks was so different from what she had felt when alone with George Falkirk. Now she was afraid of the words she *longed* to hear, longed to shout out herself!

"Maggie," Ian went on with stammering determination, "you've . . . you've given me something since I came here—different from anything I've felt with anyone before."

He stopped and breathed deeply, then jumped to his feet and paced about nervously, trying to find the right words. Then he dropped to the ground again at the foot of a rowan tree and leaned his head back against its trunk. Maggie slid to her knees next to him.

"Oh, it's no use!" he exclaimed.

Maggie turned toward him and gently placed her hand on his arm. "Try, Ian," she said. "What were you going to say?"

"I would never have noticed that insignificant flower without you," he said at last. "I might have even tried to step on it if I had seen it— unknowing, uncaring, unfeeling. Now I can never again look at the plainest of flowers, at a mountain stream, at a desolate moor, at a heather hill, without—"

Her lips were silent, but Maggie's eyes said, *Yes?*

"—without thinking of you."

Now that he had said it, Ian was finally able to turn and look Maggie in the face. She was smiling, a silent tear running down her cheek.

"I did nothing, Ian," she said softly. "You must have always had that love for God's creation within you. But you were too bound up in the distractions of your life, afraid to open yourself to that kind of beauty, afraid to let out your true feelings, afraid of being vulnerable."

"But it's more than a sensitivity to all this beauty around us," he said.

"I know," she said softly. She wanted to say, *It's more for me, too,* but she couldn't make the words come out.

"It's *you,* Maggie," he said. "The reason I can love that flower or the heather is that for the first time I really care about someone—about you."

He turned away, embarrassed at the awkwardness of his speech, and fearing her reply.

Maggie, too, remained silent. What could she say? Did she even know what she felt herself? She had been holding back for so long; now suddenly something cried out within her to open her heart again. With every ride she and Ian took, with every chance meeting of their eyes, each time she heard him laugh in such high-spirited joy, the crevice in her heart opened a bit wider. Something was driving them together, and she could no longer resist its force.

Misconstruing Maggie's silence, Ian was overcome with self-consciousness. If the forest around them remained silent one second more, he feared he would burst; to break the hush he suddenly blurted out the thoughtless remark—

"Of course, I know that you and our friend Mr. Falkirk—"

"George Falkirk!" interrupted Maggie. "What about *him*?"

"Aren't you and he. . . ?" Ian completed his sentence with a look of questioning.

"Ian," said Maggie, "George Falkirk means nothing to me."

A stab of hope shot through Ian's heart. He turned toward Maggie, eyes aglow with the laughter he was for the moment content to keep inside.

"Don't you know . . . haven't you seen, Ian?"

Only his eyes spoke, searching her face for the final words he sought.

"Don't you know that I feel the same way about you?"

At last he could contain his delight no more. Ian burst into a hearty laugh, more exuberant than Maggie had yet heard from him. She could not keep from joining him.

When the verbal expression of their shared joy was spent, Ian rose, took her hand and raised Maggie to her feet. Arm in arm they walked silently back through the forest the way they had come.

31 / The Locket

Ian wanted to give Maggie a present. Perhaps his gift would never mean as much as Lucy Krueger's simple handkerchief, but nevertheless, he wanted her to have something from him. He had looked through the belongings he had brought from London, but nothing was suitable.

The day was drawing to a close. On a sudden impulse he decided to ride into Port Strathy. Surely he could locate something there. Maggie so loved this valley that a gift from its quaint fishing village would be the best thing, anyway.

Pat Brodie was about to hang his *Closed* sign on the door of the mercantile when Ian rode up in a gallop and quickly dismounted.

"Weel, ye're in a fine rush, ye are, lad," he said with an amiable smile.

"I've a mind to buy something," Ian replied, approaching the front of the shop. "I won't keep you long."

"I've ne'er been one t' keep away a customer . . . come in." The shopkeeper opened the door and with a sweep of his hand welcomed Ian inside.

One look at the interior of the store made Ian wonder if he'd overestimated his chances of finding something. The place was crammed with a vast array of merchandise, none of it appearing to be in any particular order. A hammer could be found with linen handkerchiefs, or a pair of shoes tucked in between sacks of chicken feed. The foodstuffs seemed generally to be along the right-hand wall, but then Ian noticed a pair of long underwear jammed between several tins of cured herring.

Ian edged his way between crates and bins and sacks, somehow hoping the right token of his feelings might miraculously jump out to greet him. He had no idea what he might be looking for; a hasty scan of the premises revealed little other than the most practical necessities of humble Scottish life, and he was about to give up. He had already overstepped the bounds of courtesy in keeping Brodie past the usual hour.

As he turned with a sigh to go, a small wooden crate perched atop a bin of plowshares caught his eye. He walked toward it for a closer look, and discovered the crate to be filled with smaller, delicate boxes.

Further investigation revealed that each box contained a ring or brooch or some particular article of jewelry. So Brodie did stock a few impractical trinkets after all! Most were large gold-colored pieces with cheap, showy imitation gems. Familiar enough with quality jewel-work, Ian realized that such costume pieces might be fine for a poor fisherman's wife who had never in her life seen a real pearl—but none were suitable for Maggie. Persistently, however, he opened each box until at last his efforts were rewarded. Near the bottom of the crate he discovered a delicate heart-shaped locket, golden in color, hanging from a delicate gold chain. Ian perceived at a glance that it could not be genuine. It was clearly the sort of thing the crofters might buy for their sweethearts— Maggie's poorest gem would easily outshine this trinket. Yet for right now it was just what he wanted: a simple momento of his feelings. There would be plenty of time to purchase a fine expensive piece in London later.

He removed it from the crate and made his way to the counter, only discernible as such in that Brodie was standing patiently behind it.

Brodie's eye twinkled as he caught sight of Ian's selection. "Ah, now I see what ye was in sich a hurry fer. 'Tis a fine locket! Will make yer lass happy fer sure. They come t' me all the way from Glasgow. An' 'tis only two shillin's."

Ian placed the money on the counter.

"Now, in the big city," Brodie continued as he carelessly dropped the coins into a tin urn, "they engrave fancy words an' such on these things—but I'm afraid I dinna hae the art."

"It'll do fine the way it is, Mr. Brodie," Ian replied. "Thank you so much for letting me in."

Leaving the shop, Ian felt great satisfaction with his purchase. He hoped this gift might, in a way mere words never could, clarify what he had been trying to express to Maggie in the Dormin. He urged the chestnut to a trot, now eager to return to Stonewycke and see the lovely face once more.

As he turned from Port Strathy's chief street toward the hill leading out of town, he spied a rider rapidly approaching down the hill. Though the features of the face were not yet visible, there could be no mistaking the golden stallion and the confident carriage of its rider. In an instant, Ian perceived that the horseman had only just come from the mansion and his spirit sank within him.

"Good evening, Mr. Falkirk," said Ian crisply as they met.

"Good, indeed," Falkirk replied sharply, the gleam in his eye revealing unspoken contempt. "Flying back to the little nest, are you?"

"What is that supposed to mean?" retorted Ian, in no mood to exchange quips with his rival.

"You think yourself pretty clever, no doubt," answered Falkirk, "getting your tentacles about the little lady of Stonewycke. But don't be too sure of yourself, Duncan. The women I have known take pleasure in a prize with more, shall we say, gratuities, than I believe you have to offer. And this wench is no different."

"Is that how you think of Maggie, as a common wench?"

"Ah, Maggie, is it?"

"I asked you a question, Falkirk!"

"Playing the shining knight—a good move. But it won't help you get your clutches around Stonewycke. That tasty morsel will be mine, along with its little lady."

"That's all you're after, isn't it, Falkirk! You care nothing for Maggie!"

Maukin moved about nervously and stamped her foot, feeling her rider's growing anger tightening in his muscles.

"Don't be plebian, Duncan."

"That's what you consider affection between a man and a woman?"

"You come from a family of breeding. You know how the game is played."

"I love her, Falkirk. That means more than your breeding!"

"Love?" sneered Falkirk. "Pshaw!"

"I'll die before I see her with you," retorted Ian angrily.

"Another challenge?" mocked Falkirk.

"Make of it what you will," replied Ian, moving his horse aside to continue along the road.

"Even if you did love the girl," Falkirk called out to him in a taunting voice, "you stand no chance with her. I have her father's approval. And I will win her in the end!"

"We shall see!" yelled Ian over his shoulder, then dug in his heels and galloped away.

The fury Ian felt for Falkirk was quickly suppressed by the impact of his own words, which now rushed back into his memory with staggering power.

I love her, he had said.

It had been an emotional outburst. Yet as his head began to clear and he slowed Maukin to a walk, he tried to recall when the exact moment of realization had come. Perhaps it had come upon him so slowly because the feeling had been there from his first day at Stonewycke.

32 / Words of Truth

By the time Ian had arrived back at the mansion, he had all but forgotten his unsettling encounter with George Falkirk. His spirits were alive with thoughts of Maggie.

Digory heard him approaching, walked to the entrance to the stables, and stood in readiness to take charge of Ian's mare and lead it inside.

Whistling happily, Ian lightly swept the groom aside. "Let me take care of the horse, my good man! Have yourself a rest. Take a walk . . . it's a beautiful day!"

Thanking him, Digory noted that both the day and his years were rather far advanced for walks of any extended nature, and then went inside. Following him, Ian, still whistling, began to unsaddle Maukin.

"Ah, Digory," he said. "I'm a lucky man. While my friends are languishing away in the stone and gloom of London, I am here in the most beautiful land on earth."

"Aye, 'tis a wondrous place."

"Truly God's land, wouldn't you agree?"

"That I would, sir," Digory replied.

"Why on a day like today, I could almost believe that God does care about us. How else could it be so beautiful?"

The words took Digory by surprise, spoken as they were with unabashed cheerfulness.

"Sir?" he said, not knowing how else to respond without seeming to offend the laird's houseguest.

"Yes," Ian went on, caught up in his exuberance. "A god could have created Scotland, with all its lovely visions. Don't you think?"

"I *know* He did, sir," Digory replied. "Not jist could hae, He *did*. But I'm also knowin' He created London, too."

"Extraordinary," Ian breathed, almost in a daze, still thinking about the magnificent countryside. He turned with a start as Digory's last words seemed finally to reach him.

"You believe in God, then?"

"I do, sir," replied Digory, "wi' all my heart."

"I think I should like to believe too," Ian said.

"An' what's stoppin' ye, sir?"

174

"I suppose if one could just see Him, or understand Him, it would make believing in Him easier," said Ian thoughtfully.

"Did ye never love somethin' that ye couldn't fully understan'?" asked Digory. "Mysel', sometimes I canna understan' these horses, but I love them nonetheless fer it."

Ian said nothing. His thoughts turned to the primrose whose beauty he and Maggie had shared in the Dormin. Just seeing it had prompted such wellsprings of delight, such love, inside him that he had hardly been able to contain it. Yet he hardly knew a thing about the tiny plant. Then he thought of Maggie. Yes, he loved her without knowing all about her or understanding her. Perhaps the old groom was right.

"I dinna ken how or why, but I ken He gives us good gifts, like the land an' horses, an'—"

"And flowers?" suggested Ian.

"Ye're right there," said Digory. "An' flowers . . . because He loves us. An' we don't need t' understan' all aboot that love, or aboot Him, in order t' receive that love o' His."

"Perhaps you're right. But how or why He would love such as us I don't know."

" 'Tis His nature t' love," said Digory. "When He made the world, 'twas because He loved. When He made man, 'twas because He loved. Whatever He does now, 'tis because He loves."

"His *nature* . . ." Ian mused. By this time he had hoisted Maukin's saddle onto its rack and was vigorously rubbing the animal down with a stiff brush. At another time, in another place he would have laughed off the groom's words, indifferent to the serious impression they made in his mind. He had never thought much about *love* before now, about its nature or its source. He had always wanted love, of course—both to give and to receive it. But he had never admitted that need, not even to himself. Now for the first time, such feelings did not frighten him. He was growing accustomed to the changes within him, even beginning to accept them.

"Does everyone know that about God?" asked Ian, stopping his work and turning to face the groom squarely.

"Ken what, lad?"

"That He loves . . . that it is His nature to love?"

"I doobt it, lad," Digory replied. "Nay, I think we'd be behavin' different if we all did. An' even those of us who *think* we ken, even we probably dinna grasp jist how deep His love fer us is."

"Yes," replied Ian absently, "yes, I suppose you're right."

"But what everyone thinks or kens dinna matter so much," Digory went on. " 'Tis that ye ken *yersel'* that God loves ye—that's what matters.''

Ian did not reply, but stood contemplating the words. At last he handed the brush to Digory and, without a word, turned to leave the stables.

33 / The Granite Pillars of Braenock _____

George Falkirk and Martin Forbes made an unseemingly pair.

Falkirk was the gentleman in every proud sinew of his body, while Forbes sat slouching in the saddle of his borrowed horse, outfitted in coarse dungarees, dreaming of the day he would be rich enough to kick dirt in the face of such as Falkirk.

Unlikely and mismatched as they were, the two now rode in common cause.

The sun had disappeared somewhere behind the Dormin, and the shadows of evening blanketed the desolate Braenock Moor. The September nights were growing longer and cooler, and without a moon the riders would have a measure of cover, at least as much as was possible until later in the winter when the sun would set by mid-afternoon.

The horses found their footing with difficulty over the rocky ledges; the fact that they had already traveled this path made little difference. Why those ancients would ever build a village out here, Falkirk could not even hazard a guess. Perhaps it was different a thousand years ago. Perhaps this unlikely location offered some advantage in case of attack— who could tell?

He recalled the gruesome tales of those days and the talebearers he had had to endure. But those visits to dark, smelly back rooms had at last paid a rich dividend. The moment of victory was almost at hand.

The first account he had heard had been at the university during a lecture on ancient history; the professor had spoken of the various ruins scattered about Britain. Falkirk's interest was mildly aroused when the professor mentioned a ruin on the Stonewycke property, only a few miles from Kairn. He would have thought little more about it except that later in the same discourse, the professor had dwelt for some time on the wealth discovered by a team of archaeologists in a dig near Craigievar Castle farther to the south, some twenty miles west of Aberdeen. The value of most of the items in such finds had, of course, been measured purely in historical terms, an issue of little interest to Falkirk. But the word *wealth* had impressed itself upon him. Further investigation stirred up shadowy stories about hastily dug vaults containing more tangible riches than mere artifacts and relics.

Whispers about the Pict ruin near Stonewycke said that over a thousand years earlier, the village had been ruthlessly attacked by marauding Viking warriors, supposedly for a few morsels of food. Though the legend was mentioned from time to time, few, if any, of the local inhabitants had ever set eyes on the place. Those who knew where it was offered differing opinions. Just a pile of rocks, some said. Boulders piled high to block the entryway to a small ravine, said others. But no one bothered to investigate further. Even young Stevie Mackinaw, who had played on the very spot, had no inkling of the history that had passed beneath his very feet.

As if fate were drawing him to the ruin, young George Falkirk's attentive ears continued to gather tidbits of information, important pieces in the puzzle.

"Who'd kill like that?" he had overheard in Culden's only public establishment, a small pub with a warm fire and cheap ale.

Falkirk glanced about him inconspicuously and eyed two farmers, apparently talking about the ruin.

". . . an' jist fer a bit t' eat?" the man continued.

" 'Tis how folks was back then," replied his companion.

"But how could even the Vikings be so cruel as that?"

"I suspect 'twas more like what *I* heard aboot it," said the other.

"An' what was that, noo?"

"Jist this, that them Pict fellows had a heap o' somethin' they was hidin' that the Norsemen found oot aboot."

"An' they killed them fer it?"

"So I heard."

His companion laughed. "So why aren't ye oot lookin' fer it?" he scoffed.

"I got a croft t' run," he answered. "An' if there was somethin' there, them Vikings got it long ago, no doobt."

His curiosity kindled, Falkirk had taken a longer route home that day, riding to Braenock in search of the ruin. He found what he thought were the granite boulders and had poked around among them. But he soon realized it would take a concerted effort to delve into the secrets of the ruin if he hoped to discover anything of value. Other cares waylaid him for a time, but through research and journeys to several of Aberdeen's universities, he did eventually manage to learn something of the original structure of that ruin. He had also learned of the stone door, which he had reason to believe was an entry to the fulfillment of his plans.

He had then discussed with his father the purchase of the ridge, ostensibly for other reasons. Lord Falkirk asked few questions and made the offer; George had been hopeful. He had to keep his keen personal passion for the site quiet, for if Duncan fell privy to the information he possessed, all would be lost. But the sale had been quelled at the last moment by Duncan's wife, who determined to hang onto every inch of Stonewycke as if it were Eden itself.

George's initial rage soon quieted into controlled determination; he now had to discover some alternate means to achieve his ends. His desire to unearth the secrets of Braenock Ridge had become so single-minded, he would have spared nothing to gain his goal, an intensity stimulated by the influence of one Sallo Grist.

Grist appeared as ancient and mysterious as the Picts themselves. More than his antiquity produced the aura of reverence which seemed to cling to him: his entire person emanated an image of legend and magic, enhanced by the coarse woolen robe belted with hemp rope, and the thick white hair massed upon his head. His medicinal remedies and cures—well known in all the lower portions of London—lent further credence to his ancestry. He lived along the Thames under bridges, or in any one of several greasy taverns on the docks. One was never sure where he might be found. Some thought him a vagrant, some considered him a doctor, still others swore he was a sorcerer in the tradition of Merlin—or worse. Most simply called him mad.

An acquaintance of Falkirk's in London had told him, "If you want to know about the Picts, go to Sallo Grist—he claims to be a descendant of Oengus. Of course," he added with a laugh, "he also claims descent from Moses."

Falkirk had laughed with his friend over two more tumblers of dark stout—the best beer to be found in London. But nonetheless, the following day he sought out Grist. Sallo knew of the Stonewycke ruin, he said, and swore a treasure remained buried there to this day. Bidding Falkirk to remain where he was, he disappeared into a darkened room and reappeared a few moments later bearing a crumbled shred of paper in his hand.

"A map," he said, "o' the veery place!"

"Why haven't you gone after it, then?" asked a suspicious Falkirk. He didn't much care for the cold glint in Grist's one open eye.

"I did . . . long ago."

He drew Falkirk close across the table, moving the flickering candle aside. "Ye see this?" he said, blowing the stench of his rotten breath into Falkirk's face. He pointed to his eye, partially closed and badly scarred. " 'Twas my reward fer that. Th' bloke nearly blinded me, 'e did. Them lairds trust no one—'specially strangers. Tried t' get someone else t' come wi' me, but no one'll believe me." His voice was raspy and low.

"So you've decided to give away your secret?" said Falkirk in a suspicious tone of contempt. "Just like that? What do you take me for, old man, a fool?"

"You look t' be a gent'man," went on Sallo in the harsh tone which seemed his only mode of expression. Heedless of Falkirk's accusation, he paused to scratch his partially bearded chin. "I s'pose ye'd 'ardly notice partin' wi' a few quid—this map's worth mor'n fifty . . . but I'll settle fer that."

"Fifty quid!" Falkirk exclaimed. "You must take me for an imbecile!"

He rose from his seat and moved toward the door. He was more than able to pay the fifty, and almost willing to go that high. But not if there was a chance of getting by with less. And the thought of being outwitted by this low-life Thames tramp galled him.

"All right, mate—twenty-five," conceded Sallo quickly, "but na a farthin' less."

Falkirk came away with the map, still far from convinced Sallo Grist wasn't London's foxiest and most cunning con man, but nevertheless intrigued with his prospects. When Forbes found the opening between the rocks, called a *door* on the map, George Falkirk gained a new respect for Sallo Grist. He did not, however, intend to pay Sallo the extra twenty-five quid from the proceeds of their findings. He was a shrewd one himself, and if he never saw Sallo Grist again in his life, it would not be soon enough for him.

Centuries earlier the so-called door had apparently been used as an entryway into a secluded cleft in the expansive moorland. But it had grown thick with brush; and as the surrounding rocks and pieces of ruin had fallen, some had crumbled into smaller pieces, so that upon first glance the ancient building sites, which had stood on both sides of the huge granite boulders, were barely distinguishable from the scattered rocks of the rugged heath. Only when one gazed upon the site for some time, from a distance, did a certain order begin to form among the vague shapes. And now George Falkirk knew what he was looking for, if Sallo's map was to be worth its price—a small cave-like opening in the side of the hill just behind the door through the boulders.

So on this cool September night his treasure hunt would, he hoped, culminate at last—if the idiot Forbes had indeed found the right spot. It would have been better to have done it all himself, but he couldn't risk being seen and recognized. If Forbes were seen wandering about, who would think anything of it? Against his better judgment, Falkirk had to trust the dullard.

The huge rocks stood in black shadows, heaps of granite and stone piled in fragmentary disarray, like the ancient memories they represented. Not even the vaguest outline of habitation still remained in the thick dusk. Moss and vines grew over most of the stones, and heather and bracken had infringed upon the rest.

Forbes led the young heir of Kairn around the east side of a particularly large mound of granite. They tied their horses and continued on foot, descending to the base of the largest two stones. There Falkirk could see that some of the smaller stones had been removed and the brush cleared away. Forbes pointed through the tight space between the two vertical boulders, a hole barely large enough to squeeze through.

"Ye said t' touch nothin'," said Forbes. "But I had t' get inside o' the thing. This here openin' looks like it might lead t' where ye want t' go. Ye see, if ye jist look through there—"

He pointed into the blackness. "Can ye see? Looks like there could be a cave o' some kin', there agin' the bank."

Falkirk could see that the area had not been disturbed beyond the initial removal of a few stones, and for that reason alone he believed Forbes. He didn't like the man. Nor did he trust him. But in this business he had to do what he could with the help he could find.

"Get the tools," Falkirk ordered. "Let's see what's inside there."

Forbes was the one to do the work, though grudgingly. He hammered and pried at the jagged edges of rock covering the entrance of what seemed to be a small opening, perhaps a cave, through the rocks. Peering after him from beside the granite towers, Falkirk could see nothing but blackness. At last, with the aid of a pick, the rocks were removed, an opening was discovered into the hillside large enough to accommodate a man—lying on his belly—and Forbes, after communicating this fact, was instructed to crawl into the crevice.

Falkirk stood and waited impatiently. The cold had begun to bite into his bones. After what seemed an interminable time, he heard a muffled yell from Forbes. Either the bloke had struck his head or had discovered something. When he emerged a few moments later, scooting out with feet first, the only evidence of his labor was a nasty gouge on his forehead.

"Ends in a solid wall o' granite," he said, wiping his head with a dirty hand.

"Are you sure?"

" 'Course I'm sure!"

"No box . . . no chest of any kind?"

"I bang my head an' the bloody place near caves in on me, an' ye ask if I'm sure!" retorted Forbes sharply.

Again Falkirk regretted bringing the rotter into his secret plan. Yet

Forbes did serve his purpose. The worst that could happen if Forbes were caught snooping around would be a short stint in jail. Falkirk himself would remain in the clear in any case.

Not having expected their initial foray to the ruins to pay off completely, Falkirk was not overly disappointed. The time would come when triumph would be his.

"Well," said Falkirk, ignoring Forbes's wound, "we're not beat yet. We've found the place, but it's too late to dig any farther tonight. Load everything up and let's get out of here."

The Clyde certainly wasn't the Thames. And Glasgow had nothing to compare with Piccadilly or Kensington Gardens. But Scotland's largest city fulfilled James's need to be in the hub of activity when he was unable to make the distance to London.

More importantly, the brewery was located just five miles outside the city. Though he knew relatively little about the actual process of making dark Scottish ale, he loved the whine and thump of the steel and wooden machinery and the smells of yeast and fermentation.

Best of all, it was his! This brewery was one of the few things he could truly claim as his own, and it represented the means to further wealth and more enterprising investments in the future. He could see now that the failure of the Braenock deal had worked to his advantage. Had he acquired funding for the brewery in that manner, Atlanta would have managed to keep her hold on this, too. The arrangement as it had finally come about was far superior. He'd much rather be indebted to men like Browhurst or Byron Falkirk than to his wife. And as it turned out, he was still able to maintain a majority financial interest in the business.

At last, after three successful years, he was ready to expand his holdings. One of Scotland's largest distilleries had recently come on the market. The owner had died, and his only heir now lived in America. The man wanted no part of overseas holdings and was thus selling off the entire British portion of the inheritance. He was no amateur, that much was plain, for he was asking a pretty penny for the distillery. But it was well worth it, James thought. Its Scotch whiskey was renowned throughout Britain and found a regular market in exports as well. Last year alone its revenues were several hundred thousand pounds. If grown men could drool, the anticipation of latching onto such a vast enterprise would doubtless have had such an effect on James. Yet he again found himself faced with the dilemma of garnering the necessary funds for a beginning. Since he was not a wealthy man on his own, he still was forced to use other people's money for his schemes.

James sat in the plush restaurant slowly sipping his brandy and wondering what this meeting with Lord Browhurst would produce. He had already obtained a commitment of sorts, and the Lord had been to London attempting to tap some of his more wealthy associates.

James shifted uneasily in his seat. He was never sure just how far to trust Browhurst. His words had always been perfectly cordial, but something in the look of his eye worried James, as if the cunning Lord were only waiting for him to make a mistake so he could move in to pick up the pieces. But then, James Duncan was hardly in the habit of trusting anyone.

Soon he spotted Browhurst's imposing figure striding across the dining room floor. He showed his white teeth in a hasty grin as he spotted James.

"Ah, Duncan!" he said, seating himself at the table. "I've not yet been to this establishment—not bad for Glasgow. But I doubt the food will measure up."

"We must take what we can get," James replied amicably. "London isn't the only place on earth, though it may be the most civilized."

"You are right—there is Paris. And even New York is beginning to attract some in the influential circles. But Glasgow, I'm afraid . . ." He let a wry chuckle complete his thought.

A waiter hurried to the table, took their order, and within moments Browhurst was holding his own glass of the house's finest brandy.

"I must say, Duncan," said Browhurst with a chuckle, "how a man of the world like yourself can stand to remain where you do, with nothing but a sleepy little fishing village for miles, surrounded on all sides by that bloody, wiry shrub—what do they call it?"

"Heather? The weed the peasant girls wear in their hair?"

"Oh, yes, heather, that's it!—as I say, how you can tolerate living there is beyond me."

"It's not so bad, once you get used to it."

"If you're going to be a businessman, you really ought to live in the city."

"Perhaps you're right."

"Certainly I'm right. Business is done in the city, not out on the bloody hills."

"But you must admit, Browhurst," replied James, "that we Scots do make the world's finest whiskey."

"You'll get no argument from me there."

"Which brings us to the purpose of this little discussion. We do have something other than geography to discuss."

"Yes, *that* . . ." For the first time Browhurst's countenance clouded. "I'm afraid I was none too successful in London."

"Your investors turned you down?"

"For the moment, yes—it appears that way."

"But they would gain from the venture," James insisted.

"They feel it's a large sum of money, and too great a risk."

"You showed them last year's figures?"

"Of course I did," Browhurst answered, a trifle annoyed. "They were impressed. But one fact did not pass their scrutiny—a large percentage of the whiskey is exported to America. With the war raging there between the North and South, who can tell what will happen to the market?"

"The war didn't affect last year's profits."

"True, but perhaps it was too early for potential ill-effects to be felt in sales."

"Bah! There won't be any ill-effects on the sale of whiskey!" James said with rising irritation. "People drink whether they're at war or not."

"You know what the experts say, that if the North didn't win the war in the first year, it could drag on interminably. There are rumors of blockades—"

"They'll always want whiskey," James argued. "Especially soldiers, far from home and lonely."

"I'm not the one you have to convince," said Browhurst. "You've made a strong case with me and have won me over."

He paused and took another sip from his glass. "Although," he went on after a few moments, "it appears there may be a slight problem with my investment as well—"

"A problem!" James exploded. Several nearby patrons turned and shot glances in the direction of the two men. "What kind of problem?" he asked in a more subdued but equally intense tone.

"Nothing major," Browhurst assured in the most conciliatory of voices. "However, in reevaluating my various investments, if it turns out that I find that I am spread a . . . ah . . . a bit too thin, so to speak— in a case such as that I would have—ah—no alternative but to, shall we say, trim back my initial commitment somewhat."

"Listen, Browhurst," said James quietly, but with a cold, determined intimidation in his voice, "if you are looking for a way to weasel out of—"

"Not in the least," Browhurst answered quickly.

James eyed the man intently. Was Browhurst toying with him for some motive of his own? What was his game?

"We both know this will be a good investment," Browhurst continued; "why else do you think I am stretching myself to the limit on this one?"

"Well, without additional funds it's a venture that may never get off the ground,'' James replied with a sour note of exasperation. He had already invested a great deal of time and effort to set up this deal and was none too pleased to see it starting to slip through his eager grasp. What could this latest stall of Browhurst's mean? James wondered. He didn't like the thought of being a pawn in anyone's scheme.

"I too have stretched myself to the limit," he said finally. "Yet there still remains a sizable portion to be obtained."

"What about Lord Falkirk?" asked Browhurst.

James did not reply immediately, for the answer was not a simple one. He was already in too great a debt to his neighbor. He had already promised his daughter. What more did he have to bargain with?

Falkirk *did* have the cash. It vexed James to be so close to his goal and yet be powerless to lay his hands on it. There was but one way to entice Falkirk to part with any further money.

A wedding.

On that day—and only on that day—would Agnes Falkirk allow her husband to invest another pound in a business venture, no matter how lucrative it might prove. Falkirk was not ambitious. He had his own motives, as did his wife. And they involved his son's future, not the expansion of their capital holdings.

But there was little time. If he did not act with dispatch, the American owner might well find another buyer. Yet . . . weddings could be hastily arranged.

"Yes . . .'' James mused after several moments of silence, "I think Byron Falkirk might come through for us."

He paused, contemplating the practicalities involved. "Yes," he added, "I think he just might at that."

He smiled at his decision, lifted his glass to Browhurst, and said—

"Meanwhile, I'm going to talk to the American's solicitor. I think the time has come to put up some earnest money to secure the deal."

35 / The Tapestry

October harshly shoved aside the tranquil days of September, leaving no doubts that it was indeed the harbinger of winter. For the first days of the month rain poured relentlessly from heavy skies. And with the rain came winds of such force that three boats in the harbor were slammed against their moorings and wrecked almost beyond repair. The fisherfolk were only thankful the herring season had ended before the storm.

That week, the Lindow reached the top of its banks. And when there was no letup in sight, the farmers began attempts to seal off as much of their property as possible. Everyone was keenly aware that if the Lindow flooded, there was little they could do to save their possessions against the deluge. Many were the stories still circulating of the flood of 1802 when every farm within ten miles of the river had been washed out to sea. Stonewycke castle had been the only refuge, and hundreds of peasants had poured up the hill, able to save only what they could carry with them.

The last fair weeks of September had been glorious. Maggie and Ian had ridden nearly every mile of the estate and ventured as far inland as Culden and as far along the coast as Gardenstown. Their deepening friendship evolved naturally, splendidly, into love of a more permanent kind. When the truth of what was happening between them dawned on Maggie, she accepted it joyfully. The walk in the Dormin had been the beginning, but she had become more sure than ever of his love when he had given her the locket. What a wonderful memory that moment was! Ian had been so shy, even blushing slightly as he pulled it from behind his back where he had been hiding it. When he had placed the locket about her neck, he kissed her lightly on the cheek. She had never thought a man could be so gentle. And as much as she loved him, she could not help a moment's surprise that such tenderness was to be found in Ian with his seemingly flippant, almost cynical personality. But the considerate care in his touch was something she would never forget. After that day she had worn the locket hidden beneath her clothing—always close to her, always a reminder of the sweet love that had finally opened her heart.

Each had wrestled through uncertainties, giving much to one another in the process; thus they came into the realization of their love stronger and more confident about one another than would have been possible before. Maggie was now ready to open her heart again, to love and be loved in return. Ian accepted the changes within himself as if his past life in London had merely been the dream of another world.

Both were in love, but with one another only. They had not yet learned to look up to the Source, to that greater Love from which all loves are born. But they were learning to love for the first time, and would look up when the time was ripe. Through their love each for the other, the Source was drawing them. And through the pain of their love, they would come to know His.

The inclement weather seemed bent on spoiling their earthly joy. On hill and moor they could be free—to laugh, to talk, to run, to jump, to delight in one another. But under the watchful eye of the household they were compelled to remain distant and aloof, still keeping their affections hidden. Though she knew the time would have to come, and soon, Maggie could not bring herself to open the subject to Atlanta. Had not James been absent from Stonewycke for two weeks, the pressure would have been unbearable.

More trying than ever were the frequent visits of George Falkirk. Far from being intimidated by the rain, he relished it, always arriving in good spirits, sweeping Atlanta off her feet with praise and shallow indulgences, and managing to isolate Maggie into some private room, there to weave his confident spells with her.

She learned to fend off his open advances with vague words, co-quettish smiles, and witty words, giving in just enough to appear charmed by his adept seduction, but keeping her distance all the while. Falkirk was thus kept off his guard, hopeful of ultimate victory and unconcerned by the threats of her buffoon of a cousin. But with each succeeding visit Maggie found it more and more difficult to rebuff him. An outright denial of his attentions, she feared, would lead to great conflict with her father, ultimately threatening her love for Ian. But how long could she hold Falkirk off before he pressed his advantage too far?

Such thoughts plagued Maggie as she sat staring out the window in the little sitting room adjacent to the east parlor. A fire crackled cheer-fully in the fireplace while the rain beat relentlessly against the window; the smaller confines of this familiar haunt offered warmth and coziness to Maggie.

The door opened and Atlanta peeked in. "I thought I left my sewing in here, dear," she said, explaining her presence. "Oh . . . there it is."

She picked it up and turned back toward the door. But something prompted her to linger.

Atlanta had seen a change in Maggie of late—a small corner of her taut fabric was relaxing. An undefined peaceful glow radiated from her eyes. When had her melancholy daughter last been so content as she had during the past month?

How Atlanta wanted to break through the distance which separated them! Both felt the strain. Each desired a closer approach. Love beat in each heart for the other, but neither knew how to break the bonds of silence.

Still Atlanta tarried.

"There's little else to do these days," she attempted, gesturing with the needlework in her hand.

"I know," said Maggie with a sigh.

"The rain keeps falling and falling."

"Will it never stop?" said Maggie, thinking aloud rather than addressing her mother. Her hands moved absently, sending the needle through the cloth.

"You've been outdoors so much lately," Atlanta replied, "it must be doubly difficult for you being inside all day."

Maggie glanced up from her work toward her mother with a questioning look. Had Atlalnta drawn her own conclusions after seeing Ian and her together so frequently?

Maggie struggled to force her trembling fingers to continue the needlework.

"It's warm in here," Atlanta continued, groping for words. "The other rooms get so drafty. We may live in a grand house, but it has its drawbacks. There's always a chill. But that must just be my age showing. You young people probably don't even notice it."

Maggie nodded, mumbling a few words of assent, assuring Atlanta that she felt the chill also. She had hardly heard anything else her mother had said.

"Speaking of young people," Atlanta went on awkwardly, "have you been able to tolerate our houseguest adequately?"

Maggie's head bounded up again. This time Atlanta could not mistake the agitated expressions on her daughter's face.

"My dear . . . what is it?" Atlanta asked with concern. "Have you had difficulties with him?"

"No," Maggie replied quickly. "No, not at all—he's been . . . he's been a perfect—gentleman. I . . . we've . . . that is—we've had a nice time together. I mean, I've tolerated him wonderfully . . . just fine—"

She stopped short, realizing that in the confusion of her thoughts she had nearly stammered out too much. She wanted to tell her mother! But the last time they had tried to talk seriously, Atlanta hadn't understood. What if she couldn't understand about Ian? She did seem altogether taken with George Falkirk. Both she and her father seemed intent on pushing her toward him.

Yet, what if . . . perhaps—what if she *would* understand?

"If there's a problem—" Atlanta began.

"No. There's no problem," Maggie insisted. "We've become . . . friends."

There was something in Maggie's tone: an urgency, more emotion than she was allowing to show. Slowly the truth began to flash across her heart.

"Friends?" Atlanta said, the hard Ramsey crust forming again. "That's nice . . . I'm glad."

"Do you mean, Mother . . . do you really mean that? I thought you would be . . . opposed to—"

"Of course I mean it," replied Atlanta, softening as she sensed Maggie's effort to tell her something deeper. "Why would you think—?"

"There's Father. You know what he thinks of Ian."

"Your father and I do not always see eye to eye."

"I thought you might also . . ."

"I know you needed someone—"

"Oh, I do need him, Mother!" burst out Maggie before realizing what she had said.

Atlanta walked closer and sat down on the chair next to her daughter. She laid aside the sewing project she had been carrying in her hand, then thought for several long moments, carefully measuring each word before she spoke. She painfully recalled the many times she had thoughtlessly quelled such rare tender moments between them. There would be few further opportunities.

"I thought I had noticed a change in you," Atlanta said at length. "You've seemed so happy."

"I am happy," replied Maggie, looking down at the floor. "That is except for—"

"What?"

"I shouldn't have thought it."

"What doesn't make you happy?"

"I know you think he's quite the gentleman."

"Who?"

"George Falkirk."

"Me? I don't think that highly of George Falkirk."

"You don't? I thought—"

"Your father and Mr. Falkirk are great friends. And on those grounds George seems to assume he has the right to consider himself a welcome guest here at any hour he chooses."

"And you don't—?"

"I must say I don't share your father's fascination with the young man. His charming ways are more than I can tolerate."

"Oh, Mother, you don't know how glad it makes me to hear you say that!" exclaimed Maggie. "All this time I thought you wanted me to encourage him."

"I take it our friend Mr. Falkirk is not the cause of your recent radiant smiles."

"No, Mother," replied Maggie with a smile. "It's someone else."

"Am I to take it that our houseguest from London means more to you than merely a distant relative?"

Maggie looked up at Atlanta full in the face.

"I love him, Mother," she said.

The words sent an involuntary chill through Atlanta's body, much like she'd felt the night of the *Maiden* when watching Maggie hold the tiny Krueger child. Her daughter had taken another step toward maturity. In Atlanta's heart pulsed both joy and sorrow—sorrow at having to let go of her baby daughter, joy at seeing Maggie so happy for the first time.

"And Ian . . . how does he feel?"

A tentative smile tugged at Maggie's lips. She nodded, then said, "He loves me also. We have even . . . spoken of marriage."

At the word a great heaviness fell upon Atlanta's heart. "Does anyone else know of this?"

"Only you," Maggie answered. "We couldn't—well, I'm simply glad that you finally know."

Already, however, Atlanta's thoughts were on James. If he should learn of this development, there would be no telling what he might do. One thing he would *never* do was accept a marriage between his daughter and the son of the Earl of Landsbury!

Atlanta's attention gradually returned to Maggie, who had risen and stood quietly gazing out the French doors at the steady stream of rain splashing against the glass and down onto the small enclosed courtyard below. *Why must it be my duty,* Atlanta thought, *to bring my daughter back to reality?* How desperately she wanted her daughter to be able to enjoy a few moments of contentment, for she knew too well how few such moments a lifetime could contain. Yet she also knew how futile was the hope that Maggie's dream world with Ian could long remain unshattered.

"Maggie," she said gently. "Are you sure this is what you want?"

Maggie spun around, every feature of her face glowing with resplendent affirmation.

"Oh, yes, Mother!"

"You know how difficult your father can make life for you."

"I don't care about him," Maggie replied flatly. "He showed a long time ago that he didn't care about me."

Atlanta winced, feeling the pain of her daughter's silent burden.

"I asked if you were certain," Atlanta continued, "only because if it truly is what you want, you may very well have to fight for it."

"I know, Mother," said Maggie.

"You know how your father feels about Landsbury."

"Yes. But what I'm more concerned with is—how do you feel about it, Mother?"

"I want you to be happy, Maggie."

"You approve?"

"Of course."

"Oh, thank you, Mother!" exclaimed Maggie, embracing Atlanta.

Slowly Atlanta's arms reached about her daughter and held her close. She felt tears filling her own eyes, the unfamiliar response of her own deep need to love and be loved. Silently they stood for some moments, as if the walls between them had never been.

"And you won't say anything to Father?" asked Maggie softly.

"No," answered Atlanta. "But your secret won't last forever. I have seen it all over your face."

Maggie laughed. Then she pulled away from her mother's embrace suddenly and said, "I must go find Ian, to tell him."

Atlanta laid her hand on Maggie's arm. It had never been her habit to act impulsively. Yet she was not yet ready for this precious moment with her daughter to come to an end.

"Maggie," she said, "before you go, I have something to show you."

Dabbing her eyes, Atlanta led the way out of the room. They walked upstairs, Maggie assumed to Atlanta's dayroom, but instead they stopped at the door next to it. Atlanta pulled the door open, and the large windows on the opposite wall admitted what was left of the afternoon light. Immediately a faint odor of mothballs assailed them.

"My old nursery!" exclaimed Maggie. "I haven't been here in years. It has hardly changed."

"I've kept it as it was when you were a child," said Atlanta. "Those memories are dear to me."

Maggie looked up at the stately woman, and to her amazement saw the tears which her mother had been unable to control.

"Oh, Mother," she said, walking toward Atlanta and again putting her arms around her. She gently laid her head against her mother's chest as she hadn't for years.

Now at last the tears flowed unchecked down the solemn cheeks of the great mistress of Stonewycke, the last remnant of the Ramsey line. Maggie wept openly as Atlanta stroked her hair. The daughter was at last a woman, and finally in this poignant moment of sorrow and bliss the two women were able to lay aside their fears and uncertainties and embrace each other in the love they had long possessed but rarely expressed.

The two stood silently in the center of the thick rug where Maggie had spent hours playing as a toddler. To one side of the door sat a small bed, canopied in lace, and a bureau lined with dolls and stuffed toys. In another corner stood Maggie's cradle.

When the embrace and the tears had accomplished their healing work, Maggie stepped back. They laughed, squeezing hands as if to say, *It is good!*

Then Maggie began to look around as memories of the past flooded her. She could not help but notice that the room was clean and dusted, although it had been twelve years since she had last used it.

Atlanta motioned her toward the bed.

Then Maggie saw it—the grand tapestry of the family tree, just where it had always been. But something was different. A fine new gilt-edged frame surrounded it, and the tapestry itself seemed brighter, fresher. She looked questioningly toward her mother.

"I've had it restored and reframed," Atlanta explained. "I had hoped to present it to you on your birthday, but it wasn't ready in time. Then I thought I'd save it for Christmas. But now . . . somehow today just seems like the right moment. I want you to have it, Maggie."

"You're giving it to me?" asked Maggie. "But, Mother . . . it's yours—it's far too precious for me to have!"

"I want you to have it."

Atlanta's words came closely, cautiously, as she continued to measure the fragile emotions which had been stirred so deeply. "There are so few things a mother can truly pass on to her daughter," she began again. "Especially things which convey the heritage she wants to transfer. This family . . . this estate—"

Atlanta stopped, unable for the moment to continue, choking back the lump which seemed so insistent on blocking the words. Now that the vault had been cracked open, the tears seemed determined to flow all the more readily.

". . . this home . . . these people," she tried to begin again in shaky tones, "it's all part of me, Maggie. It's my lifeblood. There is so much I want to give you. Let this be a start."

Sensing the tenderness of her mother's emotions, Maggie stretched out a hand and laid it on her arm.

"You will marry soon," Atlanta continued, "and become part of a new family. The Ramsey name may fade in your memory—"

"Mother," interrupted Maggie. "That will never happen! Don't you know how dear it is to me? I regret that I have never borne the name, but it is no less real to me. I shall *never* forget that half of my blood is Ramsey blood, and all I am is bound up in the ancestry of Stonewycke."

Atlanta's eyes smiled first, and then her lips.

"Then all the more reason for you to have the tapestry."

"But it means so much to you."

"That is why I want you to have it," Atlanta said. "I always intended to pass it along to my daughter, though at the time I stitched it you were only an idea in God's mind."

Maggie gazed at it for some moments, remembering her own awkward attempts to reproduce it. Then, she was a child; the years which had passed seemed a lifetime ago. Suddenly within Maggie rose the strong sense of being part of something deeper and more permanent than anything she had felt before. All those names from generation to generation belonged to her, and in some mysterious way, she belonged to them, too. Years from now her descendants would stand where she was standing now, admiring it and wondering about the person who had been called Margaret Duncan.

Examining the tapestry more closely, Maggie suddenly became aware of the new addition.

"Mother, there's my name!"

In its own special block directly under those of her parents stood the words *Margaret Isabel Duncan*. "Surely you didn't embroider that in place when you first made it? I don't recall seeing it there before."

"I added it only recently," said Atlanta with pride.

"But where is Alastair's name?" she asked.

"Come," said Atlanta quickly, apparently heedless of Maggie's question. "Let's take it down and move it to your room."

"Take it down?" Maggie questioned. "But it has always hung here. It seems like it belongs in the nursery. How could we hang it somewhere else?"

"But you won't be able to enjoy it if it hangs where you never see it," Atlanta insisted.

"It will take some getting used to," said Maggie thoughtfully. "It belongs in the nursery. But it is such a great treasure, I do want to be able to see it.''

Together they lifted the large frame from its hook and Maggie carried it carefully to her room. There they hung it above her bed in similar position to its original location in the nursery. She stood back to admire it, realizing for the first time that this tapestry was far more than a simple family heirloom. Not only was it a line backwards in time, but also a line forward into the future . . . the unknown. What the years ahead would hold, she had no idea.

''Thank you, Mother,'' Maggie said at last. ''It's beautiful. It really is a treasure.''

36 / Atlanta's Discovery

Atlanta had always tried to respect the sanctity of James's cubicle. She had never once set foot inside his private retreat since their marriage, never even alluded to its existence. He had never told her about it, and she rarely so much as ventured into the corridor where it was located. She knew about it, of course, and its contents and uses occasionally played upon her curiosity. But she believed every person needed a refuge, one place to which he could retreat that was entirely his own. Perhaps it was her way of subtly admitting to the pressure he faced from her, though she would never have admitted it outright.

She loathed, therefore, what she was about to do. Her heels echoed on the bare stone floor of the hallway. Though she knew James was not expected back from Kairn for hours, impulsively she glanced back over her shoulder. But her step continued firm and determined. Since his return from Glasgow the situation had grown intolerable. George Falkirk visited nearly every day; he and James grew more familiar by the hour. Ian was rarely to be seen, and Atlanta knew Maggie was miserable.

Something had to be done.

Atlanta had never been one to allow obstacles to deter her from her goals. She had known fear from time to time, but for her it had served as a driving force, compelling her to do her part to preserve her ancestral estate intact. And she knew to achieve that end she had to maintain her power over James, who would wrest it from her if he could.

Anxiety compelled her again—this time, through concern for her daughter. Fear for Maggie's future forced her to make this furtive journey. She had to find something to bargain with, something which would constrain James to give his blessing to Maggie and Ian and their future together. Even as she thought it, Atlanta realized the impossibility of her quest. James's hatred was so concentrated that the very name of Landsbury was enough to send him into a rage. And the fascination of his hatred, his desire for revenge, precluded any possibility of a change of heart. For true hatred, as well as true love, is long-suffering and will make any sacrifice in order to expend itself upon its object.

Atlanta stood before the door as if to finalize her resolve. She placed her hand on the latch. It yielded to her pressure, but almost as quickly she drew back. *Had he trusted her so much that he did not lock this most private of rooms?*

The thought was staggering. Their relationship had endured over the years, but she would never have numbered trust among the causes. Was she now betraying the only thread of decency left to their marriage?

Seconds passed; but it could have been an hour. Did this temporary indecision spring from some dormant sense of guilt, some notion that she owed a loyalty to the man who was her husband? What did such loyalty mean at this point in their marriage? Were the inevitable lines between them at last being drawn? Was the choice no woman should have to make finally being thrust upon her—the choice between husband and child?

But why should such a moment of crisis come as any surprise? The choice had been made long ago when she had produced an heir to Stonewycke—the only heir there would ever be from her body. The battle had been enjoined when she knew she would have to fight for her daughter's place—a battle she could not now abandon for any brief moment of sentimentality.

She pushed, and the door swung open.

Stepping inside, Atlanta was astonished at the sight. She had considered James a meticulous man, but this, his most private of rooms, was in complete disorder. Books, papers, maps, journals, folders, swords, guns, boxes, and other paraphernalia were strewn about at random. Whether or not he actually worked here was doubtful. Rather than an office, it appeared to be simply a storage closet for rubbish of all kinds.

But she had work to do. Laying aside her initial shock at the disarray, Atlanta set immediately to her task, glad at least that her little foray into James's forbidden world would not be noticed. She approached the desk, looked about, and began randomly to sift through the several piles of papers scattered over the top. Then she glanced around. If she didn't discover anything here, she would have to concentrate her attention on the drawers in the bureau and cabinet, of which there were many. There might not be time to sort through every drawer, especially since she didn't know what she was looking for. This place was such a mess. It would take forever to investigate every nook and cranny.

She turned her attention back to the desktop.

Within a few moments her search was rewarded, and she need worry no longer about having to rummage through the endless drawers. The bureau could keep its secrets; this was all she needed. A small note, written on formal business paper, was nestled between a sheaf of business documents. It had clearly been thrown down on top of the desk, then inadvertently covered with other papers. As she read it, Atlanta wondered why James had not destroyed it. Perhaps it had arrived with other documents, for the two men were involved in several financial arrangements together.

As she read the words on the page, Atlanta's hand, then her entire body, shook with outrage. She had been told, of course, that the Falkirks had asked that their son be permitted to visit Maggie, even to court her. She had been upset to begin with, after their first visit to Kairn. But later visits had proved more cordial, and she had reconciled herself to the idea of his presence, though she was not particularly enamored of the conceited young man. He did have a way of flattery that could beguile even her at times. Maggie had seemed to enjoy his company at first. But then after learning her true feelings for Ian, Falkirk's very presence had become an aggravation. She never dreamed that James's duplicity could extend to such a businesslike manipulation of his daughter to gain his own financial ends.

The words of the note left little doubt. But this time James had gone too far. It was one thing to seal an agreement with a horse or some other token of friendship. But his own daughter!

In a frenzy of passion, Atlanta read the words again—

I am pleased with the progress of your ventures and I trust our bargain will further pledge our future together in ways profitable to us both. My son is taken with your daughter and has assured me that a marriage will be announced soon. From this I see my investment and my confidence in you was well placed. As I said, I will certainly be eager to consider future liaisons once the wedding has taken place. But first things first, I always say. I remain

Yours most sincerely,
Falkirk

Atlanta stuffed the paper into her pocket, slammed the door behind her, and marched down the corridor in a rage. She would never lower herself to try to win James's favor again. He had forfeited his right to bless his daughter's marriage! He had forfeited whatever rights of fatherhood he had ever possessed!

She walked straight to the sitting room, locked the door behind her, and sat down to think.

That this development changed the complexion of everything there could be no doubt. Falkirk's more frequent visits and private discussions with James, as well as James's repeated rides to Kairn, all fit into a grand and cunning scheme. When she had blocked his sale of Braenock, his twisted genius had found another opportunity, now making use of his daughter instead of her land.

But she would stop him . . . somehow!

As the heat of her anger gradually settled into cold, silent wrath, Atlanta's only alternative became clear. To thwart James's cruel design she had to move, if not quickly, certainly decisively. She contemplated the implications, settled her resolve firmly in her mind, rose, placed the letter of treachery in a drawer, and left the room with a fixed look and an unswerving gait.

She found Maggie and Ian in the dining room. She had not heard the call to dinner, and her stomach was too knotted to feel hunger.

Her face revealed her passion instantly.

"Mother . . . what is it?" asked Maggie in alarm.

Atlanta closed the door behind her, excused the maid who had been serving, then continued to pace the floor searching for the right words with which to begin. Ian glanced at Maggie with a questioning look, but said nothing.

After several minutes Atlanta spoke.

"I don't know how to . . . the words to say what I must tell you are difficult to find—"

She paused, continued pacing, then took a deep breath and began again.

"There are some circumstances which have just come to my attention—developments . . . which affect both of you, your father, Maggie—and even the future of Stonewycke."

She stopped again for another breath, for her heart was still pounding. "Maggie," she continued, looking at her daughter, "you have told me that you and Ian are in love."

Maggie glanced down and blushed.

"Excuse me, Ian, for being so blunt. But you will soon see why events compel me to speak thus. So I must ask you too, Ian, I must ask you both. Is what Maggie told me true? Are you in love?"

Ian glanced over at Maggie beside him at the table, took her hand, then returned his eyes to Atlanta.

"Yes . . . yes, it is. Insofar as I can speak for Maggie, Lady Duncan, yes—we are in love."

"Maggie?" said Atlanta.

Maggie nodded.

"And you have spoken of marriage?"

"Yes," replied Ian.

"Then as sudden as this seems," said Atlanta, "I am now going to urge you to move with haste."

A puzzled expression came over Ian's face.

"What exactly are you saying, Lady Duncan?" he asked. "That we should make an announcement of our betrothal?"

"More than that, Ian," Atlanta replied. "I am suggesting—if you are truly serious in your intent—that you marry without delay, at the soonest moment to present itself."

The forceful words shattered Atlanta's two listeners into speechlessness.

"Mother . . ." began Maggie, too incredulous to know whether to weep or laugh.

"But there are so many considerations," faltered Ian. "Our families . . . a proper period of engagement."

"There's no time for all that," insisted Atlanta. "I told you, there have been developments. You'll just have to trust me when I say the matter is urgent."

"I don't understand—what would Father say?" asked Maggie.

"Maggie," Atlanta returned flatly, "your father has given up his right to any say in the matter."

"What do you mean?"

"Your father has deceived us and we must act without delay . . . and without his knowledge or consent."

A silence came over the room, each lost in his private thoughts. Finally Ian broke the quiet.

"I believe you, Lady Duncan," he said. "And I value the trust you place in me by desiring that your daughter be my wife. But I want to consider what is best for Maggie. I wouldn't want to act in haste if she were in any way unsure about—"

"Oh, Ian," said Maggie, "I *am* sure. I love you."

"If you wait," Atlanta broke in, "all could be lost. Believe me, it will be in Maggie's best interest for you to move without delay."

"Naturally," said Ian, "I am eager for us to be married. I love Maggie. But I do not want her pressed into it."

"The choices before my daughter are severely limited," said Atlanta. "If you wait, she may never be able to marry you at all."

The two young people were silent.

"Don't you understand?" implored Atlanta. "I didn't want to have to tell you. Oh, Maggie, I don't want you to be hurt anymore."

"Mother, Mother . . . what is it?"

"Oh, Maggie . . . your father—he has—your father has pledged you—in marriage—to George Falkirk."

Maggie looked at Ian, stunned.

"It's true," said Atlanta, then slumped to a chair where she too remained silent.

"No wonder he has been so cocky and confident," said Ian at length. "That explains everything."

Atlanta nodded.

"Then you are right," Ian went on, "we do have little choice. But how . . . what should we do?"

"James is planning another trip to Glasgow in two or three weeks," said Atlanta. "He will be away several days. That will be the best time. I will handle Falkirk and will keep you appraised of any developments. The two of you can go away—Fraserburgh would be good; there's a kindly old vicar there—and be back to Stonewycke before James returns. By then he will have a new son-in-law."

"And when he finds out?"

"We'll decide how to handle that when the time comes. For now you have my blessing . . . and that is enough."

37 / An Unexpected Encounter————————

Days passed, stretching into a week, then two. The visits of George Falkirk continued; gradually, Maggie became barely able to endure his presence. Fair weather held, yet Ian and Maggie—confined to brief moments when there was no danger of discovery by James—dared not go out together. Angered by Falkirk's presence, Ian nevertheless kept calm and waited patiently. Maggie wanted to tell her father everything, to have it out in the open, yet she feared for Ian's sake of the result. Likewise, Ian favored a full disclosure rather than their secretive plan. But in the end, both submitted to Atlanta's persuasion to wait until after the wedding, when James would be powerless to stop them.

Maggie dared not look her father in the eye for fear of betraying herself. James began to question Atlanta about their daughter's moodiness. Mealtimes were strained, with Maggie sitting stiff and silent. Ian's attempts at humor and conversation were rebuffed by James, whose fondness for Falkirk had grown more and more blatant. He began to question Ian as to the time of his return to London. Ian vaguely sidestepped his questions. "Isn't your month about over?" James asked. Ian laughed and commented that he hadn't anticipated enjoying the north so much. James muttered something about taking advantage of hospitality and then said no more; his face, however, revealed his keen displeasure.

Days continued to slip by. Storm clouds again rolled in, and Maggie announced she was going for a ride before the rain descended. Waiting long enough to arouse no suspicion, Ian excused himself, left the house by another door, then followed Maggie to the stables. He found her saddling Raven.

"I don't know how much longer I can take all this sneaking around," he blurted out, revealing the tension that had been building inside. "I'm not so sure we should have followed your mother's advice. We ought to just tell your father how things are between us and suffer the consequences."

"I've tried to summon the courage . . . several times," Maggie began lamely.

"We can't go on like this."

"The time hasn't seemed right."

"Don't you see? There's never going to be a *right* time! I want to tell him I love you and want you to be my wife. Then I want to tell Falkirk to stay away!"

The sharpness of his words stung, and tears began to form in Maggie's eyes. Realizing he had taken his frustrations out on her, Ian approached Maggie and gently placed a hand on her shoulder.

"I love you, Maggie," he said tenderly. "I just want him to know."

Maggie rubbed a quick hand across her face.

"I'm sorry," said Ian.

Maggie pulled the cinch tight and pulled it down through the round brass buckle, then moved to lead Raven to the door. "I have to think," she said. "I know what Mother says. But I want to tell him. Still, I need courage to face him. Maybe it takes more strength than I have."

"Oh, Maggie," said Ian. "Why won't you let me tell him? I can bear his anger. It's my place—my responsibility."

"No, Ian . . . I have to do it."

Why she insisted so strongly that she be the one to confront James, Maggie didn't know exactly. But she had to prove that she was no longer bound to her girlhood relationship with her father, that she could stand on her own feet as a woman and face him squarely.

Ian fell back and watched her swing easily up into the saddle. *Is she regretful about this hasty decision?* he wondered. As if reading his thoughts, Maggie looked down and smiled in reassurance. But she could force no words beyond the tightness in her throat. How she wanted to jump down and run into his arms and let the man she loved hold her! But for the moment, she kept that longing inside, spurred Raven around and sped down the road.

She gave no thought to where she rode. If she had stopped to choose, she would have chosen to ride on the beach, for the stormy tide was always magnificent in its frightful power. Instead, Raven carried her south. Perhaps her downcast spirit subconsciously sought the mournful comfort of the barren moor. Its harsh tenacity might give her the strength she needed. Hadn't Digory said that Braenock held a tender place in God's heart?

While the rains had held back, the winds had redoubled their mighty efforts at blowing away every frail leaf or loose twig left on the countryside. It lashed at Maggie's face like a whip of ice, but in her present mood she welcomed it as tangible proof there was strength beyond her own weakness.

"Oh, God!" she wailed. And indeed, only the Almighty could have heard her above the howling winds. "Oh, God . . . help me to do what

I must do, and bear what I must bear. Help me stand up to him, though he has never loved me . . . and will now hate me for what Ian and I are going to do.''

On she rode, the wind whipping against horse and rider, her hair streaming behind her violently, tears running down her cheeks as she struggled to form into definite prayers the painful, mingled memories of childhood and maturity. Then her hand found its way to her throat as it had so often of late, to seek the firm reality of Ian's love. She eased the locket from its hiding place and touched the fine chain, but it only brought new pain to her aching heart.

"Dear God . . . why must I choose between a father and a husband? All I wanted was to be loved by him . . . but now I will never know even that. He will hate me—and he will hate my husband even more. Dear God . . . how can I bear it?''

The wind lashed about her from every direction. Was it a messenger in answer to her prayers, or a cruel rebuttal? Raven continued up the ridge while Maggie closed her eyes against the sting of the wind. But the cries of her heart overshadowed the terrific power of nature.

"Dear God . . . help me!'' was all she could say.

A brief lull in the blast jolted Maggie awake. She stopped Raven, opened her eyes, and listened. All was calm.

Almost as quickly as it had died down, the wind picked up again and soon resumed its efforts to unseat her. Still Maggie sat unmoving on Raven's back, wondering if the passing moment of tranquillity had not come from within her own heart. What was it that Digory had once told her about a still small voice?

Had that lull been the still small voice of God speaking His presence to her, offering the gift of His strength, assuring that her future was in His hands?

She could not question it, for she had no other way to turn. She could not refuse the gift. She could only accept that God had indeed heard her cries and had, in that brief glimpse of time, promised to help her as she had asked.

The winds continued to sweep over her with their fury, but a tiny recess of inner calm remained in a corner of her heart. Suddenly Hector and Stevie Mackinaw filled the eye of her mind. The thought of a brief respite from the icy wind, a warm fire, and perhaps a hot cup of tea was especially inviting to her and might also help crystallize her thoughts before returning to the tensions of Stonewycke.

She turned Raven immediately toward the cottage and urged her forward, judging herself about a mile away.

In the flurry of wind and in the turmoil of her thoughts, however,

Maggie had lost her bearings. For all at once looming before her Maggie saw the granite heaps of the ancient Pict ruin. And there, tethered to a scraggly tree, were two horses—one of which was unmistakably George Falkirk's golden stallion.

The last thing Maggie wanted at this moment was to be seen by that man, yet curiosity compelled her forward. There was no one to be seen. Maggie judged the men—whoever they were—to be in the hollow surrounded by the rocks. If so, they would be unable to see her—or hear her approach because of the wind. What could they be doing here, alone late in the day on her father's land? She had no idea. But thoughts about James temporarily suspended, and her sense of danger and adventure aroused, Maggie tied Raven to a low shrub, and inched her way closer to the two horses.

She walked straight on until she came to within a hundred feet of the horses. She could make out figures in the small sheltering ravine below in the gathering dusk. She crept nearer, keeping behind the formations of rock as much as possible. Reaching the point where the moor began its steep descent, she stopped behind a boulder, and peered carefully down.

There were two men. One was definitely Falkirk, stooped over a mound of freshly dug earth. The other was on his knees with his back toward Maggie alternately wielding a pick and shovel, enlarging the hole they were apparently making in the opposite embankment.

The wind had subsided slightly, but it still muted their voices. Maggie dared go no nearer and strained to hear as best she could.

"There's na other way," said the other man.

". . . too noticeable . . ." came the remnant of Falkirk's words.

". . . do us na good t' steal the laird's . . ."

". . . belonged to the Picts . . . not his at all—"

"Picts or no," replied the man on his knees, whose face Maggie had still been unable to see, ". . . the laird wouldna take kindly . . . still his land."

". . . could be right," Falkirk conceded. ". . . can't risk . . . found out now . . ."

". . . need more horses . . . I'll get twa more an' . . ."

". . . tonight . . . late . . . wait no longer . . . too many delays . . ."

". . . rain's likely . . ."

"Don't argue!" snapped Falkirk. "This is the best time. You won't be seen." Raising his voice, Maggie could hear him clearly now. He stood and turned partially toward her and Maggie slipped back behind the protection of the rock. "Now let's get out of here."

Together they shoved what appeared to be a heavy chest beneath the projection of some rocks, then headed toward their mounts. Long before they had climbed back up to their horses, Maggie had run to Raven, mounted, and galloped for cover behind a low hill covered with shrubbery some two hundred yards distant. Her precaution mattered little, however, for the two conspirators did not even glance in her direction, so bent were they on getting out of the torrents of wind.

Abandoning her visit to the Mackinaws, Maggie turned and made her way homeward as soon as the two men had disappeared from sight. Falkirk was up to no good. What they had found she didn't know. And whether it, in fact, belonged to her father she didn't know either.

But one thing was certain. This land was the property of the Stonewycke estate, hers as much as her father's. She couldn't let them get away with their scheme, not until she at least knew what they had found.

She would have to decide what to do quickly. From the fragmentary conversation she had heard, she gathered that one of the men was planning a return visit to Braenock Ridge later that night.

As Maggie neared home, she recalled the reason for her ride in the first place. The immediacy of the events on Braenock suddenly faded as she remembered the awesome task that lay ahead of her. She could not wait until after they were married to tell her father. An inner resolve of her maturing womanhood compelled her to take a stand. She must tell him about Ian—tonight! She recoiled at the thought of such a confrontation. But at last she knew she had been given the strength necessary to see it through.

A shock of panic surged through Maggie when she saw the golden stallion in front of the stables. Falkirk must have departed from his companion somewhere on the valley road and hastened directly here.

Maggie dismounted and cautiously walked Raven inside, wishing to delay the inevitable meeting as long as possible. He was probably in the house by now, sharing a glass of brandy with her father. She dropped the reins and turned to unsaddle the mare.

"Ah, back from a windy ride, eh?" came a voice from deep inside the stable.

Maggie gasped. "You startled me," she said, turning. Her voice wavered.

"That was certainly not my intention, Lady Margaret," returned the smooth tones of George Falkirk. "The groom said you had gone for a ride and I decided to wait for you out here."

"I'm sure my father would have been delighted to entertain—"

"I didn't come to see your father, Margaret," replied Falkirk with an air of confidence. "This time I didn't want to go into the house and have to vie with your parents and servants, and even your houseguest, for your attentions. I thought I would have a better chance of speaking with you alone out here.

"Alone?" said Maggie.

"Oh, come now, Margaret," said Falkirk. "Surely you don't mean to suggest that you are unaware of the reason for my visits. Clearly, it isn't simply to pass the time with your father."

"I'm afraid I don't know what you mean," stalled Maggie.

"Oh, Margaret," he replied, his moderate tone thinly disguising the cocky self-assurance he felt. His discovery on Braenock Ridge had so intoxicated him with his own importance and good fortune that he could barely keep from telling her everything. How could she waste her time with that ridiculous fellow Duncan when he—the future earl of Kairn *and* Stonewycke—was right before her eyes? In addition, he was soon to be rich in his own right. How could she act so disinterested? He knew she longed for him. He must simply help her overcome her girlish fears.

"Margaret," he said, "you are so lovely with your hair blown by the wind and your face flushed from the ride—'' He moved toward her and reached out to touch her hair.

''Mr. Falkirk, please!'' Maggie backed away, more irritated than afraid.

''Margaret,'' he said, with a hint of insistence, ''I've waited long enough for you to come to your senses. It's time—''

''Come to my senses?'' she interrupted. ''What do you mean?''

''You know very well what I mean. You know our parents have spoken about us.''

''I know of no such thing!''

''Then it's time you found out. What else do you think my visits and my words of affection mean?''

''I'm sure I have no idea.''

''Margaret, don't you see? It's time we make definite plans. I want you, Margaret. I want to marry you.''

''Please . . . no,'' Maggie said, trying to back away.

He continued to press himself toward her. ''We have your father's blessing, Margaret. You need but say the word and the estates of Kairn and Stonewycke—''

''No . . . no—I can't. I—''

''*Can't!* Come, Margaret. Don't pretend to be so naive. I know you want me also. I know you. I've seen the look of love in your eyes.''

He continued the advance, backing Maggie against the rough side of Raven's stall.

''Mr. Falkirk,'' Maggie began again, ''I . . . I don't want to marry you. I'm sorry if you inferred otherwise.''

Her eyes darted about for a way to flee, but Falkirk's arms blocked her on either side.

''I tell you, I've seen it in your eyes, Margaret,'' he insisted, undaunted by her words. ''I know what love looks like.''

''If you have, Mr. Falkirk,'' said Maggie, breathing deeply and trying to utter calmly the words she wanted to scream at him, ''I'm sorry. Perhaps you have seen love in my eyes. But it was not meant for you.''

He colored slightly and his voice quavered momentarily; then he swiftly regained his composure.

''Am I not good enough for the grand lady? Are you insinuating you would rather bestow your favor on that rascal of a cousin—''

His careless words were ill-chosen if he thought to win Maggie's favor by insulting her fiancé.

''Don't you dare speak that way of him!'' she cried, her fear of Falkirk at last giving way to anger.

"So that's it, is it?" he snarled as his hands inched closer and then clamped down on her two shoulders. Then he laughed, still convinced his menacing charm could overpower any impressionable young girl. "You'll change your tune after you have tasted a *real* man!"

He pulled her to him and forced her lips to his. She struggled, but his hands on her shoulders held her fast.

"Please—don't—" she managed to say before his passionate breath suffocated her.

After a moment he released her. Her hand flashed to his cheek with a resounding slap so that her palm stung; his face reddened with the force of the blow.

Falkirk staggered backward, stunned at the affrontery of her scorn. Then a grin of malicious intent crept over his face, and he rubbed his cheek ruefully.

"So that's how we would play this game, is it?" he said as the leer grew wider. "Well, my captivating little heiress, let me give you the feel of a man with power."

He pressed his body against her, his arms holding Maggie's tiny frame in a vise-like grip, his lips ardently crushing down on hers. "Don't worry," he said, "you'll enjoy it once you're taught what love is all about." He kissed her again, and again.

Terror seized Maggie. With both hands against his chest she tried to repel him, but fighting was useless against his superior strength.

"Digory!" she tried to call out. But her voice was dulled by Falkirk's nearness.

"Don't worry about him . . . I sent him away."

In one final surge, Maggie shoved with all her might, wrenched herself partially free, and lurched toward the door. Falkirk grabbed at her sleeve and the leather of her jacket tore with a sickening rip. In shock she stared at the torn sleeve, then up at him, incensed at what he had done. His grip loosened, then he retreated a step.

"I'll be back," he said. "And make no mistake, Margaret. I *shall* claim you as my wife—with or without your consent!"

He spun around and was gone.

Maggie slumped to the ground and burst into tears, hardly aware of the pounding retreat of the stallion's hooves. She was still weeping several minutes later when Digory ambled into the stable.

Hearing her choking sobs, he hurried to her side. "Lady Marg'ret!" he exclaimed, kneeling down beside her. "Are ye ailin', lass?"

She shook her head, but no words would come. At last she struggled to whisper the single word, *Ian.*

Digory understood and hurried away as quickly as his arthritic bones would carry him. When he returned, Ian was at his side. He rushed to Maggie, still lying on the stable floor, and his face turned ashen. His mind reeled as he reached out his hand to her trembling body; he dropped to her side and wrapped his arms about her.

"What happened?" he asked softly.

She tried to speak, but every word caught in a sob.

Ian tried to calm her, then glanced up at Digory with a questioning look.

"Were it the gentleman, lassie?" asked Digory.

"What gentleman?" asked Ian sharply, his hot blood rising.

"Mr. Falkirk," Digory replied. "He were here jist a few moments ago—he was a-ridin' off jist before I came in."

Suddenly the scene before Ian's eyes took on deeper and more sinister meaning. He saw the torn sleeve for the first time and suddenly realized the reason for Maggie's sobs.

"Maggie. . . ?" he said. "Was it him?"

She managed a nod.

Ian leaped to his feet. "Which way did he ride, Digory?"

"I couldna tell, sir, but—"

"Ian, no!" exclaimed Maggie. "Don't go . . . please!"

"I'll kill the miserable scoundrel!" he cried.

"No, Ian!" implored Maggie, rising.

But Ian had already thrown himself on Raven's back, where she stood still saddled from Maggie's ride.

"Ian . . . Ian! This isn't the way!" Maggie screamed after him. But he was gone.

Maggie numbly fell back against the wall. Fear and darkness surrounded her, and for a moment she forgot Digory's presence altogether.

Gradually she felt Digory's loving hands reaching out and pulling her to her feet. Then she became aware, as if coming to her from a distance through a fog, of his gentle voice repeating tender words she could not understand. Her first thought was that he was attempting to console her. Then suddenly it dawned on her that he was praying, and that his mellow words of compassion and healing were not intended for her at all.

By degrees she relaxed, and the tears abated. But with the calming of her spirit came the reawakening of her thoughts.

"I have to stop him," she said.

"In time, lass," Digory soothed, ". . . in time."

"There is no time. We must stop him!" Her voice rang through the quiet that had descended on the stable.

"Noo, lass," Digory tried to calm her. "The lad will do na harm—

only cause a bit o' a row, as lads'll do.'' Then his voice rose with the uncharacteristic outrage he had been hiding for Maggie's sake. ''An it'll serve that yoong de'il right!''

Immediately he repented his words. ''Dear Lord, forgi'e me—but the man deserves na better.''

''But Ian could be hurt! Falkirk had rage in his eye when he left.''

''I'm thinkin' yer yoong cousin can take care o' himsel'.''

''He'll be back. I know he will!'' said Maggie, hardly heeding Digory's attempts to calm her.

''Then the bla'gart'll hae the whole Duncan clan t' fecht!'' said Digory, his highland blood rising at the thought, as if he were himself the chief member of the clan he had given his life to serve.

Maggie had now come to herself. Thoughts were finally crystallizing in her mind. If she were indeed, as people had been saying all her life, the heiress of Stonewycke, now was the time for her to step into that calling. She couldn't help Ian, not right now at least. But maybe there was something she could do—something which would thwart Falkirk's scheming designs, and possibly keep him out of their lives forever.

She sprang up, her strength reviving with renewed purpose.

''Digory,'' she said, ''saddle us two horses. And bring out a work-horse too—and sacks. We'll need several.''

''I don't think we'll be able t' get t' town in time t'—''

''We're not going into town, Digory,'' interrupted Maggie.

The groom stood staring at his young mistress, wondering if the stress had finally been too much for her.

''Hurry!'' Maggie urged, heading for the stalls to begin preparations by herself.

Two hours later the three horses plodded heavily back past the iron gates of Stonewycke, their covert mission accomplished under the cloak of darkness. The rain still withheld its torrents, and only the wind impeded their step; their labored journey was nearly at an end. At the back of the house the horses stopped near the walled garden where Digory and Maggie unloaded from their weary backs the heavy bags they had carried all the way home. They had ridden hard to the granite mounds of Brae-nock Ridge, covering the distance in half the usual time. Finding it still deserted, Maggie located the spot without difficulty and flew to the task with the aid of her trusted groom. The return trip, though slower, was no easier for the faithful beasts of burden with their cumbersome cargo. When the bags were off their backs, Digory led them to the stables while Maggie—making sure they were not seen—began lugging their find into the little-used and overgrown arbor which would, until she could devise a better permanent cache, serve to conceal their find from Falkirk and her father. There was a breach in the back wall she thought would do just fine. There remained many difficulties, but she would manage them somehow, as soon as Ian returned. At least she had it out of Falkirk's scheming grasp.

As Maggie tucked the key in her pocket a plan began to form in her mind. Perhaps, had she thought it through, she would have seen its folly. But in her desperation from the heightened fervor of the evening's events, it seemed the only way. Falkirk would return to the ridge tonight with his accomplice—whoever that was—and find his treasure gone. In the morning she would send him a cryptic message: if he wanted his treasure, he would have to meet her conditions, the most important of which was never to set foot on Stonewycke again.

Perhaps it was foolish. In the light of day she might find herself unwilling to yield the long-hidden cache. But at this moment all she could think of was ridding her life of Falkirk forever. No price seemed too great to ensure her happiness with Ian.

Oh, if only he would return so she could tell him everything! He would know what was best—to expose Falkirk; or to employ any number of other possibilities.

Meanwhile, Maggie entered the house by a little-used back door and, still unseen, hurried up the flights of stairs in search of a place to hide the key to the garden.

Back in her room a short while later, she paced in front of her window, her ears straining for sound of Ian's return. She tried to pray, but no prayer could find coherent expression in her harried mind. There was only confusion, fear. On Braenock Ridge hours ago she had felt so confident in her resolve—but now it was gone. The image of her father crossed her mind and unconsciously her hand crept toward her neck and to the locket.

It was gone!

Despair flooded her. Was this the final horrible answer she had dreaded to face? Once more something precious had been lost to her. And could this be anything but a sign that the giver of the beloved object would be torn from her as well?

Maggie desperately tried to focus her mind—where could she have lost it? She had had it earlier on Braenock Ridge. Had it fallen off since? Could it have been snagged on something when she and Digory were digging? If so, how could she dare return for it? *Oh, where is it?* her heart wailed.

Why had Ian not yet returned?

39 / The Fight

The shadows of dusk had given way nearly completely to night. Raven, little more than a swift black streak, raced down the valley road leading south.

In his fury Ian dug his heels in relentlessly. The miles to Kairn should have cooled his wrath, but they only served to sharpen and further define it. Unaware that she was, even now, making her way in the same direction on an altogether different mission, all Ian could see through the distorted images of his agitated brain was Maggie crumpled on the floor of the stable. Her sobs tore painfully at his memory. *I should have been there*, he thought. *I could have protected her.*

His own selfish words still vibrated in his ears. He had only been thinking of himself. He should never have let her ride off alone! In anguish and guilt, Ian drove Raven on.

Falkirk had no right! Whether he knew about the betrothal or not, he had behaved like a fiend. But the dog would pay! He would force the miscreant to his knees before this night was through. He needed no weapon. With his bare hands he would teach Falkirk to behave like a gentleman!

He had never been to Kairn. He eased into a trot when he reached the rows of trees lining either side of the road. He could barely make out their shapes in the darkness, but he knew he must be approaching the estate. Soon the silhouette of the house loomed in front, dark, too, except for two or three pale windows. Ian brought Raven up short at the doorstep of the mansion. Flying from the saddle, he ran up the few steps and pounded on the door.

The wait was long and he continued to pound. Finally the door swung open.

"Do ye want t' wake the veery dead wi' yer poundin'?" bawled a woman who appeared to be the housekeeper.

"I want Falkirk!" shouted Ian. The woman retreated a step or two, as if Ian would attack the portress herself.

"The laird be t' bed," she replied, unabashed by his insolent tone.

"The young Falkirk!"

"He's na here."

"Where then?" demanded Ian.

"How should I ken?"

"I tell you, I want him," said Ian, moving forward.

"An' I tell ye, I dinna ken his whereabouts," she said, ready to slam the door. But Ian caught it with his foot and glared at her.

"The yoong lord comes an' goes," she continued, at last feeling the intimidation of this wild stranger who would not be turned aside by her gruffness. "He went t' Port Strathy this mornin'—"

Ian waited to hear no more.

He spun on his heels, leaving the woman at the open door with her unfinished sentence in her mouth, flew back down the steps, leaped on Raven's back, spurred her on mercilessly, and tore back down the road the way he had come.

The long ride back to Port Strathy moderated Ian's initial passion, but a steely determination replaced it. What would he do if his suspicion as to Falkirk's location proved to be wrong? But he needn't have worried. The golden stallion was tied in front of the inn where Falkirk had come both to celebrate the good fortune of his find on the moor, and to deaden the humiliation of his rebuff by Maggie.

A storm of renewed violence assailed Ian. He quickly dismounted, hardly bothering to tether Raven at the hitching post outside, and strode angrily toward the door.

Inside, Falkirk had already passed the midpoint toward complete intoxication. The combined emotions of exhilaration and mortification operating upon him, he had been loud and boisterous, at one moment toasting the health of his companions with elation, the next lapsing into the despondency of solitude, ready to break out suddenly in a challenge against any and all present. He was anxious to reconcile his defeat at Stonewycke by demonstrating his virility, itching to vanquish with his fists any farmer foolish enough to stand up against him. For the young lord was no stranger to the arena, having boxed with greater than average ability in the ring at the university. To this point in the progress of the evening, however, the locals had prudently managed to sidestep his slurs against everything from their town to their wives in an attempt to incite someone to stand against him. The effect of his impotence, working in combination with Queenie's drink, had by now raised the neighboring lord to such a pitch of agitation that he was ready to find provocation to violence in the slightest pretense.

A glass of ale was raised to his lips when the door suddenly burst open with a crash.

"Falkirk!" shouted Ian, "Step outside!"

Turning toward the threat, Falkirk's lip curled into an evil sneer. He set his drink on the table.

"You must be jesting, Duncan," he drawled, rising slowly from his chair and starting toward him.

"You will pay for what you have done!"

"Playing the knight again, are you?" replied Falkirk, skillfully covering the wobbly sensation in his knees.

"If you want it here, that's fine with me!"

"So you're upset that the little flower has a crumpled petal," Falkirk went on, the alcohol working in his brain to instill confidence where he had no reason for it. "But no, that's not it," he taunted with a sardonic grin of disdain. "You're just a poor loser!"

But the words were unwisely spoken. If there had been any restraint in Ian, it now broke before the full force of his anger. He took two strides toward his opponent, who was still not fully apprised of his danger.

Falkirk opened his mouth to speak once more as Ian approached.

"Why, you good-for-nothing b——!"

But before he had the chance to finish the word, Ian's fist smashed directly into his face. Falkirk stumbled backward, stunned, caught himself on a bench, then touched his lip and felt a slow trickle of blood.

"You scum!" he shrieked in a diabolical voice. "You will pay for this, you mangy cur!"

Sobered from the pain and the sight of his own blood, Falkirk sprang on Ian with a flurry of well-placed blows. His experience quickly regained him the upper hand and Ian found himself thrown back against the wall with a sharp stinging sensation over his right ear, from which he, too, felt a warm oozing down the side of his cheek.

But he had not come to be on the defensive, warding off Falkirk's punches. Ian had experience too, not from the university but from the streets of London. He struck back without restraint, attacking Falkirk with the fury of righteous indignation, battering his fists about the other's head and midsection. The two fell across a chair which crashed to pieces, and then to the floor.

The small gathering of men in the common room were content to stand by and observe—not often were they provided with such splendid entertainment, and they had long since tired of Falkirk's abusive behavior and coarse tongue. But Queenie was not about to stand by while her new tables and chairs were demolished by the two ruffians. She ran forward as quickly as her oversized frame would allow and frantically exhorted the onlookers to do something. Receiving no help from that quarter, she hastened into the midst of the fray herself.

"Ye bloody blokes!" she cried, "Ye can kill each other if ye want. But not in my place!"

Then turning again to her customers. "Grab 'em, will ye, afore my place is in shambles!"

The two combatants tried to push Queenie aside, but by that time several of the men had approached them where they rolled and wrestled on the floor. They pulled Ian off Falkirk, who had just received a volley of tormenting punches about his head. Seeing his quick advantage, Falkirk jumped to his feet and lunged forward, delivering a punishing blow to Ian's ribs. Ian crumpled to the floor where the men, still holding him, attempted to help him back up.

Painfully Falkirk gathered his hat and staggered toward the door, then outside. Regaining his breath, Ian shrugged off the help of his supporters and struggled toward the door.

"I'll kill you!" he yelled. "Do you hear me, Falkirk? If you ever touch her again, I'll kill you!"

The small gathering of men remained silent in the aftermath of the row, but Queenie—anxious to soothe tempers and calm the atmosphere in her respectable establishment—hastened to Ian's side.

"I dinna ken what the bloke did t' ye," she said. "But I'll warrant he ne'er does it again."

She led Ian, in a state of mental and physical exhaustion, back into the room and to a table. "An' na doobt he deserved it!" she added as if to seal the matter for all present.

"Sit ye doon," she said with a husky gentleness. "Ye'll be needin' a drink."

She brought out a bottle of her prime Scotch from behind the counter and poured him a large measure. "This'll put the starch back int' yer bones."

Slowly the others resumed their former places, one or two of the men helping Queenie straighten the furniture and pick up the broken chair, and gradually the buzz of conversation resumed. Ian sat alone in a daze. The voices around him were but a subdued blur. Even Queenie's friendly tones registered only vaguely in his consciousness. For the moment all the latent violence within him had been spent. The energy which had driven him to such convulsive hysteria only a few moments before was gone, and his body sagged in weariness.

The only action of which he seemed capable was to raise the glass in front of him to his lips and let the whiskey burn down his throat.

He signalled for Queenie, and she poured him another.

Maggie hurried from her room the moment she heard the hoofbeats.

It was very late, but sleep had been impossible. She hastened down the stairway, the long wait at last over, desperately hoping the horse she heard bore Ian and not Falkirk returning as he had threatened.

She forgot her coat, and the rush of cold wind bit through her thin frock as she stepped outside. Gingerly she crept toward the stable through the darkness of the yard. Peering inside, the blackness was deeper still.

"Ian . . . Ian . . . is that you?" she whispered.

The jingling and creaking sounds of bridle and saddle being unfastened stopped. Ian stepped out of the shadows. She could just barely see his face, but it was enough.

"Ian . . . oh, dear Lord!" Maggie cried. "You're hurt!" Carefully she reached up and touched his bruised and bloodied face.

He took her hands and wrapped them around him instead.

"Ian, I was so worried . . . so afraid—"

"You don't need to worry anymore, my love," he replied.

"Did you . . . did you find him?"

"Yes. And he will not hurt you again." The chill of his voice frightened Maggie; the words sounded so decisive and final. She could smell that he had been drinking.

"Ian, while you were gone," she began, then stopped. "Ian," she continued after a moment, "I know how we can keep him away—"

"Hush, my Maggie . . ." he interrupted in a soft, strained voice. "Just hold me. I need so much for you to hold me." He tried to focus his muddled vision on her face, barely visible in the darkness. "He won't bother us ever again."

"How can you be sure? Ian . . . what happened?"

"Not now, Maggie . . . not now."

His voice contained a cold foreboding; Maggie shuddered involuntarily.

"I've done something I want to forget," he went on. "I need you to help me forget. Just hold me."

She complied. For a few moments nothing else existed for the two lovers who were yet compelled to hide their love from view. And even before it could be made public, outside forces threatened to destroy their love and wrench them apart. But for now, in this one moment of quiet bliss, even the smells of horses and hay, the howling wind, and the gentle squeaking back and forth of the stable door all receded into the distance. All that mattered was their love, and they clung to one another, holding tight to that solid reality.

They did not hear the footsteps approaching across the cobblestone drive, and saw the light from the lantern too late.

"So!" growled the voice they knew all too well. "This is how I am repaid for my kindness!" James Duncan's voice resounded with the hatred of a lifetime against the offspring of Landsbury.

The couple fell apart and gaped with horror at the man as if they were thieves caught in the very act of stealing his treasures. Through the unfolding of the events of this evening, James had been the furthest thought from their minds. Maggie had all but forgotten her earlier resolve to tell him everything.

"Father—" she tried to begin.

James ignored his daughter and turned instead to the cousin whose father he loathed.

"What have you to say for yourself, Duncan?" he shouted angrily.

Ian stepped forward. Despite the pain from Falkirk's blows, he stood straight and tall. He had already faced one foe tonight; he would not be easily cowed by another, even Maggie's father.

"Your daughter and I are in love," he began in a calm, unflinching voice.

"Love!" replied James with a spiteful laugh. "What do you know of love, you baseborn son of a swindler!"

"We intended to tell you—"

"You intended to tell me!" James roared. "But you knew I'd never allow it! And I won't—not for an instant!"

"We weren't intending to ask your permission," said Ian resolutely. "Your approval, or lack of it, cannot change our love for one another. We only wanted you to hear it from us first."

"You blackguard!" shouted James, seething with rage. The impudent scoundrel was challenging him to his face.

"I'm sorry, sir," began Ian again, "we had hoped—"

"You get out of here!" James ordered. "You'll never lay eyes on my daughter again!"

"Father, you must listen to us!" implored Maggie.

"Quiet, Margaret!" James commanded. "You get to the house immediately. I'll deal with you later."

"Please, Father," returned Maggie, standing her ground, "please hear what we have to say."

"Why, you insolent hussy! By Jove, I tell you to get—"

"No, your lordship," said Ian, his composure at last giving way. "You'll not speak to my fiancée in such a tone. You no longer control what she may or may not do."

"What!" he shrieked. "You . . . what right have you? By heaven, if I were a younger man, I'd thrash you and throw you out myself! Now, begone, you charlatan. I command you—"

"No!" Ian resounded. "You do not command us. We are going to be married!"

The words hung in the air like a thunderhead ready to burst at any instant. In disbelief James stared at the audacious couple before him as if he recognized neither of them.

His countenance slowly turned to ice. When he spoke, his voice was low like a distant thunderclap, portending another explosion of lightning soon to follow.

"What evil hoax you are trying to deceive me with, I do not know," he said. "But this I do know—before I am finished, I will destroy you. As for you, my slut of a daughter, I will never—so long as you take up with this vile excuse for a man—look upon your face again!"

Maggie burst into tears.

"We had hoped to reason with you," Ian tried again. "We had wanted your blessing!"

"My blessing!" James spat out the words like bile. "You'll have *nothing*—do you hear me, Duncan . . . nothing! And you'll never have my daughter! She *will* marry George Falkirk. That is what she shall do. And you shall go to the devil!"

"I tell you, sir," said Ian, fighting with all his might to control his rising temper, "we *will* be married—with or without your consent."

"Do you think that matters?"

"There is nothing you can do to change it."

"How naive you are! That marriage will mean no more than an old birch shilling by the time I get through! I have influence, and I will grind you, and your so-called marriage, into the dust beneath my feet!"

Ian opened his mouth to speak again, then hesitated.

Suddenly the desperation on his face was unmasked, as exposed in stark reality as the wounds on his face. Suddenly a voice inside said that James could win after all, that his words were not mere empty threats. All at once the weight of the evening's events crashed in upon him. The throbbing in his head, the numbing effect of the alcohol in his blood, and the onslaught of James's verbal abuse pressed mercilessly against his brain.

"I warn you, Duncan, if you try to take my daughter away, any so-called *marriage*"—James spat out the word with revulsion—"you contrive to arrange will be over—ended forever—within two days! It will never have been! I will have my way. Margaret will marry George Falkirk!"

Ian heard only a few words of James's final odious speech— ". . . over . . . ended . . . marry George Falkirk!"

"No!" he screamed like a madman. "She will never marry Falkirk. I won't let it happen—never!"

Ian stumbled past James out of the stable. He could barely see in front of him. He had no destination in mind, no intent. He just had to get away. His old self welled up from deep within and cried out to him— "Flee! . . . Flee from Stonewycke . . . Flee from Scotland!"

The rain, so long pent up in the swelling clouds overhead, at last poured down and enveloped Ian as he ran into its dismal darkness.

41 / A Midnight Plot

Rain pelted the granite embankments as if after a thousand years it might finally beat the boulders back to the dust from which they had been forged.

The dark figure cursed aloud, then spat on the ground.

"Tha' dirty bla'gart!" he growled. "Thinks 'e can dooblecross me, does 'e? Cheat me oot o' my share?"

In spite of his tattered woolen overcoat he was soaked to the skin, and now he bitterly realized that all his efforts had been in vain. The empty wooden cask told him all.

"Thinks 'e can do what 'e pleases cause o' him bein' a gent'man . . . thinks I'll stan' fer't, does 'e?" he muttered with revenge in his voice. "Oh, I'll get my share, my fine earl," he snarled greedily, kicking at the ancient box and knocking the fragile wood to splinters, "or I'll get all o' it!"

He pulled a crude wooden-handled dagger from his belt. Even in the dark it flashed with evil intent. He tested the edge with a calloused finger. "Jist let him try t' cheat me! He'll pay . . . that 'e will!"

He mounted his horse and sped off, already having forgotten that his own traitorous design had brought him to the ruin well over an hour ahead of the appointed rendezvous. He had forgotten that he, too, had planned to fleece his partner by making off with the loot himself. But even had his own felonious motives crossed his mind, he would not have been hard-pressed to convince his feeble conscience that he somehow possessed a greater right to the treasure. The fine-talking lord had more than enough wealth for one lifetime and certainly had no need for more. Besides, he reasoned, he had himself been kicked around for years by such noblemen with nothing to show for it. "Highborn rascals!" he mumbled.

Hatred and indignation rose within him, and mounted with every hoofbeat.

He flogged his horse pitilessly down the ridge, across the darkened fields, and to the valley road. Reaching it he spun toward the left, dug

221

in his heels, urged his steed on at still a more furious gallop, and was soon out of sight, lost to view in the gathering hills to the south.

The storm-blackened sky grew only vaguely lighter as dawn approached. The angry clouds permitted but the vaguest intimation of light—enough to show that, though unwelcome, morning would eventually come.

Leaning heavily on the door of the Bluster 'N Blow, Ian pounded his fist on the hard oak. Rain-soaked, mud-splattered, with dried blood on his face, he gave the appearance of a London street vagabond. His fine clothes drooped on his beaten frame, evidence of a lost battle. When a surly and sleepy-eyed Queenie Rankin opened the door some moments later, he lifted a bloodied hand to her but could only mumble incoherently.

"I . . . I need—"

"Good Gaud!" Queenie exclaimed, her perturbation at being roused at such an untimely hour dissolving in the shock of his appearance. More disturbing than the tattered look of his clothes was the vacant stare in his eyes which seemed to say that life no longer meant anything because he had done the unthinkable.

"Look at ye!" she cried. "Ye'll catch yer death in them wet clothes!"

She led him to the hearth and gently pressed him into a chair. "Ye sit doon here by the fire."

She stooped down, poked and blew at the dying embers from the previous evening's blaze, added a few sticks of dried oak, and coaxed the coals once more to give off their warmth. When the crackle of flames had resurrected to her satisfaction, she rose, and saying, "I'll be right back," hurried off toward the kitchen. She returned with a basin of water to which she had added several drops from a vial in her cupboard, and laid Ian's hand in it. He winced sharply and withdrew the hand, but she guided it back into the stinging potion of water.

" 'Tis a fine gash ye got there," she said. "Ye must soak it or 'twill fester sure as ye blink."

Ian said nothing, only closed his eyes and took a deep breath. The pain awoke him gradually to reality. "I knew a young bloke once," Queenie went on, trying to ease Ian's mind with random conversation, "got jist a wee cut in his hand. He didna clean it proper, an' afore ye know it, he lost his whole hand. Had t' cut it clean off, they did. Wears a hook now—an' that's God's trowth! Ever seen a man wi' a hook fer a hand? 'Tis a gruesome sight—and these eyes o' mine hae seen jist aboot everythin' there is t' see."

Ian allowed Queenie to nurse his wound, thinking she came as close to a compassionate mother and ministering angel as could be found under the circumstances.

How a gentleman like this could get into such scrapes, thought Queenie, she couldn't guess. He had everything he could want. Why did he go out and get himself into such trouble?

Yet she was drawn to this poor lad. He had shown her a courtesy all too rare among those of his breed, and taking him in now was a thing hardly to be questioned.

"Whate'er brings ye oot on such a foul mornin'?" she asked.

"I don't know." His voice had no tone. "I was out."

"Weel, ye should be at Stonewycke where ye can get proper fixin'."

"No!" said Ian with some alarm. "Not Stonewycke . . . I can't."

"Weel, a han'some lad like yersel' dinna want t' be goin' round wearin' no hook!"

"I didn't know where else to go."

"Dinna ye worry. I'll take care o' ye the best I can. Don't hae no clothes fer ye, though. My husband was a small man—dropped dead a week after this place was built. Still canna believe it mysel'. His clothes would ne'er fit the likes o' yersel'. Weel," she added, "maybe the fire'll do the job."

When his hand was clean and a warm cup of tea had passed his lips, she led Ian upstairs. She stripped him of his outer garments and eased him into bed, pulling a thick layer of blankets over him.

"A guid night's sleep's what he'll be needin'," she murmured, softly closing the door.

Ian slept. Perhaps that was what his body needed. But his soul could not rest. When he awoke several hours later, fatigue still wracked his aching frame and a vague apprehension had settled on his heart.

Dreams had disturbed the refuge of his sleep, dreams that were in a tangled mass of disarray—filled with a terror of the unknown, with a premonition he couldn't quite lay hold of. He rode, like the wind but he was not on Raven's back, nor on Maukin's, but on a mighty steed of great power and fierce, red eyes. Its coat was black as death and its long tail flew in the wind as he bolted across the moor with a speed no animal of equine origins could match. Now he was surrounded by heather, the very heather that had filled his heart with such joy when he had first seen it with Maggie. But now there was no joy—only desolation and loneliness. Suddenly a figure on the ground before him arrested the mad flight of his courser. Ian was on the ground walking toward the heap before him. He stooped down amidst the full blooming heather. Suddenly, to his horror, he realized the lovely blossoms of purple had altered their hue and had changed to the color of blood. In terror he jumped to his feet and tried to scream. But no voice would come . . .

Ian pulled himself up in bed, dripping with cold sweat. *Thank God!* he thought, easing back onto the bed, still breathing deeply from the panic of the nightmare.

All at once words came into his mind. Were they from his dream or were they words he had heard somewhere before? " *'O choose, O choose, Lady Marg'ret,'* he said, *'O whether will ye gang or bide?'* "

What choice? he asked himself, as wakefulness gradually returned. *What Margaret? Was his own dear Maggie wrestling with a choice?*

He tried to shake the jumble of questions from his mind. Where had he heard those verses?

Then the old ballad he had heard that peaceful night around the huge fire so many weeks ago flooded back upon his memory.

No! he wanted to shout. *This can't be!*

He clasped his hands to his ears, as if to keep out the thoughts and accusations, the threats and fears.

But he could not escape them. If Maggie were struggling with a choice between himself and her father, even as the maiden in the Douglas ballad, then at least he had to know. He had to face it. Then, if her choice was against him, he could run once more. But he would have to return in order to discover what his future held.

42 / Constable Duff

Amid the fury, pain, and stupor of the previous night, Ian had no recollection of retrieving the chestnut mare. But when he stumbled out of the inn about an hour before noon, Queenie brought Maukin around to him. The horse had been tied out in front, she said, and while he slept, she had fed and cared for the animal.

He looked at the woman for a long moment, incredulous that he could remember nothing of returning to Stonewycke for the horse following his altercation with James. Then, coming to his senses and realizing all the rough old woman had done to befriend such a vagrant as he, Ian swallowed hard, wondering how to thank her.

A woman not given to shows of emotion, Queenie laid a pudgy hand on his sleeve.

"Noo, where might ye be off to, if ye canna gang t' Stonewycke, as ye said last night?" Her tone was full of concern, for she could still see in his eyes the look of fatal hopelessness.

"I must go back," Ian replied flatly.

She scrutinized him carefully. He looked a bit better than he had several hours earlier. And his clothes, while still untidy, were at least dry. His hands no longer trembled, but that wound on his left hand required attention, as did the nasty cut above his ear. She wondered if he would get it at Stonewycke.

Ian mounted Maukin. Queenie was glad she had had sense enough to tend to the poor animal during the night, for it had been in nearly as bad shape as its master. Wherever the lad had ridden the mare during the night, it must have been long and hard.

Ian threw her one more glance, nodded in thankful salute, and spun around toward Stonewycke.

During the night the storm had blown out its fury, leaving the land washed with gloom. Little evidence of the summer just past remained. Ian recalled riding in the valley with Maggie—how lovely the heather hills had been beneath their feet, with the deep blue of the sky overhead! Gentle breezes had carried the odors of warmth and freshness on their wings. All had been so new, so delicious. Maggie's laughter, her smiling face rose into Ian's mind. It had been such a short time ago, yet it seemed another lifetime, a time when their budding love was joyous in its innocence. Hardly had they had the chance to realize they were in love before the blossom of that love seemed to be crushed, snatched from them. He could not believe summer would ever come again for him. Here, in these fields and hills, he had found his greatest joy. Would his greatest agony be here as well?

"Oh, God!" he cried. "Why do you allow a man to possess a tiny moment of ecstasy only to tear it from him? Do you delight in breaking our hearts?"

On he slowly rode. All the pleasures of the times so soon past soured within him. The treasured memories became instead knives of pain.

I would rather never to have lived than face this! he cried within himself. *God, I curse you for giving me breath!*

His hopelessness had turned to complete despondency by the time he approached the manor gate. Even if Maggie still wanted him, what could she do against her father's threats? If only they could go away . . . far away . . . to America! But she could never leave Stonewycke. What could he do? The man had threatened him. Just to show his face again could jeopardize Maggie's safety and happiness.

The gate stood open. Two strange horses grazed on the front lawn. Another impulse to turn back, to run, to flee, swept over him. Still he forced himself forward, approaching the house with trepidation. He dismounted, tied Maukin, walked to the door, and raised his hand to knock. Almost immediately the sound of approaching feet could be heard from within as though they had been waiting for him.

The door opened, and beyond the silent figure of the answering butler stood James with two men Ian had never seen before. The confrontation was more sudden than he expected.

"You have your impudence!" James said, spitting the words at him, "showing your face around here! But I'm glad you did."

Then turning to one of the men, "Constable, I believe this is the man you are seeking."

One of the strangers stepped forward toward Ian. He was shorter than Ian, somewhat stocky, and dressed in a coarse but respectable tweed coat and woolen trousers. His round face sported a thick moustache. His sharp black eyes left no doubt that he was wise as any serpent, but they also held an affability—as anyone viewing him with his grand-daughter in his lap would have discerned in less than a moment.

"Mr. Duncan?" the man said.

Ian nodded.

"I'm Angus Duff, the constable from Culden."

"Culden?" said Ian, perplexed.

"Yes. But my duties extend to Strathy."

Ian did not reply, still unable to tell what the unusual scene portended.

"I've come to ask you some questions," Duff went on. The constable had never been a man to judge another by his appearance. But this young Duncan definitely looked as if trouble were no stranger to him.

"What questions?" asked Ian flatly.

"About the gentleman who was killed," Duff answered, carefully making note of Ian's reaction. "Seems you two had words last night—"

"Killed?" Ian said in a hoarse voice, barely able to get the words past his dry throat. "Who?"

"Come now, Duncan," James cut in with derision in his tone. "We can all see well enough past your attempted ignorance. I told the constable how you left here last night with blood in your eyes."

"Who?" asked Ian again, hardly aware of anything but the pounding in his skull.

"The young master of Kairn," the constable answered. "Mr. George Falkirk. Stabbed to death in the middle of the night, as far as we can tell."

Ian's face turned ashen.

"The folks in town said your words at the inn last evening came to blows. It would be good to know where you were for the rest of the night?"

Ian did not respond. For an instant the thought crossed his mind to turn and run back through the door through which he had just come. But his legs had suddenly been drained of their strength. *My God*, he thought, *the night was so hazy. Could it be possible . . . what if . . .*

His thoughts were suspended as something all at once drew his eyes to the stairway above him. There stood Maggie on the landing, her eyes red-rimmed, her skin pale. She started to descend the stairs but James's voice shot out at her.

"Margaret! Remain where you are!"

She froze.

It is a choice, Ian thought. *Between her father and myself. O choose, O choose, Lady Margaret . . . whether you will go or stay.*

With eyes riveted upon the young woman he loved, Ian's heart sank as she paused in fearful obedience to her father. He could not sustain his gaze, and looked away.

But then hope rose again at the sound of her footstep continuing on down the stairs. With each step she seemed to say to her father that he would not—could not—vanquish the love she bore in her heart for Ian.

Reaching the floor, Maggie walked straight to Ian's side, ignoring the astonished look of supreme offense on her father's face at her flagrant disobedience of his command. *I have made my choice, Father,* she seemed to say, *and I make it with the man I love!*

"Mr. Duncan," said the constable patiently, "you still have not answered my question."

Ian looked toward Maggie; hers was the only trust he had needed.

"I was out," he said, ". . . thinking."

"By yourself?" the constable pressed.

Ian nodded.

"Could you tell me," Duff asked, "where you went?"

"Places. I was just . . . out—I don't remember . . ."

Ian's head was hot. He had no idea where he'd been. He could not stand up under many more of Duff's unrelenting questions, for he had no defense. But suddenly the constable said—

"Well, Mr. Duncan, I won't be troubling you any further right now. But I will be talking to you later."

It was James who spoke now. "What! Is that all you're going to do?"

"I'm sorry, your Lordship. We have more investigating to do. We mustn't act too hastily."

"You'd let him go free because he's the son of the Earl of Landsbury!"

"Your Lordship," rejoined Duff, miffed at Lord Duncan's interference, "the boy's father has nothing whatever to do with this. When the time is right and the facts are straight, justice will be done. For now, I thank you for receiving us into your home."

Then turning to Ian, he added, "You are planning to remain in the area for some time yet, I presume?" But he did not await Ian's reply, for his words—though framed as a question—carried the ring of an order. He and his associate turned and strode from the room. Just as they reached the door, Duff paused as if the question had only just occurred to him, and once again addressed Ian:

"Oh . . . one more thing, Duncan," he said. "That's a nasty cut you've picked up there on your hand . . . mind telling me how you got it?"

Ian shot a quick glance at Maggie, then back at the constable. "I'm afraid I don't know, sir," he said. "It must have happened sometime during the night. Maybe in the fight with Falkirk. I don't remember."

Duff nodded with knowing expression, then turned and disappeared out of the house.

As the door closed behind the two men, James flung a hostile and menacing glance toward Ian and his daughter.

"I tried to tell you what kind of man this was!" he said to Maggie scornfully. "Now, you would marry a murderer!"

"He is no criminal," answered Maggie quietly.

But James Duncan cared little for any defense; he had already convicted the man who stood before him. Whether or not he was guilty of murdering Falkirk hardly affected his opinion of Ian. It simply provided a convenient way of allowing the law to do his work for him. But if that fool of a constable did nothing, he would see to it himself. One way or another he *would* destroy this imposter, the so-called betrothed of his moonstruck daughter. No matter that Falkirk was now gone, and with him his father's money; he would repay these two idiots for what they had done to him!

"Mr. Duncan," James continued as if Maggie had never spoken, "you will leave these premises immediately. You will not return! If you ever set foot on Stonewycke again, I shall consider you an intruder and will be justified in whatever I may do. Is that understood?"

But it was Maggie, not Ian, who answered him: "We will leave right away, Father."

"You, Margaret, are going nowhere." James replied dispassionately, as one who knows his victory is assured.

"No!" she screamed.

"Don't force me to carry out my threat here and now," said James, leveling his icy stare at his daughter as if she were the enemy.

Suddenly from over James's shoulder came Atlanta's voice, quiet and controlled:

"Maggie, let Ian go for now," she said. "We will work this out. You will be with him soon."

Maggie shook her head in agony, desperately afraid that once he was gone, in some hideous way her father would keep her from Ian forever.

"This is best," Atlanta said. "By tomorrow you will be together again. Ian . . . will you go peaceably?"

Ian stared blankly at Atlanta. Could he believe that in one more day it would all be over? Yet even as he doubted, something in her resolute, unflinching tone spoke assurance to him, communicating more than her mere words that she would be able to deliver what she promised.

Ian looked at Maggie, his heart crying out to hold her one more time. Slowly he walked toward the door. He turned his eyes away, afraid to look at her again for fear of losing his resolve.

"Ian!" Maggie cried out after him. "Ian . . . I love you!"

He turned, cast her one quick glance, blinked back the rising tears, then hastened through the door. On he walked through the great iron gates of Stonewycke, leading Maukin, down the road, and on.

As the west wind stung his face, even as a few rays of sunlight beat down trying to warm the chilly earth, Ian looked toward the sky in anticipation of tomorrow.

Perhaps in another time, summer will come again after all. He could only hope . . . and wait.

43 / An Unknown Assailant

Stonewycke became a prison to Maggie.

All that was dear in life now stood outside those somber stone walls. She could think of nothing but Ian—out there somewhere.

Even Raven remained out of reach. For Maggie knew that if she once drew near to the horse, she would inevitably be drawn directly to him. Only one thing kept her from seeking out her love: the glare of hatred in her father's eyes. She had little doubt of the lengths he was prepared to go against Ian.

Thus she wandered about the solitary house; each hour seemed an eternity as she waited for her mother to fulfill her promises. On the second day she overheard two servants speaking with concern about Digory. He had risen as usual in the morning and had begun his regular tasks. But around midday, Sam had unexpectedly found him sitting in his chair in the loft, staring straight ahead with fixed gaze, shaking with chills and a low fever.

Without considering the consequences, Maggie rushed from the house and toward the stables. Sam had helped Digory to his bed, and there Maggie found him, apparently asleep. As Maggie stood silently over him, her mind was filled with fearful visions of Bess Mackinaw, helpless and dying.

Oh, God, she thought, *don't take him now!*

After a brief moment an eye cocked open and a gentle smile formed on the lips of the old man.

"Weel, lassie," he said in a cheerful, but noticeably weak voice, "I canna gi' ye a proper welcome today."

"Oh, Digory," she said, "is there anything I can do?"

He chuckled. " 'Tis na so bad, lass. Jist a touch o' ague. I'll be na up t' give the lads an lassies below their evenin' feedin'."

"You most certainly will not! I'll feed them myself if I have to. But you must stay right where you are."

"Ye hae enough on yer mind, lassie," Digory replied, "wi'out tryin' t' do my chores, too."

"Oh, Digory," Maggie sighed, a flood of childhood memories flowing into her confused mind. The long past days of her childhood may have contained hurts of their own, but they now seemed sweet and carefree in comparison to the present. Would she trade Ian for a return to those days of innocence? Her sigh caught in a sob, and before she could stop them, tears rose in her eyes and spilled down her cheeks.

"Dear child," Digory whispered, "dinna ye forget that our God will turn everythin' t' good in the end. I ken 'tis hard t' believe when ye're in the midst o' yer trial. But if ye can hold on t' that truth, it'll help ye through the pains o' life."

Digory always spoke as if God were so kind, Maggie thought: He spoke of God as his loving Father. But the only father she had ever known was cold, selfish, and vengeful. She wanted to believe that God was a *good* Father like Digory said. How delightful it would be to have such a Father whose loving arms were warm and inviting and full of tenderness and forgiveness!

"Jist remember," the groom had gone on, "God'll never forsake ye. He loves ye an' will make everythin' come t' good when ye trust Him."

"I'll try," Maggie replied, forcing as much conviction into the words as she could. As much as she envied the simplicity of Digory's trusting faith, at this moment God seemed too distant to help.

Yet Digory knew Maggie even better than she knew herself. He formed a silent prayer in his heart. "Oh, Lord, keep yer hand on this dear child. Dinna let her from yer care, whate'er comes her way."

To Maggie he then said, "Child, could ye read me a bit from the Book? It would help me t' rest."

She glanced around, found the worn leather Bible on Digory's table, and took it to him. He pointed out several Psalms, and she read them aloud to him. But the words came out toneless and Maggie could scarcely hear her own voice. The words which Digory hoped would speak life into her troubled spirit would have to wait to do their work. But as the rector had read at the funeral of Bess Mackinaw, that time would come as surely as the rain came down from heaven to nourish the plants of the earth. At this moment, however, Maggie was no more aware of the work of heavenly rain from this old man and his oft-read Bible than she was of the surgery of God's scalpel deep within her heart in the midst of her tribulation.

Digory was soon asleep and Maggie gently closed the book, sighed deeply, and rose to go.

As she stepped from the stable after descending from Digory's room, the shadows of evening lay across the grounds. Hoping to avoid a confrontation with her father, yet not ready to return to the house, she turned toward the left and walked along the outer hedge which led around to the courtyard at the front of the mansion. She had just passed the rusty iron gate of the forsaken little garden, thinking of the first time she had shown it to Ian, when suddenly a hand shot out from the shadows and clamped down roughly on her.

"Dinna say a word!" threatened a deep voice in little more than an evil whisper.

Maggie tried to force a scream but her sounds were cut off by the harsh pinching of fingers against her lips. Terrified, she felt herself being dragged into the cover of the shrubbery where her assailant had been hiding.

"I'm na goin' t' hurt ye, ye little jade!" the unfamiliar voice grated.

Maggie twisted and struggled, but the cruel hands held her tight. The stale smell of ale and the stench from his unwashed body sickened her. Maggie gagged, then wrestled again to free herself.

"I'll not hurt ye," the voice went on, "long as ye cooperate. Now I got my knife here an' if ye scream oot, I'll use it." He poked the blade into her back until she winced.

"Now," he went on with rasping voice, "I'm goin' t' take my hand from yer mouth. If ye try t' yell . . . weel, blue blood'll flow as easily as any. Am I makin' my meanin' clear t' ye?"

Maggie stiffly nodded her head.

By slow degrees he loosened his grip on Maggie's mouth. But he only lowered his arm enough to keep a tight grip on her shoulders. His foul breath was overpowering, but Maggie did not struggle further, for the steely reminder of his purpose remained pressed against her back.

"I been hearin' ye was pretty friendly wi' Master Falkirk," he said, settling into the business for which he had come, for his prey was now safely in the spider's power.

"I—I don't know what you mean . . ." Maggie replied, her feeble voice quivering in fear.

"Ye're in on this wi' him! I ken it!"

"No!"

He loosened his grip for an instant and fumbled in his pocket. The knife continued to press against her. "Deny that this is yers then, leddy!" he said, shoving a shining object into her face.

She gasped. "Where did you get that!" she cried, not realizing how dangerous her impulsive words could be. "Give it to me!" she gasped out, grabbing for the locket. She could not bear to see the gift from Ian in that vile hand. She watched it drop into the dirt and the man's hands closed more tightly around her.

"Ha, ha!" he snarled. "What better place fer the laird t' hide his booty than wi' his sweetheart!'' A villainous laugh followed, which gave way to a low, hacking cough.

"I hardly knew Mr. Falkirk.''

"Come, lassie,'' the man replied, growing angry, "ye wouldna be so foolish as t' be thinkin' t' keep it all yersel', would ye?'' He purposely jabbed her with the tip of his blade, still poised in readiness in the event she should scream. "Weel, ye can ferget that, ye trollop! I earned my share, an' I mean t' get it . . . one way or the other. Now talk!''

"I don't know what you mean,'' said Maggie, her voice trembling as she realized, indeed, *exactly* what he meant. Could she make him believe her lie?

"Ha! I dinna believe that any more than ye believe I'll let ye go alive if ye dinna tell me!''

His grip tightened and she felt the knife tearing through her clothes.

"*You* killed him, didn't you!'' she accused, hardly realizing what she was saying until it was too late.

The muscles of his arm tensed in momentary anger, then relaxed. "Ne'er bite the hand that feeds ye, I al'ays say,'' he replied. "The way I hear it, that fancy gent'man fr' Lonnon killed the laird. They're sayin' he swore t' kill him that very night.''

"It was you I—''

She stopped short, realizing anything she said about the murder would reveal her knowledge of the treasure, thus endangering her all the more.

"No more o' yer accusations, ye hear? Me an' the laird hardly laid eyes on each other. Now . . . where's the loot!''

"I . . . I don't know.''

" 'Tis a good week fer the spillin' o' blue blood,'' he sneered. "I suppose ye'll be joinin' yer lover.''

Suddenly the reflection from an approaching lantern illuminated the darkness where they stood, and the assailant's grip slackened for an instant. Maggie thrust her elbow into his ribs with all her might and struggled to free herself. A sting of pain shot through her back, and she screamed in terror.

She heard footsteps running toward her, saw the lantern swinging in the darkness, and could make out vague yells. The foul grip loosened, and she fell to the ground in a swoon.

"What is't, my leddy?'' asked Sam as he knelt at her side.

The sound of his voice brought Maggie's mind back into focus, but when she opened her mouth she found herself unable to speak. She shook her head, reached for his hand, and pulled herself partly up, still trembling. Then she felt again the sharp throbbing in her back.

"Is he gone?" she gasped.

"Who, mem?" he asked. "I thought I heard voices. Were it an intruder, mem? I'll gang after him."

"No, Sam!" Maggie replied, grabbing his arm. "It's too late. I'm sure he's gone by now."

Sam helped Maggie to her feet, then caught up something from the ground.

"Look, my leddy," he said. "This be yers?"

She snatched the locket from his hand as if he were the thief. Clutching it tightly in her trembling hand, she sped to the house. She managed to make it to her room without being seen, and lay facedown on the bed. She had to think.

Surely a report of what had just happened would lift suspicion from Ian. Yet her father might well twist her report around somehow to suit his own designs. Constable Duff had appeared sympathetic. But if she tried to get a message to him, James might well intercept it.

She had to see Ian!

She rose from the bed, changed the blood-splotched dress and tended the wound in her back as best she was able. The cut was merely superficial and, though painful, would not be serious. Then she sat down once more to sort out her jumbled thoughts. But before she came close to arriving at a course of action, she fell into an exhausted sleep.

44 / Preparations

Because Maggie had not rested well in days, she slept till almost noon. When she finally awoke she jerked up with a start, and cried out sharply as the pain cut through her back. She reached behind her, still forgetful of the events of the previous night. Gradually her numbed mind began to clear. She had to see Ian, that much was certain.

Outside the sky was blue and thin rays of sunlight beat against the windowpane. It was turning into a fine day, one the harried land well deserved. *But what is one more day of sunshine?* Maggie thought. *Only a cruel reminder of the joys that may never again come.* Would even Atlanta be able to bring her and Ian together again? Was the hope of marriage but a fading dream?

As if in answer to her silent question, a soft knock came to the door.

"Maggie," came Atlanta's welcome voice.

Atlanta entered bearing a tray with breakfast for her daughter. But Maggie set it aside and urgently faced her mother.

"I must see Ian," she said.

"The time will come, Maggie," replied Atlanta. "But we have to be patient. Your father has postponed his trip to Glasgow. We must simply wait until—"

"It can't wait!" interrupted Maggie with urgency in her voice. "There is someone who may have had reason to kill George Falkirk."

"Who?" asked Atlanta. Though she would have supported Ian for the sake of her daughter, she yet believed him guilty of the crime.

"I don't know."

Atlanta eyed her daughter inquisitively, as if to say, "Is that all?"

"I don't know what he looks like," Maggie went on, "but . . ."

All at once it dawned on Maggie how sketchy her notions about the mysterious attacker really were. Unable to identify him, even if she told everything she had seen and heard that night on Braenock Ridge, it would still not remove the guilt from Ian's head. He *had* threatened Falkirk. And to divulge what she knew would only increase the danger to herself. With a stab of dismay, Maggie suddenly realized the treasure would implicate her and Ian all the more.

"I have to see Ian," she repeated lamely.

"It's too dangerous," Atlanta replied. "Your father is watching me. He is doubly on his guard after what I said the other day."

"But surely you see that Ian is innocent!"

"He can't account for his whereabouts," said Atlanta, voicing her doubts.

"Even if he *did* kill Falkirk," said Maggie in despair, "that would change nothing for me."

"You are still determined to marry him, even though that could make you the wife of a murderer?"

"Oh, Mother, I love him. There is nothing that could change that."

Atlanta needed no further inducements. She knew it would be foolhardy to oppose them once their minds were made up. And she knew arranging a marriage now would be dangerous with James on the prowl. But she doubted whether any more suitable opportunity would present itself in the near future. Better she have a hand in it than to force the two lovers into some reckless course of action. A meeting between Ian and her daughter was ill-advised; the preparations must be made under the cloak of secrecy. Then they could flee Stonewycke cleanly and safely and remain away for as long as necessary. She could no longer stand against the despairing tone in her daughter's voice. Whatever James's threats, she could not refuse her daughter the happiness she so desperately wanted.

"I will return soon," Atlanta said, turning to leave the room. "All will be arranged."

Atlanta did return to Maggie that afternoon with news. From that moment on the choices made themselves.

Before two more days had ended, in response to a brief letter Atlanta had smuggled into town, a visitor appeared at the great door of Stonewycke mansion. The maid opened to a stout, rough-hewn creature, only a vague semblance of a woman, who spoke in hard, masculine tones.

"What do ye want?" asked the maid, filled with suspicion. There had been such strange goings-on lately, she wasn't about to offer any extra hospitality to such a creature as this.

"The name's Queenie," the woman answered, undaunted. "I'm bearin' a message fer the mistress o' the house."

"I'll take it t' her," said the maid.

"I'm t' give it int' her hand my own sel'," said Queenie firmly.

The maid stood indecisive for a moment, then decided to find Lady Atlanta. But before she turned to leave she said, "Ye wait here . . . dinna move!"

Moments later Atlanta appeared with the dutiful maid scurrying along behind her. Atlanta also eyed Queenie cautiously.

"Yes," she inquired, "what is it?"

Queenie stepped forward and, for one of the few times in her life, felt intimidated. Atlanta was perhaps the grandest lady she had ever seen; so close to the regal presence, Queenie suddenly felt her own roughness more acutely than ever before.

"Weel, my leddy," she began. "I got a message here." She handed it to Atlanta and prepared to make a quick retreat.

"Wait," said Atlanta. "A reply may be necessary." Atlanta scanned the paper, then returned her attention to Queenie. She handed the inn-keeper a sovereign and said a brief, "Thank you."

"No. Thank ye, my leddy," Queenie protested. "I dinna do this fer the money." She began to back toward the door. "I jist hope ye can help the lad." Then she turned and exited quickly, if not gracefully.

Atlanta stood motionless for some time. When she finally did move, it was toward the stairs.

She did not go directly to Maggie's room. She walked straight to her own sitting room, quickly sat at her elegant French desk and began to sort through several sheaves of papers. She had already been through them several times in anticipation of this moment, though she had all the while prayed that circumstances would never come to this extreme. Even now as she placed two of the papers into a thick brown envelope, she tried to convince herself that her precaution would not be needed. Even if it were, there remained one more document which she kept from the others. Maggie would be back, of that she was sure, and she would carry on the fight for the land. But just in case something happened, she wanted to be doubly certain James could never have the power to do the unthinkable.

Yes, it was best she keep this one paper secret.

She tucked it into a drawer and locked it securely. She would have to find a better hiding place for it later. But there was no time now. She hoped she would be able to forget about it altogether, just as it had lain forgotten for nearly half a century.

Now she must think of Maggie. James was nearly mad; Ian's life was in danger, and—whether guilty or innocent—he was soon to be the husband of her daughter. Banishing her last-minute hesitations, Atlanta reminded herself that she had to help them in every way she could, for the sake of her daughter's happiness, and for the sake of Stonewycke. She rose and made her way to Maggie's room.

She walked in without knocking. The drapes were drawn against the afternoon sun, giving the room a dim, deathlike appearance.

"Maggie," Atlanta said with an urgent tone. "I've a reply from Ian."

Maggie jumped up and faced her mother with a look of radiant expectation.

"He wants me to get you out of the house tonight. He says he has made all the arrangements."

"Oh, Mother!"

Up until that moment Atlanta had spoken with a calm urgency. But with the words of excitement from her daughter, her lip began to quiver and a tear brimmed over, tracing a path down her cheek.

"Oh, my baby!" she cried, embracing Maggie.

The two women stood thus, bound in the mutual embrace they had known all too seldom, until the tears of their varied emotions were exhausted.

At last they separated.

"I have given your father a sedative," said Atlanta. "He is asleep now and will remain so until morning. But you must waste no time. He will not know where you have gone, but he is bound to search until he learns the truth. So do not stay more than two or three days in one place. Go to Aberdeen or Edinburgh if you can. In his present temper, if James finds you I do not doubt he would kill Ian. So the two of you must stay away for at least a month. Get word to me of your whereabouts through the woman at the inn in Port Strathy. Then I will advise you as to developments here and when you may safely return."

"Yes, Mother."

"Your father is mad with rage. He blames Ian for Falkirk's death and the failure of his latest schemes. Who is to tell what he may do? He may seek his revenge on me, Maggie; I do not know what evil lurks in that man's heart. So you must plan for the possibility of being away for a very long time. Whatever is very dear to you, take with you. I will hope to see you within a month, my daughter. But if it should not be, we must be prudent. Do you understand me?"

Maggie nodded.

"I'll be back soon," said Atlanta, leaving the room. "And quickly, dear. Ian will be waiting for you within the hour."

Maggie began to sort through her things, and one by one filled a single carpetbag with the most important. The essentials left little room for even the smallest keepsakes of the home and land she loved. She glanced up at the grand tapestry her mother had made and regretted she couldn't take it with her. There was a place in the bag, however, for her own smaller reproduction—paltry by comparison, she thought, but at least a reminder of the mother she loved so dearly. This was a thrilling moment of anticipation, and a painful moment of separation.

Sorting through her bureau, Maggie unexpectedly discovered a small music box hidden deep in the back of one of the drawers. Tears fell afresh as she picked up the delicate instrument. She wound the key and lifted the lid, and once again the sweet strains of Brahms' lullaby filled the room as they hadn't for years. As the nostalgic tune played on, sobs shook her body and she snapped the lid shut. Her father had presented the gift to her on her fifth birthday. The memory rose in her mind, as clear as an image in a polished mirror. He had chosen it himself, he had said, in one of London's finest shops. All she remembered was that it was the only gift he had ever given her. *Yes,* she thought bitterly, *the memory is clear. But like the reflection in the mirror, it is not real.*

Maggie's immediate impulse was to smash the box against the wall, but she found herself dropping it into the carpetbag along with her other possessions. Why, she could not tell. Neither did she ask.

Atlanta returned some moments later.

"Your father is sleeping soundly," she said. "You and Ian will be safe for the rest of today and tonight."

Then she held the envelope she had prepared out to her daughter. "Maggie, I want you to take this with you. You need not open it; you may scarcely even grasp its significance. But I want you to have it, in the event that something should happen to me, or in case you are gone longer than we anticipate. It is yours. It is the promise not only for your return but for the safety of this land we love. I love you, my dear! God forbid that I will not see you again! This will always be your home, whatever happens. Do you understand me? *It is yours!* When all this is settled, you must come back. I will be waiting for you!"

"Mother, I love you!" said Maggie, embracing her again. Fresh tears streamed down both faces.

Maggie's mind was racing too fast to try to grasp the meaning behind all of Atlanta's words. She could not think of such things now. All she knew was that Ian was waiting for her, and that she was going to marry the man she loved! She tucked the envelope into the pocket of her coat. Then she wrapped her heavy woolen cloak about her as an added protection against the cold of the fast-approaching winter.

Atlanta placed a strong, motherly arm about her daughter, and together they walked downstairs to the stables. There, Maggie realized, a different farewell faced her. Raven was waiting saddled, and by her side stood Digory, looking as though he had never been ill.

"You look better," said Maggie huskily, her voice betraying the emotion she felt inside.

"Didna I tell ye?" Digory replied. His voice, too, was strained and taut with tenderness for the girl he had seen grow from a baby into a young woman.

"Oh, Digory!" cried Maggie, flinging her arms around the groom's bony shoulders. "I shall miss you so!"

"An' I will miss ye too, lass."

"How will I ever get along without you?"

"Oh, ye will, lass," he replied, the tears streaming down his wrinkled cheeks glistening in the failing sunlight. "The Lord'll be goin' wi' ye, an' so will my prayers. Ye dinna need an auld groom when ye hae all that."

Maggie's heart found little comfort in his words, though she treasured them because they were Digory's. She tried to impress his voice on her memory so she would never forget.

She walked again to where Atlanta stood, weeping openly, and gave her a final squeeze.

"I shall miss you, Mother."

"And I you. But we will pray it will not be longer than a month!"

"Thank you for everything!"

"I wish you happiness, Maggie! How I would like to share this time of joy with you!"

"We will think of you when we say our vows, Mother. You have made it possible. Thank you. I love you."

Maggie mounted Raven, thankful that at least she did not have to give up *this* friend.

She cast one more wistful glance toward Digory and her mother as they stood side by side in the yard. Then Maggie turned and urged her horse forward. She sucked in a deep breath of the late afternoon air, wiped her eyes, and tried to think of the joyous hope within her. Sad as these good-byes were, her future did not lay here, but with the man she loved and to whom she had pledged herself. Whatever happiness her life would hold lay in that future, and not in her past.

She walked Raven from the stables around the house, then urged her forward at a trot out the gate and along the road.

The sun was just beginning to set when she reached the main road leading down the hill into Strathy. Her heartbeat increased at the sight of Maukin standing alongside the road. The chestnut mare stood quietly grazing by a clump of trees with a small field of clover at her feet. Maggie jumped from Raven's back and ran forward, her chest heaving not from the exertion of her short ride, but from the thought of at last seeing Ian.

He was seated on an incline with his back to her, as if fearing to believe he would actually see her face. She ran up behind him shouting his name. He turned and beheld her, and his radiant face told her that she was the fulfillment of every dream of his heart.

He jumped to his feet and embraced her. They clung to one another for a long while, neither willing to add the dimension of speech to that glorious moment of reunion.

At last Ian broke the silence.

"Don't you know it's bad luck to see your future husband before the wedding?"

Maggie laughed. "I love you!" she said.

"And I love you," he replied. "And now, my bonny lassie," he went on, "what would you say to us going and getting married?"

They turned, hand in hand, ran back to where Raven and Maukin were patiently waiting, leapt on the horses' backs, dug in their heels, and galloped up the hill along the eastern road toward Fraserburgh.

45 / A Decision

The sun had long since set on the two riders. The winding dirt road spread out before them like a silver thread, illuminated by the half-moon caught in the treetops. With the anxieties of the past days behind them, it was a peaceful ride. Ian and Maggie almost felt as if they were again riding upon the heather-covered hills, laughing and sharing and growing in their love. For the moment, neither wanted to admit that the wondrous purple blossoms were now gone and the barren brown of dormant life signified that winter was quickly approaching. In their hearts it was summer again, and all was fresh and bursting with possibilities.

Maggie glanced over at Ian. His gaze was straight ahead as he concentrated on the darkened road. How she loved him! It hardly seemed possible after all that had happened that they were actually going to be married. But Fraserburgh was less than an hour away!

Ian reined Maukin to a stop.

"Let's take a rest," he said.

"I don't need a rest!" exclaimed Maggie exuberantly.

"Well, the horses do, at least," he laughed. It felt good to laugh again. "And Queenie insisted on packing us some food. We'd best fortify ourselves for what lies ahead."

"You sound as if we're on our way to a funeral," said Maggie with a playful scowl.

"Isn't that how most men look upon their wedding day—the death of their freedom?" He laughed again. Then with a more serious tone, he added, "But I am not among them, Maggie! Today is the true beginning of life for me." He leaned over and kissed her lightly on the cheek.

"It will be a beginning for both of us, Ian," Maggie replied.

Then they dismounted and Ian began to rummage through his saddle pouch. He withdrew the packet of food prepared by Queenie.

"That's odd," he murmured.

"What is it?"

"My dirk—it's gone. I last remember putting it here . . ." But his voice trailed away as the feared images of forgotten horrors began to creep into his mind. When had he put the dirk there? A week, two weeks ago? Three days ago. . . ? The night hid the cold pallor on his face.

Maggie caught the faltering in his voice and cheerfully broke into his thoughts. "We don't need it," she said. "Let's eat like the country folk!"

She led him to a dry patch of ground thickly covered with pine needles and drew him down next to her. She opened the packet and found bannocks and cheese and dried herring.

They ate in silence for a while, then Maggie said, "Shall we go to London after Fraserburgh?"

"London?" Ian asked in the detached tone of one whose mind is elsewhere. "London was another lifetime ago for me," he said. "I could never go back. My father would make life unbearable for us. My future is here . . . with you."

"My father will not make life easy for us, either. We may not be able to return to Stonewycke for some time."

"We will have to come back eventually. I won't have us trying to start our marriage on the run, always looking over our shoulder for your father. I'll stand up to him."

"Ian," Maggie interposed, "as long as I'm with you, I'll be happy. I don't care if we never go back. I don't want you in any danger."

"But, Maggie, if we go away it will look as if I'm truly guilty of murdering Falkirk. I have to clear myself."

"You are innocent," said Maggie firmly. "You could never have done something so horrible."

A cloud came over Ian's face as self-doubts overwhelmed him.

"Maggie," he began in a disconsolate tone, "what if . . . *could* I have—is it possible?"

"No . . . no, my dear Ian!" persisted Maggie.

"I had been drinking, and was so filled with rage."

"Please, Ian, don't talk like this!"

"You don't know what it's been like," Ian said. "I've relived that night in my mind a hundred times . . . *but I still can't remember!*"

"It will come back," Maggie said, trying to soothe him. "Then it will all be made right."

"But it may be too late. By then they'll have hanged me."

"Ian! don't say that . . . it frightens me."

"I'm sorry . . . I didn't mean to—"

"Ian, let's just go away—as far away as we can! They'll find the real killer eventually. Then it will be safe to return. But not now, not anytime soon."

"I can't run. Don't you see? I have my pride, my honor to think of.

I have to face your father like a man. And I have to face the charges, too.''

"My father is wild," Maggie implored. "Your guilt or innocence in Falkirk's death has nothing to do with it anymore. If we stay here, I'm sure he'd try to kill you. Maybe even me. I'm afraid for you. I want you as far away from him as we can get. We can start over, at least for a while, somewhere far away."

"Maybe you're right," sighed Ian. "And unless I can remember what happened, there is no way to prove I'm not a murderer."

"There might be a way to prove it—" Maggie said suddenly.

"What do you mean?" interrupted Ian. "Is there something I don't know?"

"I wanted to tell you before," Maggie answered. "but so much has happened—it almost seemed unimportant. The other night I was walking on the grounds and a man accosted me—"

The sudden look of anxiety on Ian's face stopped her short.

"Sam frightened the man off," she assured him. "He and Falkirk were conspiring to steal a cache of gold. He thought I had it and threatened me—"

"My God!"

"But don't you see? He must have been the one to kill—"

"Did he hurt you?" asked Ian with panic in his voice, not even stopping to wonder why Maggie knew of Falkirk's plot.

"No . . . a small cut—Ian, don't you see? He must have killed Falkirk over the gold. If we can only persuade the constable to listen."

"Who was the man?"

Maggie shook her head dismally. "I don't know. I never saw his face."

Any hope this development may have sparked in Ian immediately died. Who would believe a story of a faceless, nameless murderer? Especially coming from the prime suspect's own wife! And if this man were the murderer, he would roam free, free to . . .

Suddenly Ian said, "You're right. We have to get away! You're in danger, too. That changes everything. I don't care if I'm branded a murderer for running. I don't care if they follow; I have to get you away from here!"

They both fell silent for a few moments. At length Maggie spoke in a soft voice. The time for decision had come, and each seemed to sense it.

"I'll go with you wherever you want, Ian," she said. "Just as long as it's far enough from here that my father can't follow. I love you. We'll do whatever you think is best."

Ian stood up as if he would take flight right then, then paced about.

Every thought in his confused brain pointed toward the same conclusion. But it was such a far-fetched notion! Maggie had said *far away*. But neither of them had meant *that* far. Yet James Duncan was an influential, compelling man. He wielded great power. Where could they hope to go to avoid his reach? Wherever they went in Scotland, even in England, he could find them and ultimately engineer an indictment for Falkirk's death. Could even his own daughter stand against him? And how could he—miserable, confused, hapless Ian Duncan—hope to keep the daughter of such a man? But the idea was too daring, too wild. Would Maggie willingly oppose such a father and thus relinquish her ties to her beloved Stonewycke? The roots of her heritage which bound her to this land extended generations into her past. Would she give all that up for him?

The conclusion remained the same. There was no alternative if this love was to endure. Could he ask it of her, knowing of her love for this land? Yet he had to ask, for he could not face the thought of what might happen otherwise.

Ian looked deep into Maggie's face. "If our marriage is to last," he said intently, "we must do as you say; we must go *far* away."

He paused, summoning the courage to say it all.

"We must, Maggie," he went on at length, "*go to America*."

Maggie returned his gaze with eyes of love. Even as he said the words, the resolve seemed already settling upon her that this was indeed the only way left to them. "Where you go, Ian, I will follow."

Ian breathed a sigh, hardly realizing he had been holding his breath, bracing himself for the most dreaded of answers. "Could you . . . Stonewycke, everything here you love?"

"I love *you*, Ian. That's all that matters to me now."

"Oh, think of it, Maggie! It's always been a dream of mine. I've read books about it. Didn't you tell me the Mackinaws had a son who migrated there?"

"Yes, their older son, Drew."

"We could be so happy away from here."

"It's so far, Ian. But I want nothing more than to be with you . . . for us to be happy together."

"Maggie," Ian said with a laugh as he sat down beside her, "just think of it—freedom from all this . . . we'd be free!"

He wrapped his arms tightly around her, kissed her, then cradled her head against his shoulder and stroked her hair.

"I love you," he said.

Maggie looked up into his face, the moonlight filling her eyes with the words of love her voice could not speak.

By common consent, they rose hand in hand, put away their provisions, mounted Raven and Maukin, and rode off on the final leg of their journey.

46 / The Groom and His Master _____

When James awoke late the following morning, it was too late to overturn the deception that had been worked on him. Pulling himself out of bed, he sensed immediately that his sleep had not been natural. He threw on his clothes and set out on a rampaging search, first for Atlanta and then for his daughter. He could find neither, though had his search been more thorough he would have discovered his wife weeping in Maggie's favorite haunt, the dayroom.

The servants cowed into the security of their tasks. What could be happening in this family they served? Certainly the master of the house had always been a hard man, given occasionally to harsh words. But they had never seen him like this.

Unsuccessful in his inspection of the house, James stormed out toward the stables. Maggie always retreated there with her four-footed friends and that old lout of a groom. Why he had kept him around all these years he didn't know.

A downcast Digory was going about his tasks in an aimless manner. Already he missed his young mistress; without the vibrancy of her life at Stonewycke, all had turned pale. But he forced himself to do what must be done. There was still a Master to serve.

James found Digory bent over a workbench, mending a broken harness.

"Where are they!" he bellowed.

Digory looked up from his work and could hardly believe what he saw. Standing before him James appeared as a wild man, his clothes hanging haphazardly on his body, his rumpled shirt uncharacteristically open at the neck. Never one to be coy, Digory answered the laird's question with silence, only because the scene before him filled his heart with such sadness that he could find no words.

"Answer me, you miserable cuddy!" James shouted.

Digory fastened his eyes on James and quietly stood his ground. "I dinna ken where the lass has gone," he replied, hoping no more would be asked of him. But in truth, he knew no more than he had told.

"You dirty traitor!" James screeched. "After all this family has done for you, you betray me in the end. Well, I'll teach you some respect!"

James caught up a riding crop and stalked angrily toward the groom. "You'll soon learn where to place your loyalties after this, you lying cur!"

Before the sound of the words had parted his lips, a painful crack of the hardened leather lashed across Digory's head. A thin red line under his ear and across the back of his neck began to ooze with blood as James whipped the tip back and sent it snapping at his shoulders and midrift. The groom stood silent with head bowed, uttering no word of defense through the agony of his pain.

"What do you have to say now?" asked James, interrupting his torture. "Where has she gone? Tell me what you know!"

"I will that, laird," answered Digory in a barely audible anguished voice. "All I ken is this, that yer daughter didna want t' go. All she wanted was yer love—"

"Why you insolent . . . how dare you!"

But James was too caught up in the renewed frenzy which Digory's words brought on to complete his cursing denouncements. His whip spoke instead.

Digory crumpled to his knees under the onslaught, nearly senseless from pain, blistering welts already rising on his skin under his shirt and breeches. Head bowed, he said no more. Instead, he did the only thing he could. He quietly prayed. But this time it was not for the two young people he loved, nor for the family whose distress made his heart ache.

Instead, he prayed for James alone, for the master of the house who knew not what he did, who was too blind to see what was happening before his very eyes. Then Digory knew no more. He did not awake until the following day when he opened his eyes to see Atlanta's compassionate face looking down on him. He was in his own loft, in his bed. A fresh cup of tea stood on the stand next to him. Atlanta clearly had been tending him for some time, for her eyes appeared weary.

She had, in fact, been at his bedside the entire night.

Later that same day James was seen in Port Strathy riding in a frenzy. He made two or three stops, after each of which he galloped off in a greater passion of rage than before. He was last seen with two other riders, both of questionable character. The three whipped their mounts up the hill, but they did not turn off the road when they reached the entrance to Stonewycke. Instead, they tore along the coast road toward the east.

47 / Ian and Maggie

The sun pierced the window with splintered shafts of cold light.

Maggie turned her head toward its rays, wondering why she felt so odd. Then she remembered—the rainclouds had gathered the night before, and she hadn't anticipated seeing the sun again for days.

Next she became aware of the sleeping figure next to her. The shining of the sun was not, after all, the only change this morning held. Would she ever again waken after a night's slumber without a thrill at seeing Ian by her side?

She lay back and exhaled a long sigh of contentment. He would always be there, of that she was confident. Nothing else mattered. How she longed to reach out and touch his shoulder! But she did not want to risk waking him; the look of peaceful repose on his face was too beautiful to disturb. Maggie wondered if he were dreaming. *If so,* she hoped, *may they be good dreams.* Even in sleep the muscles of his arms and chest rippled with vitality. She murmured a prayer for him, for them both, that they would have only good dreams from this moment on.

Slowly she took in their surroundings. It had been dark as they had entered the previous night, but even then she had realized that they could hardly have chosen a more perfect setting for their first night together. Now, in the daylight, she was sure of it.

They had not arrived in Fraserburgh until the evening was well advanced. When the vicar had answered their knock on the parsonage door, his puzzled expression and his nightclothes both testified to the unusual circumstances of their visit. Explaining themselves, the light finally began to break over his countenance as he recalled Ian's letter of several days earlier. He admitted the two unlikely aristocrats, simply clad in traveling clothes, then disappeared for what seemed ages before he and his wife returned fully dressed. The ceremony had been awkward, brief, scarcely mirroring the depth of love the young bride and improbable groom felt in their hearts for one another.

When it was done they shared a cup of tea with the older couple. Then they bid them good night, but not before receiving directions to the cottage where they now lay, a place which would always harbor fond memories of their first moments as husband and wife.

250

They had planned to stay in the inn, but arriving late and unaware of a local late-autumn festival, they had found it full to overflowing without a single room to spare. Explaining their difficulty to the vicar, he directed them to an empty dwelling some four miles from town. The tenants had been forced to leave for an undetermined period of time a month earlier. The wife had come down with a severe case of pneumonia; the doctor said he would treat it as best he could, but that in the wet climate of the north it would probably recur, and he therefore recommended their spending the winter as far to the south as possible. Poor though they were, the wife had a sister in Liverpool, and with the help and generosity of the parish they had been able to make the journey. The vicar had been asked to keep watch over their cottage until their anticipated return in the spring, and to the young bride and groom he now offered their simple abode as honeymoon cottage.

Entering in the dark, Ian managed to build a fire. The place was humble indeed, reminiscent of the Krueger cottage, but missing Lucy's homey touch. But that night, with the rain pouring down on the thick thatch roof overhead, they had noticed little of it other than the welcome fact that it was dry. Maggie was glad Atlanta had insisted they take along an extra blanket. "Those inns are never warm enough," she had said. Maggie smiled as she thought of her mother, thankful for the recent healing and strengthening of the bonds between them.

The warm fire and blanket, along with the few other provisions which had been left behind, could hardly have been sufficient to keep out the blasts of cold penetrating the cracked walls of the cottage. But the newlyweds, discovering the wonders of each other, were oblivious to the cold. Maggie had always dreamed as a child of being a simple crofter, with no pressures and anxieties other than to raise her children and serve her husband. Now she could almost lay her head back and dream it had come true.

Her husband . . .

She could barely comprehend the truth that she and Ian were married! How good God was to provide her with this one most important wish. Digory had told her many times there was always hope. She would never again give up hope, not as long as there was a God who cared.

Had it all been worth it? The bitterness of her father's rebuff? All her life it seemed she had only been able to see people grasping for what they could get themselves. She had closed herself off, never considering anyone worthy of her trust again. Repelling her father, she had unknowingly shut out Atlanta's reluctant but tender heart as well. Both mother and daughter had suffered in silence as a result.

But when Ian had stumbled into her life, laughing and gay, a crack began to open in that wall of self-protection. Slowly it widened. Before long she and Ian were sharing open expressions of love, and she and her mother were reaching out to one another in ways she had never thought possible.

Maggie glanced over at him.

Yes, she thought, *he has made me believe for the first time that relationships do not have to be founded on isolation and resentment. He has made me believe that trust is possible, that I can truly give myself to another without the danger of being hurt.* He had shown her what love could be like.

Part of her had resisted, still afraid of the risk of being hurt again by someone she loved. But Ian loved her in return. He would never do anything to hurt her. Only hours ago, as he had pledged his love, he had said, "I will never leave you or forsake you."

Maggie believed him. As impossible as it would have seemed to her a year earlier that she would ever believe such words from anyone, she was confident of Ian's love. His simple, honest, trusting manner had dissolved her doubts. His gentle voice reverberated with understanding, compassion, and caring. Though his own past remained unknown to her, he had changed just as she had. He, too, had learned to rise out of past hurts into present love. Together they had struggled to overcome their painful histories and together were now ready to face the future— whatever obstacles were thrown against them.

Ian rolled sleepily over and she watched him stir into gradual wakefulness. A smile came to his lips as he beheld her watching eyes.

"Good morning!" he said. "You were right. There is no finer bed than the straw mattresses of these northern peasants!"

"What a sleepy sluggard you are," she replied playfully. "I've been waiting for hours."

"Then why isn't my breakfast prepared?" he asked with a mock frown.

She laughed. "Ah, yes . . . breakfast," she said. "One detail I overlooked. Now we're simple rustics . . . no pantry . . . no servants."

"And I am the simple farmer," laughed Ian, "who has not even provided my wife the food for our sustenance. Come on!" he said, jumping out of bed. "Let's see what we can find in this *wee but an' ben.*"

"*Your wife . . .*" repeated Maggie reflectively. "I like the sound of it."

Ian turned, then eased himself back down onto the bed beside her and pulled her close to him. "Oh, Maggie, is it right to be so happy?"

"Yes," she breathed as he kissed her. Then after a moment, she said reluctantly. "We're not finding our breakfast this way."

"Who needs breakfast? Besides, we brought no food." He kissed her again.

"That's your London upbringing showing through," she said. "Now if you were a true Scotsman, you'd know that food abounds all around us. All you have to do is know where to look."

He leaned back on his elbow and grinned. "Weel, my wee highland lassie, then ge' yer guidman sommat t' eat."

She laughed. "You're a Scotsman at heart at least, *aren't ye noo, my guidman*?" she replied, imitating his brogue accent. "Wherever did you pick up our native tongue?"

"Here and there. You forget—you married a man of diverse and hidden talents."

They did not have far to search for food. The garden at the back of the cottage contained unharvested potatoes, carrots, and turnips. Weeds had overgrown portions of it, but they easily found sufficient for their present needs. Within an hour a large iron pot boiled over the fire with a frothy mixture of potatoes, carrots, turnips, and salt bubbling cheerily away.

Later, as they partook of their simple breakfast of boiled vegetables, they found themselves savoring every moment, knowing they were storing away each one as a precious memory of their first day together—memories which would never grow dim. For that morning, their lives started and stopped in that rough-hewn hut. There had never been a past, and the future would continue on and on as a joyous extension of the blessed present.

"Ian, this is how I always dreamed it would be," Maggie sighed with deep contentment. "And when we get to America, we could have a cottage just like this."

"In America they call them log cabins," said Ian. "That's how people live out in the American west. There's so much land that everybody can have as much as he wants. And it's good land, Maggie." His eyes brightened in anticipation. "We'll start over . . . build a new life together!"

48 / A New Beginning

Once the decision had been made, Maggie and Ian's enthusiasm mounted by the moment.

"How will we arrange it, Ian?" asked Maggie.

"Ships leave from Aberdeen every week. Passage to London will be easy enough to arrange. Then we can transfer to one bound for New York. I tell you, Maggie, we can do it!"

"The thought of freedom sounds so wonderful. But I'll miss Stonewycke and my mother."

"You'll be able to see them before we leave. We'll go back to say good-bye."

"But my father?"

"He can't do anything to us now. We're married, Maggie!"

"Oh, yes!" Maggie exclaimed. "How could I forget?"

"I've always thought of sailing to America, but just as a lark. Now we can leave our past completely behind us."

"We'll have our own little house—or log cabin, or whatever you call it. I'll plant flowers and put up curtains."

"Just like two peasant newlyweds?"

"Such a life sounds so peaceful."

"But honestly," replied Ian, "I don't know what I could actually *do*. I have enough money to get us there. But I'm hardly wealthy. My father has seen to that. I'm afraid you have married quite a good-for-nothing—"

She raised her finger to his lips and shook her head. "You won't have to do anything but be there with me," she said, her earnest tone communicating far more than her words. "Whatever we do, wherever we go, whether we come back to Scotland or stay in America, whether we live as royalty or as crofters on the land, I will still need you. I will go anywhere with you. I love you far more than I do any country or home."

"I suppose I could try my hand at farming. The Mackinaw fellow in New York would surely help a fellow countryman make a beginning. But I doubt I'm cut out for it."

"It sounds wonderful to me," Maggie replied dreamily. "I have confidence that you can do anything. And when Stonewycke becomes mine we can return here.''

"We may prefer our little log cabin by that time and not want to leave,'' he said. "And besides, won't Alastair inherit Stonewycke?''

"Alastair will inherit the title and be the marquis, I suppose. But I'm to get Stonewycke, I think. It's all so confusing. I think Father has some other property that's tied up in it too. But I've never tried to understand it.'' Then she threw back her head and laughed and sighed all at once. "Who cares! As long as we're together, I don't care if it's in Hector Mackinaw's old place.''

"I wonder if we might not be happier there anyway . . .'' Ian mused, but he let his words trail away unfinished.

What will we find when and if we ever do return to Stonewycke? Ian wondered. *Will James ever moderate his hatred of me? Could he ever accept me as a son-in-law?* Only the future could answer such questions. At present, that gnawing feeling of apprehension was a reality Ian did not want to admit existed. Now was not the time for any thoughts but those of joy.

At last they were one—now and forever. Nothing else mattered. Ian remembered when he had been a boy, so alone, so empty of anything that deeply mattered to him. But Maggie had changed that. He would never lose the sense of belonging Maggie had given him.

He reached for her hand and brought it gently to his lips.

"Thank you, my Maggie,'' he whispered.

"For what?''

"For loving me,'' he answered. "For giving yourself to me.''

"I have given you no more than you have given me,'' Maggie replied. "And is that not what makes our love so right? We have grown in a way we never could have apart.''

Neither spoke again. Ian knew she was right. That love would continue to sustain them whatever the future held, for it was a love that would never die. All that mattered at this moment was the glow in the eyes of his bride as they anticipated their new beginning in America together.